RANDOM HOUSE

LARGE PRINT

THE KISS

*Also by Danielle Steel available
from Random House Large Print*

The House on Hope Street
Irresistible Forces
Journey
Leap of Faith
Lone Eagle
The Wedding

DANIELLE STEEL

THE KISS

RANDOM HOUSE
LARGE PRINT

Copyright © 2001 by Danielle Steel

Published in the United States of America by Random House Large Print in association with Delacorte Press, New York, and simultaneously in Canada by Random House of Canada Limited, Toronto. Distributed by Random House, Inc., New York.

The Library of Congress has established a cataloging-in-publication record for this title.

0-375-43132-2

Random House Web Address:
www.randomlargeprint.com

FIRST LARGE PRINT EDITION

10   9   8   7   6   5   4   3   2   1

This Large Print edition published in accord with the standards of the N.A.V.H.

*"Courage is not the absence of
fear or despair,
but the strength to conquer them."*

*To my wonderful children,
who are my heart, my soul,
my courage,
To Beatrix, Trevor, Todd, Nick,
Sam, Victoria, Vanessa, Maxx,
and Zara,*

*With all my love,
Mom
d.s.*

A single moment,
etched in time,
shining brightly
like a star
in a midnight sky,
an aeon, an instant,
a million years
pressed into one,
when all stands still
and life explodes
into infinite dreams,
and all is changed
forevermore,
in the blink of an eye.

THE KISS

Chapter One

Isabelle Forrester stood looking down at the garden from her bedroom window, in the house on the rue de Grenelle, in the seventh arrondissement in Paris. It was the house she and Gordon had lived in for the past twenty years, and both her children had been born there. It had been built in the eighteenth century, and had tall, imposing bronze doors on the street that led to the inner courtyard. The house itself was built in a U-shape around the courtyard. The house was familiar and old and beautiful, with tall ceilings and splendid boiseries, lovely moldings, and parquet floors the color of brandy. Everything around her shone and was impeccably tended. Isabelle ran the house with artistry and precision, and a firm but gentle hand. The garden was exquisitely manicured, and the white roses she'd had planted years before were often called the most beautiful in

Paris. The house was filled with the antiques she and Gordon had collected over the years, locally and on their travels. And a number of them had been her parents'.

Everything in the house shone, the wood was perfectly oiled, the silver polished, the crystal sconces on the walls sparkled in the bright June sun that filtered through the curtains into her bedroom. Isabelle turned from the view of her rose garden with a small sigh. She was torn about leaving Paris that afternoon. She so seldom went anywhere anymore, the opportunities were so rare. And now that she had a chance to go, she felt guilty about it, because of Teddy.

Isabelle's daughter, Sophie, had left for Portugal with friends the day before. She was eighteen years old and going to university in the fall. It was Isabelle's son, Theodore, who kept her at home, and had for fourteen years now. Born three months premature, he had been badly damaged at birth, and as a result, his lungs had not developed properly, which in turn had weakened his heart. He was tutored at home, and had never been to school. At fourteen, he had been bedridden for most of his life, and moved around the house in a wheelchair whenever he was too weak to do so under his own steam. When the weather was warm, Isabelle wheeled him into the garden, and depending on how he felt, he would walk a little bit, or just sit. His spirit was indomitable, and his eyes shone the moment his mother came into the room. He always had something funny to say, or something to tell her. Theirs was a bond that defied words and time and years, and the private terrors they had faced together. At times she felt as though they were two people with one soul. She willed life and strength into him, talked to him for hours, read to him, held him in her arms when he was too weak and breathless to speak, and made him laugh whenever she could. He saw life as she did. He always reminded her of a tiny fragile bird with broken wings.

She and Gordon had spoken to his doctors of a heart-lung transplant, performed in the States, but their conclusion was that he was too weak to survive the surgery or perhaps even the trip. So there was no question of risking either. Theodore's world consisted of his mother and sister and was limited by the elegant confines of the house on the rue de Grenelle. His father had always been uncomfortable in the face of his illness, and Teddy had had nurses all his life, but it was his mother who tended to him most of the time. She had long since abandoned her friends, her own pursuits, and any semblance of

a life of her own. Her only forays into the
world in recent years were in the evening, with
Gordon, and only rarely. Her entire mission in
life was keeping Teddy alive, and happy. It had
taken time and attention away from his sister,
Sophie, over the years, but she seemed to understand it, and Isabelle was always loving to
her. It was just that Teddy had to be the priority. His life depended on it. In the past four
months, ever since the early spring, Theodore
had been better, which was allowing his mother
this rare and much-anticipated trip to London.
It had been Bill Robinson's suggestion, a seemingly impossible one at first glance.

Isabelle and Bill had met four years before at a
reception given by the American ambassador to
France, who was an old classmate of Gordon's
from Princeton. Bill was in politics, and was
known to be one of the most powerful men in
Washington, and probably the wealthiest. Gordon had told her that William Robinson had
been responsible for putting the last president in
the Oval Office. He had inherited a vast, almost
immeasurable fortune, and had been drawn to
politics and the power it afforded him since his
youth. It suited him, and he in fact preferred to
remain behind the scenes. He was a power broker and a king maker, but what had impressed
Isabelle was how quiet and unpretentious he

was, when they met. When Gordon explained Bill's circumstances to her, it seemed hard to believe that he was either as wealthy or as powerful as he was. Bill was enormously unassuming and discreet, and she had instantly liked that about him. He was easygoing, and looked surprisingly young, and he had a quick sense of humor. She had sat next to him at dinner and enjoyed his company immensely. She was pleased and surprised when he wrote to her the following week, and then later sent her an out-of-print art book they had discussed, which she had told him she had been hunting for for ages. With far more pressing pursuits at hand, she had been amazed that he remembered, and touched that he had gone to the trouble of finding it and sending it to her. Art and rare books were his passion.

They had talked endlessly about a series of paintings that had been found at the time, lost since the Nazis absconded with them during the war, which had turned up in a cave somewhere in Holland. It had led them to speak of forgeries, and art thefts, and eventually restoration, which was what she had been doing when she met Gordon. She had been an apprentice at the Louvre, and by the time she retired when Sophie was born, she had been thought to be both skillful and gifted.

Bill had been fascinated by her stories, just as she was by his, and over the next months, an odd but comfortable friendship had formed between them, via telephone and letters. She had found some rare art books to send to him, and the next time he came to Paris, he called her and asked if he could take her to lunch. She hesitated and then couldn't resist, it was one of the rare times when she left Theodore at lunchtime. Their friendship had begun nearly four years before, and Teddy was ten then. And over time, their friendship had flourished. He called from time to time, at odd hours for him, when he was working late, and it was early morning for her. She had told him that she got up at five to tend to Teddy every morning. And it was another six months before he asked her if Gordon objected to his calling her. In fact, she had never told him. Bill's friendship had become her secret treasure, which she diligently kept to herself.

"Why should he?" she asked, sounding surprised. She didn't want to discourage his calls. She enjoyed talking to him so much, and there were so many interests they shared. In an odd way, he had become her only real contact with the outside world. Her own friends had stopped calling years before. She had become increasingly inaccessible as she spent her days and

nights caring for Teddy. But she had had her
own concerns about Gordon objecting to Bill's
calls. She had mentioned the first art books he
sent when they arrived, and Gordon looked
startled but said nothing. He evidenced no particular interest in Bill's sending them to her, and
she said nothing to him about the phone calls.
They would have been harder to explain, and
they were so innocent. The things they said to
each other were never personal, never inappropriate, neither of them volunteered anything
about their personal lives, and they rarely spoke
of their spouses in the beginning. His was simply a friendly voice that arrived suddenly in the
dark hours of the early morning. And as the
phone didn't ring in their bedrooms at night,
Gordon never heard them. In truth, she suspected Gordon would object, if he knew,
which was why she had never told him. She
didn't want to lose the gift of Bill's calls or
friendship.

Bill called every few weeks at first, and then
slowly the calls began to come more often.
They had lunch again a year after they had met.
And once, when Gordon was away, Bill took
her to dinner. They dined at a quiet bistro near
the house, and she was stunned to realize, when
she got home, that it was after midnight. She
felt like a wilted flower soaking up the sun and

the rain. The things they talked about fed her soul, and his calls and rare visits sustained her. With the exception of her children, Isabelle had no one to talk to.

Gordon was the head of the largest American investment bank in Paris, and had been for years. At fifty-eight, he was seventeen years older than Isabelle. They had drifted apart over the years, she was aware of it, and thought it was because of Teddy. Gordon could not tolerate the aura of constant illness that hung over the child like a sword waiting to fall. He had never allowed himself to be close to him, and they all knew it. His aversion to Teddy's illness was so extreme, it was almost phobic. Teddy himself was acutely aware of it, and had thought his father hated him when he was younger. But as he grew older, he saw it differently. By the time he was ten, he understood that his father was frightened by his illness, panicked almost, and the only way he could escape it was to ignore him entirely, and pretend the child didn't exist. Teddy never held it against him, and he would speak of it openly with Isabelle, with a wistful look, as though talking about a country he wished he could visit, and knew he never could. The child and his father were strangers to each other, almost as though they had never met. Gordon blocked him out, and put all his energies into his work, as he had for years, and removed himself as much as possible from life at home, particularly his wife. The only member of his family he seemed even slightly drawn to was Sophie. Her character was far more similar to his than to her mother's. Sophie and Gordon shared many of the same points of view, and a certain coolness of outlook and style. In Gordon's case, it was born of years of erecting walls between himself and the more emotional side of life, which he perceived as weakness in all instances, and had no appeal to him. In Sophie's case, she simply seemed to have inherited the trait her father had created in himself. Even as a baby, she had been far less affectionate than her brother had been, and rather than turning to anyone for help, particularly Isabelle, she preferred to do everything for herself. Gordon's coolness had translated to independence in her, and a kind of standoffish pride. Isabelle wondered sometimes if it had been her instinctive reaction to her brother needing so much of her mother's time. In order not to feel shortchanged by what was not available to her, she had convinced herself and her own little world that she needed nothing from them. She shared almost no confidences with Isabelle, and never spoke of her feelings if she could avoid it, which most of the time she could and did. And if she confided in anyone, Isabelle knew, it was not her mother but her friends. Isabelle had always cherished the hope that once Sophie grew up, they would find some common ground and become friends. But thus far, the relationship with her only daughter had not been an easy one for her.

Gordon's coldness toward his wife, on the other hand, was far more extreme. Sophie's seeming distance from her mother could be interpreted as an attempt to stand on her own two feet, in contrast to her brother's constant neediness, and to be different from him. In her case, it seemed almost an attempt to prove that she did not need the time and energy her mother did not have to give, due to Teddy's being constantly ill. In Gordon's case, it seemed to be rooted in something far deeper, which at times seemed, or felt to Isabelle at least, like a deep resentment of her, and the cruel turn of fate that had cast a handicapped son on them, for which he appeared to blame her.

Gordon had a dispassionate view of life, and generally observed life from a safe distance, as though he were willing to watch the game but not play it, unlike Teddy and Isabelle, who were passionate about everything they felt, and expressed it. The flame that she and the child shared was what had kept Teddy alive through a

lifetime of illness. And her devotion to her son
had long since distanced Gordon from her.
Emotionally, Gordon had been removed from
her for years, since shortly after Teddy's birth.
Years before she met Bill, Gordon had moved
out of their bedroom. At the time, he had explained it by saying that she went to bed too
late and rose too early, and it disturbed him. But
she had sensed accurately that there was more
to it than that. Not wanting to make things
worse between them or confront him, she had
never dared to challenge him about it. But she
had known for a long time that Gordon's affec-
tions for her had at first diminished, and then
finally disappeared.

Isabelle could no longer even remember the
last time they had touched or kissed, or made
love. It was a fact of life she now accepted. She
had long since learned to live without her husband's love. She had often suspected that he not
only associated Teddy's illness with her, but
blamed her for it, although the doctors had reassured her that his infirmities and premature
birth had not been her fault. She and Gordon
never actually discussed it, and there was no
way to acquit herself of his silent accusations.
But she always felt them, and knew they were
there. It was as though just seeing Isabelle reminded Gordon of the child's sickroom, and

just as he had rejected his son from birth, out of a horror of his defects and illness, he had eventually rejected Isabelle as well. He had put up a wall between himself and his wife to shut out the images of illness he detested. He hadn't been able to tolerate what he perceived as weakness since he was a child himself. The wall between them was one Isabelle no longer attempted to scale, although she had at first. Her attempts at drawing closer to him after Teddy's birth had been futile, Gordon had resisted all her efforts, until finally she accepted the vast, lonely chasm between them as a way of life.

Gordon had always been cool and businesslike by nature. He was said to be ruthless in business, and not a warm person in any aspect of his life, but in spite of that, he had been affectionate with her at first. His standoffishness had almost seemed like a challenge to her, and was unfamiliar to her. But because of that, each smile won, each warm gesture, had felt like a victory to her, and all the more impressive because he showed no warmth to anyone else. She had been very young then, and intrigued by him. He seemed so competent, and so powerful in her eyes, and in many ways impressive. He was a man in total control of every aspect of his world. And there had been much about Isabelle that Gordon had liked, and which had reassured him that she would make a perfect wife. Her ancestry certainly, her aristocratic heritage and name, her important connections, which had served him well at the bank. Her family's fortune had evaporated years before, but their importance in social and political circles had not. Marrying her had increased his stature socially, which was an important factor for him. She was the perfect accessory to enhance both his standing and his career. And in addition to the appeal of her pedigree, there had been a childlike innocence about her that had briefly opened the door to his heart.

In spite of whatever social ulterior motives he may have had, there was a basic sweetness to Isabelle as a young girl that would have been hard for any man to resist. She was compassionate, kind, without guile. And the loftiness of Gordon's style, his considerable attentions toward her, and his exquisite manners when he courted her, had elicited a kind of hero worship from her. She was fascinated by his intelligence, impressed by his power and success in the world, and Gordon had been smooth enough with the advantage of being seventeen years older than Isabelle, to say all the right things to her. Even her family had been thrilled when he proposed. It had been obvious to them that Gordon would be a perfect husband and take extraordinarily good care of her, or so they thought. And in spite of his reputation for being tough in his dealings at the bank, he seemed extremely kind to her, which ultimately proved not to be the case.

By the time Isabelle met Bill Robinson, she was a lonely woman standing vigil over a desperately ill child, with a husband who seldom even spoke to her, and leading an unusually isolated life. Bill's voice was sometimes the only contact she had with another adult all day, other than Teddy's doctor, or his nurse. And he appeared to be the only person in her world who was genuinely concerned about her. Gordon rarely, if ever, asked her how she was. At best, if pressed, he told her that he would be out for dinner that night, or that he was leaving in the morning on a trip. He no longer shared with her what he did in the course of his days. And their brief conversations only reinforced her feeling of being shut out of his life. The hours she spent talking to Bill opened the windows to a broader, richer world. They were like a breath of fresh air to Isabelle, and a lifeline she clung to on dark nights. It was Bill who had become her best friend in the course of their conversations over the years, and Gordon who was now the stranger in her life.

She had tried to explain it to Bill once in one

of their early-morning phone calls, in the second year of their friendship. Teddy had been sick for weeks, she was feeling run-down and exhausted and vulnerable, and she was depressed over how cold Gordon had been to her the night before. He had told her that she was wasting her time nursing the boy, that it was obvious to everyone that he was going to die before long, and she had best make her peace with it. He had said that when the boy died finally, it would be a mercy for all of them. She had had tears in her voice and her eyes, when she spoke of it to Bill that morning, and he had been horrified by the callousness of the child's father, and his cruelty to Isabelle.

"I think Gordon resents me terribly for all the years I've spent taking care of Teddy. I haven't had as much time to spend with him as I should have." She entertained for him, but not as frequently as she knew he felt she should. Gordon had long since convinced her that she had failed him as a wife. And it irked Bill to hear how ready she was to accept what Gordon said.

"It seems reasonable, under the circumstances, that Teddy should be your first priority, Isabelle," Bill said gently. He had been quietly researching doctors for her for months, in the hope of finding a miracle cure for Teddy, but he hadn't been encouraged by what he'd been told by the physicians he'd consulted. According to Isabelle, the child had a degenerative disease that was attacking his heart, his lungs were inadequate, and his entire system was slowly deteriorating. The consensus of opinion was that it would be a miracle if he survived into his twenties. And it tore at Bill's heart knowing what Isabelle went through, and would have to face someday.

Over the next few years, their friendship had deepened. They spoke on the phone frequently, and Isabelle wrote him long philosophical letters, particularly on the nights she spent awake, sitting at Teddy's bedside. Teddy had long since become the hub of her life, and not only had it alienated her from Gordon, but there were times when it also kept her from Sophie, who berated her mother for it on more than one occasion. She had accused her mother of only caring about her brother. And the only one Isabelle could talk to about it was Bill, in their lengthy conversations in the heart of the night.

The moments they shared transcended their daily realities, the pressures of the political arena seemed to vanish into thin air when he talked to her. And for Isabelle, she was transported to a time and a place when Teddy wasn't ill, Gordon hadn't rejected her, and Sophie was never angry. It was like being lifted out of the life she led into the places and topics that she had once cared about so deeply. Bill brought her a new view of the world, and they chatted easily and laughed with each other. He spoke to her of his own life at times, the people he knew, the friends he cared about, and once in a while, in spite of himself, he spoke of his wife and two daughters, both of whom were away in college. He had been married since he was twenty-two years old, and thirty years later, what he had left was only the shell of a marriage. Cindy, his wife, had come to hate the political world, the people they met, the things Bill had to do, the events they had to go to, and the amount of time he had to travel. She had total contempt for politicians. And for Bill for having devoted a lifetime to them.

The only things Cynthia was interested in, now that the girls were gone, were her own friends in Connecticut, going to parties, and playing tennis. And whether or not Bill was part of that life seemed unimportant to her. She had shut him out emotionally years before and led her own life, not without bitterness toward him. She had spent thirty years with him coming and going, and putting political events ahead of everything that mattered to her. He had never been home for graduations and holidays and birthdays. He was always somewhere else, grooming a candidate for a primary or an election. And for the past four years, he had been a constant visitor at the White House. It no longer impressed her, and she was only too happy to tell him how much it bored her. Worse than that, she had dismissed the man along with a career she detested. Whatever there had once been between them was long gone. She had had a face-lift the year before, and he knew that she had been having discreet affairs for years. It had been her revenge for a single indiscretion he'd committed ten years before, with the wife of a congressman, and never repeated. But Cindy was not long on forgiveness.

Unlike Isabelle and Gordon, he and Cindy still shared a bedroom, but they might as well not have bothered. It had been years since they'd made love. It was almost as though she took pride in the fact that she was no longer sexually interested in her husband. She was in good shape, had a constant tan, her hair had gotten blonder over the years, and she was almost as pretty as she had been when he married her thirty years before, but there was a hardness about her now, which he felt rather than saw. The walls she had erected between them were beyond scaling, and it no longer occurred to him to try. He put his energies into his work,

and he talked to Isabelle when he needed a
hand to hold or a shoulder to cry on, or someone to laugh with. It was to Isabelle that he admitted he was tired or disheartened. She was
always willing to listen. She had a gentleness
about her that he had never found in his wife.
He had liked Cindy's lively spirit, her looks, her
energy, and her sense of fun and mischief. She
had been so much fun to be with when they
were young, and now he wondered, if he disappeared off the face of the earth, if she would
even miss him. And like their mother, his
daughters seemed pleasant when they were
home, but essentially indifferent to him. It no
longer seemed to matter to anyone whether or
not he was home. He was treated as an unexpected visitor when he arrived from a trip, and
he never really felt he belonged there. He was
like a man without a country. He felt rootless.
And a piece of his heart was tucked away in a
house on the rue de Grenelle in Paris. He had
never told Isabelle he loved her, nor she him,
but for years now, he had been deeply devoted
to her. And Isabelle greatly admired him.

The feelings Bill and Isabelle had expressed
toward each other over the years were officially
never more than friendship. Neither of them
had ever admitted to each other, or themselves,
that there was more to it than simply admira-

tion, ease, and a delight in the lost art of conversation. But Bill had noticed for years that when her letters didn't come, he worried, and when she couldn't take his calls, because Teddy was too ill, or she went somewhere with Gordon, he missed her. More than he would have cared to admit. She had become a fixture of sorts to him, someone he could count on and rely on. And he meant as much to her. He was the only person, other than her fourteen-year-old son, whom she could talk to. She and Gordon had never been able to talk to each other as she and Bill did.

Gordon was in fact more English in style than American. His parents had both been American, but he had been brought up in England. He had gone to Eton, and was then sent to the United States for college, and went to Princeton. But immediately after graduation, he returned to England and from there moved to Paris for the bank. But no matter what his origins were, he appeared to be far more British than American.

Gordon had met Isabelle one summer at her grandfather's summer house in Hampshire, when she was visiting from Paris. She was twenty years old then and he was nearly forty, and had never married. Despite a string of interesting women in his life, some of them racier

than others, he had never found anyone worthy
of a commitment, or marriage. Isabelle's mother
had been English and her father was French.
She had lived in Paris all her life, but visited her
grandparents in England every summer. She
spoke English impeccably, and she was utterly
enchanting. Charming, intelligent, discreet, affectionate. Her warmth and her light and her
almost elfin quality had struck him from the
moment they met. For the first time in his life,
Gordon believed that he was in love. And the
potential social opportunities offered by their
alliance were irresistibly appealing to him. Gordon came from a respectable family, but not
nearly as illustrious as Isabelle's. Her mother
came from an important British banking family,
and was distantly related to the queen, and her
father was a distinguished French statesman. It
was, finally, a match that Gordon thought worthy of him. Her lineage was beyond reproach,
and her shy, genteel, unassuming ways suited
him to perfection. Her mother had died before
Isabelle and Gordon met, and her father was
impressed by him, and approved of the match.
He thought Gordon the perfect husband for
Isabelle. Isabelle and Gordon were engaged and
married within a year. And he was in total
command. He made it very clear to her right
from the first that he would make all their deci-

sions. And Isabelle came to expect that of him. He had correctly sensed that, because of her youth, she would pose no objections to him. He told her who they would see, where they would live, and how, he had even chosen the house on the rue de Grenelle, and bought it before Isabelle ever saw it. He was already head of the bank then, and had a distinguished position. His status was greatly enhanced by his marriage to Isabelle. And he in turn provided a safe, protected life for her. It was only as time went by that she began to notice the restrictions he placed on her.

Gordon told her who among her friends he didn't like, who she could see, and who didn't meet with his approval. He expected her to entertain lavishly for the bank, and she learned how to very quickly. She was adept and capable, remarkably organized, and entirely willing to follow his directions. It was only later that she began to feel that he was unfair at times, after he had eliminated a number of people she liked from their social circle. Gordon had told her in no uncertain terms that they weren't worthy of her. Isabelle was far more open to new people and new opportunities, and the varied schemes and choices that life offered. She had been an art student, but took a job as an apprentice art restorer at the Louvre when she married Gordon, despite his protests. It was her only area of independence. She loved the work and the people she met there.

Gordon found it a bohemian pursuit, and insisted that she give up her job the moment she got pregnant with Sophie. And after the baby was born, in spite of the joys of motherhood, Isabelle found that she missed the museum and the challenges and rewards it offered. But Gordon wouldn't hear of her returning to work after the baby was born, and she got pregnant again very quickly, and this time lost the baby. Her recovery was long, and it wasn't as easy afterward to get pregnant again. And when she did, she'd had a difficult pregnancy with Teddy, which resulted in his premature birth, and all the subsequent worries about him.

It was then that she and Gordon began drifting apart. He had been incredibly busy at the bank then. And he was annoyed that, with a sick child under their roof, she was no longer able to entertain as frequently, or pay as close attention as he liked to her domestic and social duties to him. In truth, in those early years of Teddy's life, she had had almost no time for Gordon or Sophie, and she felt at times that they banded together against her, which seemed terribly unfair to her. Her whole life seemed to revolve around her sick child. She could never bring herself to leave him, in spite of the nurses they hired, and unfortunately by then, her father had died, her mother years before. She had no one to support her through Teddy's early years, and she was always at his side. Gordon didn't want to hear about Teddy's problems, or their medical defeats and victories. He detested hearing about it, and as though to punish her, he removed himself almost instantly from any intimacy in their marriage. It had been easy to believe eventually that he no longer loved her. She had no concrete proof of it, he never threatened to leave her, not physically at least. But she had a constantly uneasy feeling that he had set her adrift and swum off.

After Teddy, there were no more babies. Gordon had no desire for them, and Isabelle had no time. She gave everything she had to her son. And Gordon continued to convey to her, with and without words, that she had failed him. It was as though she had committed the ultimate crime, and Teddy's illness were her fault. There was nothing about the boy Gordon was proud of, not the child's artistic abilities, nor his sensitivity, nor his fine mind, nor his sense of humor despite the burdens he bore. And Teddy's similarity to Isabelle only seemed to annoy Gordon more. He seemed to have nothing but contempt for her, and a deep, silent rage that he never expressed in words.

What Isabelle didn't know, until a cousin of Gordon's told her years later, was that Gordon had had a younger brother who suffered from a crippling illness as a child and had died at the age of nine. He had never even mentioned his brother to Isabelle, nor had anyone else. The subject was taboo to him. And although his mother had doted on Gordon when he was younger, the latter part of his childhood was spent watching his mother nurse his brother, until he died. The cousin wasn't entirely sure what the illness had been, or what had exactly happened, but she knew that Gordon's mother had fallen ill after the boy died. She had lingered then, with a long illness, and died a slow, painful death. And what seemed to have stayed with Gordon was a sense of betrayal by both of them, for stealing attention from him, and tenderness and time, and eventually dying and abandoning him.

The cousin said that her mother had been convinced that Gordon's father had died of a broken heart, although several years later, but he had never recovered from the double loss. In effect, Gordon felt he had lost his entire family as a result of one sick child. And then he lost

Isabelle's time and attention to Teddy's illness. It had explained things to her when the cousin explained it to Isabelle, but when she had tried to speak of it to Gordon, he had brushed her off, and said it was all nonsense. He claimed he had never been close to his brother and had never had any particular sense of loss. His mother's death was a dim memory by then, and his father had been a very difficult man. But when Isabelle spoke to him of it, despite his protests, she had seen the look of panic in his eyes. They had been the eyes of a wounded child, not just an angry man. She wondered then if it was why he had married so late, and remained so distant from everyone, and it explained, finally, his resistance to Teddy in every possible way. But whatever she had come to understand did not help her with Gordon. The gates to Heaven never opened between them again, and Gordon saw to it that they remained firmly closed, and stayed that way.

She tried to explain it to Bill, but he found it impossible to understand, and inhuman of Gordon to desert her emotionally. Isabelle was one of the most interesting women he'd ever met, and her gentleness and kindness only made her more appealing to him. But whatever he thought of her, Bill had never suggested any hint of romance to her, he didn't even allow himself to think it. Isabelle had conveyed to him clearly right from the first that that was not an option. If they were going to be friends, they had to respect each other's respective marriages. She was extremely proper, and loyal to Gordon, no matter how unkind he'd been to her, or distant in recent years. He was still her husband, and much to Bill's dismay, she respected him, and had a profound regard for her marriage. The idea of divorce or even infidelity was unthinkable to her. All she wanted from Bill was friendship. And no matter how lonely she was with Gordon at times, she accepted that now as an integral part of her marriage. She wasn't searching for anything more than that, and would have resisted it in fact, but she was grateful for the comfort that Bill offered. He gave her advice on many things, had the same perspective on most things as she did, and for a little while at least, while they talked, she could forget all her worries and problems. In her eyes, Bill's friendship was an extraordinary gift that he gave her, and one that she treasured. But it was no more than that.

The idea of the trip to London had come up purely by accident, during one of their early-morning conversations. She'd been talking about an upcoming exhibit at the Tate Gallery, which she was dying to see, but knew she never would, as it wasn't scheduled to come to Paris. And Bill suggested that she fly to London for the day, or even two days, to see it, and enjoy a little time there on her own, without worrying about her husband or her children for a change. It had been a revolutionary idea to her and something she'd never done before. And at first, she insisted that she couldn't possibly go. Leaving Teddy was something she never did.

"Why not?" Bill asked finally, stretching out his long legs, and resting his shoes on his desk. It was midnight for him, and he'd been in the office since eight that morning. But he had stayed just a little later, so he could call her. "It would do you a world of good, and Teddy's been better for the past two months. If there's a problem, you could be home within a couple of hours."

It made sense, but in twenty years of marriage, she had never gone anywhere without Gordon. Theirs was a remarkably old-fashioned European marriage, unlike the very liberated arrangement he had shared in recent years with Cindy. In fact, these days, it was far more common for Bill and Cindy to travel separately than together. He no longer made any effort to spend vacations with her, except for an occasional week here and there in the Hamptons. And Cindy seemed much happier without him.

The last time he had suggested they take a trip together, she had come up with a million excuses, and then left on a trip to Europe with one of their daughters. The message was clear between them. The spirit of their marriage had long since disappeared, although it was something neither of them was willing to acknowledge. She did whatever she wanted, and with whom, as long as she wasn't too obvious about it. And Bill had the political life he loved, and his phone calls to Isabelle in Paris. It was an odd disparity between them.

In the end, after several conversations, Bill convinced Isabelle to go to London. Once the decision had been made, she was excited about it. She could hardly wait to see the exhibit, and do a little shopping in London. She was planning to stay at Claridge's, and perhaps even see an old school friend who had moved to London from Paris.

It was only days later that Bill discovered he needed to meet with the American ambassador to England. He had been a major donor to the last presidential campaign, and Bill needed his support for another candidate, and he wanted to get him on board early, to establish a floor for their contributions. With his support, Bill's dark horse candidate was suddenly going to become a great deal more attractive. And it was a pleasant coincidence that Isabelle would be there at the same time. She teased him about it when he told her he would be in London when she was.

"Did you do that on purpose?" she asked with her slightly British-tinged English. And along with it, she had the faintest of French accents, which he found charming. At forty-one, she was still beautiful, and didn't look her age. She had dark brown hair with a reddish tinge, creamy porcelain skin, and big green eyes flecked with amber. At his request, she had sent him a photograph two years before, of herself and the children. He often looked at it and smiled while they were talking during their late-night or early-morning phone calls.

"Of course not," he denied it, but her question wasn't entirely inappropriate. He had been well aware of her travel plans, when he made the appointment with the ambassador in London. He had told himself that it was convenient for his schedule to be there then, but in his heart of hearts he knew there was more to it than that.

He loved seeing her, and looked forward for months to the few times a year he saw her in Paris. He either found an excuse to go, when he hadn't seen her in a while, or stopped to see her on his way to somewhere else. He usually

saw her three or four times a year, and when he
was in Paris, they saw each other for lunch. She
never told Gordon about it when they met, but
insisted nonetheless to Bill, and herself, that
there was nothing wrong or clandestine about
their seeing each other. The labels she and Bill
put on things were polite, concise, appropriate.
It was as though they met each other carrying
banners that said "friends," and they were of
course. Yet he had been aware for a long time
that he felt far more for her than he ever could
have said to her, or anyone else.

He was looking forward to being in London.
His meeting at the embassy would only occupy
him for a few hours, and beyond that, he
planned to spend as much time as possible with
her. Bill had assured her that he was dying to
see the exhibit at the Tate as well, and she was
thrilled at the prospect of sharing that with
him. It was after all, she told herself, her princi-
pal reason for going to London. And seeing Bill
was going to be an unexpected bonus. She had
it all sorted out in her head. They were the perfect friends, nothing more, and the fact that no
one knew about their friendship was only because it was simpler that way. They had nothing
to hide, she told herself. She wore a cloak of respectability in his regard that seemed to be des-

perately important to her. It was a boundary she had long since established for them, and one that Bill respected, for her sake. He would never have done anything to upset her or frighten her away. He didn't want to jeopardize anything, or anyone, that had become so infinitely precious to him.

As she stood in her bedroom in the house on the rue de Grenelle, she looked at her watch, and sighed. It was time to leave, but at the last moment, she hated the thought of leaving Teddy. She had left a thousand instructions for the nurses who would be caring for him while she was away. They were the same nurses he always had, but they were going to be sleeping in the same room with him while she was away. And as she thought of Teddy, she tiptoed softly next door, to the bedroom next to her own. She wanted to check on Teddy one last time. She had already said good-bye to him, but she felt her heart give a tug as she thought of leaving him. And for just an instant, she wondered if it was a good idea for her to go to London. But he was sleeping peacefully when she looked in, and the nurse looked up with a smile and a wave, as though to shoo her on her way. The nurse on duty was one of Isabelle's favorites, she was a large, smiling, sunny-faced girl from Bretagne. Isabelle waved back at her, and then gently backed out of the room and closed the door. There was nothing left for her to do, it was time for her to go.

Isabelle picked up her handbag and a small overnight case, straightened the simple black suit she wore, and glanced at her watch again. She knew that at that exact moment Bill was still on his plane traveling from New York. He had been working there for the past few days. Most of the time, he commuted to Washington.

She put her suitcase on the backseat of her car, and put her black Hermès Kelly bag on the passenger seat next to her. She drove onto the rue de Grenelle with a smile in her eyes as she turned the radio on, and set off for Charles de Gaulle, as Bill Robinson sat staring out the window of the Gulfstream he owned and used constantly. He was smiling to himself as he thought of her. He had coordinated his flight to arrive in London at the same time as Isabelle's. And he was overwhelmed by a sense of anticipation.

Chapter Two

Bill Robinson went through customs at Heathrow
with a purposeful air, looking as though he
were in a hurry. And he was. It took him only a
few minutes to collect his bag, and with his
briefcase in his other hand, he strode toward
the driver from Claridge's, standing discreetly
to one side with a small sign bearing his name.
He stayed at Claridge's whenever he was in
London, and had convinced Isabelle to stay
there as well. It was full of ancient traditions,
was always cited as the best hotel in town, and
he had been staying there for thirty years. In
great part, the hotel appealed to him because
they knew him.

As the driver put Bill's suitcase and briefcase
in the trunk of the limousine, he glanced at the
tall gray-haired American, and was instantly
aware of a noticeable aura of power and success
about him that was impossible to ignore. Bill

had bright blue eyes, that shone with a kind expression, and once sandy blond, now graying hair. He had sharply etched masculine features, and a noticeably square chin. He was wearing gray slacks, a blazer, blue shirt, and a dark blue Hermès tie, and his black leather loafers had been perfectly shined before he left New York. There was a subtle elegance about him, he was well dressed without wearing anything remarkable or showy. And as he opened a newspaper to read in the back of the car, a woman would have noticed that he had beautiful hands, and he was wearing a Patek Philippe watch Cindy had given him years before. Everything about him, and that he wore, had a subtlety and quiet elegance to it that drew the right kind of attention to him. But for the most part, Bill Robinson preferred to be a behind-the-scenes man. In spite of his obvious connections in politics, and the opportunities that could have afforded him, he had never had the need to be a front man. In fact, he much preferred things as they were. He was fueled by power and political excitement, he loved the ins and outs of the ever-changing political scene, and had no desire to be publicly known. In fact, it was often far more important to him to be invisible and unseen. He had no need or desire to make a lot of noise, or draw attention to himself.

It was in fact an aspect of his personality that he and Isabelle shared. In her case, it manifested itself in shyness, in his it was one of the tools he used to wield his power behind closed doors. And although one might have noticed him walking into a room, just by the way he looked, or the way he seemed to take over without saying a word, he commanded respect and attention more by his silence than by anything he did or said. And in just that same way, people noticed Isabelle without her saying a word. She was actually uncomfortable when attention was focused on her, and it was only in private one-to-one conversations like theirs that she felt free to be herself. It was one of the things he loved about her, the way she opened up with him. He knew her every emotion, every reaction, every thought, and she had no hesitation anymore in sharing her deepest secrets with him. It was something Isabelle told him she and Gordon had never shared.

Bill checked into Claridge's, and Thomas, the concierge, instantly recognized him, and was pleased to see him again. Bill found himself engaged in polite conversation as he chatted amiably about the weather and recent local elections with the assistant manager, who escorted him to his room. It was a large, sunny suite on the third floor, decorated in flowered chintzes, pale blue silks, and antiques. And he waited only an instant after the assistant manager left the room. He picked up the phone as he glanced around the room. And he smiled as soon as he heard the familiar voice.

"How was the trip?"

"Very easy," Isabelle smiled when she heard him. They had synchronized their arrivals, and she had checked in twenty minutes before. "How was yours?"

"Fine." He looked like a boy, as he smiled. He had that all-American boyish quality that had always attracted women to him. "It felt like it was taking forever, I couldn't wait to get here," he said, as they both laughed a little nervously. It had been nearly six months since they'd last seen each other in Paris. He had planned to come back sooner, but unexpected political complications had kept him away longer this time, and he was anxious to see her. "Are you tired? Do you want some time to relax?"

"After an hour's trip?" She laughed. "I think I'm all right. How are you?"

"Hungry. Do you want to go out and get something to eat?" It was three in the after-noon.

"I'd love that. We can go for a walk afterward. I haven't moved all day. I've just been sitting on the plane." She was excited to see him, and he could hear it in her voice. Their meetings always filled them both with anticipation, and when they met, they talked endlessly for hours and hours, just as they did on the phone. There was never any awkwardness between them, no matter how long it had been since they last met.

"How was Teddy when you left?" As always, he sounded concerned. He knew what a constant worry Teddy was for her.

"Sleeping. But he had a good night. And Sophie called from Portugal last night. She's having a great time with her friends. How are the girls?"

"They're fine, I think. They're coming over here in a few weeks with their mother. Nobody tells me anything anymore. I can tell where they are by the charges on my American Express bill. Cindy's taking them to the South of France, before they go to Maine to see Cindy's parents." And then he was going to meet up with them in the Hamptons at the end of the summer, as he always did. But he had his own plans before then. He was going to be working in Washington all summer. Cindy no longer asked him to join them anymore, she knew it was a lost cause, and would have been stunned if he'd wanted to. "What's your room number?" he asked, glancing at his watch. They had time for a quick lunch, and he already knew he wanted to take her to Harry's Bar for dinner that night.

"Three fourteen."

"We're on the same floor," he observed. "I'm not sure where you are. I'm in three twenty-nine. I'll pick you up on the way out. Ten minutes?"

"Perfect," she smiled shyly then, and there was a moment's pause. "I'm happy to see you, Bill." For a moment, she sounded very French, and he felt suddenly very young. She meant something to him that he couldn't have explained. She was what he had always thought women should be, but couldn't have defined if he'd had to put it into words. Gentle, loving, patient, understanding, interested in all his doings, compassionate, funny, kind. She was like an unexpected gift in his life, as he was in hers. He was the life preserver she hung on to when everything else around had vanished over the years. There was nothing she could count on anymore, Teddy's health was a constant worry to her, and she knew that she could lose him at any moment, and Gordon was simply the man she shared a house with, and who had given her his name, but she often felt that he was no longer a part of her life. Except for occasional public appearances, he no longer had any need for her in his. And, as was appropriate at her age, Sophie had flown the nest. More than ever these days, Isabelle felt alone. Except when she was with Bill, in person, or on the phone. He was her mainstay, her joy, her laughter, her comfort, and her best friend.

"I'm happy to see you too," he said gently. "I'll pick you up in ten minutes. We can figure out our plans then." He knew they were going to the Tate the next day, and there were some private galleries she had mentioned she wanted to visit. He was planning to take her to dinner both nights. He would have liked to take her to the theater as well because he knew how much she loved it, but he hated to waste hours of precious time that he could spend talking to her. It was Tuesday afternoon, and they had until Thursday night. She had said she might be able to stay until Friday morning, but it depended on how Teddy was. And she felt she should be back in Paris for the weekend. It was like a race against time, and an extraordinary gift to have these few days. They had never been able to do anything like this. And he had no ulterior motives, no intentions or plans. He was just looking forward to the opportunity to be with her. There was something wonderfully pure and innocent about what they shared.

Bill washed his face and hands, shaved quickly, as he thought about seeing her, and ten

minutes later was walking down the hall looking for her room number. It was around two
corners and as confusing as possible, but he
found her at last. He knocked on the door, and
the wait seemed interminable, and then she
opened it and stood there looking at him for a
moment with a shy smile.

"How are you?" she asked, her creamy skin
faintly flushed, her long dark hair brushed and
gleaming as it hung past her shoulders, and her
eyes looked straight into his. "You look wonderful," she said as she stepped out of the room
and he gave her a hug. He had never kissed
more than her cheek, as he did now. He had a
faint tan from a weekend he'd spent at home in
Greenwich several weeks before, in sharp contrast to her creamy white skin. Her summers of
tanning in the South of France had ended years
before. Gordon still went occasionally, to see
friends, or with Sophie, while Isabelle stayed
home with their son.

"So do you," Bill said admiringly. Each time
he saw her, he was struck by how beautiful she
was. He forgot about it sometimes, when he
got caught up in her words and her thoughts
and their exchange of ideas. More than her
looks, he was captivated by her soul. But she
was strikingly beautiful, and she stepped next to
him and slipped a hand into his arm with the

grace of a young doe. She still moved like a girl, rather than the woman that she was. And he noticed instantly the chic black suit, the Hermès bag, and the elegant high-heeled shoes. She wore only her wedding ring, and on her ears a pair of small diamond studs. And looking at her, it was hard to believe she had a care in the world. She had a warm, welcoming smile, and just seeing him, there was joy and excitement in her eyes. "My God, Isabelle, you look great." She never changed, hadn't in the last four years, she was a little thinner than she'd been six months before, but with her classic beauty, she seemed to stand still in time. He felt like a kid again, as they walked down the stairs arm in arm, chatting about the trip, the galleries they wanted to see, the exhibit at the Tate, and they talked about his girls. He loved telling her funny stories about them, and she was laughing as they walked past the concierge to the main doors.

"I was so worried something would happen to interfere with this trip," he confessed. "I was afraid Teddy's health might make it impossible for you to come." He always told her everything he had on his mind, as she did with him. And Teddy certainly could have caused her not to come. Or Gordon, if he had decided she shouldn't go. But he had seemed totally uncon-

cerned with her plans to go to London for a
few days, and Teddy had been happy for her
that she could go. He knew nothing about Bill,
but he loved seeing his mother smile, and had
understood immediately how much she wanted
to go, and didn't want to stand in her way.

"I was worried too," she admitted to him.
"But he's so much better now. I don't think he's
been this well in the past five years." Adoles-
cence had been hard on him, and his condition
had worsened in the last few years, as he grew,
and his heart and lungs strained to keep up with
him. "He really wanted me to come." Bill felt as
though he knew him and had for years. Although he didn't see how, he hoped he could
meet him one day.

They stepped out onto Brook Street, and
Isabelle took a breath of air, as she stood close
to Bill, her hand still tucked in his arm. It was
a magnificent day, and unseasonably warm
for June.

"Where would you like to go?" he asked,
making a mental list of the possibilities, all he
wanted was to be with her. It was like a vacation
for him just being there. He never took the time
for leisurely afternoons, casual lunches, or strolls
down the street with a woman next to him. His
entire life centered around his work, and everything he did was tied into politics. There was no

such thing as free time in his life, except when he was with Isabelle. At her side, time seemed to stop, and his entire tempo and focus changed. No one who knew him well would have recognized him as he stood, looking relaxed and smiling at the beautiful woman with the long dark hair. "What about a pizza somewhere?" he asked casually, and she nodded. She was so happy, smiling up at him, she could hardly concentrate on what he was saying.

"What are you smiling at?" he teased, as they ambled slowly down the street, in no particular direction. They both felt that, for now at least, they had nothing but time on their hands.

"I'm just happy. I've never done anything like this. I feel so far removed from all my worries here." She knew Teddy was in good hands and all was well with the world.

"That's the way I want it to be for you. I just want you to relax and forget about everything."

They hopped in a cab a few minutes later and went to a little place Bill remembered in Shepherd Market, it was near the embassy, and he had gone there many times to catch a quick bite to eat between meetings. It had a garden, and the owner was delighted to see them when they arrived. They were well dressed and elegant, and there was something enormously charismatic about both of them. He showed them to a quiet table in the back. He brought the wine list to Bill, handed them both menus, and then disappeared.

"This is perfect," Isabelle smiled as she sat back in her chair and looked at him. The last time she'd seen him had been in Paris the previous winter, just before Christmas, he'd given her a beautiful Hermès scarf, and a first edition of a book they'd talked about. It was leather bound and extremely rare, and she cherished it, as she did everything he'd given her over the past four years. "I feel very spoiled."

"Good," he said, patting her hand. They agreed on a pizza, he ordered salads, too, and a bottle of Corton-Charlemagne.

"Now you're going to get me drunk in the middle of the afternoon," she teased. He knew from previous lunches that she hardly drank, but it was a wine he knew she liked, and a very good year.

"I don't think there's any risk of that, unless you've acquired some bad habits in the last six months. I'm much more likely to get drunk than you are," he confessed, although she'd never known him to drink too much on any of the occasions she'd seen him. He was a reasonable person with no apparent vices, other than a tendency to work too hard. "So what are we going to do this afternoon?"

"Whatever you like. I'm just happy to be here." She felt like a bird that had escaped a gilded cage, and he suggested wandering through some galleries and antique shops, which sounded very appealing to her. They chatted all through lunch, and it was four-thirty by the time they left the restaurant, and he hailed another cab. He had a limousine waiting for him at the hotel, but they were both enjoying the freedom of simply wandering around London on their own. And after the galleries and the shops, they strolled back to the hotel. It was after six o'clock by then.

"Dinner at nine?" he asked, smiling at her. "We can have a drink in the bar here, and then go to Harry's Bar." She had admitted long since that it was her favorite restaurant, and it was his as well. It was all very respectable, and neither of them felt awkward about being seen there. They had nothing to hide, and even if Gordon heard about it eventually, she had no qualms about telling him she'd seen Bill Robinson. She didn't intend to volunteer it to him, but she had no cause for guilt, and nothing to apologize for. "I'll pick you up at your room at eight," Bill said, and he had an arm around her shoulders as they walked into the elevator. No one who saw them would have believed that they had separate rooms and weren't married to each other. They looked so totally familiar and at ease, that at the very least it would have been easy to believe they were having an affair. But they seemed oblivious to all that as they talked on the way to the third floor and he walked her to her door.

"I had a wonderful afternoon," she said, and then stood on tiptoe to kiss his cheek. "You're very good to me, Mr. Robinson. Thank you, Bill," she said solemnly, and he smiled.

"I don't know why I should be good to you. You're such a dreadful person, and such a bore. But I have to do a little charity work now and then. You know, political wives, the halt and the lame . . . and time with you. Brownie points." She laughed, and he gently touched her arm as she opened her door. "Have a little rest before we go out tonight, Isabelle. It'll do you good." He knew how stressful her life was, how on duty she felt all the time, caring for her son, and he wanted her to relax and have a real vacation here. He knew from what she said that no one took care of her normally, and he wanted to do that for her now, for the short time he could. She promised him she'd take a nap, and then lay there thinking about him once she was alone in her room, lying on the bed. It was remarkable to think about how he had come into her life, by sheer happenstance years before, and how lucky she was.

She wondered why he stayed with his wife sometimes. It was easy to figure out that there was no real communication between them, and he deserved so much more. But she also knew that he didn't like talking about it. The state of his marriage to Cynthia was something he accepted, and a balance he chose not to disturb. She suspected it would have been awkward for him to challenge that anyway, he wanted no breath of scandal near him, to draw attention to him. Part of his strength was keeping well out of sight, so he could wield his power without any focus on him. A divorce would have brought too much attention to him, particularly if it was acrimonious, and he often said that Cindy liked things just the way they were. She wouldn't have gone quietly into the night, she liked the practical advantages of being Mrs. William Robinson, particularly in Washington, or anywhere. Although she said she hated politics, having a husband who had considerable influence over the president was not a bad thing in her mind. But Isabelle felt sorry for him. He deserved so much more than he had with Cindy. But he said the same thing about Isabelle. The life she led with Gordon was certainly not the marriage she'd envisioned or hoped for twenty years before, but it was something she accepted now. She had made her peace with it, and she didn't think of it, as she lay on the huge bed at Claridge's, anticipating an evening of conversation and laughter with Bill. At that exact moment, Gordon seemed part of a distant, almost nonexistent world. Bill always made her laugh and feel so safe and comfortable. And being in London with him was everything she had hoped it would be.

She dozed for a few minutes, and then got up at seven o'clock, and took a bath. She chose a narrow black lace cocktail dress and a silk wrap, with black satin high-heeled pumps, a pearl necklace she'd brought, and a pair of pearl and diamond earrings that had been her mother's. The dress was very respectable, but very feminine, and just like Isabelle, it had a faint air of subtle sex appeal to it. She brushed her hair into a smooth French twist, and applied her makeup carefully, and when she stood back and looked at herself, she saw nothing remarkable. But she was startled by his reaction when he came to her door at exactly eight o'clock, just after she'd called home and talked to Teddy's nurse, and was relieved to hear that all was well. Gordon was out, and Teddy was already fast asleep, so she didn't talk to him, but she was happy to hear that he'd had a good day. Knowing that would allow her to have a good time that night with Bill.

"Wow!" Bill said, taking a step back to admire her. She had the silk wrap thrown easily around her shoulders, one nearly bare shoulder peeked through, and the lace dress molded her figure exquisitely. She looked elegant and very lady-like, but far prettier than she realized, which was part of her charm. "You look incredible. Who did the dress?" he asked knowledgeably, and she laughed. She didn't think he knew anything about dress designers nor cared to.

"Saint Laurent. You surprise me. Since when are you interested in fashion?" He had never before said anything like that to her. But things were different here. They had the luxury of time, knowing they had two days stretched out before them.

"Since you've been wearing it. That was a Chanel suit today, wasn't it?" he asked, looking proud of himself, and she laughed at him again.

"I'm very impressed. I'll have to be careful what I wear from now on, and be sure it's up to your standards."

"I don't think you need to worry. You look lovely, Isabelle," he said warmly. They rode down in the elevator standing close to each other, and whispering in quiet conversation. She told him she had spoken to the nurse and Teddy was doing well, and she looked happy when she said it. He wanted so much for her to relax and have a good time, and so far the fates were conspiring in their favor. He had spent a great deal of time thinking about what he wanted to do with her during their two days. He wanted it to be a trip they would both remember for a lifetime, because who knew when their paths would cross in just this way again. He was almost afraid to think about it, he knew it was very likely that this one extraordinary opportunity would never come their way again.

Bill walked into the bar at Claridge's just behind Isabelle, and a number of heads turned as they entered. They made a handsome couple as they sat down at a corner table, and Bill ordered a scotch and soda for himself, and a glass of white wine for her. As usual, she barely sipped it as they chatted about art, politics, the theater, his family's summer home in Vermont, and the places they had both loved to go as a child. She talked about visiting her grandparents in Hampshire, when they were alive, and the rare but impressive times she had met the queen. He was fascinated by her stories, and she was equally intrigued by his. As always, there was a striking similarity of reactions and philosophies, the things that had mattered to each of them, the people, the places, the importance of family ties. It was Isabelle who commented later in the limousine, on the way to dinner, that it was strange how for people to whom family meant so much, their marriages had become distant and remote, and they had chosen people who were anything but warm.

"Cindy was a lot warmer when we were in college, but she grew up to be somewhat cynical. I'm not sure if that's my fault or not," Bill said pensively. "Mostly, we're just very different, and I don't think I've met her needs in a lot of years, and I think for a long time she was angry at me, or disappointed at least, about that. She wanted me to play the social game with her, in Connecticut and New York. She was never really interested in the political scene in the early days, when it fascinated me and I was up to my ears in it. And now that I'm in a more rarefied atmosphere, I think she's just fed up with it and it turns her off. And privately, we've just grown apart." But Isabelle thought there was more to it than that. He had already intimated to Isabelle for several years that he thought his wife had been unfaithful to him. And he had confessed to Isabelle about his one affair. But more than that, Isabelle sensed, both in what he said and didn't say, that Cynthia was anything but warm. She was not only distant from him now, but punished him, when they met, for what she seemed to feel were his fail-

ings in regard to her. Isabelle never heard stories about closeness between them, or kindness,
or any kind of emotional support. And she
couldn't help wondering if it was too painful to
Bill to admit that his wife simply didn't love
him anymore. From all that he said, Isabelle
wondered if she ever had. She had the same
questions in her own mind about Gordon. But
she didn't want to press Bill about his wife.
Whatever he saw in her, whether it was emotion or simply history, she didn't want to force
him to face something that would be too
painful for him, or awkward to admit or discuss.

"I think Gordon is a lot colder than Cynthia,"
he said honestly, and Isabelle didn't disagree
with him, although in great part Isabelle was all
too willing to blame herself.

"I think I've been a great disappointment to
him," she said quietly, as they rolled along in the
limousine toward Harry's Bar. "I think he expected me to be far more social and outgoing
than I am. I'm perfectly willing to entertain for
him, but I'm not very good at opening up to
people, or impressing them. That's hard for me.
I felt like a puppet in the early days of our marriage, and Gordon was pulling all the strings.
He told me what to say to people, how to act,
how to behave, what to think. And then, once
Teddy was sick, I didn't have the time or the

patience to play that game anymore. Even when Sophie was small, I was far more interested in her than I was in all those silly people he wanted me to impress. All I wanted was a family life and a home. I suppose you could say I failed him in that sense. I think Gordon is far more ambitious than I." Bill thought there was more to it than that, and the kind of coldness and cruelty she had described to him seemed calculated to make Isabelle feel that the distance between them was entirely her fault. It was as though Gordon was implying that, if she had done a better job of it, he would still be actively involved in her life. And Bill suspected that the reasons for his absence now had nothing to do with her, or with Teddy, but with things Isabelle didn't even begin to suspect. But he never wanted to hurt her by suggesting that to her, and she was so willing to take the blame. In spite of Gordon's unkindness to her, she was loyal to him and always made excuses for the things he did and said to her. As far as Bill could see, the generosity of spirit she extended to him was undeserved but typical of her.

"I don't see how you could disappoint anyone, Isabelle. I've never known anyone to try so hard, to extend themselves as much as you do, in every possible way, and I'm sure you did to him as well." She was able to forgive almost anything, and had. "And the fact that Teddy was sick from the moment he was born was not your fault."

"Gordon thinks I did something in the pregnancy that caused him to be premature. The doctor says it would have happened anyway, but I've never been able to convince Gordon of that." Which only confirmed the unpleasant things Bill thought of him.

Bill hadn't liked Gordon on the two occasions they'd met. He had found him pompous and overbearing and arrogant, and the sarcastic way he spoke to Isabelle had made Bill's skin crawl. He treated her like a child, and publicly dismissed her with sharp words, open criticism, and a wave of the hand. But he had gone out of his way to be nice to Bill, because he was impressed by him, while all the while seeming to ignore his wife. Gordon was charming when he chose to be, with people he thought were important or could be useful to him, but it was almost as though he needed to punish Isabelle for who she was. All her kindness and compassion and decency only seemed to inspire his contempt. Bill suspected that underneath it all Gordon was impressed by her family, and felt inadequate somehow, perhaps because of her ties to the royal family, and he needed to put her down to reassure himself. It wasn't a style, or a point of view, that warmed Bill's heart. But for Isabelle's sake at least, he feigned a moderate amount of respect when she spoke of him. He didn't want to put her in the position of defending the man. Her loyalty was evident, and he was her husband after all. But she no longer pretended to Bill that she was happy with Gordon, she simply accepted their marriage as her lot in life, and refused to complain about the way things were. She was just grateful to have Bill to talk to, and listen to her, and she loved the fact that he always made her laugh.

There was a big crowd at Harry's Bar that night, they could hardly get in the door, there were women in evening suits and cocktail dresses standing elbow to elbow at the bar, with men in dark suits, white shirts, and dark ties. The crowd looked sophisticated and fashionable, and Isabelle fit in perfectly in her black lace dress. Bill looked distinguished and elegant in a double-breasted dark blue suit he had just bought before the trip.

Their table was waiting for them, and the headwaiter acknowledged him instantly, and greeted Isabelle with a smile. He gave them a corner table he knew Bill liked, and they both recognized faces at the various tables all along the walls. There were several actresses, a major movie star, some literary figures of note, a table of businessmen from Bahrain, two Saudi princesses, and a table of fashionable Americans, one of whom had made a fortune in oil. It was a noticeably distinguished crowd, and several people stopped to say hello to Bill. He introduced Isabelle without hesitation simply as Mrs. Forrester, and offered no explanation as to who she was. And halfway through dinner, she noticed a well-known French banker she had met years before, he knew Gordon certainly, but he paid no attention to her, and never acknowledged either of them on the way out.

"I wonder who people think we are," she said, looking not worried, but amused. Her conscience was clear, even if it was unusual for her to be in London and dining with a man at Harry's Bar.

"They probably think you're a French movie star, and they think I'm some boorish American you picked up." He laughed as the waiter poured Cristal with their dessert. They had had a fabulous meal, and two excellent wines so far. But neither of them was drunk, just sated and happy and relaxed.

"Hardly," Isabelle looked amused. "Everyone knows who you are, Bill. In spite of the fact that you think no one does. But they have no idea who I am."

"I could make an announcement if you like. Or we could go table to table on the way out, and I could introduce you to everyone, and then I could tell them you're my best friend. Do you think that would tell them what they want to know?" What they could see was an extremely attractive couple, enjoying each other's company. Watching them made people smile.

"It might. Do you suppose Cynthia would be upset if she heard you were dining out with another woman?" Isabelle was always curious about her.

"Honestly?" he asked, smiling at Isabelle. He was always honest with her. It was a promise he'd made himself a long time ago, that he would never dodge the truth with her, no matter how awkward the truth was. And as far as he knew, she had done the same with him, and she always assured him she had. She cherished the candor and openness they shared. "In all honesty, Isabelle, I don't think she'd care. I think she's long past that now. As long as I don't make a fool of her, publicly at least, I think she figures what I do is my business. She wouldn't want me asking her questions about her life. And she has a lot more to hide than I." He had heard rumors about her for years, and only the first couple of times had he questioned her, after that he had decided that he didn't want to know.

"That strikes me as sad somehow," Isabelle

said, looking at him. "That isn't what marriage is about."

"No, it's not. But marriage seems to cover a broad spectrum of possibilities. Yours and mine are not exactly the stuff that people dream about. We have what people settle for, for a variety of reasons, after a long time."

"I suppose you're right," she said pensively, as the waiter poured them each a glass of Chateau d'Yquem. "Is that good enough for you, settling I mean?" The wine she'd drunk so far made her a little braver than she normally was.

"I don't have a choice. If I don't settle, my only choice is to get out. And for very different reasons, neither of us wants that. Cynthia wants the aura of respectability I provide for her, and the way of life. And I don't want the shock waves it would cause if we got divorced. So here we are. And besides, if we got divorced it would upset the girls. I don't see the point. I've never seen anything or anyone I wanted more." Nothing that was available to him, at least. He had made his peace with his own situation, as Isabelle knew, a long time before. But sometimes she wondered why. At fifty-two, he was young enough to start another life, and he deserved happiness, she thought, at least more than most. He gave so much, and got so little back. But Bill thought the same of her.

"You're never going to find anything or any-one else, as long as you're tied to her," she said as she took a tiny sip of the Yquem.

"Are you suggesting I get divorced?" He looked surprised, she had never said it as di-rectly before, and he couldn't help wondering why she was saying it now.

"I'm not sure. I just wonder sometimes if we're wasting our lives. I have no choice be-cause of Teddy, and I wouldn't get divorced anyway. No one in my family ever has. And at my age, it's too late to start over. But it's differ-ent for a man." It surprised him to hear her words, he didn't think she'd ever thought of leaving Gordon, and this was the first hint of it he'd ever had.

"It's not different for a man," he said quietly, "and you're eleven years younger than I. If any-one should be thinking of a new life, it's you, Isabelle. You and Gordon haven't been married in any real sense for years. You deserve a lot better than that." It was the first time he had ever been that blunt with her, but she had opened the door for him to say it to her, and he was glad he had.

"I couldn't do that, and you know it," she said calmly. "Everyone we know and are related to would be horrified, and I couldn't disrupt Teddy's life. He's too frail to survive a major change like that. Besides which, Gordon would never tolerate it. He'd kill me before he'd let me go. I have no doubt of it." Divorce wasn't even remotely an option in her mind. She sounded sobered as she said it, but tonight for the first time, she realized that she felt like a prisoner on parole. She had never allowed herself to realize how depressing the house in Paris was, how limited her life, how totally absent Gordon was. And suddenly, sitting at Harry's Bar with Bill, she was totally aware of what she had never had. But much of that, she insisted to herself, was because her life revolved around a sick child. She was not ready to see that the lonely life she led was in great part due to the fact that she had been emotionally abandoned years before by the man she'd married.

"I've never heard you talk like this before," Bill said as he put his hand over hers. She had never before been willing to admit to him or herself how deeply unhappy she was, she always made excuses for it, and she had also never openly admitted how potentially destructive Gordon was. Bill wondered if he had ever threatened her. But whether or not he had, Isabelle seemed to be well aware of the measure of the man, and how cruel he was, not only to her, but to their child. "What's making you say this now, Isabelle? Has he threatened you?" She had never before said that Gordon would kill her if she left, and he wondered now if she had brought up the subject with Gordon at some point. Bill watched Isabelle's eyes as she smiled at him. Her eyes were deep and wise and sad beneath her smile. She could foresee no life in her future other than the one she had. Hope for a better life had eluded her years ago.

"I think you got me drunk," she said apologetically, but she felt like a prisoner who had escaped, and she no longer wanted to keep the vow of silence she had once made. On the other side of the English Channel, she suddenly felt just slightly less loyal to Gordon than she did at home. And Bill knew her so well.

"I wish I had gotten you drunk," Bill laughed as he took another sip from his glass. "I would love to see what you'd do if you were drunk, Isabelle. Should we try?"

"You're awful. Here you are, worried about being the object of a scandal, and you're inciting me to behave scandalously. If you keep pouring champagne and Yquem for me, I'm sure you'll have to carry me out of Harry's Bar."

"I'll just throw you over my shoulder and tell them I found you under my table. I don't think anyone would mind."

"And then what would you do?" She giggled

at the image he painted, she was in great spirits, and wanted the evening to go on forever. In the back of her mind, she could hear the time ticking away. After tonight, she and Bill only had one night and two days left. Two nights if she stayed till Friday. But after that, they both had to go back to their real lives. She felt like Cinderella at the ball, and she didn't want the coachmen to turn back into white mice. Not for a while.

"I think if I had to carry you out of here, I'd give you a cup of coffee and sober you up just enough to take you to Annabel's to dance." The idea had just come to his mind, and Isabelle laughed.

"That does sound like fun. I haven't been to Annabel's in years, not since before I was married. I spent my eighteenth birthday there, and my father took me there once after Gordon and I were engaged. I haven't been back since. Gordon absolutely hates to dance."

"Then that settles it. We'll go there tonight. As soon as you empty your glass." He was teasing her, and knew she would probably only have another sip or two, the glass was still nearly full. She had only had one glass of each of the two wines he'd ordered and another of champagne, and no more than a sip of the Yquem. But it was still more than she ordinarily drank.

They were both happy, but not drunk. If anything, they were inebriated by the pleasure of each other's company, but not the wine.

"I can't finish it," Isabelle said plaintively, with huge eyes that looked into his, while he fought off an urge to put his arms around her. But he was not foolish enough to do anything of the sort, and he had no desire to jeopardize her reputation or put her in an awkward spot.

"If you can't finish your Yquem, then we can't go to Annabel's," Bill said with a determined look, as the waiter brought them a plate of chocolates and candies, which delighted Isabelle. She had had a wonderful time, and didn't expect to go anywhere else, except back to the hotel. She wasn't greedy and didn't expect to go out to dance. "I have an idea," he said then, teasing her again. "If you eat two chocolates, I'll accept that instead, and I'll take you to Annabel's." He wanted to take her there now.

"Are you serious?" She looked amused and surprised as she popped a small chocolate truffle into her mouth with a menacing look. "That's one."

"And here's one more," he said, handing her another chocolate.

"That's terrible. Not only do you want me drunk, you want me fat."

"That would take a lot longer than getting

you drunk," he said with a grin, and ate one of the truffles himself. "That settles it. We're going to Annabel's," he said as he signaled for the bill as the waiter walked by.

"I don't think I can even dance anymore. Besides, you're too young and I'm too old. The men there are all as old as my father, and they're dancing with girls Sophie's age."

"You can pass, and I'm afraid so can I. We'll just have to do our best. I'm not much of a dancer myself, but I think it would be fun." He looked relaxed and happy as he said it, and several heads turned as they left. They were a very handsome pair.

It only took them a few minutes to get to Annabel's, and when they arrived, once again everyone seemed to know Bill. He had been to Annabel's six months before with the ambassador, and he dined there occasionally with friends whenever he was in London. Isabelle was smiling as they were led to their table. She suddenly felt young and silly being there, but very flattered that Bill would take her.

There was a good crowd at Annabel's that night, and a number of them were couples like the ones Isabelle had described to Bill, older men with very young women, but there were a lot of couples Bill's and Isabelle's age as well. There were people at tables all along the walls having dinner, and a number of people chatting and drinking in the cozy bar. And as Bill and Isabelle sat down at a table near the dance floor, she was startled by something she saw in Bill's eyes. It was a look she had never seen there before. She put it down to the wine they'd been drinking, and the closeness they'd always shared, but there was something tender and warm in the way he looked at her, and he led her onto the dance floor a moment later without saying a word. They were playing an old song she had always liked, and she was surprised to find that Bill was not only a wonderful dancer, but he seemed to be in perfect harmony with her. He held her close to him, with a strong arm around her, and she glided around the floor with him feeling happier and more at peace than she had in years. They moved from one song to another without leaving the dance floor, and it seemed hours later when they finally went back to their table, and he ordered more champagne.

She only sipped at hers, and their eyes met again over their glasses, and after a moment, she looked away. She was afraid of what she was beginning to feel for him.

He saw her look instantly and was concerned. "Are you all right?" He was worried that he had done something to upset her, but on the contrary, what she felt ran so deep and moved her so much, she couldn't find the right words.

"I'm fine. I'm just having such a nice evening, I never want it to end."

"We won't let it," he said gently, but they both knew it might be years before they could do this again. She couldn't make a habit of flying off to London, and if Teddy took a turn for the worse again, it might be years before she could get away. And she didn't feel as free about seeing him in Paris as she did here. Gordon would never understand, and there was no way she could explain it to him. "Let's not think about later, Isabelle. Let's just enjoy this now, while we can." She nodded, and smiled at him, but when she did, there were tears in her eyes. It was as though she knew that only moments after she had said hello to him, she would soon have to say good-bye, and all they would be would be voices on the phone again. And he hated to see her go back to her lonely life. She was young and vital and beautiful, and she deserved to have someone beside her who appreciated all she had to give. "Shall we have another dance?" he asked finally, and she nodded. He held her hand this time as they walked back onto the floor. And this time, when he held her, she seemed to move infinitesimally closer to him. He said nothing to her, and closed his eyes as he held her in his arms. It was, at that exact instant, the most perfect moment in time, like a single sparkling diamond hanging suspended in a night sky.

They were both quiet when they left Annabel's, and they were halfway back to the hotel before either of them spoke again.

"I had such a good time tonight," Isabelle whispered softly, acutely aware not only of how handsome he was, but of how kind he was to her.

"So did I," he said, with an arm around her shoulders, enjoying her warmth as she nestled next to him. There was no artifice between them, no awkwardness, nothing uncomfortable or strange. But what she felt when she was with him, as much as happiness, was an extraordinary sense of peace. And neither of them moved for a minute when they got to the hotel, and the driver waited politely outside without opening the door.

"Shall we?" Bill said regretfully as he moved slowly away from her, and seeing the movement inside the car, the driver opened the door.

Bill followed Isabelle into the lobby, through the revolving door. It was two o'clock in the morning, and two workmen were polishing the marble floors. Isabelle yawned sleepily as they rode up in the elevator, and it stopped on the third floor.

"What time do you want to get started in the

morning?" he asked her, wishing in spite of himself that he could spend the night with her. He knew it was out of the question, and would never have jeopardized their friendship by asking her, or doing something she might regret. He knew how proper she was.

"How does ten sound? I don't think the museum opens before then." They were standing at her door by then, and she seemed subdued. The evening had made an enormous impression on her, in a number of ways.

"What about breakfast at nine? I'll pick you up on the way downstairs," he offered, standing very close to her.

"That would be nice," she smiled again. "I had such a good time tonight . . . thank you . . ." she whispered as he opened the door with her key, and then kissed the top of her head.

"I had a rotten time," he said, smiling at her as she stepped into her room and looked back at him and laughed.

"I'm glad," she said as he waved and then disappeared down the hall to his room. And all she could think was how lucky she was to have a friend like him, as she quietly closed her door and took off her shoes.

Chapter Three

Bill knocked on the door of Isabelle's room the next morning, and she was dressed and waiting for him, this time in a beautifully cut navy blue linen suit. She was wearing a navy blue Kelly bag, and navy alligator shoes, and she had a bright green scarf around her neck, and emerald and sapphire earrings. She looked pretty and young and fresh, and as always, very chic.

"You look wonderful today," he commented as they walked down the stairs side by side. "How did you sleep?"

"Like a rock," she said with a smile. "How about you?"

"I think I had too much to drink. I'm not sure if I fell asleep or passed out, but I feel great today." He hadn't seemed drunk to her the night before, and she didn't think he was. He was just teasing her, and he looked in good spirits as they walked into the dining room. He had called and reserved a table, and he ordered a huge breakfast for both of them.

"I can't eat all that," she complained. She looked at what he had ordered—eggs, waffles, bangers and bacon, croissants, oatmeal and fruit, orange juice and coffee—more than enough for a starving army, she commented with a smile.

"I didn't know what you like for breakfast," he grinned at her sheepishly, "so I ordered everything. What do you usually eat?" he asked with curiosity, he liked knowing every little detail about her.

"Usually, coffee and dry toast, but this is more fun," she said, putting waffles and eggs and bacon on her plate, and then adding some strawberries. And much to her own surprise, she ate a huge amount of what he had ordered, and he polished off most of the rest. And by the time they left the hotel, they were both in high spirits and teasing each other about how much they'd eaten and how fat they would get. "It's a good thing I only see you a few times a year," she said as they got into the waiting limousine. "I'd be obese if I saw you more than that," she added, but he looked odd as he glanced at her. He'd been thinking how nice it would be to have breakfast with her every day. She was such good company, and so easy to be with. It was rare for him to hear her in a bad mood, even when he called her several times a week on the phone. Cindy always said that she hated dealing with humans before noon. But Isabelle was chatty and informative all the way to the Tate.

She was telling him all about the paintings they were going to see, their history, their provenance, the technique and details that were most remarkable about them. She'd done her homework and was excited about seeing the exhibit with him. It delighted him to share her enthusiasm with her. And once they got to the exhibit, she was totally absorbed in each painting, studying intricately the most minute details, and pointing everything out to him. It was a whole new experience going to a museum with her, and by the time they left at noon, he felt as though he had taken an extensive art course.

"You're incredibly knowledgeable. Why don't you do something with all that, Isabelle? You know too much about art to just waste it."

"I don't have time anymore," she said sadly, "I really can't leave Teddy."

"What about doing restoration work in the house, so you could be near him? From the sound of it, you could set up a studio somewhere. The house must be big enough for you to do that."

"I think Gordon would make it very difficult," she said quietly, with a tinge of regret in her voice. "He never liked the idea of my working. He thought it was a far too bohemian existence when I was working at the Louvre. I don't think it would be worth the headaches it would cause." She had given up the idea of working long since, not only for Gordon, but for their son.

"I think it would be great for you," Bill said practically. He admired her knowledge, and the gentle way she had shared it with him. It was like sharing her passion with him, he never felt that she was showing off or making him feel ignorant, although he was far less knowledgeable than she was about it. But there was an amazing grace and humility about everything she did and said to him. "Do you paint yourself?" he asked with interest.

"I did. I'm not very good at it, but I used to love it."

"You could do that too, if you had a studio. I think it would be a wonderful outlet for you." She smiled at the idea, but she knew how angry Gordon would be. He had been constantly irritated by her work before she had Sophie, and he had absolutely insisted she stop all of it once the child was born. He thought it was beneath her somehow, and her artwork didn't suit the image he had of her, or wanted for her. All he had wanted from her at that point was to have his children and run his home. All that she had been before they married, everything she had once done and loved, was no longer of any consequence to him. She was his now, to direct and control, and treat as an object he owned. Possession was important to him.

"I think Gordon would take it as an affront if I went back to painting or restoring now. He made it very clear to me when we had children that that was part of my youth, and not a suitable pastime for a married woman."

"And what is a suitable pastime for a married woman?" Bill asked, sounding annoyed. Bill realized that he hated the man, and everything he stood for. He was snobbish and superficial and controlling, and it was obvious to Bill that he had absolutely no respect for her. And no interest whatsoever in what she liked to do, or who she was. She was just a "thing" he had acquired to enhance his career and his social position, and once she'd done that for him, he had no further interest in her. It seemed so incredibly unfair to Bill. She deserved so much more.

"I think running a home is pretty much all Gordon wants me to do. Taking care of the children. Keeping out of the way until my presence is required, which isn't often anymore. I think he might tolerate it if I did some kind of charity work someday, as long as it's on a committee that meets his approval, perhaps with other people he considers useful or worthy of him. Gordon never believes in doing anything unless it serves some useful purpose, otherwise he thinks it's a waste of time."

"What a sad way to live," Bill commented dryly.

"He's gotten a long way on that. He's probably the most important banker in Europe, certainly in France, and his reputation is very established in the States as well. Everyone on Wall Street and in all the major countries in Europe knows who he is."

"And then? At the end of the day, Isabelle, what does that give you? Who are you when it's all over and all you have is your career? What kind of human being are you? I've been asking myself that a lot in recent years. I used to think that was all that mattered too, that your business connections think you're important. But then what? What does that do for you if you have no family life, your wife doesn't care if you live or die, and your kids can't even remember the last time they had dinner with you? I want people to remember more than that about me." It was one of the many things she loved about him, the fact that Bill's values and sense of priorities were crystal clear. But she also realized that they hadn't always been as well established, and he had paid a high price for the lessons he had learned. His marriage was as empty as hers, and there was no denying that, although he loved them, he wasn't close to his girls. He had been gone too much of the time, chasing politics and making presidents, at times that would have mattered to his daughters when they were little girls. In recent years, he had made an effort to spend more time with them, with fairly good results. Both his daughters enjoyed his company and were proud of him, although he still traveled a lot of the time. But now when he was gone, he made a point of calling the girls. But his increasing estrangement from Cindy had taken a toll on the family. They rarely spent time together as a group, and when he saw his daughters, it was usually one on one, which worked too. In many ways, Isabelle was luckier than he, the one thing that truly mattered to her was Teddy and Sophie, and she spent a lot of time with them, and always had. But Gordon couldn't have said the same. His children were strangers to him, even Sophie, whom he preferred.

"I don't think Gordon has reached your state of enlightenment," Isabelle said honestly, "and I don't think he ever will. Those things don't matter to him. He's very happy with just being important in the financial world. The rest is of no importance to him."

"He'll wind up a sad man one day. But then again," Bill said, looking ruefully at her as they walked back to the car, "maybe I will too. I figured it out for myself eventually, but a little late in the day. I share more real life with you, Isabelle, than I ever did with Cindy or the girls. I'm afraid I missed that boat a long time ago. I was never there for them."

"I'm sure they understand why," Isabelle said gently. "The girls are nearly grown up now, they still have a lifetime to share with you."

"I hope they see it that way. They have their own lives now, and their mother has tried to convince them of what a selfish bastard I am. And maybe she's right," he said, and then smiled down at his friend. "You've brought out the best in me. She never did. She's not a warm person. I'm not sure she ever really wanted me to be who I am now. I think this would actually be frightening to her, the kind of intimacy we share, even if it is on the phone most of the time. She didn't want to bare her soul to me, or deal with mine, she just wanted me to be there, to go to parties with her. And that's not who I am. I like having a good time, but I never realized how much I missed having someone to talk to. Cindy and I manage to miss the point with each other completely, and wind up feeling alone, even if we're sitting in the same room. That's never going to change."

"It might," Isabelle said, trying to sound encouraging and hopeful for his sake, "if you did. Maybe if you gave her a chance and opened up to her, she might learn to be intimate with you."

"That's not Cindy," he said as something hardened in his eyes, "and that's not what I want anymore. It's over for us, and actually, I think it's better that way. There's no disappointment, no pain. As long as I show up once in a while for one of her benefits, and keep paying the bills, and don't forget to come to the girls' graduations, that's all she wants from me now. We live in different worlds. I think we both feel safer that way." He was remarkably sure of what he felt, and was afraid to feel.

"It's amazing what we do to our lives, isn't it?" Isabelle said with a sigh as they settled into the back of the limousine again and he gave the driver the address of the restaurant where they were having lunch. Isabelle had heard of it, but didn't know where it was. It had been a favorite with Princess Di for years. "You've allowed yourself to drift apart from Cindy and your children. I've allowed Gordon to shut me out without saying a word. Why are we so willing to let people do that to us? Why do we let others make that choice without speaking up, and at least making ourselves heard?" Thinking about it now amazed her. It all seemed so clear, more than it ever had before.

"Because that's who they always were. At some level, we both knew going in that this was how it would wind up. Cindy was adorable when she was in college, she was bright and cute and a lot of fun, but she was never warm. She's probably the most selfish, manipulative, calculating woman on the planet. And Gordon is cruel, cold, and controlling. Nothing we did would ever have changed that. The trouble is, that was what we were willing to settle for, whether we admit it or not. The question is, why did we think that was all we deserved?"

"My parents were like that," Isabelle said softly, looking at him with her enormous green eyes, and he nodded. "I loved them, but they were very distant and reserved."

"So were mine. My parents hated kids, and had decided not to have any, and then I came along in their forties, as a surprise. They never let me forget it, and always let me know, or made me feel, that they were doing me a huge favor having me around at all. I couldn't wait to get the hell out when I went to college. And they both died in a plane crash when I was twenty-five. I never even cried. I felt as though strangers had died when the airline called. I didn't know what to say. I don't even know who they were, just two very intelligent people who let me live with them for eighteen years, and were relieved when I finally moved on. I don't know what they'd ever have done if I'd hugged them, or kissed them or told them I loved them. I don't remember my mother ever hugging or kissing me as a child. She always spoke to me from across the room, and my father never spoke to me at all. Cindy's like that. She always speaks to me from ten feet away, farther if she can."

"It's a wonder you're as sane as you are," Isabelle said sympathetically. She could barely imagine his childhood, in some ways, and yet hers hadn't been much different. There had been hugging and kissing, but mainly the form of it, and beneath the form, there had been very little love. "My mother was very English. I think she wanted to love me, and she did probably, but she didn't know how. She was very proper and very cold, she had lost her own mother when she was a baby, and her father had been very cold to her. He sent her to boarding school when she was nine, and left her there until she married my father. She met him at her presentation at court, and I think my grandfather arranged the marriage to get her out of the house. And once she was gone, he remarried, a woman he'd been involved with for years, even before his wife died. The British side of the family was full of skeletons and secrets, and people we weren't allowed to mention or talk about. All we had to do was dress properly, be polite, and pretend that everything was fine. I never had any idea how my mother felt about anything, and my father was so involved in politics, I don't think he knew we were alive. My mother died when I was in my teens, and my father never had time to talk to me, or be with me, although I think he was a nice man. Their marriage was a little like mine and Gordon's, which may be why it doesn't shock me more than it does to have a husband who has shut me out. I've never given it much thought, but it's the only model I know."

"I guess me too," he said philosophically. There was nothing he couldn't say to Isabelle. "I suppose if Cindy had been warmer than my parents, I wouldn't have known how to deal with it in those days. I was twenty-two when we got married, and I think part of me has been frozen for years." It was only when he had begun talking to her four years before that so much had become clear to him, and so many of his views had changed. He had been drawn to

Isabelle's warmth and light like a moth to flame, and in some ways, she had kept him alive ever since. But the contrast between her and his wife had made him feel even more distant from Cindy after so many years. He could see now how vastly separate and distant they were, and had been for so long.

"I wonder how different it would have been if we had known then, when we married them, all that we know now."

"I'd never marry Cindy if I met her today," Bill said without hesitation. "I can't talk to her, never could. She hates talking about feelings, has no need for real conversation, in fact she detests it. All she's interested in is a marriage that looks good, what lies beneath it is of absolutely no interest to her. I hate to make her sound so shallow, and she has some wonderful qualities, but I've been married to a stranger for thirty years."

"And you're willing to stay that way for another thirty?" she questioned him.

"It looks that way, doesn't it?" he said honestly, but lately he'd been wondering why himself. But divorce would have been a serious handicap for him. Keeping a low profile, and his nose clean, was essential to him. No president or presidential candidate would want to be associated with him, if Cindy ever made things rough, and he had long since suspected she would. She was not about to let go of a good thing. The last thing Cindy wanted was a divorce. She liked the status quo. "Aren't you ready to do the same thing? To stay in a loveless marriage for the rest of your life?" Bill questioned her. He knew the answer without asking her. They had discussed it before.

"I have no choice."

"We all have choices, if we're brave enough to take them. But you and I have a lot to lose. My career would be impacted if Cindy and I split up now. And you have a desperately sick child. I understand why we're both doing what we're doing. I can explain it. But in spite of that, sometimes I think we're both fools. If we really had any courage, and believed in our ideals, we'd get the hell out of Dodge. And I don't think either of us ever will." It was not a judgment he was making of her, or himself, it was a simple statement of fact as he saw it.

"I suspect you're right," she said, sounding sad.

"I just hope we don't regret it one day. Life is short. My parents died in their sixties, and I'm not sure they ever enjoyed their life. They just did what they thought they had to, and what they should. I want more than that. I just haven't figured out how."

"I don't let myself think about it," Isabelle said

honestly. "I made a choice twenty years ago, and I've stood by it."

"That's noble of you," he said, taking her hand in his as they sat in the car, "but they don't give prizes for that. In the end, no one's watching, no one cares. No one's going to pin a medal on us one day for being brave."

"What are you saying?"

"I'm not sure. I get tired sometimes of all the reasons I give myself for the way I live. I'm not even sure I believe my own bullshit anymore. To be honest with you, Isabelle, when I see you, and talk to you, I wonder what the hell we're both doing."

"With each other?" She sounded frightened and wondered if he was telling her he wouldn't see her anymore. As she looked at him, her eyes were wide.

"No, with everyone else. You and I are the only ones who make sense. I've never been able to talk to anyone the way I talk to you. Isn't that the way it's supposed to be?"

She nodded, thinking of all that he had said. "It is now, but I wouldn't have understood it at twenty-one when I got married. All I knew then was to do what I was told. Gordon was just like my father. He told me when to get up, when to go to bed, what to say, what to do, what to think. I think I found it comforting then. I never realized I had a choice, and there were other ways to live."

"And now?"

"I still don't have choices, Bill. You know that. What choice do I have?"

"Whichever you want. That's the point. We both talk about the high price of changing our lives. What about the high price of staying in them as they are? Do you ever think of that?"

"I try not to," she said honestly. "I'm there for Teddy's sake, and Sophie's, whether they recognize it or not."

"Are you sure that is why you're there? Are you sure of that?" he asked, watching her intently. He had never been this forceful with her, and Isabelle was surprised. She wondered what had changed. It was as though he was no longer satisfied with his life, or hers. "Are you sure you're not there because you're too scared to do anything else? Because I am. I think I'm too goddamn scared to just throw all the cards up in the air and walk out. Someone might actually think I'm human and less than perfect, and even that I have real needs. Imagine that."

"Are you telling me you're going to leave her?" Isabelle was stunned. In all the years they had talked to each other, he had always said he'd never break up his marriage, and so had she.

"I'm saying, or at least I think I am, that I

wish I had the guts to leave her." And then he decided to take a big step. Even if she was furious and walked off, he had to say it, because it was what he felt. And it meant too much to him to ignore. "Just for your sake, I wish you had the guts to leave him. It kills me to listen to you when I call, you sound like a prisoner in that house, you're being starved and deprived and disregarded and disrespected, and you have been for years. It makes me want to come over and kidnap you, and Teddy, anything to get you away from him and that house. Gordon doesn't deserve you, Isabelle, any more than Cindy deserves me. And what's more, they never did. Both of them have been getting away with murder for years. I wish life were simpler than it is. But it's not. It's goddamn complicated for both of us. I just wish it weren't. I wish we could both start all over again."

"So do I," she said quietly. "But we can't. You know that as well as I do." Isabelle loved the idea of his getting out of his marriage. But in truth, she knew it would be disastrous for him. And so did he. "If Cindy creates a scandal, your entire political life will come down around your ears. You've spent thirty years building that. Are you really willing to give that up? For freedom? Are you so sure? For your ideals? And then what will you do? And I? Gordon told me

a long time ago that if I ever left him, he would
see to it that I starve in the street. I inherited
nothing. It all went to my brother. And when
he died, in an accident, it went to his sons. I am
completely dependent on Gordon. I cannot afford to walk away from him. I couldn't provide
for my son. I couldn't get him the medical assis-
tance he needs. It costs a fortune, and as little as
Gordon may care for me or Teddy, he pays for
absolutely everything he needs without blink-
ing an eye. What would you suggest, Bill? That
I subject Teddy to abject poverty, on a whim,
or leave him behind? No, it's impossible and
you know it. Besides, Teddy wouldn't survive
the upheaval and the change. And it's all very
noble to think of leaving Gordon because he
appears not to love me. But love is a luxury in
my life. It's one neither Teddy nor I can afford."
It was a hard thing to say, and to live with, but
for her it was true. She was dependent on Gordon to provide the very best she could for her
son. But it broke Bill's heart to see her willingness to live like that, although he had done virtually the same thing. They were both so
willing to settle for what they had. And at such
a high price to themselves.

"I guess we just have to make the best of it,"
Bill said quietly, as they pulled up in front of the
restaurant he'd chosen for lunch. It was Italian,

and immensely popular, and once again very chic. "Maybe you're right. Maybe we don't have a choice, although I hate to believe that." But in her case, he could see no way out, although he found it hard to believe that the French courts would allow Gordon to starve her and their sick child, but maybe she was right, and they would.

"If I leave him," Isabelle said, looking unhappy, "it would be the most selfish thing I could ever do. Gordon wouldn't give me a penny more than he had to, and I wouldn't be able to make Teddy as comfortable as he is. I would be doing it strictly for myself, and how could I do that to him? The balance is already precarious enough for him as it is."

"You can't do it," Bill said simply. "I don't mean to taunt you. I think I get greedy when I spend time with you. I see what life could be, and has never been for either of us."

"Maybe it's only like this between us because all we have are phone calls, and a few hours together every few months. Maybe if we had married each other, it wouldn't be like this."

"Do you really believe that?" he asked, looking her straight in the eye.

She hesitated for a long time, and then silently shook her head. "No, I don't. But we'll never know. We can't even allow ourselves to think of it," she said, closing a door in her head.

"Is dreaming about it another luxury we can't afford, like love?" he asked, looking unhappy.

"I think so. If we ask for more than we have now, or try to take it, we'll only hurt each other in the end. I think we just have to be grateful for what we have, and not ask for more. You're the dearest friend I have in the world, and I love you for it. Bill, you know that. Don't let's spoil it by wanting more." She had felt the same pull he had since the night before. It was so wonderful being together, walking, talking, laughing, dancing, sharing waffles and croissants. But then what? What would happen when they went home? She wasn't going to allow Bill to do anything foolish, even if he wanted to, she knew that the rest was something they couldn't have. Just as he would, she would have loved it, but she was willing to accept knowing that it wasn't theirs to have. But Bill looked stubborn as he looked at her, before the driver opened the car door.

"I want more," he said bluntly, and suddenly she laughed.

"Well, you can't have it. You're being a spoiled brat."

"I feel alive for the first time in years." He

looked it too. And so did she. She felt as if she had dropped ten years since the day before.

"It was the bangers at breakfast. I think they went to your head." She had decided that the only way to handle it was to refuse to take him seriously, but she was startled by all that he had said. "Maybe we can promise to meet here once a year, for a few days like this. Maybe that will be enough." It was all she could think of in lieu of a life with him.

"You know as well as I do that it's not enough," he said stubbornly.

"What do you suggest? That we run away to Brazil? Bill, be serious. Think of what you're saying. Don't be crazy. And don't expect me to be crazy with you. I can't." He knew her well enough to know that she would never jeopardize her child, that was the crux of it for her. But he wasn't sure she'd ever have left Gordon anyway. She was too proper to do anything as outrageous as that. And even though he was rotten to her, she was incredibly loyal to him.

"You can't like taking his abuse."

"I don't. And it's not. He has simply removed himself from me."

"He abandoned you emotionally years ago. What's left, other than the fact that he pays Teddy's bills?"

"That's enough. It's all I need."

"That's insane. You're forty-one years old. You need more than that."

"I don't even think about it anymore," she said firmly, trying to resist all that she felt for him.

"Then you should."

"I think you need a drink, and a nap. Maybe sedation." She had never seen or heard him like this. It touched her, but there was nothing she could do about any of it. And she knew it. In another day, she had to go back, two days at most. All she could do was enjoy the time they had, and not spoil it by wanting more. But suddenly he was refusing to see that, and he seemed to want to jeopardize everything by wanting too much. "You have to be sensible now."

"Why?" he asked her as they got out of the car.

"You know why. Because like it or not, we have no choice. You're only torturing yourself. Or me at least. You have a right to get free if you want to, and maybe you should. But my situation is more complicated than that. Teddy's life depends on what Gordon provides for him." And she couldn't afford the uncertainty of counting on someone else, not even Bill. Gordon was the boy's father, and owed at least that much to him.

"He'd have to be a monster to withdraw that

from you." She didn't comment for a moment and then looked Bill in the eye again, and spoke clearly and firmly so he would know she meant what she said.

"I'm not going to put it to the test. I can't."

"I understand," he said quietly, and followed her into the restaurant. He didn't speak again until they sat down. "I'm sorry I brought it up. I didn't mean to upset you. It's just that none of this makes sense. We're both living with people who make us unhappy, and when we're together, it feels so right." Suddenly he wanted to risk it all for her.

"Maybe it feels right because we're not really together. Maybe we'd make each other as unhappy as they do. We don't know." Everything that had been unspoken between them was now suddenly out in the open, and in some ways it was a relief. They had been hiding behind their friendship, and suddenly he was making it clear that he wanted more. But she was making it just as clear that it was impossible for her, no matter what she felt for him. There was far more at stake than that. And she wasn't going to throw Teddy's life or health away for the dream of a romance. She was far too sensible for that. No matter how much she cared about Bill, and admired him, her son came first. And he respected her for that, he always had, and always would.

"I accept what you're saying, Isabelle," he said clearly, as they sat at a table under an umbrella, protecting them from the June sun. "I would never jeopardize Teddy's health. But I want you to know how much I care about you. I won't put you or your son at risk. In fact I'd like to help you with him if I can. But I'm not willing to pretend I don't give a damn, or that I don't want more. I want you to know that."

"I know that, Bill," she said softly. "You've been so good to me for so long." For the past four years, other than her children, he was all she had.

"Not good enough. Not as good as I'd like to be. I'm just tired of the hypocrisy of our lives. You pretend to be his wife, I pretend to give a damn when I go to black-tie events with Cindy. I'm not sure I can fake it anymore. I'm not sure I want to. I don't think the rewards are worth the price."

"You may pay a much higher price if you don't play the game anymore." She had questioned it all herself, and he had caught the bug and tried to incite her to riot. But Isabelle was prepared to be the reasonable one.

"Maybe one of these days I'll toss it all into a hat, and give it up. You never know," Bill said calmly.

"You need to give it a lot of thought," she said quietly, as he nodded, and took her hand in his. She had long, slender fingers, and beautiful, graceful hands.

"You're a remarkable woman," he said quietly, with eyes full of emotion, "and a lot more sensible than I."

"Maybe that's a good thing." She lifted his hand to her lips then and kissed it. "You are my very dearest friend." He couldn't speak for a moment, and she nodded. There was so much he wanted to say to her, but he knew from everything she had said to him that morning that it wasn't the right time.

"What would you like for lunch?" he said, trying to de-escalate the emotions that had nearly gotten the best of him. He couldn't even imagine what it would feel like when she left for Paris again. But there was no point thinking of it now.

They decided on pasta and salads, and they both stuck to safe subjects like books and art. And she thought he should write a book of his own about the political scene. She had said as much to him before. But what would have made the book interesting were the secrets he couldn't divulge.

"Maybe when I retire," he said as they got to dessert.

They had both calmed down by then. He wasn't sure why things had gotten out of hand that morning, except that he was so happy when he was with her, and it was hard to accept that there could never be more. He knew that in Teddy's lifetime she would never even think of leaving Gordon, and he hoped for her sake that her son would live for a long time.

After some earnest consultation, they went to the British Museum that afternoon, and didn't come out again until four. They went for a walk down New Bond Street, looking into the shop windows at paintings and jewelry, and walking along slowly arm in arm. He couldn't help thinking to himself again how comfortable he was, being with her. It was nearly six o'clock when they got back to Claridge's and decided to have tea. They had cucumber sandwiches, and others with tomato and watercress and egg salad and little biscuits that reminded her of her grandfather when she was a child. High tea was something she had always loved. It seemed so civilized to her, and he teased her about it. Bill said he'd much rather eat eclairs and petits-fours at Angelina's in Paris, or have ice cream at Berthillon. And she said she loved that too.

"When are you coming to Paris again?" she asked casually as they ate their sandwiches and she poured him another cup of tea.

"How about next week? I'm going to have terrible withdrawal after this week."

"So am I," she confessed. For all her brave statements about what they couldn't have, she felt the same pull that he did. When they were together, or even talking on the phone, it all seemed so right, to both of them. But it was forbidden fruit. Just being with him was a great gift.

"Where do you want to have dinner tonight?" he asked, as she rolled her eyes and laughed at him.

"How can you even think of eating again after all this? I won't be able to eat for a week." But as far as they both knew, it was their last night. She was planning to leave the next day, late in the afternoon. She didn't really think she should stay over the following night, although she was tempted to, and he didn't want to push. He knew she felt she should get back to her son. And maybe, if he didn't press too hard this time, she'd be willing to do this again. It had been absolutely perfect for both of them.

"What about Mark's Club?" he asked, ignoring her protests about eating dinner again. "We can go late if you prefer."

"That would be fun. I haven't been there in years. Actually," she laughed, "I haven't been anywhere."

"I'll make a reservation for nine o'clock." He left the table for a moment to cross the lobby and speak to the concierge as she watched him go. He had an almost irresistible male grace as he sauntered across the lobby and spoke to the clerk at the hall porter's desk. And she continued to watch him as he walked back. "Why were you staring at me?" he asked, looking amused and faintly embarrassed. She was so beautiful, it made his heart ache sometimes just to look at her. He wanted to give her so much more, to go places with her, spend time with her, introduce her to his friends, take her to Washington and show her off. But he knew that neither of them could do that. This was as far afield as she could go.

"I was admiring you," she confessed. "You're a very handsome man, Mr. Robinson." She had felt that way about Gordon a long, long time ago. But not anymore. She knew him too well now, and the icy coldness of his heart.

"You're either crazy or blind," Bill said, and then laughed, looking slightly uncomfortable, and then they got up and went upstairs. It was seven-thirty by then, and he said he was going to have a massage in his room while she dressed, and called home. "I'll pick you up at a quarter to nine. Does that give you enough time?"

"It's fine." All she wanted to do was check on Teddy again, have a bath, do her hair, and dress, and she didn't take long.

"See you in a little while," he said as he put an arm around her and kissed her cheek. And as he did, he was tempted to ask if she wanted to stay another night, if Teddy was doing well. But he thought he'd wait and see what she said after she called home, and spoke to the nurses and the boy.

And when she did, she was pleased with what she heard. Teddy had had another good day, and he was laughing when he talked to her. He and the nurse had been reading a book of jokes she'd bought for him before she left. He read her a couple of them, and she laughed with him, and she was smiling when she got in the bath. She had promised him she'd be home the following night. She was booked on a six o'clock flight, and it would be around nine o'clock Paris time when she got home. She had thought about staying another night, but it didn't seem fair to him.

She wore a simple white silk cocktail dress that night, with a white cashmere stole, her pearls again, and white silk Chanel shoes with black toes. She carried a white evening bag with nothing more than a lipstick and her room key in it. She didn't need more than that. And this time, she decided to wear her hair down. And Bill looked even more impressed than the previous night when she opened the door. He was obviously taken with her, and it pleased her no end.

There was such a softness to her, such a gentleness, and so much femininity. She defined everything he had always wanted in a woman, and all Bill could do was regret he hadn't found her years before.

"How was Teddy when you called?" he asked as they walked downstairs. Neither of them had the patience to wait for the elevator, and they preferred walking, down at least.

"He was in great form. He read me half a dozen jokes, and the nurse said she's never seen him so well. I don't know if it's the medication he's been on, or the weather, or just good luck. But whatever it is, I hope it holds. I told him I'd be home tomorrow night."

"Oh," Bill said, and she saw the look in his eyes as he turned to her on the last step. "I was hoping you might want to stay another night. I have to see the ambassador tomorrow, and I don't think I'll be free much before noon. That doesn't give us much time before your flight."

"I know," she said, as she tucked her hand into his arm. "I thought about that, but I didn't have the heart to tell him I wanted to stay another night. I suppose I could call tomorrow."

"I wish you would," he said honestly. "Why don't you ask him if he'd mind?" He didn't want to steal her from her son, but he wanted her to stay. And she wanted to stay too. She felt torn between her son and him, which was an unfamiliar feeling for her.

"I'll call in the morning and see how he feels. But I can't promise anything. If he has a bad night tonight, I should go home." She was responsible above all.

"I understand," Bill said gratefully. He was glad she was at least willing to consider it. "Maybe if you have to go, I'll fly back to Paris with you. It wouldn't do any harm for me to visit the embassy there." Even if he couldn't see much of her, he wanted to be close to her. But it was going to be different once they were on her home turf. They might be able to have lunch, but she couldn't have lunch or dinner with him as easily as she did here. If Gordon became aware that she was seeing him, no matter how chaste it was, it could be awkward for her. But Bill knew and understood all that. He had seen her in Paris before. "Thank you for being willing to call. I've got to fly back to New York on Saturday anyway." And he knew his daughters would be home then.

"It's going to be strange," Isabelle said sadly, "once you're gone." They had only been together for a day, but it was so comfortable being together night and day that neither of them could imagine leaving each other now.

"I was thinking the same thing," he said as they drove toward Mark's Club. "You could become a habit that would be hard to break." She nodded in answer, and he gently held her hand. They were crossing barriers they had both respected before, and traveling into regions that had been heretofore unknown. And they both knew that if they ventured too far, it could be a dangerous thing.

They had drinks in the comfortable, elegantly shabby atmosphere of the bar at Mark's. The shabbiness was intentional, as they sat chatting with each other in oversized battered-leather chairs, and then they were escorted to their table in the dining room. In some ways, Isabelle preferred Harry's Bar, but the atmosphere was cozy and romantic here. They talked for hours, and Isabelle had a sense that she wanted to stop time and turn back the clock. The moments were ticking by too fast, and she didn't want the evening to end. And neither did Bill.

"What about Annabel's again?" he asked when they finally left, and their eyes met and held for a long time. She wasn't sure if they would get into deep water if they went dancing again, but neither of them could resist. It was very probably going to be their last night, and the last chance they would have for a long, long time. It could be years. They knew they had to seize the moment now.

"I'd like that very much," she said quietly. There were suddenly unspoken words hanging thick in the air between them, as they sat in the car and held hands. And they were both quiet as they walked into Annabel's and went to sit in the bar.

Bill ordered champagne, and he toasted her, and after her first sip, he set down his glass, held out a hand to her, and invited her to dance. She was only too happy to follow him onto the floor, beneath the ceiling of tiny sparkling stars. It was the most romantic place she'd ever been, and this time, as she danced with him, their bodies felt like one. They moved slowly to the music, and the songs they played were familiar to them. Neither of them spoke, they just held each other close as they danced, and Isabelle closed her eyes.

It was a long time before they left the floor, and they both seemed subdued. Neither of them wanted to think of leaving each other the next day, but there was no avoiding it. They knew the moment would come.

They danced again before they left, and as they left the dance floor, Isabelle had tears in her eyes. And Bill had an arm around her as they walked outside. It was a beautiful, warm, starry night, and he was looking down at her with a warm smile as an explosion seemed to go off in their faces. Isabelle wasn't sure what it was at first, she was blinded by a flash of light, and it was only when her vision cleared that she realized that a photographer had taken their photograph, but she couldn't imagine why.

"What was that all about?" It had frightened her at first, and she had nearly jumped into Bill's arms. He still had an arm around her, and as she stood close to him, he was holding her tight.

"They do that sometimes. The paparazzi hang around outside. They shoot first and then identify their victims afterward. They catch a lot of movie stars and politicians like that. And if they happen to get someone who doesn't matter to anyone, I guess they just toss it out."

"That would be me, I guess. But what about you? Could they cause a problem for you?"

"Not really. I don't think the gossip sheets give a damn who I am. I think that was a wasted shot."

"I didn't even know what it was at first. All I saw was a flash of light." They had used a strobe, and had put the camera only inches from her face.

"It must be miserable to live like that," Bill

commented. He was thinking about the photo-graph they'd taken, and wondering if someone would identify him. But he didn't say anything about it to Isabelle. There was nothing they could do about it now. The only one who might care would be his wife. And Isabelle was certainly unknown. There was no reason why Gordon Forrester would ever see the shot. As they got into the car, Bill put it out of his mind.

Isabelle sat close to him in the car, and as he was growing accustomed to doing now, he held her hand. They were both thinking about leav-ing the next day, and there was a tangible aura of seriousness in the car, as he instructed the driver to take them for a little drive on their way back to the hotel. They were in no hurry to get back, and it was a beautiful night.

It was Isabelle who spoke first, her voice was husky and soft. "I don't know how I'm going to leave tomorrow." Teddy was the only thing pulling her back.

"Maybe you won't. See how he feels when you call." All Bill could do was pray that he had a good night. He couldn't imagine watching her go.

Isabelle nodded and smiled at him, and then put her head on his shoulder. "I had a wonder-ful time tonight, Bill."

"So did I." And then he turned to look at her

again. And he startled her with his next words. "What are we going to do now, Isabelle?" he asked in a voice that she knew too well. It was the voice that always gave her a thrill when she answered the phone.

"About what?"

He was looking down at her with more serious eyes than she had ever seen, and she didn't know if she wanted him to answer or not.

"About us. I'm in love with you. I swore to myself I wasn't going to say those words to you. I know it's not fair, but I want you to know. I want you to take that with you when you go back tomorrow, or whenever you do. I love you, Isabelle. I have for a long time." As he said it, he had never felt as vulnerable in his life.

"I know," she whispered as she looked up at him. "I've loved you since the first time we met. But there's nothing we can do about it." They both knew that. And she had never wanted to say those words to him, she knew it would complicate everything, but neither of them could stop now. And as he gently touched her cheek, their driver rolled slowly toward an intersection, and for a moment Bill thought of asking him to stop. He wanted to be alone with her. This was a moment he wanted neither of them to forget.

"We can't do anything about it now, Isabelle.

But maybe one day. You never know. But whatever happens, I wanted you to know . . . I'm going to love you for the rest of my life." It was something he had been absolutely certain of for a long time. She was everything he had always wanted, and knew now that he couldn't have.

"I love you, Bill," she whispered as he held her close to him, ". . . so very much. . . ." And as she said the words, he put his lips on hers, and he was only sorry he hadn't done it before. It was a moment they had both waited a lifetime for, and it brought them closer than they had ever been. He kissed her as she put her arms around him, and time seemed to melt into space. All she knew was that she had never been as happy in her life, and she never wanted this moment to end. Her eyes were closed and he was holding her, and for the first time in her entire life, she felt totally safe. He was kissing her as they entered the intersection, and the driver was watching them in the rearview mirror, so mesmerized by what he saw there, and so fascinated, that he never saw the red double-decker bus bearing down on them at full speed. It was only yards from Isabelle's side of the car as he pulled into the intersection, and there was no way it could stop. Bill was still kissing her as the bus sheared off the entire front of the car, and the driver literally vanished into thin air. They never caught their breath, never looked up, never knew what had happened to them. They were still kissing as the bus seemed to devour the entire limousine, and within seconds, the car and the bus were a tangle of mangled steel, and there was broken glass everywhere. The bus dragged the car halfway down the street, and in the end it was crushed under it, and it lay on its side with spinning wheels. Isabelle was still lying peacefully in Bill's arms, she was lying on top of him. The roof of the car had caved in, they were both unconscious, and her entire dress was no longer white but red with blood. There were two long gashes on the side of Bill's face, and Isabelle looked as though she were sleeping peacefully. Her face was untouched, but her entire body appeared to have been crushed.

There were sounds in the distance then, the honking of horns, and the horn on the bus was stuck. The driver had flown through the windshield, and was lying dead on the street where he fell. And two people came running with a flashlight and shone it into the mangled car. All they could see was the blood on Bill's face and the bright red dress. His eyes were open and he appeared to be dead, and judging from the amount of her blood smeared everywhere, it was inconceivable to think that Isabelle might have survived. The two men holding the flashlight just stood and stared at them, and one of them whispered, "Oh my God . . ."

"Do you think they're alive?" the other man asked.

"No way, mate." And as they looked, they saw a small stream of blood trickle from the side of her mouth.

"How are they going to get them out of there?" The one holding the flashlight couldn't even imagine how to extricate them. The roof of the car was pressed against Isabelle's back.

"It doesn't matter now, I guess. But it'll take them all night."

They went back to check on the people lying on the floor of the bus then, and a few of the luckier ones were straggling out of the bus, with bloodstained shirts, and gashes on their heads. Some were limping, and others just looked dazed. And someone said that there were half a dozen dead bodies inside. It was one of the worst accidents the police had ever seen with a bus that size, and as they talked to witnesses who had happened by just as the bus hit the limousine, there was the sound of sirens screaming toward them, and within minutes, there were ambulances and fire trucks and paramedics everywhere. They started toward the limousine, and the two men who had glanced into it told them that the only two passengers in it appeared to be dead.

They went to check anyway, and at first glance they saw that the men were right, but as one of the paramedics reached in, and took their pulses just to be sure, they realized that Isabelle and Bill were still alive.

"Hold on!" The paramedic reaching into the car shouted back toward a fireman standing nearby. "I've got two live ones here, but just. Get the trucks over here. We've got to get them out." He had a sense that it was too late and it would be futile by the time they got them out, but at least they had to try. The driver of the limousine had been found by then, and he was dead of a massive head injury. And there was no telling yet if either of the passengers would survive. She appeared to be losing vast quantities of blood from massive injuries, and as the paramedic felt for Bill's pulse again, it was so weak he could barely feel it. They were losing both of them fast. And as the Jaws of Life approached and they attached them to what was left of the car, there were men climbing everywhere, attaching claws, and shouting instructions to the men driving the trucks that would pull the car apart. The noise was deafening, but neither Isabelle nor Bill heard a sound.

Chapter Four

It took them nearly two hours to pull the limousine apart. They had to work carefully to keep
Isabelle and Bill from being even more crushed.
They had gotten IVs into both of them by then,
and they had managed to get a tourniquet on a
gash on Isabelle's artery in her left arm. The
men who had been working on both of them
were smeared with blood, and no one could
believe that they were still alive. There was no
way of telling that Isabelle's dress had ever been
white. The entire dress had been saturated with
her blood. They still had no idea who either of
them were, and by the time they got them both
into an ambulance, the victims from the bus had
all been removed. One of the paramedics had
Bill's wallet in his hand by then, and they'd been
able to identify him, but they still had no idea
who Isabelle was.

  "She's wearing a wedding band," one of the

paramedics offered as the ambulance careened toward St. Thomas' Hospital, "must be his wife." He radioed back to the police officers on the scene to keep an eye out for a handbag in the car, just in case.

Neither of them had regained consciousness during the entire process of being lifted out of the car, and they were both in deep comas when they were carried into the trauma unit, and were immediately attended to by separate teams. It was rapidly determined that both were in need of surgery, he for a spinal cord injury and a fractured neck, and she for a head injury, extensive internal injuries, and the severed artery to which they'd applied the tourniquet. They had to operate immediately or risk losing the arm.

"Jesus, that's an ugly one, isn't it?" one of the nurses whispered about the accident as they were wheeled into separate surgeries. "I haven't seen damage like that in a long time."

"I can't believe they're still alive," the other nurse commented as she scrubbed up. She had been assigned to Isabelle, who had just been assessed as the least likely to survive. They were worried about her head injury, but the greatest damage she had sustained had been to her liver, lungs, and heart, all of which had virtually been crushed.

Within moments, both were lying on operating tables in separate surgeries, with anesthesiologists working on them and bright lights shining overhead, as the members of the surgical team listened to the assessment from the trauma teams. It was difficult to decide which of the limousine's passengers was in the worse shape. They were both classified as extremely critical, and as the surgeries began, both patients' vital signs began to deteriorate at almost exactly the same rate.

As they began operating on Bill to set the many vertebrae that had been broken in his spinal column, he could feel himself sitting up, and within seconds, he found himself walking along a brightly lit path. He was aware of sounds all around him, and far ahead in the distance, there was a bright shining light. And he was surprised, when he looked around, to find Isabelle, sitting on a rock just ahead of him on the path.

"Are you okay?" She looked strange to him when he glanced at her, as though she had fallen asleep for a while. But she stood up, and waited for him to join her on the path.

"I'm fine," she said, but she didn't look at him. As he had been at first, she was mesmerized by the bright light. "What is that?"

"I don't know," he said, he was feeling con-fused, and he was aware of having looked for her, and not being able to find her for a brief time. "Where were you?"

"I was here, waiting for you. You were gone for a long time." Her voice was very soft, and she looked very pale, but she seemed strangely calm.

"I was right here. I didn't go anywhere," he explained, but she didn't seem to be listening to him, and she seemed anxious to move on to-ward the light.

"Are you coming?" She turned to look at him, and he could feel himself hurry to catch up. But she was moving too quickly for him, and he wanted to ask her to slow down.

"Why are you running like that?" he asked, and she just shook her head, and walked steadily on toward the bright light.

"I want you to come with me," she said, and then reached back toward him with her hand. He took it, and he could sense her next to him, but he couldn't feel her hand. He could see that she was holding his, but he couldn't feel any-thing. All he knew was that he was desperately tired. He wanted to lie down and go to sleep somewhere, but he didn't want to lose her again. He knew that, in spite of what she said, he had for a little while. And then she turned and looked at him and spoke barely audibly. "I love you, Bill," she said, and he wanted to ask her to slow down.

"I love you too, Isabelle. Can we rest for a while? I'm very tired."

"We can rest when we get there. They're waiting for us now." She was sure of that, and she had a sense of urgency. He was slowing her down.

"Where are we going?" he wanted to know.

"Up there." She pointed at the light, and he followed her for a while. Getting there seemed to be taking a long time, and when they were almost there, he could hear voices behind them calling her name. And when he turned to look, he saw it was a small child. He couldn't see for sure, but he thought it was a young boy. He was waving at them, and he started shouting "Mommy" until Isabelle finally turned around, and she looked at him for a long time. And in the distance, behind him, was the shadowy figure of a young girl.

"Who is that?" Bill asked, but he knew before she said the words.

"It's Teddy. And Sophie. I can't go to them now. It's too late." She started to turn away, and then suddenly the boy and girl who had waved were joined by two more girls. They looked like children to him, but when he turned back to look at them, he could see that they were his daughters, Olivia and Jane, and they were calling for him just as Teddy had called Isabelle.

"Wait . . ." He was struggling to keep up with her and get her attention now, but she was moving far ahead of him, and he wasn't sure if he should follow her or go back to see Olivia and Jane. "We have to go back to them," he explained, but Isabelle only shook her head.

"I'm not going back, Bill. Are you coming with me?" She seemed very determined, and he was getting more and more tired with each step. It seemed to be an endless path.

"I can't keep up with you," he complained, "why can't we go back to them? They need us now. . . ."

"No, they don't," Isabelle said, and turned away. "I can't go back again. It's too late for me. Tell Teddy and Sophie I love them," she said as she prepared to go on alone.

"You have to come with me," Bill said suddenly, grabbing at her arm. "Listen to me . . ." he said, sounding angry at her. She wasn't listening to him, and she was nearly at the light. "You have to listen to me . . . Teddy and Sophie need you to go back. . . . I have to go back to the girls. Come back with me, Isabelle. . . . We can come back another time."

She hesitated, but only for a fraction of an instant, as he touched her hand. "What if we don't get another chance?"

"We will someday . . . but now it isn't time."

"It is for me. I don't want to go back. . . ." She looked at him imploringly, and he could feel her slip away. "Please, Bill . . . come with me. I don't want to go alone."

"I want you to stay with me. I love you, Isabelle. Don't leave me now." He was crying as he said the words, and he hung his head, not wanting her to see, but she stood there looking at him, and then he looked up and held his hand out to her. "Take my hand . . . I won't let you go, I swear. You have to come back with me." And as he said it, she suddenly looked very tired, and she looked back at Teddy and the girls. She hesitated for a long time, and then slowly, she began to inch her way back toward him. It seemed to be a great deal harder to go backward than to move forward. And he could see the light behind her now, as she started to come toward him again. And a moment later, he was holding her in his arms. He was kissing her and holding her and she was smiling at him. Neither of them was sure where they had been, but all they knew was that they had to go back to their children now. And he could feel her hand tightly holding his.

"Are you sure you want to do this?" she asked as they walked along. They couldn't hear the children's voices, but they knew they were waiting for them. It was growing dark, and the light behind them seemed much dimmer now.

"I'm sure," he said, and kept a tight grip on her hand.

"It's getting late . . . it's so dark . . . how will we find our way back?" she asked. She had a sense that they had both gotten lost before, and she didn't want to get lost again.

"Just hold on to me," Bill said. He could breathe more easily again. The air around them didn't seem quite as thin. "I know the way back." He put an arm around her then, and they kept walking for a long time. It was Isabelle who was tired now, and Bill who was getting strong.

"I need to stop for a while," she said. They could both see the rock where she had been sitting before while she waited for him, but he wouldn't let her stop this time. They had to get home.

"We don't have time. You'll be all right. You can rest when we get back."

And without saying another word, she followed him. It was dark around them by then, but she had a sense that he knew where he was going. All she wanted was to sleep, and lie

down by the side of the road. But Bill wouldn't
let go of her hand, and he wouldn't let her slow
down, and she didn't know how they got there
or when, but after a time she had a sense that
they were home.

They were in a room she didn't recognize,
and she felt safe next to him. There were children everywhere, and she could see Teddy and
Sophie laughing with some friends, and Bill's
girls were talking to him. And while he was
hugging them, Isabelle finally lay down. She
knew it was safe to by then, and all she wanted
to do was sleep next to him. She looked over at
him and smiled, and he smiled back to her. And
as she drifted off to sleep, she knew he would
always be there with her.

"Jesus, I never thought we'd make this one,"
the surgical nurse said to the anesthesiologist as
they left the operating room. They had been
battling for four hours to keep Isabelle's blood
pressure high enough to keep her alive while
they were operating on her. Her crushed organs
had been repaired, and her arm, and for the first
half hour everyone in the operating room had
been absolutely certain she would die. She
had lost an enormous amount of blood. They
had no idea why she'd turned around in the

end, if it was the medications they'd administered, the transfusions, the surgery, or just sheer luck. But whatever it was, everyone agreed, it was a miracle she was alive.

"I've never seen a surgery like that. She's damn lucky to be alive," one of the attending surgeons agreed. "She's not out of the woods yet, but I think she actually might make it. Cases like this restore my faith in God." He smiled as he left the operating room, dripping with sweat. It had been a long night, and an exhausting uphill fight.

Two of the other nurses were coming out of the surgery next door where they'd operated on Bill, and they looked as tired as everyone else.

"How was yours?" one asked the other.

"We nearly lost him four or five times. He pulled through, but he's got a lot of damage to his upper spine. We had to pull him back again and again. We nearly gave up the last time."

"Sounds like ours. It's amazing that they survived."

"How is she?"

"Still critical. And I thought she'd lose the arm. We managed to save it for her. We had a hell of a problem with her liver and her heart. I've never seen so much damage, and seen the patient come out of it alive."

"It shows that you never know, doesn't it?" It

was eight in the morning by then, and both teams went to the cafeteria for coffee and scones, as Isabelle and Bill were wheeled into separate rooms. Both were still in a deep sleep after surgery, and by then Isabelle's handbag had been found. Her room key from Claridge's was in it, the police had called the hotel, and were told that her name was Isabelle Forrester, she was French and had a Paris address. The assistant manager had promised to go to her room immediately to see if her passport could be found, so he could get information on who to call in an emergency. But as yet no one had called.

They had all the information they needed on Bill. His home phone number was in his wallet, and he listed his wife as his next of kin. The desk clerk at the hospital was planning to call Cynthia and tell her about the accident and that Bill had survived.

Bill and Isabelle were both listed as critical. Isabelle's head injury was a factor too, but it was not nearly as severe as her internal injuries. And their greatest fear for Bill was that his spinal cord injury might have compromised his ability to walk, if he survived. It was just low enough, mercifully, that he had avoided total paralysis. The big question for him was going to be the use of his legs. They both had a long stretch of road to travel before their survival would be assured. It had been one of the worst accidents the police had seen in recent years, and eleven people had been killed: the drivers of both vehicles and nine passengers of the bus. For most of the night, as they worked on Isabelle and Bill, the surgical teams had been almost sure the death toll would reach thirteen. Only by a minor miracle were both Isabelle and Bill still alive.

The desk clerk in the ward filed some papers on her desk before she sat down with a sigh. The assistant manager at Claridge's had gone into Isabelle's room, and found her passport, which listed her husband as next of kin. They had the number in Paris, and Bill's number in Connecticut. She hated making calls like that. She took a sip of coffee to steel herself and then dialed Paris first. The phone rang several times before a man answered, and the clerk at the hospital took a breath.

"Monsieur Forrester, *s'il vous plaît*," she said in heavily British-accented French.

"I am he," he said in clipped tones. She recognized the accent as American, and asked him quickly in English if Isabelle was his wife.

"Yes, she is," he said, sounding concerned. The clerk rapidly told him that she was calling from St. Thomas' Hospital and that Isabelle had been injured in a car accident the night before. She explained that her limousine had been hit by a bus.

"She's listed in critical condition, she's just come out of surgery, Mr. Forrester, and I'm afraid there's been no improvement so far. She had extensive internal injuries, and a moderate head injury. We won't know anything more for the next few hours. But it's encouraging that she survived the surgery. I'm sorry," she said, feeling awkward, and at his end there was another long pause, as he pondered what she'd said.

"Yes, so am I." He sounded shocked. "I'll come over sometime today," he murmured vaguely, wondering if he should speak to her doctor first. But the woman on the phone had given him enough details that he felt there was nothing more to ask for now. "Is she conscious?"

"No, sir, she's not. She hasn't regained consciousness since the accident, and she's sedated now. She lost a lot of blood." He nodded, looking pensive, not sure what to say. It seemed incredible to him that this was Isabelle they were talking about. As little as they shared, and as distant as they had become, she was still his wife. He wondered what he should tell Teddy, or if he should call Sophie in Portugal, and as he thought about it, he decided he'd say nothing to either of them. All it would do was frighten them. And there was no point calling Sophie and worrying her, until he knew more. Gordon thought it was best not to say anything to anyone until he saw the situation himself, unless of course she died first. The clerk at the hospital had made it very clear to him that that was a real possibility, and as he hung up, he sat at his desk for a long moment, staring into space. He had had no feelings for her for a long time, but she was the mother of his children, and they had been married for twenty years. He hoped she hadn't suffered when the car had been hit, and for an instant he was grateful she hadn't died. But he was startled by how little he felt. The only emotions he was aware of were of sympathy and regret.

He called the airlines and asked about flights, and then he made a decision. No one knew about the accident, she was unconscious, and he needed time to absorb what had happened himself. He had important appointments in the office that afternoon. He didn't want to rush off in a panic. There was nothing he could do there anyway, and he hated hospitals. After only an instant's hesitation, he made a reservation on the five o'clock flight. It would get him into Heathrow at five-thirty local time, and he could be at the hospital by seven that night. If she died before he got there, it was meant to be, he told himself. And if she was still alive by then, it would be a hopeful sign. But he felt that lying there in a coma, it would make no difference to her if he was there or not. His time would be better spent elsewhere, he thought. Or at least that was what he told himself.

He left for the office shortly afterward, and said nothing to his secretary except that he was leaving the office at three o'clock. He didn't want a big fuss made about it. There was no point, unless she died.

In London, at the hospital, after speaking to Gordon, the clerk at the intensive care desk steeled herself for her next call. Calling Gordon had unnerved her somewhat. He had asked so few questions and sounded so terrifyingly calm. It was most unusual for anyone to respond to a call like that as he had.

The desk clerk at the hospital had the Robinsons' number in front of her, and two nurses walked by her desk as it rang at the other end. They were talking about Isabelle and holding her chart. And from what Gordon had said on the phone, the clerk had no idea when he would come. He had just thanked her, and hung up.

Olivia, Bill's twenty-one-year-old daughter,

answered the phone at the Robinson home. It was six o'clock in the morning, and no one was up, but Olivia heard the phone. A voice with an English accent asked if Mrs. Robinson was there.

"She's asleep," Olivia said, rolling over in bed. "Could you call back in a couple of hours?" she asked with a yawn, about to hang up.

"I'm afraid I can't wait or call back. Would you ask her to come to the phone?"

"Is something wrong?" Olivia started to come awake, and sat up in bed. She had no idea what the call was about, but the voice sounded strained.

"I'm afraid I'll have to speak to Mrs. Robinson herself." Olivia looked worried as she put her on hold and got out of bed. She hurried down the hall to her mother's room, and at the sound of footsteps in the hall and the door opening, Cynthia woke up.

"Hi, are you okay?" she whispered in the darkened room. She'd been sound asleep, but even after all these years, she still had a sixth sense for her kids. "Are you sick?"

"No, there's some English woman on the phone who says she has to talk to you." Mother and daughter exchanged a glance, and Cindy had an eerie feeling. She knew instinctively that it had something to do with Bill. She had never been confronted by it before, but she suddenly wondered if there was another woman in his life.

"I'll take the call," she said quietly, and sat up. "It's okay, Ollie, go back to bed." But Olivia didn't move. She had had the same eerie feeling too. "This is Mrs. Robinson," Cynthia said into the phone, and then, as she listened, she was silent for a long time, but Olivia saw her close her eyes. "How serious is it?" was all Olivia could hear at her end. "When? Is he conscious?" And with that, her daughter's eyes grew wide.

"Is it Dad?" Her voice was filled with panic, as her mother opened her eyes and gestured to silence her. She wanted to hear everything the clerk in the intensive care unit said. But she nodded in answer to Olivia's question, as the young woman sat down on her bed. "Is he okay?" Her mother didn't answer her as she continued to listen to the voice on the other end.

"What's his doctor's name?" She quickly jotted a name down on the pad at the side of her bed, asked a few more questions, and asked them to call her if anything changed. "I'll be there as soon as I can. I want to be called if anything happens, and I want to know as soon as he regains consciousness, if he does. I'll call back in half an hour, and tell you when I'll be there." She sounded calm, but her eyes said she was anything but. She looked stunned as she hung up the phone and Olivia flew into her arms.

"What happened?" There were tears in her daughter's voice, and Cynthia could feel a lump in her own throat. What they had told her was terrible, and she could only hope that it wasn't as bad as it seemed. A fractured neck, a spinal cord injury, spinal surgery, possibly permanent paralysis, internal damage, broken bones. And they weren't even sure he'd survive. And if he did, it was questionable that he'd ever walk again. The thought of Bill in a wheelchair was unthinkable. In some ways, she almost thought, for his sake, he'd be better off if he died. He would hate being in a wheelchair for the rest of his life. And she couldn't see herself as his nurse. What if he were a paraplegic, or worse? What if he were bedridden and unable to move? Her mind was racing over everything the woman had said, and her own terrors were running wild.

"Dad had an accident. He's in London. I forgot he said he'd be there for a few days. I talked to him a couple of days ago in New York. He was in a car that was hit by a bus, and it sounds pretty bad," Cynthia said honestly. "His neck is fractured, and his spinal cord is damaged. He just came out of surgery, and it's very serious stuff."

"Is he going to die?" Olivia's eyes looked huge.

Cynthia hesitated for a long moment as tears flooded her daughter's eyes. "He could," she said gently. "But Dad's pretty tough. I think he'll be okay, but we don't know that yet. I'm going to go over there today."

"I'm coming with you," Olivia said. She was a tall willowy blonde with a lovely figure and a pretty face. She was going to be a junior at Georgetown University in the fall, majoring in foreign policy. She was a terrific student, and a great kid, and both her parents were justifiably proud of her. And in spite of the little time she spent with him, she was crazy about her dad. She had idolized him when she was a child, and in recent years she'd been fascinated by everything he did.

"I think you girls should stay here," Cynthia said as she threw back the covers and got out of bed. She had to call the airlines and pack. She was hoping to get a noon flight, and it would just complicate things to take Olivia with her. And she didn't want them upset. From everything the woman at the hospital had said, it sounded very bad.

"I'm coming with you, Mom." Olivia raised her voice to her, which was rare. "If I have to, I'll buy the ticket and go by myself."

"What's going on?" Jane asked sleepily as she wandered into the room. She was small and blond with a tantalizing figure, and she looked almost exactly the way Cindy had at her age. She had just finished her freshman year at NYU, and was turning nineteen. She had heard their voices, and she could see that Olivia was angry at their mother, from the look on her face. "What are you two fighting about at this hour?" Cynthia and her elder child had always had battles about everything. It was Jane who was the peacemaker and the easygoing one. And as she yawned, she climbed into her mother's bed.

"Dad had an accident," Olivia told her younger sister, as Jane's eyes grew wide, and her mother got on the phone to call the airlines.

"Is he okay?" It was hard for her to imagine that he might not be. Olivia was much more high-strung than she was, and could have been exaggerating. Jane couldn't be sure.

"It doesn't sound good," Olivia said, choking on a sob, and then sat down on their mother's bed to put her arms around Jane, as she started to cry. "He fractured his neck, and his spine is hurt. Mom says they're not sure he'll ever walk again. He just had a surgery. His car got hit by a bus."

"Oh shit," Jane said, clinging to the older sister she had always comforted, rather than the reverse. But Jane had always been the calm, competent one, even as a very young child. She could take care of herself anywhere, or anyone else who needed her help. She had Cindy's cool unemotional side, but this time she looked panicked as she started to cry.

"Mom's flying to London, and I'm going too," Olivia said through her tears.

"I'm coming too," Jane said, and then hopped out of bed, to tell her mother her plans. She stood right in front of her, as Cindy made her flight arrangements on the phone. "We're both going with you," Jane spoke right over her, and Cindy waved her away. She could hardly hear, they were talking so loud. And then she put her hand on the phone, and spoke to Jane.

"I think you should both stay here. I'll call you if I think you should come."

"Either we go with you, or we'll go on our own," Jane said purposefully, and her mother knew from experience, it was futile arguing with her. Olivia could be talked out of things, but once Jane made up her mind, she had the flexibility of a rock. "What time do we leave?"

"There's an eleven-forty flight," Cindy answered, and then changed her reservations on the phone. She told the agent she'd need three seats in business class. And a moment later, she hung up, and told the girls they had to leave the house at nine. They had two hours to get organized, dress, and pack. There wasn't even time for Bill's plane to come back to New York for them.

"I'll make breakfast," Jane volunteered, as Olivia sat on the bed and cried. "Go pack," she told her older sister, and then looked at her mother, as Cindy opened her closet and took a suitcase off a shelf. "Is Dad going to make it, Mom?" Jane asked quietly. Ever the sensible one, she was fighting to stay calm, as her mother turned and looked at her with troubled eyes.

"I don't know, sweetheart. It sounds like it's too soon to tell. But he's hanging in, and he came through the surgery." She didn't tell her that the clerk in the ICU had told her he had almost died twice, and it had taken them two hours to pry him out of the car. "He's healthy and strong, and he's in great shape. That can't hurt."

"How did it happen?" Jane asked, dabbing at her eyes.

"I don't know. All I know is that his limousine was hit by a bus. It must have been a terrible accident, eleven people were killed. Let's be grateful your father wasn't one of them," she said as Jane left the room, and she tried to figure out what to pack.

But as she threw slacks and T-shirts and sweaters into a suitcase, all she could think of were the implications for Bill. She was absolutely certain that if he was going to be severely impaired, he would prefer not to live. She wasn't sure what she wished for him now, it all depended on how badly damaged he was. But she didn't want to say any of that to the girls. As she packed underwear and shoes into her bag, she realized that she wasn't even sure what she felt herself. She had been married to him for more than half her life, and she wasn't in love with him anymore, but if nothing else they were friends. He was the father of her children, and had been her husband for thirty years. There had been other men in her life, and their marriage had run out of gas a long time ago, she had even thought about divorcing him once or twice, when she was involved with other men. But it had never once in all these years occurred to her that he might die. Just thinking of that now changed everything.

All Cynthia could think of suddenly was what he had been like when they were kids, how desperately in love with him she had been, how happy they were when they were first married. It was like seeing thirty years of history race before her eyes as she walked into the bathroom and turned on the shower. And as she stood beneath the spray of hot water, and thought of him never walking again, all she could do was cry.

They left for the airport shortly after nine, Cynthia drove, and the girls were quiet in the backseat. Cynthia never said a word, and both girls stared out the window and were lost in thought. They were all wearing jeans and T-shirts and Nikes, and had brought very little with them. Cynthia figured they probably wouldn't leave the hospital much, and none of them cared how they looked. The girls had barely taken the time to comb their hair. And when Jane made them breakfast before they left, no one ate. All they could think of was Bill in a hospital in London, fighting for his life. And as their plane took off, Gordon Forrester was in the air, on a flight that had just left Charles de Gaulle. He was due to touch down at Heathrow in less than an hour.

At the hospital in London, nothing had changed. Isabelle and Bill had been put in separate private rooms in the intensive care ward. Both of them were covered with monitors, had their own separate teams, and were in such dire straits that they were being kept apart from the ward. Isabelle had been running a high fever since three o'clock that afternoon. Her heart was beating irregularly, her liver had been badly damaged, her kidneys were threatening to fail, and they knew, from the trauma and the surgery, that she had some slight swelling of her brain. But at least an EEG had determined that her brain was functioning. The doctors were fairly sure there would be no permanent brain damage, if she survived. It would have been hard to determine which of her many injuries was causing her temperature to rise, and she was still in a deep coma, as much from the trauma as from the anesthetic and the drugs. Looking at her clinically, it was hard to believe she was going to live.

And Bill was faring only slightly better than she. His neck was set in a torturous-looking apparatus with steel bolts and pins, he had an iron brace on his back, and he was on a board that allowed them to move him, although he was unaware of it. He was still in a coma too.

"His family is arriving from the States around midnight," one of the nurses said at six o'clock that night when they changed shifts. "His wife called from the plane. They're on their way." The other nurse nodded and adjusted a beeping sound on one of the monitors. At least his vital signs were good, better than Isabelle's, who seemed to be fluttering between life and death constantly. Her survival seemed even more unsure than his. And one of the nurses asked if anyone was coming to see Isabelle too.

"I don't know. I think they called Paris this morning, and spoke to her husband, but he didn't say when he'd come. Katherine said he sounded very cool. I guess he was in shock."

"Poor man. This is one of those calls you have nightmares about," one of Bill's nurses said sympathetically. "I wonder if she has kids." They knew almost nothing about either of them, no medical history, no personal details, just their nationalities and the names of their next of kin, and what had happened in the accident. No one even knew the relationship between the two of them, if they were business associates, related in any way, or just friends. And there was no point guessing at any of it. Right now all they were were two patients in the intensive care ward, fighting for their lives. They were talking about operating on Isabelle again, to relieve the pressure on her brain. The surgeon was due back at any moment to make a decision about it. And when he came shortly after six, he checked the monitors and, with a grim look, decided to wait. He didn't think she'd survive another surgery, and might not anyway. It seemed unreasonable to him to challenge her more at this point.

It was after seven, and the doctor had just left, when Gordon arrived. He walked into the intensive care ward quietly, spoke to a male clerk at the desk, and told him who he was. The clerk looked up at him, nodded, and asked a passing nurse to take him to Isabelle's room. And without a word, Gordon followed her with a somber expression. He had had all day to prepare himself for this, and as he stepped into her room, he had expected to find her looking very ill. But nothing he had imagined had prepared him for this. To him, she seemed like an almost unrecognizable hunk of flesh, there were bandages and wires and tubes and monitors everywhere, even her head was swathed with gauze, and the arm with the severed artery was heavily bandaged as well. The only thing familiar about her was her deathly pale face peeking out of the gauze. It was the only part of her that seemed untouched.

There were three people standing next to her when he walked in. One of them was changing an IV, another was checking the monitors, and a third was checking her pupils as they did constantly, but just looking at her, Gordon felt ill. He didn't feel anything for her except horror at what he saw. It was as though she were no longer there, and the shell of what was left meant nothing to him. She was a broken body, nothing more. He said nothing, and did not approach, as one of the nurses spoke softly to him.

"Mr. Forrester?" He nodded his head and cleared his throat, but he didn't know what to say. And it embarrassed him to have to see her with an audience focused on him. He wasn't sure what they expected of him. To throw himself on the foot of her bed perhaps, kiss her fingers, touch her lips. But he couldn't bring himself to come any closer. Watching her was like staring at the angel of death, and it frightened him.

"How is she?" he asked in a gruff voice.

"She has a fever. The doctor just left. They were considering another surgery to relieve the pressure on her brain, but he thinks she's too compromised to tolerate it. He wants to wait. He said he'd be back at ten o'clock."

"And if he doesn't do the surgery? Will she be brain-damaged?" He couldn't imagine anything worse than her surviving with almost no brain function, or even severely impaired, and he wanted to tell the surgeon that. If she was going to be anything less than she had been, he thought their efforts to save her were a travesty. She had been beautiful and intelligent and talented, and whatever their differences, she had been a good wife to him, and a good mother to their children. To save her in order to lie in a bed like a living corpse was abhorrent to him, and he was prepared to fight to see that that didn't happen to either of them. He didn't want their children to remember her that way. Or to live with it himself.

"It's impossible to tell at this point what the prognosis is, Mr. Forrester. But the brain scans have been encouraging. It's too soon for anyone to know." It was impossible to believe that she would survive hours, let alone months, in the condition she was in.

"Is there a physician here that I can talk to?" Gordon asked one of the nurses, without any visible sign of emotion. The nurse thought he looked like a distant friend, or a remote member of her family who had come to the hospital dutifully. He kept his emotions to himself.

"I'll let the surgeon on duty know that you're here," the nurse said as she slipped past him into the hall, leaving the remaining two nurses with Isabelle. Gordon Forrester made her acutely uncomfortable. Looking at Isabelle tore at her heart. She was so beautiful and so young. But the man who had flown from Paris to see his wife seemed to feel nothing at all. She had never met anyone as cold.

Gordon stepped out of the room, and walked

slowly down the hall, waiting for someone to come and talk to him. It was another ten minutes before a young surgeon appeared. He confirmed to Gordon what he already knew, more or less, and acknowledged the grave danger she was in. He said they were debating performing another surgery on her, but were hoping to avoid it if they could. All they could do was wait and see how her own body responded to the trauma it had endured. And in his estimation, it was going to be a long wait before they had good news. But he felt that the fact that she had come this far was a hopeful sign, the only one they had. Hope for Isabelle was still slim.

"I'm sorry, Mr. Forrester," he said finally. "Given the nature of the accident, it's a miracle that they survived at all." Gordon nodded, and then his attention caught on something the younger man had said, in direct conflict to what he'd heard earlier in the day.

"I thought the driver was killed."

"He was, instantly, as was the driver of the bus, and nine passengers."

"I thought I just understood you to say that 'they' had survived." It made Gordon pause.

"Yes, I did. There was another passenger with her. He survived as well, though he's not in any better shape than your wife. His injuries are different than hers, but they're equally grave. He's listed in very critical condition too." Gordon had an eerie feeling as he listened to him, and couldn't imagine what she'd been doing in a limousine with another man, particularly at that hour of night. He knew she had come to London to see an exhibit at the Tate and to go to some other museums and galleries, and he'd seen no harm in it, but now this all seemed very strange.

"Do you know who it was by any chance?" Gordon asked, appearing casual. Absolutely nothing unusual showed on his face.

"We know his name, but we don't know much more than that about him. His name is William Robinson, he's American. I believe his family is flying over now. They're due here tonight." Gordon nodded, as though he was expecting old friends, and he turned the name over in his mind for a moment, as it clicked, and he wondered if it was the same man. There was a William Robinson he had met several years before, an important figure in the political world. And he knew that Robinson and the ambassador to France were old friends. But he couldn't imagine what he'd been doing with Isabelle. He wasn't even sure they'd ever met. He couldn't remember if Isabelle had been with him when they were introduced at the embassy. It was so rare that she went out. It was a complete mystery what Isabelle had been doing with him.

"Will he be all right?" Gordon asked with a look of concern, which masked the unspoken questions on his mind.

"We don't know. He fractured his neck, and damaged his upper spinal cord. There are some internal injuries as well, but none as severe as your wife's."

"It sounds like she took the worst of it," Gordon said, "but not by much. Will he be paralyzed from the spinal injury?"

"It's too soon to tell. He's still unconscious, he never regained consciousness after the surgery. It could simply be a reaction to the trauma of the accident, or something more complicated as a result of his neck. He's in critical condition as well." It occurred to Gordon as he listened to him that they might both die without ever explaining to anyone what they had been doing together that night. Gordon was wondering if it had just been a coincidence. If she had old friends in London from her youth that he didn't know about that she had gone to see, perhaps she and Robinson had shared a limousine leaving the hotel. But why would she be out at that hour? Where were they coming from? Where were they going? Where had they been? Why were they together? Did they even know each other? Had they just met? There were a thousand possibilities and questions racing through his mind. And there was no way of getting answers to any of them, certainly not if they didn't survive. He thought he knew Isabelle well, he was sure he did. She was not the kind of woman to be having an affair, or even having clandestine assignations with a man. And yet they had been together, in a limousine, at two A.M., and whatever the reason was, there was no way to discover it now.

"Would you like to spend the night here at the hospital with your wife?" the young doctor asked him, but Gordon was quick to shake his head. He had a horror of sickrooms and hospitals and sick people. They reminded him of his mother in a sinister way.

"As she's not conscious, I don't see what purpose I'd serve here. I'd just get in the way of your staff. I'll stay at the hotel. I'll be at Claridge's, and you can call me if anything changes here. That seems more sensible. I appreciate your time, and your efforts on my wife's behalf," Gordon said formally, and looking uncomfortable, he stood up again. It was obvious that he was extremely ill at ease in the hospital, and had no desire to go back to his wife's room. "I'll just stop in and see her again for a moment before I leave." He thanked the doctor again, and walked back down the hall, and when he reached her door, there were five members on the team working on her, and there was still no sign of life. He made no attempt to enter the room, watching them for only the briefest moment, and then turned and left, without saying another word. He had never touched her, never kissed her, never approached Isabelle's bed, and he took an enormous breath of fresh air as soon as he reached the street.

Gordon detested hospitals and sick people and infirmities. It was why Teddy had always been hard for him. It was something he simply couldn't tolerate, and as he hailed a cab, with his overnight bag in his hand, and gave them Claridge's address, he felt slightly ill. He was enormously relieved to have escaped the intensive care ward, and in spite of the fact that he felt sorry for her, he hadn't been able to bring himself to walk into the room and touch even so much as her hand. It was merciful that she was unconscious, he thought, and it would be more so if she didn't survive to be brain-damaged. That was a fate that he didn't wish for her. But in spite of how sorry he felt for her, he couldn't seem to feel anything about it for himself. He had no sense of loss, no despair, no terror of losing her. She seemed like a stranger to him now, lying so broken and still in her hospital bed. She looked like a lifeless doll, and it was hard to understand that the woman he had just seen had been the young girl he once married, let alone his wife of twenty years. Her spirit already seemed to have fled, and all he wondered as the cab pulled up in front of Claridge's was what she had been doing in a limousine with Bill Robinson. But there was no one except Isabelle whom he could ask. She alone knew the answer to the mystery, and Bill of course, but he was just as unable to answer Gordon's questions as his wife.

The doorman took Gordon's overnight case from him. He had only brought a few shirts and some underwear. He wasn't intending to stay long. He had come to assess the situation, and he was planning to return to Paris in a day or two. And come back to London again if need be. She might be dead by then, or she may have remained the same. The young surgeon had told him that night that she could stay in the coma, without change, for weeks or even months. And there was no way he could stay in London with her. He had to go back to tend to his own affairs, to monitor Teddy now, and see what was happening at the bank. If he had to, he would go back and forth between London and Paris every few days. But he realized that if this was going to take a while, it was going to be best if he called Sophie in Portugal and asked her to come home. If nothing else, she could take over watching Teddy for him. He dreaded calling her, but after what he'd seen tonight, he was beginning to think that he should. He needed to prepare her in case Isabelle died.

Gordon stopped at the desk, and asked for Isabelle's key, and an assistant manager came out from an office instantly, and told Gordon how sorry he was.

"It must have been a dreadful accident. We're all so sorry . . . such a terrible thing . . . such a lovely person . . . no idea it had happened until the police called . . ." He went on for several minutes as Gordon nodded his head and agreed with everything he said. "How is she doing, sir?" the assistant manager asked solicitously.

"Not very well." And then he decided to see what else he might know. "Apparently Mr. Robinson was severely injured too." He searched the young man's eyes for whatever he could discover there, but it was just more of the same. Sympathy and an endless wringing of hands.

"So we understand" was all the young man said. It was awkward asking him if he knew why they'd been sharing a limousine, and Gordon was searching for the appropriate question to satisfy his needs. But it was not an easy thing to do.

"So unfortunate, such a shame they were riding together," Gordon said noncommittally. "He's an old friend of mine, they must have run into each other here."

"Yes, I suppose," the assistant manager said, nodding his head. "I believe I saw them having tea together in the lobby yesterday afternoon."

"Do you know where they might have gone last night?" Gordon inquired, as though investigating the accident, but the young manager shook his head.

"I can ask the hall porter if he made reservations for them anywhere, perhaps he did." He stepped away for a moment and inquired, and the hall porter said Mr. Robinson always made his own reservations when he was in town, and rarely asked anything of them, except hiring a car, as he had this time. But he believed the other hall porter had made a reservation for them at Mark's Club. "He's off today. I can ask him when he gets back. Or I can call Mark's Club, if you like. Unfortunately, the driver died, as I'm sure you know. One of our best men, an Irish fellow, he had a wife and four boys. A terrible tragedy," he said, obviously distressed by what had happened, and Gordon thanked him as he took the key, walked to the elevator, and rode upstairs. He was still thinking about what the manager had said about their

having tea in the lobby the previous afternoon.
He wondered if they had met through art circles somehow, or if he had just picked her up.
She was such an innocent that she might just be
naive enough to befriend someone like that,
and tea in the lobby was certainly a relatively
harmless pursuit, but in Gordon's mind being
out at two in the morning in a limousine with a
man was not. He still couldn't imagine what
Bill Robinson had been doing with her. He
didn't like the sound of it, and if it were anyone
other than Isabelle, he would have jumped to
the obvious, but in Isabelle's case, there may
well have been some foolish, benign reason
why she had been in the car with him. Gordon
was still puzzling over it when he stepped
into her room.

There was an eerie feeling to it suddenly, as
though she had just gone out, and as he looked
around, it made him feel almost as though she
had already died. Her makeup was spread out
on the table next to the sink. Her nightgown
was hanging on a hook behind the bathroom
door. Her clothes were neatly hung in the
closet, and there was a collection of pamphlets
and brochures from museums and art galleries
sitting on the desk. And then he saw that next
to them, there was a book of matches from
Harry's Bar, and as Isabelle didn't smoke, he

thought that was somewhat odd. And what on earth would she be doing at a place like Harry's Bar? Or Mark's Club? And then he saw that next to the matches from Harry's Bar was another matchbook from Annabel's. And when he saw it, he felt a finger of anger run down his spine. Perhaps the evening with Bill Robinson hadn't been as innocent as he hoped. He wondered if she had been to those places with him. He looked around the room for further evidence, but there was no sign of a man's clothes, no letters, no notes, no flowers with cards from him. There was nothing but two matchbooks from two fashionable watering holes that he somehow knew she had kept as souvenirs. Maybe Robinson had just picked her up, and she had been vulnerable to it. In all likelihood it was innocent, and whatever had happened between them that night, or before, they had certainly paid a high price for it. But he couldn't help wondering what their bond to each other was, or if there was one at all. He slipped the two matchbooks into his pocket, sat down, and looked around the room, and then rang for the waiter and ordered himself a stiff drink.

When Cynthia Robinson and the girls got off the plane, it was eleven-thirty P.M. in London.

Both of the girls had slept on the plane, for a while at least. But Cynthia had spent most of the flight lost in thought, and staring out the window. The full impact of what had happened to Bill was beginning to hit her. And she was anxious to see him. Maybe, with any luck at all, he would be out of the coma by the time they got to the hospital, and maybe, just maybe, the blow to his neck and spine wouldn't have any long-term effects. It was all she could hope for, for his sake.

It took them half an hour to get through customs, and Claridge's had a car waiting for them. They went straight to the hospital, and were there at one o'clock in the morning. The intensive care ward was still bustling at that hour, and four new trauma patients had come in just before Cynthia and her daughters arrived. But Cynthia had no problem making herself known to the nurses, or finding a doctor to talk to her about Bill. Cindy was good at things like that. She managed to stop a doctor on his way to Bill's room.

The same young surgeon who had spoken to Gordon earlier sat down with her in the hall, and spelled it all out for her, as Jane and Olivia listened. Bill was still in a coma, and there was no sign of any improvement so far. He had begun having a considerable amount of swelling in the spinal area, which was pressing on damaged nerves, and the fractures in his neck were severe. By the time the doctor had finished explaining it all to her, the outlook for Bill seemed very grim. And when Cynthia saw him, she was only slightly better prepared for the way he looked. He was trapped in a hideous-looking contraption on his neck, a full body brace, and he was covered with stitches and cuts and small lacerations and bruises. The nurses were watching him, the monitors beeped endlessly, and he was so deathly pale that both girls started crying when they saw his face. All Cindy could do was stare at him, and suddenly all the emotions she'd resisted since she'd heard the news overwhelmed her all at once. Tears welled up in her eyes, and he was no longer a conglomeration of symptoms and broken parts anymore, he was the boy she had fallen in love with in college, and she could see how desperately injured he was. It took all the strength she had to get control of herself again, and be of some support to her girls.

Jane and Olivia just stood in a corner of the room, hugging each other and crying silently, as one of the nurses adjusted the respirator, and Cindy slowly approached his bed. She touched his hand, and it didn't even feel like him, and she was crying too hard to bend down and kiss him. There was a terrible smell of disinfectant in the room. His chest was bare, and there were monitors taped to him everywhere.

"Hi, baby," she whispered as she stood next to him. "It's me, Cindy." She felt like a girl again, as she watched him, and a thousand images raced through her head, of the day she had met him, and the day she'd married him, the day she told him she was pregnant. So many memories and moments, and now he was lying here, and their lives were forever changed. She couldn't imagine how they would ever achieve normalcy again. And suddenly, she knew she didn't want him to die if he was impaired, she didn't care how damaged he was, she didn't want to lose him. And for the first time in years, she realized that she still loved him. "I love you," she said again and again, "I want you to open your eyes now. The girls are here. They want to talk to you, sweetheart."

"He can't hear you, Mrs. Robinson," one of the nurses said gently.

"You don't know that," Cindy said firmly. She wasn't a woman one would have wanted to argue with, at the best of times, and at this particular moment, she did not want to hear what the nurse was saying to her. Besides, for years she had heard stories about people in comas who had heard what the people around them were saying. Cynthia continued talking to him, and she and the girls stayed with him for two hours, until a doctor checking him suggested that they get some rest themselves, and come back in the morning. There was no change whatsoever in Bill's condition so far.

"Do you think I should stay here with him?" Cindy asked the doctor. She hadn't come all the way from Connecticut to sit at Claridge's and not be with Bill. Besides, she wasn't entirely sure yet if she trusted them with him. She wanted to watch what they were doing. But at least she was impressed by the care he was getting, from all she could tell.

"I think you should go to the hotel. We'll call you if there's any change in his condition," the doctor said firmly. He could see that this was a woman he would have to be direct with. There was no messing around, no hiding the facts from her. She wanted to know it all, and would settle for nothing less than that from him. "I promise you, we'll call you." It had taken another half hour to convince her to leave. Their driver was waiting downstairs for them, and by then, it was nearly four o'clock in the morning. And Cynthia and the girls were exhausted when they left.

She had reserved a room at Claridge's for Olivia and Jane, and she was planning to stay in

Bill's room. And as she opened the door with the key they'd given her, she had the same eerie feeling Gordon had had when he walked into Isabelle's room. She felt as though she were intruding. His briefcase was there, there were papers on several tables around the room, and a bunch of brochures from art galleries and museums, which seemed odd to her. When did he have time to visit museums? There were half a dozen American Express receipts too, and she saw that there was one from Harry's Bar, and another from Annabel's. But she also knew that he went there with friends and business acquaintances whenever he was in London. She didn't find that unusual, and it made her cry again when she put on his pajamas. She was suddenly terrified of losing him, and when she called the girls to see if they were all right, they were both crying. It had been an emotional day for all of them, and seeing their father had frightened them even more than it had their mother. It was hard to hold on to hope after seeing him. He looked so severely broken, and nearly dead.

Cynthia couldn't get the sound of the girls crying out of her head, so she put on a bathrobe over Bill's pajamas and walked down the hall to see them. She just wanted to give them a hug, and reassure them. And in the end, she sat down and spent a half hour with them. It was nearly five A.M. when she finally left them and went back to Bill's room. She lay there and cried into the pillow that still smelled of him, and she didn't fall asleep until six o'clock Friday morning.

When Cynthia awoke later that morning, she called the hospital to check on Bill, and they told her nothing had changed during the night. His vital signs were a little more stable than they had been, but he was still deeply uncon-scious. It was eleven in the morning by then, and Cindy felt as though she had been beaten with lead pipes all night. She checked on the girls, letting herself quietly into their room, and she found that they were still asleep. She went back to her own room, bathed and dressed, and shortly before noon, she was ready to go back to the hospital. She hated to wake the girls, and left them a note instead. She left it in their room, and told them she'd call from the hospital to let them know how their father was doing. She went downstairs to the car they had waiting for her, and gave the driver the address. And he talked about the accident on the way. The driver who had been killed had been one of his best friends. He told Cynthia how sorry he was about her husband, and she thanked him.

She found things much the same once she got

to the hospital, and settled into the waiting room after talking to him for a while. She was waiting to see one of Bill's doctors. And as she sat there, she saw a man walk by. He was tall and distinguished looking, wearing a well-cut suit, and he had an aristocratic air of command that instantly caught her eye. He stopped to speak to the nurses at the desk, and she saw them shake their heads and look at him with a discouraged expression. His mouth set in a grim line, and he disappeared down the hall then, in the direction of Bill's room.

Cynthia couldn't help wondering what had brought him here. And later, she saw him come out of a room across the hall from Bill's, and come back to speak to one of the doctors in the hall. And then he left again, but Cynthia had the impression that he was locked in the same agonizing waiting game she was trapped in, waiting to see what would happen to someone severely ill. And she didn't know why, but she thought there was something odd about him. He seemed extremely uncomfortable in the intensive care ward, and she sensed both resistance and anger in him, as though he was deeply resentful that he had to be there at all. He seemed restless and awkward and ill at ease. She commented on it to one of the nurses when she went back into the room to see Bill.

What Cynthia didn't know then was that Isabelle had taken a turn for the worse, and they had just told Gordon that his wife's situation had become markedly less hopeful. Her numerous injuries were getting the best of her, and she was slipping deeper into the coma. They had decided not to operate again, they were certain that she couldn't withstand further trauma to her system. And he had gone back to the hotel, to call his office and wait for further news. He told his secretary he was staying in London over the weekend, without saying why, and then he called Teddy's nurses to check on him. Suddenly, he felt extraordinarily burdened by the responsibility of his son. He had never had to deal with any of that before. And he said nothing to Teddy, or the nurse, about his mother's situation. But Gordon was not pleased that these responsibilities had suddenly fallen on him.

He told the boy he'd be gone for the weekend, and that he was in London with his mom.

"Mommy said she was coming home yesterday," he said, sounding disappointed. "Why is she staying?"

"Because she has things to do here, that's why," Gordon snapped at him, but his brusqueness didn't surprise Teddy. His father had never had any interest or patience to offer him.

"She didn't call me. Will you ask her to call me?" Teddy sounded faintly plaintive, and Gordon was irritated. His nerves were suddenly on edge, and he had no satisfactory explanation for Teddy about why his mother hadn't called him.

"She'll call you eventually. She has things to do with me," he lied to the boy, but he felt he had no other choice. And right now, lying to him was far kinder than telling him the truth. Teddy was too frail to even hear the truth about what had happened, particularly at this distance. If he had to be told eventually, Gordon intended to do so in person, with the boy's doctor present. And Gordon hadn't called Sophie yet either. He wanted to see how things developed. There was no point terrifying them, and if she was going to die without regaining consciousness anyway, he didn't think Sophie should see her. He had made that decision that morning.

"Tell Mommy I love her," Teddy said as his father rushed him off the phone. He was not enjoying the conversation. He didn't like lying to the boy, nor did he want to tell him what had happened to Isabelle.

And shortly after that, Gordon went back to the hospital himself to see her. When he arrived, he stood in the farthest corner of the room, looking agonized, and observed a variety of things they were doing to her. And unlike

Cynthia Robinson with Bill, he did not approach, didn't speak, and never touched her. His revulsion was so great, he simply could not deal with it.

"Would you like a moment alone with your wife?" one of the nurses asked him gently. He looked so uncomfortable that she felt sorry for him.

But Gordon didn't hesitate when he answered. "No, thank you. She can't hear me anyway. I'll be in the waiting room, please call me if anything changes." And with that he escaped, and went to sit in the waiting room with Olivia and Jane. Cynthia came to check on them after a while, and Gordon had no idea who they were, nor did he care. And he was surprised when Cynthia smiled at him. She looked tired and pale. And she had spilled something on her T-shirt, but the look in her eyes was sympathetic to him.

"I'm sorry about your wife," she said, she had heard the nurses talk about her, and knew only that she was in a situation even more critical than Bill's. But they had said very little about it to her.

"Thank you," Gordon said tersely. He had no desire to develop friendships in the waiting room of the intensive care ward. But he didn't want to sit in the horror of Isabelle's room either. He had nowhere else to go except back to Claridge's, which he'd been contemplating when Cindy spoke to him. And then much to his surprise, she held out a hand to him and introduced herself. She could hear that he was American, and felt a strange bond to him. They were both far from home, trapped in desperate situations.

"I'm Cynthia Robinson," she said simply as one of her daughters dozed, and the other was engrossed in a magazine she had bought in the lobby of the hospital. Neither of them seemed to be paying attention to Cynthia or Gordon. But Gordon's eyes widened in obvious recognition the moment he heard her name, and Cynthia noticed it. "I'm here with my husband. He had a car accident two days ago. We just flew in last night." He wondered, as he listened to her, if she had a full grasp of their situation. If she did, it didn't seem to upset her. All she seemed to be worrying about was her husband's condition, which Gordon thought was gracious of her. He was far more concerned about what might have brought them together than she was. And Gordon decided to be frank with her.

"I assume you're aware of the fact that my wife was in the car with your husband when the bus hit them." As he said it, she looked as though the bus had just hit her. And he suddenly realized from the look on her face that no one had told her about Isabelle. She was rendered speechless by what Gordon had just said to her.

"What do you mean?" If it was at all possible, she looked even paler than she had at first.

"Exactly what I just said. They were in the limousine together. I have no idea why, or how they knew each other. I met your husband several years ago, in Paris, but I have no recollection if my wife was even with me. Apparently, they had tea together on Wednesday, and she was in the limousine with him. She is now in critical condition, in a deep coma, and we may never know what they were doing together. I assume your husband is in no condition to explain it to you either."

Cynthia sat down across from him, in a chair, and looked as though someone had slapped her. Hard. "No one told me. I thought he was alone, with the driver." Cynthia looked puzzled.

"Apparently not, I'm afraid. She came over from Paris to see some art exhibits. She has a passionate interest in art. And I have no idea what else she did while she was here in London." Cynthia stared at him as she remembered the art brochures in Bill's room from assorted galleries and museums. "Has your husband ever

mentioned her? Her name is Isabelle Forrester."
It embarrassed him to discuss it with her, and it
was certainly awkward, but there were questions to which he now wanted answers, and this
woman was, at the moment at least, his only
way to get them. But she shook her head at the
question. She knew even less than he.

"I've never heard her name before. I didn't
even know he was in London. The last time I
talked to him, he was in New York. But we
don't stay in very close contact," she said
quietly.

"Are you divorced?" Gordon asked, intrigued, and she was stung by the question.

"No, but he travels a lot, and he's very independent." She didn't want to tell him that their
marriage had been limping along for years.

"My wife isn't. We have an invalid son whom
she has cared for, for fourteen years, and she
rarely leaves the house. This trip is the first one
she's taken in years, and I think it was quite innocent. I was thinking that she may have just
met your husband at Claridge's, in the lobby
perhaps. I don't think we should jump to any
conclusions. But it seems odd that they were
together in a car at two o'clock in the morning." He seemed almost to be talking to himself.

"Yes, it does seem odd," she said, looking
pensive. There was more than adequate reason

to think that Bill might have been having an affair. She had had several herself in recent years,
and she and Bill hadn't been physically involved
with each other in years. But the woman Gordon Forrester described hardly seemed like a
likely candidate for a romantic weekend in another city. Cynthia couldn't even imagine how
he'd met her. And she didn't love the idea of
their being together. And as she and Gordon
talked, she realized that both of her daughters
had been listening to the conversation with interest. "It's a shame we can't ask them," Cynthia
said, but she couldn't get the art brochures out
of her head now. And then she remembered the
receipts from Annabel's and Harry's Bar. Maybe
this woman was far less innocent than her husband thought, in spite of her invalid son and the
fact that she was married.

"If they die, we'll never know the answer,"
Gordon said bluntly.

"If they hadn't had the accident, we would
probably never have known anyway. Maybe we
just have to accept that," Cynthia said softly. She
wasn't even sure she wanted to know, there
were questions she wouldn't have wanted him
to ask her, and others she wouldn't have asked
him. Particularly now, as he fought for his life
after the accident, there were dark corners of
their lives that she didn't want to look into. But

Gordon was holding up an investigative light and shining it brightly on them both. It was obvious that the mystery disturbed him.

"I don't suppose anyone else will ever tell us," Gordon said thoughtfully.

"If they're smart, and they were involved in some way, hopefully no one knows," Cynthia said practically.

"One would hope not. The driver might have been able to tell us."

"Maybe what we need to do is put it behind us, and not look for the answers. They're both fighting for their lives, and if they survive, maybe that's all we need to know. What happened before may be none of our business."

"That's very generous of you," Gordon said, looking less than satisfied with her suggestion. If Isabelle had been cheating on him, he wanted to know. He was far less convinced of her innocence than he had been.

"My husband is a very discreet man. Whatever happened will never come to light. It wouldn't be like him to behave inappropriately or cause a scandal, for you or himself."

"It wouldn't be like my wife to get involved with another man," Gordon said somewhat fiercely, more in defense of his pride than her reputation, and Cynthia sensed that. "And I don't think she was involved with him.

I'm sure there's some very sensible, innocent explanation."

"I hope so," she said quietly, and then looked Gordon in the eye. She wanted him to know where she stood on the situation. "I think you should know that I don't intend to ask."

"I do however intend to ask my wife if she comes out of the coma. I think they owe us that much."

"Why? What difference would it make?" she asked, much to her daughters' amazement. "What would it change? And if they die, we don't need to know that."

"I do. If she was dishonest with me in some way, I think I deserve to know that, and so do you. If not, it would be nice to absolve them."

"Absolving my husband is none of my business. He's a grown man. I wouldn't like it if he was involved with your wife, but there are some things in life one is better off not knowing about."

"I don't share your point of view, Mrs. Robinson," he said tersely, and he couldn't help wondering what kind of marriage they had. In fact, hardly different than his own, but he would never have admitted to anyone that his marriage to Isabelle was a sham, and had been for years. In fact, it wouldn't have been so remarkable if Isabelle was having an affair, she was young and loving and human. Gordon knew better than anyone how very lonely she was, thanks to him. Which was why he wanted to know what she'd been up to, if she had betrayed him, or was simply very foolish and had had dinner with a strange man. But it was late to be out under any circumstances. He couldn't even begin to imagine where they'd been at that hour, or what they'd been doing. At any other hour of the day, he'd have been willing to believe they were at an art show, but not at two o'clock in the morning.

Cynthia went back in to see Bill then, and the girls stared at Gordon in silence after she left. And after a few minutes he went back to the desk to tell them he was going back to Claridge's, and they could call him there if there was any change. He had had enough of the hospital waiting room, and he didn't like Cynthia Robinson, or her liberal attitude about her husband. He probably cheated on her regularly, and she seemed perfectly willing to accept it. And he had no doubt that she cheated on him too. But in fact, as Cynthia stood at Bill's bedside, watching him, knowing what she did now from Gordon Forrester, she felt her heart sink as she looked at Bill. Maybe Gordon could tell himself that they had been together at that hour in all innocence, but with her entire heart and soul, Cynthia didn't believe it. And as she stood looking at Bill with tears running slowly down her face, she wondered if she had finally lost him after all these years. She had been so indifferent to him for so long, and so unkind at times, she knew how cold and distant she had been, how critical of the life he led. She hadn't wanted to be part of his life in years, and now that she had possibly lost him forever, all she wanted was to tell him that she still loved him. She didn't know if she'd ever get the chance again, but all she wanted was to tell him one last time how much she loved him. She hadn't even known that she still did until the night before, but she knew it now, and she wanted Bill to know it too. She couldn't help wondering what Isabelle Forrester meant to him, or if he was in love with her. And Cynthia knew that if she had lost him finally, because of her own stupidity, she deserved it. She had no doubt about that. She realized suddenly, in the face of losing him, how foolish she had been for so many years.

Chapter Five

Gordon spent Friday night at Claridge's reading a book he had bought on the way back from the hospital. He had nothing else to do. He could have called friends in London, but he wasn't ready to tell people what had happened. He wanted to see what happened to Isabelle first. And he was distracted as he read the book. He called the hospital late in the evening, before he went to bed, but there was no change. It had been forty-eight hours since the accident, and she was hanging on, but that was about it. There had been no improvement yet, she just wasn't any worse. It occurred to him that he could have gone back to the hospital, but he couldn't bear the thought of seeing her in that condition again. He wouldn't have admitted it to anyone, but the sight of her frightened him. He detested hospitals, the patients, the doctors, the nurses, the sounds, and the smells.

When Gordon called, Cynthia was still sitting with Bill. The girls had gone back to Claridge's at dinnertime, but Cynthia had decided to stay. She went to the nurses' station to help herself to a cup of tea from time to time, and they were pleasant to her. But Cynthia had a lot to think about, and she was happy keeping to herself. She was wondering, as she watched her husband fight for his survival, if she would ever get the chance now to tell him the things she wanted to say. She had a lot of explanations and apologies to make for a lot of years. She knew that, although he had never said as much to her, he was probably well aware of all her affairs. Some of them had been fairly obvious, although others had been more discreet.

After a while, once she gave up on their marriage, she just didn't care. And she wasn't even sure now why she had turned away from him with such determination. Jealousy maybe, she thought, for the interesting life he led, and the people he met. She had never liked being dependent on him, and she wondered now if she had wanted to prove to him that she didn't need him. It had always annoyed her that, as a wife on the political scene, she had to behave like an appendage to him, and emotionally at least, she had walked away from him. And he had been

so busy and traveled so much, she felt rejected
at times. She hated the image of being a subur-
ban mother with two kids, she wanted to be
more glamorous and exciting than that. She realized now that she had tried to put excitement
in her life in the wrong ways. She knew that
now, but her greatest fear was that she had figured it all out too late.

She was still thinking about it at midnight, as
she sat in a chair, in the corner of Bill's room,
and for just a fraction of an instant, she thought
she heard him stir.

"Bill?" She got up and looked at him more
closely, the nurses had just left the room to get a
fresh IV for him, and she thought she could see
his eyelids move as though he were having a
dream. She was standing next to him when
they returned. They glanced instantly at the
monitors, but all was well.

"Is everything all right, Mrs. Robinson?" one
of the nurses asked as she switched IV bags, and
smoothed the covers over his legs.

"I think so . . . I'm not sure . . . for a minute,
I thought . . . it sounds ridiculous . . . but I
thought something moved." The nurses looked
at him more closely, but there was no sign of
life, and they took his vital signs again. He had
stabilized somewhat that day. It had been almost

exactly forty-eight hours since the accident, and Cynthia had been there for twenty-four. It felt like an eternity to her.

The nurse in charge was adjusting his heart monitor, and this time she felt a faint movement in one of his hands, she watched him carefully, and then checked his eyes. She shone a thin beam of light into them, as Cindy watched, and this time there was no mistaking it, he made a small muffled sound, like a soft groan of pain. It was the first sound he had made, and Cynthia's eyes filled with tears as she looked at him.

"Oh my God," she whispered as he made the same noise again. It was almost an animal sound, and his eyelids trembled as she touched his fingers. The nurse pushed a buzzer that would summon the doctor on duty in charge of the case. A light went on at the desk, and within seconds the attending doctor was there.

"What's up?" he asked the nurse as he strode into the room. He had been on duty for hours, and he looked as tired as Cynthia felt. "Any change?"

"He groaned twice," the nurse said.

"And I think I saw him move his hand a minute ago," Cynthia added as he shone the beam of light into Bill's eyes again. And this time Bill made the sound in response to the light. Cynthia was sure of it, and the doctor glanced up at the nurse. There was a question in his eyes, and she nodded at him. They didn't want to say it prematurely to his wife, but he was coming around. It was a major sign, and the first encouragement they'd had in two days.

"Bill, can you hear me? It's me, I'm here. . . . I love you, sweetheart. Can you open your eyes? I want to talk to you. I've been waiting for you to wake up." He tried to shift his shoulders then, and this time he groaned louder, presumably in pain.

"Mr. Robinson, I'm going to touch your hand. If you can hear me, I want you to squeeze my finger as hard as you can." The doctor spoke directly into his ear, leaning close to his face, and then he put a finger into Bill's hand, and waited to see if there was any response. There wasn't at first, and then slowly, ever so slowly, Bill's fingers curled around the finger the doctor had pressed against his palm. There was no other visible sign of recognition from him, but he had clearly heard the doctor's voice and understood his words.

"Oh my God, he heard," Cynthia said, with tears pouring down her face. "Can you hear me, sweetheart? I'm here . . . open your eyes, please. . . ." But nothing moved on his face, and then ever so slowly, with his eyes closed, he frowned, and his lips parted, as he ran his tongue around his parched lips. It was like watching a miracle occur as he started to come around.

"That's very good, Mr. Robinson," the doctor said close to Bill's face. "I want you to squeeze my finger again." Bill groaned in protest this time, as though they were annoying him, but he did it again, this time with the other hand. Both nurses and the doctor looked at each other victoriously. He was coming back. It was impossible to determine how much he could hear or understand, but he was definitely responding to them. Cynthia felt as though she were going to jump out of her own skin, and she wanted to shove them aside and throw her arms around his neck. But she didn't move from where she stood. She wouldn't have dared risk hurting him.

"Do you think you could open your eyes, if you try very hard, Mr. Robinson? I would like it very much if you could." The doctor urged him on, and there was no sign from Bill for a long time, and Cynthia was afraid he had slipped into the coma again. He looked like he was asleep. The doctor touched both of Bill's eyelids then, as though to remind him of the command, and his brain of where his eyelids were. Bill let out a small sigh, and then without a sound, he opened both eyes and looked at him.

"Well, hello," the young doctor said with a smile. "That was jolly good. It's nice to see you, sir."

Bill let out a small "Hmmm . . ." and then closed his eyes again, but he had looked right at the doctor for a second or two. It was the best he could do for now. And Bill drifted slowly back into the place where he had been. He had been dreaming of Isabelle.

"Would you like to try that again?" This time there was a sharp groan that clearly meant "no," but after another minute, he did it anyway. "We've been very anxious to see you," the doctor said with a smile, and as he said it, Bill's eyes seemed to sweep the room, and he saw Cynthia standing at the foot of his bed, and he looked confused.

"Hi, baby, I'm here. I love you. Everything's going to be okay." And with that, his eyes closed again, as though it was all too much for him, and he didn't want to see any of them. And a moment later, he went back to sleep. But it had been a major event, and all of them were beaming as Cynthia followed the doctor out of the room.

"Oh my God, what does that mean?" she asked, trembling from head to foot. She had never been as shaken by anything in her life, and the doctor was happy for her.

"It means he's out of the coma, although not entirely out of the woods. But I think it's an enormously hopeful sign."

"Can he talk?"

"He will eventually, I'm sure. His head injury wasn't such that his speech should be affected. He's just been very badly traumatized." Bill's neck and spine were his worst injuries, although even the minor concussion he had sustained had kept him in a coma for two days. "His brain needs to adjust to what happened to him. I'm sure he'll speak when he wakes up again. His body has experienced a tremendous shock. It's like getting the wind knocked out of you, multiplied by ten thousand possibly. I'm not worried about his speech." He was worried about everything else. The real problem in the long run was going to be his spine and the use of his legs. But the fact that he could use his hands was a good sign. He was obviously very weak, but it meant that he would be able to move his hands and arms, particularly once his neck had healed. "I think we can assume he's going to sleep for several hours, and tomorrow we should see some forward movement again. You might want to go back to the hotel and get some sleep, Mrs. Robinson. Tomorrow will be another long day." But she was so excited, she hated to leave.

"You don't think he'll wake up again? If he does, I want to be here."

"I think it's far more likely that he's exhausted from the effort he just made. It must have been like climbing Everest for him. He just made the first base camp, and he's got a lot more climbing to do in the next few weeks." And possibly the next few years, but he didn't want to say that to her. This was just the beginning, and they had a long way to go, but the entire medical team was enormously encouraged by what they'd just seen.

"All right," Cynthia agreed. "Maybe I'll go back to the hotel." She hadn't seen her daughters in hours. They had been planning to order room service and watch TV until she got home. She had promised to call them as soon as she got back to her room. And she could hardly wait to tell them what had just happened. When she did, when she got back to Claridge's, Olivia let out a scream of joy, and Jane did a little dance.

"God, Mom, that's so great! Did he say anything?"

"No, he just opened his eyes a couple of times, and moaned. He squeezed the doctor's finger twice, and he saw me standing there. But then he went back to sleep. The doctor thinks he might talk tomorrow. And the nurse said that once he's regained consciousness, he should be alert pretty quickly after that." Cynthia was hoping he would talk to her the next day.

The next morning, when she got back to the hospital, he was lying in bed with his eyes open and looking around the room, as though he still wasn't sure where he was. He seemed half asleep, as though he'd just woken up, which he had.

"Hi, sleepyhead," Cynthia said gently as she approached his bed. "We've been waiting forever for you to wake up." He blinked his eyes at her as though to say "yes," but he looked sad, almost as though he were disappointed to see her, and had expected to see someone else. She had the feeling that he would have nodded at her, if he could, but he couldn't move his head in the brace around his neck. "Do you feel better today?" He blinked again. And then she ever so gently touched his face. "I love you, Bill. I'm so sorry this happened. But you're going to be okay." He didn't take his eyes from hers, and then she saw him wet his lips as he had the night before, and close his eyes again. She wanted to offer him something to drink, but she didn't dare. The nurses had left him alone with her for a few minutes. The monitors would warn them if anything went awry. "Can I get you anything you need?" she whispered as he opened his eyes and looked at her face. He looked as though he was worried about something, and she stood next to him so she could hear him if he had anything to say to her. His mouth opened then, but no sound came out. "What do you want, sweetheart? Can you say the words?" She spoke to him as she would have to a child. And he looked frustrated at the difficulty he was having at making himself understood. He lay there in silence for a long time, and then tried again, as though he had been gathering strength while Cynthia talked. "The girls are here," Cynthia chatted on. "They came to London with me." He blinked as though to acknowledge her, and then frowned again, as he fought to unlock his jaw. She wondered if the brace on his neck was hurting him. It didn't look comfortable, but he didn't seem to be in any particularly acute pain.

"Where . . ." he finally whispered at her, as she strained to hear and waited patiently. But he seemed to take forever with the next word. ". . . is Izzz . . . ahh . . . bell?" It had been a huge effort for him, as he stared at his wife. She wasn't even sure Bill recognized her. His entire focus seemed to be on the woman who'd been in the car with him. She also suspected he wanted to know if Isabelle was alive. And his words, so agonizingly formed, and at such effort and cost to him, struck Cynthia like a blow. Asking for Isabelle had been his first words to his wife, and told her all she needed to know.

"She's alive," she said quietly. "I'll ask the nurse how she is." He blinked twice then, as though to say thank-you to her, and then he closed his eyes. A moment later, Cynthia walked outside, and her daughters pounced on her as soon as she did. She didn't tell them what he had just said.

"How is he, Mom? Did he say anything?"

"I think he's better. He's trying to talk a little bit. And I told him you were both here." Cindy was shocked by what he had said to her. His first words had been for Isabelle, and she couldn't help wondering how much Isabelle meant to him. It was surely more than just chivalry that had caused him to ask for Isabelle the moment he woke up.

"What did he say?" They were thrilled. They were ecstatic that their father had survived.

"He blinked twice," she said, with a smile, covering her own pain.

"Can he talk?" Jane asked, looking like her mother's mirror image. It was Olivia who was the portrait of Bill. They were both like two clones of Bill and herself.

"He said a couple of words, but it's still hard work for him. I think he's resting now." She sounded strangely subdued as she promised the girls she'd be back in a minute, and then walked to the desk and spoke to the nurse. "How is Mrs. Forrester?" she asked quietly. If nothing else, she could tell Bill what he wanted to know. He had a right to that, if he cared about her, and even if they were just friends. They had been to hell and back together. The least she could do for him was give him news of Isabelle, since he had struggled so hard to ask about her.

"She's not doing very well, I'm afraid. She's about the same. She had a fever again last night. Her husband is with her now."

"Has she regained consciousness?" Cynthia asked dutifully.

"No, but that's not surprising given her injuries and the surgery the other night." Cynthia nodded, and thanked her, and then walked back into Bill's room to see if he was awake. But he was snoring softly as she stood next to him. And then as though he sensed her, he stirred and opened his eyes. He had been dreaming of Isabelle again. He had been for two days.

"I asked about Isabelle for you. She's about the same. She's been in a coma, and she hasn't come out of it yet, but I hope she will." He blinked his eyes as though he wanted to nod at her. And after a long time, he started working on another set of words.

"Thhh . . . ankk . . . youuu,   Cinnn . . . I thought . . . you . . . were her," he said, closed his eyes again, and drifted back into a dream about Isabelle. He had no desire to see his wife, or talk to her.

"Do you want to see the girls?" Cindy interrupted his dream again, and this time, he blinked three times, and she smiled. "I'll go get them, they're just down the hall." And a moment later, they were in his room, chattering at him, and Cynthia actually saw him smile. And when he talked to them, it took less effort than it had before. His ability to speak was coming back, it was just a little slow, but his mind was obviously clear.

"I . . . love . . . you, girls. . . ."

"We love you too, Dad," Olivia said as Jane leaned down and kissed his hand. He had an IV running into it, and another one in the other arm. He was still covered with monitors and tubes, and IVs. But the girls were just happy he was alive.

"Greatt . . . gggirlsss," he said to Cynthia when they left.

"You're pretty great yourself" was all she said, and he looked surprised. "You scared us for a while," she went on. "Do you know what happened to you?" she asked. It had occurred to her that he might not know.

"No." He had no memory of it at all, only of the evening he'd spent with Isabelle before the accident.

"Your limousine got hit by a bus. It took them a couple of hours, I gather, to get both of you out."

"I . . . was . . . afraid . . . she . . . died." He struggled with the words, and Cynthia couldn't help thinking how odd it was that he was talking about Isabelle to his wife, but he didn't seem to mind. His eyes filled with tears as he looked at her.

"I think she came very close to it." Cynthia didn't tell him that she still might die. "Her husband is here with her now." As Cynthia said it to him, it was almost like a warning to Bill that he also had to return to real life. Isabelle had a husband. And he had two daughters and a wife. It was their turn now. He knew that, no matter how much he loved Isabelle, he had a responsibility to them. But he had been dreaming of Isabelle for days.

The nurses came back into the room then, they had things to do to him, and Cynthia went back outside to join the girls. She had to digest what had just happened with Bill. There was no question in her mind. Isabelle Forrester was important to him, she was no stranger, as her husband had hoped, or even a casual friend. Asking about her had been Bill's first words. And his eyes were full of anguish and concern for her. He had even thought he was seeing Isabelle when he woke up, and not his wife.

And as she sat in the waiting room, waiting for the nurses to finish their tasks with him, Cynthia picked up a copy of the *Herald Tribune,* and saw that there was an article about the bus accident in it, and she was startled to see a photograph of Bill and a woman, next to the photograph of the badly mangled bus. The article said that eleven people had died, and well-known political power broker William Robinson had been in the limousine that had been hit by the bus. The caption under the photograph said that the picture had been taken just moments before. It said that he and an unidentified woman had been at Annabel's, their car was hit only blocks away, and their driver had been killed. But it didn't mention Isabelle's name, or whether or not she'd been injured in the crash. But Cynthia knew as she looked at her face that it had to be her. She looked attractive and young, with long dark hair, and she'd obviously been startled by the photographer as she stared at him with wide eyes. And in the photograph, Bill was smiling with an arm around her shoulders. It made Cynthia catch her breath as she saw them to-

gether that way. They looked happy and relaxed, and Bill looked as though he were about
to laugh. It brought the potential seriousness of
the situation home to her again. She wondered
if Gordon Forrester had seen it too. Whatever it
was that his wife and her husband had shared,
it was unlikely, as far as she was concerned, that
it was inconsequential to either of them. Particularly now.

The girls exchanged a glance as they saw her
reading the article. They didn't say anything,
but they had seen it too. But they couldn't even
be angry at their father now, for whatever he
had done with her. What had happened was so
much more serious that they could forgive him
almost anything. And Cynthia felt the same
way. What worried her was not what he had
done, but the possibility that he really cared
about Isabelle. The look in his eyes when he
asked about her had told Cynthia that this was
no casual affair. She found it hard to believe that
they were just good friends. She and Gordon
would have been even more stunned to know
that they had been confidants for more than
four years.

One of the nurses came back to get them
then, and Cynthia followed her daughters into
Bill's room. She noticed just before the door
closed that Gordon Forrester was leaving

Isabelle's room. She didn't dare, but she would have liked to ask him if he'd seen the *Herald Tribune.* But he looked as if he had bigger things on his mind.

Isabelle was showing no sign of recovering, and although the doctor said she could remain in a coma for a long time, Gordon was increasingly worried that she would be brain-damaged if she survived. In addition, they had just told him that her heart was beating irregularly, and she was developing fluid in her lungs. There was a growing risk of pneumonia, and Gordon knew that if that happened, Isabelle would die. The situation seemed to be worsening. He had been there for an hour, talking to the doctors about further surgery, and he was on his way back to the hotel when Cynthia saw him leave Isabelle's room.

It was only after Cynthia and the girls left late that afternoon that Bill asked about Isabelle again. His speech had come back to him through the day. The girls hadn't stopped talking to him, and he had been forced to respond. This time Bill asked his nurse how Isabelle was, and she was cautious about what she said.

"She's about the same, she's still comatose, and her damage is more internal than yours." He had broken more bones, but all of her internal organs had been compromised. It would have been impossible to decide which was worse.

But he had survived, and would now for sure, while Isabelle's life still hung in the balance, her survival unsure. All he could think of was that he didn't want her to die, and would have given his life for hers.

"Can I see her?" he asked quietly. It was all he could think of all day, when he wasn't being distracted by Cynthia and the girls.

"I don't think that's possible," the nurse said. She was sure his surgeon would object. He had to lie as still as possible. There was no way to get him out of bed with his back and neck injuries, and Isabelle wouldn't be aware of his visit anyway.

But Bill asked his doctor the same question that night. "Just for a minute. I just want to see her, and see how she is."

"Not very well, I'm afraid," the doctor said honestly. "Her entire system has been traumatized. I was explaining that to her husband today. He wants her moved to France. I told him that's impossible. In the delicate state she's in, it would kill her to move her now." Bill felt the doctor's words like a knife through his chest. He didn't want Isabelle taken anywhere, at least not until he saw her again. And certainly not if it put her at greater risk. Forrester was crazy to even think of moving her so soon. The doctor had said as much to him. It wasn't hard to figure that out. "I don't think it's wise for you to see her, Bill," the doctor said sympathetically. They were on a first-name basis, and he was struck by how pleasant and personable Bill was now that he could talk. He thought him a very nice man. Unlike Gordon Forrester, who had been terse and arrogant, and offended everyone on the floor. He had started out the day by demanding to have her moved. No one would hear of it, and he had backed down when the head of the intensive care ward told him in no uncertain terms that he was out of his mind for suggesting it. And then he explained very bluntly to him that it would kill his wife, so Gordon agreed to leave her there. But the entire staff was sure he would try it again. He was obviously far too stubborn to give up.

"Can't you roll my bed into her room when no one else is there?" Bill asked plaintively, in full possession of his verbal capacities again, and obviously upset. "I want to see her for myself." The doctor was thoughtful for a long time, and Bill was agitated. The doctor knew nothing of their relationship, and he didn't want to ask, but clearly it meant a great deal to Bill to see Isabelle, and it couldn't do either of them any harm. He just didn't want Gordon Forrester to be angry if he found out.

"They could take me in tonight, couldn't they? I don't have to be there long."

"Why don't we wait and see how you feel to-morrow? And how she is, as well. Neither of you is going anywhere." It was driving Bill crazy knowing she was right across the hall. If he could have, he would have wheeled himself in, but he was entirely at their mercy to do that for him. He was trapped in his bed in a neck brace and a full body brace, and he was unable to move. He couldn't even lift his head, and his arms were extremely weak. He had no sensation or mobility from the waist down. And no one had any idea for the moment if it would return. He was as helpless as a baby lying in his bed, but he had a calm but forceful way of convincing the doctor that it was a good idea. "I can see I'm not going to be able to talk you out of it," the doctor said finally with a smile. It was after midnight by then, and there were no visitors left in the halls. He disappeared then to find Bill's nurse and send her in with some medication, and when she came back into Bill's room, she was followed by two men. Bill looked anxious for a moment, worried about what they were going to do to him, but without saying a word they took their places at the head and foot of his bed and the nurse stood aside as they began rolling his bed slowly toward the door.

"Where are we going?" he asked, looking

concerned, and then as the nurse smiled, he understood. The doctor had granted his wish, he was waiting for them in the hall, and he spoke to Bill as he rolled by.

"If you breathe a word of this, I'll put you back in a coma myself," he said softly, and Bill laughed. "This is highly irregular." But he thought it would do Bill good, and it wasn't likely to do Isabelle any harm. She would never even know he was there.

It took a little maneuvering, but they got his bed next to hers. He moved his eyes sharply to see her, and he could just see her head swathed in bandages out of the corner of his eye. But if he moved his left arm as far as he could, he could touch her fingers with his hand. The two nurses assigned to her were watching what was happening, and the doctor had instructed them to turn a blind eye. It was obvious to all of them why Bill was there. He held her fingers in his hand for a few minutes, and then he spoke to her, totally impervious to whoever heard him in the room. Tears filled his eyes as he touched her hand.

"Hello, Isabelle . . . it's me . . . Bill. . . . You've got to wake up now. You've been asleep for long enough . . . you have to come back. . . ." And then in a soft voice, "I love you. . . . Everything's going to be fine." They let him stay a few more

minutes, and then rolled him back. He was exhausted and pale when he got back to his own
room. And as he lay there, thinking about her afterward, he suddenly remembered a dream he'd
had, and wondered when it had been. They had
both been walking toward a bright light, and just
before they reached it, he had forced her to turn
back, and she had been very annoyed. Their
children had been there, and he had wanted to
go back to them. But Isabelle had wanted to go
on. And he wanted to tell her the same things
now that he had then. She had to come back. He
wanted her to wake up. And all he could think of
was seeing her again. It panicked him thinking of
Gordon trying to take her back to France. It was
obvious even to Bill that she was in no condition
to be moved. But at least the doctor had reassured him that they wouldn't let that happen. Bill
was relieved for her sake, but he also liked knowing that she was nearby.

He drifted off to sleep that night thinking of Isabelle, and there was a smile on his face. Lying in
his bed at Claridge's, Cynthia was also thinking of
her. And in the room Isabelle had occupied only
days before, Gordon Forrester was lying awake in
his bed, and thinking of Bill. They all had a lot to
ponder that night, and the only ones who knew
the answers to their questions were Bill and
Isabelle.

Chapter Six

The nurse was feeding Bill when Cynthia arrived
the next day. It was Sunday, four days after the
accident, and he still looked utterly worn out.
But they were both grateful that he was awake,
and alive.

"How's it going, babe?" Cynthia asked, looking cheerful and fresh. It was warm outside, she
was wearing a T-shirt and shorts, and a pair of
sandals she had borrowed from one of the girls.
Olivia and Jane were going to spend some time
walking around London, and they wanted to go
to a flea market. The hours Cynthia spent at
the hospital were too long for them, and they
were planning to come by later that afternoon.

"How do you feel?" Cynthia inquired as she
approached his bed. Because of the angle of
the brace on his neck, it was hard for him to
see very far. And as she came into his field of
vision, he smiled.

"I thought I'd play a couple of sets of tennis today," he said. He sounded hoarse, but he was able to speak clearly now.

They had just shaved him for the first time, and he felt a little more human again, but he still had a long way to go. He had told the doctor that his vision was blurred, which came as no surprise. The impact to his head had been considerable, and he was going to be feeling the effects of the coma for a while. A specialist was due in to examine his legs and his spine again, and the attending physician had told him they might want to operate, depending on what the specialist found. It was obvious to everyone by then that Bill's recovery was going to take a very long time. And the extent of that recovery hadn't been determined yet. Whether or not he would ever walk again still remained a question in everyone's mind. Bill was aware of it, but it was a subject he and Cynthia had avoided so far, although they both knew that given the damage to his spinal cord, there was a real possibility that he'd be in a wheelchair for the rest of his life.

Cynthia was in no rush to discuss it with him, he had enough on his mind. But for the past four days, she had thought again and again about what it would be like to be married to him now. She had no idea if he would ever go back to work, or what his life would be like if he was forced to retire. She couldn't even imagine it, and neither could Bill when he tried. But it could have been far worse, they both knew. He could have been completely paralyzed. And they were both relieved to realize that he would eventually have full use of his upper body and arms. Although whether or not he could use his lower body was an open question that was terrifying him.

"How are the girls?" he asked as Cynthia pulled up a chair and sat down. She could see that he was anxious and tense.

"They're fine, they're going to a flea market today. They said they'd come to see you after that." Both girls were immensely relieved that their father had survived. And Cynthia had encouraged them to go out for a change of scene.

"They should go home this week, Cyn. There's nothing for them to do here."

"We were coming to Europe anyway in a couple of weeks. I don't think they'd want to leave you now." His wife smiled at him, and for a moment he avoided her eyes. "Maybe I'll take them to Paris for a few days, if you feel better in a couple of weeks. You'll be coming home soon anyway." But she wasn't as sure of that as she wanted him to think. The doctor had warned her that Bill would be hospitalized for months, and she had asked about flying him to the States in an air ambulance, but all his doctors agreed it was far too soon for him to be moved.

"I don't know when I'll be able to go home, Cyn. And they can't sit here all summer waiting for me. Neither can you."

"I've got nothing better to do," she said easily, and he smiled.

"Things must have changed a lot then in the last few weeks. You never stop, Cyn. Aren't you in some tennis tournament, or going somewhere, or giving a party for someone? You're going to go crazy if you just sit around here, watching me."

"I'm not leaving you here, Bill," she said quietly. "I'll send the girls back eventually, unless they want to go somewhere on their own. 'For better or worse,' remember that part? I do. I'm not going home and leaving you all alone."

"I'm a big boy," he said, looking unusually serious, and she saw something ominous in his eyes. It worried her, she was trying to keep things light, but she couldn't stop him from what he wanted to say to her. "I was going to talk to you about that. The 'better or worse' thing, I mean. We've had a lot of the 'worse' in recent years. It's my fault, I was gone all the time, and I've been so caught up in politics for so long, I haven't been around much for you and the girls." He felt guilty about it, and had for a long time, but they had established a pattern of distance between them, and eventually it became impossible to turn things around.

"We got used to it. No one blames you for it. I have a life, I have things to do. I'm not complaining about our marriage, Bill." She looked serious as she spoke to him. The nurse had left them alone when they started to talk.

"You should be complaining, Cyn. You should have complained a long time ago, and so should I. We don't have a marriage anymore. We haven't in years. We don't do the same things, have the same friends. I don't even know what you're doing most of the time, and lately I even forget to tell you where I am. To be honest, I'm not even sure you care. I'm surprised you came over here. I figured by now you'd be just as happy if I got lost one of these days."

He wasn't feeling sorry for himself, it was all true, and he didn't mention to her that he knew about her many affairs in recent years, although they had talked about the one he had had years before. Cynthia had been furious over it, and said it had humiliated her. But he had been a gentleman and never pointed out to her that her brief flings with her tennis instructors and golf pros and the husbands of her friends had humiliated him for years. Fidelity was no longer an aspect of the marriage she offered him. At first it had been her revenge for feeling rejected by him when he became obsessed by politics, and at times he thought it was a way of getting attention from him, but it had been the wrong way to go. Eventually, he had just detached and forced himself not to care anymore. He didn't say anything to her when he did, because it was easier to close his eyes to what was happening, but he was certainly aware of it, and eventually it had killed his love for her. What he had once felt for her, thirty years before, had been dead for a long time. All that was left was friendship, and he was grateful that she was there with him, but he wasn't in love with her, and that was no longer enough for him. He had realized it during the hours he had spent with Isabelle days before.

"That's a mean thing to say," Cynthia said, looking hurt. "How could you think I wouldn't come over here after you had an accident? You must think I have absolutely no heart at all."

"No, baby, I know you have a heart," he smiled sadly at her, "it just hasn't been mine in a very long time. I wish it had been, and sometimes I wish it still were, but it hasn't been, and I think we have to face that now. I was going to talk to you about it when I got home."

Cynthia looked at him in pained silence for a long time, with tears in her eyes. She couldn't believe he was saying this to her. It was ironic, just as she had realized that she was still in love with him, or maybe in love with him again, he was telling her that he didn't love her anymore, and that it was over. She wasn't even sure what he was telling her. But so far, the preamble didn't sound encouraging.

"Is this about Isabelle Forrester?" she asked, trying to sound calm. "You're in love with her, aren't you?" This was no time to hide behind words. She wondered if he'd been planning to marry her. It wasn't like Bill to just go off and have affairs, he had only done that once, and never again, as far as she knew. And the affair with the congressman's wife had gotten very serious before he ended it. He had put a stop to it because he knew that if he stayed involved with her, he would have left Cynthia and the girls.

"This isn't about Isabelle," he said, honest with her. He had to be, for all their sakes. "It's about me. I don't know why we've stayed married this long. Habit, I guess. Or laziness, or some illusion that things would get better, or a willingness to settle, or maybe because the kids were young. But is this the way you want to live? Married to a guy you never see? We never talk anymore, we have no common ground at all except the girls. You have your own life, and I have mine. You deserve a lot better than that, and so do I." It was true, Cynthia knew, but they were words she didn't want to hear.

"We could still make it work, if we wanted to. I realized once this happened to you, that I still love you. I'm the one who's been stupid for all these years," and they both knew how and why, she didn't need to spell it out for him. "I think at first I was angry that you had so much fun, and such a big part of your life that didn't include me. So I decided to have some fun too. I did it in all the wrong ways, and I wound up feeling like shit, about myself, and about you. But that could change. I see now how much we still have, how much we love each other." The tears that were brimming in her eyes suddenly spilled onto her cheeks, and she leaned over and touched his hand. "I was terrified when I thought I'd lose you. I love you, Bill. Don't give up on us now. It's too soon."

If he could have, he would have shaken his head, but his eyes said the same thing. "It's too late, Cyn. There's nothing left, all we really have are the girls and the fact that we're good friends. That's why you're here. I'd do the same for you. You're not losing me, Cyn. You can't. That's why I want to end it now, so it stays that way. If we hang on, if we keep doing this, we'll wind up hating each other eventually, and I don't want that to happen, for us, or the girls. If we give it up now, we'll always be friends."

"I'm your wife." She was fighting for her life now, but she wasn't winning with him, she could see that too. "I don't want to just be your friend."

"It's better than the alternative. One of these days, you're going to get involved with the wrong guy, maybe one of my friends, or someone I care about, and I'm going to get seriously pissed off at you and him. It won't be pretty between us after that." He was also amazed that she hadn't caused some real scandals for him, but at least she'd been careful about that.

"I won't do that anymore." She cried and blew her nose, it was humiliating to have him speak so openly of her indiscretions to her. It was embarrassing to hear that he had known about them all along, she had always told herself that he never knew. And she liked to tell herself that he was probably doing the same thing. But he was too serious for that, too loyal, and too deep, and she knew she should have realized it then. It was why he probably was in love with Isabelle. Because he was a profoundly decent man, and what he felt was far more dangerous. When he loved someone, it was the real thing. "I won't have any more affairs. I'll stop. I swear.

I'm not involved with anyone now." She had broken off her last liaison only four weeks before, after three months, with a man she'd met at their country club. He had a wife and three kids, and he drank too much. He'd been great in bed, in spite of it, but she was afraid he would talk about their affair when he was drunk. And she didn't want to risk the embarrassment he might cause.

"You'll do it again. We both know you will. And maybe you're right. We're both lonely as hell. We're a million miles apart, even when we're together. That's not what either of us wants, or what we deserve." As he spoke to her, he thought of Isabelle again. He was haunted by worry about her in the daytime, and dreams, where he wandered aimlessly, looking for her, all night long.

"Are you going to marry her?" She ended the question on a sob, and he hated what he was saying to her, but it was time. He had realized it when he was with Isabelle, and in spite of the accident, he wanted to end it with Cynthia now. It was only going to get worse, and it wasn't fair to be dependent on her. She would come to hate him eventually. She wasn't the kind of woman who could spend years, and surely not the rest of her life, nursing a man. And if he wound up in a wheelchair for the rest of his life, that was the last thing he wanted to inflict on her. He had only one choice, he knew, and that was to get out and take care of himself.

"No, I'm not going to marry her. She won't leave Forrester, if she lives. He's a son of a bitch, and he's rotten to her. But she has a very sick child. I told you, this isn't about her. It's about us. You'll thank me for this one day, when you find the right guy. I never was. We had a hell of a good time at first, but we never wanted the same things. And I don't believe in all that 'opposites attract' crap anymore, not at our age. At this point in life, we both need people who want the same things we do. You've always wanted a very different life than I. I didn't think it mattered when we were kids, but I was wrong. You need some fun-loving, happy-go-lucky guy who wants to go to parties and has lots of time to spend with you. You don't need a maniac who's obsessed with his work and gone all the time, and worries more about who's going to be the next president than he does about his own kids." He knew he would feel guilty forever for the time he had missed with the girls, no matter how close he felt to them now.

"You're a great father, Bill. You've always been wonderful to the girls. And they couldn't love you more." She meant it too, both his daughters worshiped him, even if they were used to his not being around. They had a deep respect for all he did, and were proud of him.

"I wasn't around enough," he said guiltily. "I know that now. I'll never be able to make it up to them. But I'm going to try one of these days. Maybe I'll slow down a little, for a while." But it was almost too late. They were both in college, and had their own lives, and he knew that too. In many ways, he had already missed the boat, and those opportunities, once lost, would never come again. All he could do now was be there for them, to the degree they would allow him to be, as adults.

"What are you saying to me?" she asked, blowing her nose again. She looked panicked and distraught.

"I think we should get divorced. It's the only way we'll manage to preserve whatever we've got left. Cindy, I want to be your friend."

"Go fuck yourself," she said, and then smiled through her tears. "I never thought you'd walk out on us." She couldn't believe this was happening to them, particularly now. All she had wanted three days ago was for him to live, and then for a flash of an instant, she could remember thinking that morning in Connecticut, when they first called her about the accident, that if he was going to be crippled for the rest of his life, he should die. She hadn't wanted that to happen to him, or to her, and now it had, and he was leaving her. And she couldn't help wondering if he was just depressed and reacting to the accident in some hysterical way. "Are you sure this is what you want? You've had a terrible shock. It's natural for you to . . ."

He cut her off before she could say the rest, and he looked calm as he spoke to her. "We should have done this years ago, Cyn. I just never had the balls."

"Well, I'm sorry you do now. I've been falling in love with you again all week. And now you want out. I'll tell you one thing, Bill Robinson. Your timing stinks," and then she started to cry harder again, and looked at him with heartbroken eyes. "Why didn't you stop me if you knew what I was doing for all those years? Why didn't you say something?" It was horrifying to realize that he'd known about her affairs. But they both knew it hadn't been his responsibility to stop her, it had been hers.

"I didn't know what to say. I didn't want to face it myself. I told myself a lot of stories at first, that it wasn't really happening. And then I just got used to it. I don't know, Cyn . . . maybe I didn't want to be that honest with myself. But now I have no choice. It's too late in the day for me to be anything else. I don't have the energy to tell myself a lot of fairy tales anymore. And maybe I'll never have anyone in my life again, after all this, but at least neither of us will be living a lie. That's got to be better. Don't you think?"

"No, I don't," she said honestly. "I'd rather live a lie than lose you. And we don't have to live a lie. We could try to do it right this time, if you give me another chance." As she said it, she looked like the girl he had married, and seeing that broke his heart. He almost did wish that he'd confronted her years ago, but he hadn't been ready to then, and it was over for him now.

"It's too late. For both of us. You just don't know it yet."

"What am I going to tell people?" It hit her like a blow. The whole idea of his divorcing her was so humiliating, she wanted to run away and hide.

"Tell them you finally got smart, and kicked my ass out. You probably should have when I went nuts and started working a hundred-and-forty-hour week. We both did a lot of stupid things. This isn't just your fault." As always he was being decent, and kind, and fair, which only made it hurt more. She knew what she was losing, and that she'd never find anyone like him again. Men like Bill were very rare.

"What'll I tell the girls?"

"That's another story. That's going to be hard. I think we should both think about it. They're old enough to understand, but they probably won't. No one likes change."

"Neither do I," she said in a choked voice. She didn't think about it, but it was going to be hardest for him. He had a long, tough road ahead of him, and he had chosen to face it alone. He had no illusions about his recovery, he knew there was an excellent chance he'd never walk again, and rehabilitation even to the degree he was capable of was going to be agonizing for him, particularly alone. But he also knew that Cynthia wouldn't have been able to tolerate it. Whatever nurturing abilities she'd once had had long since been spent on the girls. She would have gone crazy living with him if he was impaired in any way. Cynthia was not Isabelle. She could never have done, or lived, what Isabelle did for her son. And Bill was willing to face his new burdens alone.

Cynthia stood up and walked to the window then, she was staring into space, looking heartbroken, when the American ambassador walked in. He had heard about the accident, and read about it in the *Tribune.* He was devastated, and he looked somber and worried when he walked in. And when Cynthia turned, with red swollen eyes, he could see that she was devastated by it too. He had no idea what they'd been talking about, and it never occurred to him that he had walked into a domestic drama, as he hurried to the bed and took Bill's hand with a look of profound concern.

"My God, Robinson, what happened to you? I was supposed to see you last week." He hadn't been able to believe the news when he heard, and he saw Cynthia and Bill exchange an odd look.

"I got in a fight with a bus moving at high speed. And the bus won. It was a damn fool thing to do," Bill said with a smile, but he looked tired. The exchange with Cynthia had worn him out, and then he said to her, "Cyn, why don't you hang out with the girls for a while? It'll do you good to get out of here." She nodded, unable to speak. She didn't want to cry in front of the ambassador, and she knew she would if she stayed. She didn't want to see her daughters either, she thought it would be better to go back to the hotel and cry for a while, on her own.

"I'll come back tonight," she said, tears brimming in her eyes again as she kissed his cheek. "I love you," she whispered, and then hurried out of the room, as the ambassador watched her go.

"Poor Cynthia, she's had a hell of a shock," the ambassador sympathized. He'd known them for years. He was from New York, and had thought of running for the presidency once, and Bill had discouraged him. He'd never have won, but he was doing a great job at the embassy, and he was loving it. He'd already been there for three years, and Bill knew that the president was going to ask him to stay for another term.

"Are you doing all right?" he asked Bill with a worried frown.

"Better now." In spite of the morning he'd just had. He hadn't been looking forward to talking to her, but he knew he'd done the right thing. He had been planning to do it when he got home. And he knew he couldn't let the accident change his mind. If anything, it had solidified his resolve. And he hadn't wanted to leave her any illusions about him, painful as that was.

"Do you need anything?" the ambassador asked as he sat down. His wife had told him not to stay long.

"Nothing much. New neck, new spine, a good solid pair of legs, the usual stuff." Bill tried to make a joke of it, but his eyes looked sad, as the ambassador smiled. If nothing else, Bill Robinson was the consummate good sport, and a good man.

"What are they saying to you?"

"Not much. It's too soon to know. I figure if FDR could run the country from a sitting position, it shouldn't make too much difference to me." But they both knew it did. His entire life had changed in the blink of an eye, not only his political life, but very probably his life as a man. The full implications of the accident were impossible to assess at this point, but aside from not being able to walk, he had no idea if he'd ever be able to make love to a woman again. He had been cognizant of that too when he told Cynthia he wanted a divorce. She would have been absolutely incapable of adjusting to that. But there were even more compelling reasons for them to get divorced, which was what had motivated him. His infirmities were just icing on the cake.

"Do you have any idea how long you'll be here?"

"Probably a long time," Bill said, sounding depressed. He was very tired. The morning hadn't been easy for him either, and it saddened him deeply to be ending his marriage. He had not only lost his wife, and chosen to, but with the accident, he appeared to have lost Isabelle, his closest friend. When he thought about it, his horizon was looking pretty bleak. He had nothing to look forward to, except a very hard year ahead of him, trying to get healthy again. But at least he was alive.

"Well, you can count on us," Ambassador Stevens said jovially. "Grace was going to come to visit you too, but she said she'd come another day. She didn't want to wear you out, and she was afraid I would. If you need anything, anything at all, I want you to call the embassy. Just have Cynthia call Grace. I assume she'll be staying with you." The poor woman had looked distraught when she left. But facing the fact that he might be an invalid forever now, Jim Stevens thought, couldn't be easy for her. "I'll have Grace call her in a few days." Bill didn't tell him that he was going to tell Cynthia to go back to Connecticut with the girls. He just smiled and let him talk. They were old friends, but he didn't want to share the news of the divorce with him. It was still too fresh. He didn't want to tell anyone till they told the girls, out of respect for them.

The ambassador looked at his watch then, and at Bill, and decided he had stayed long enough. Grace was right. He looked terrible, and within five minutes he left. And to Bill suddenly, the older man who had seemed like his father only days before, now seemed vital and young and full of life, and all because he could walk out of the room under his own steam.

The hours seemed to drag by after that. Bill slept for a while, and the specialist came in late that afternoon. Bill hadn't heard from Cynthia, but he suspected she was at Claridge's, licking her wounds. He was still certain that, however painful this was, she'd be better off in the end.

The specialist didn't have anything very encouraging to say. He spelled all the possibilities out for Bill, from worst case to best. From the X rays he'd seen, and the documentation of the surgery, he thought it unlikely Bill would ever walk again. He might regain some sensation eventually, but enough damage had been caused to his spine that he would most probably never regain full control of his legs. Even if he could feel them eventually, he would not be able to stand. They could fit him for braces, and with training, he might be able to use crutches and drag his legs, but he thought Bill would have more mobility and greater ease if he used a wheelchair. That was the good news. The bad news was that if the nerves degenerated further, combined with the damage to his neck, he might not regain any sensation at all below his waist. Arthritis could set in, and cause further deterioration to the bones, and coupled with what he already had, he could endure a lifetime of pain as well. But at fifty-two, he thought Bill had a good chance of recapturing at least some use of his legs, even if he never walked again. The doctor estimated that Bill's neck would take four to six months to heal, and the rehabilitation work on his legs would take a year or more. There were one or two additional surgeries they could do, but he felt that the benefits would be minimal, and the risks far too great. If they tried to improve on what he was left with now, he could end up fully paralyzed from the neck down, and he strongly urged Bill not to take that risk. He warned Bill that some surgeons might want to experiment with him, and promise him improvements they couldn't guarantee, but he was very outspoken in saying that any surgeon who took it on would be a fool to take the risk, and listening to him, Bill agreed. The picture he painted was a livable but not an easy one, and it took immense courage to face. He told Bill honestly that he would have to work like a dog for the next year to achieve some degree of use of his legs, and he would have to strengthen his upper body to compensate, not to mention the work he had to do on his neck. But with time, and hard work, he felt certain that Bill could lead a good life, if he was willing to make the psychological adjustment to the limitations that had befallen him in the accident. He said bluntly that it was a damn shame, but it was not the end of the world.

And then, reading Bill's mind easily, he answered the question that Bill was still too afraid to ask. It was clear that he would never walk again, and he would be wheelchair bound. But he had no idea whatsoever of what was in store for him in terms of a sexual life, if he would have any at all, and he was silently panicked over it. The doctor explained practically and openly that there was a good possibility that Bill would regain sensation sexually and be able to lead a relatively normal life, although it was still a little too early to tell. He told Bill that it was difficult to predict. But he was hopeful and encouraging, and anxious to relieve Bill's mind, as best he could. Eventually, Bill would have to try it out, but he hadn't progressed far enough in his recovery yet. It was bad enough to never walk again, but the doctor didn't want Bill to lose hope entirely about the rest.

"If your wife is patient for a while," the doctor said, smiling at him, "things could go very well." Bill didn't explain to him that in a short time, he would no longer have a wife, and he couldn't imagine experimenting with women he tried to date. But at the very least, he wanted to know that if he chose to experiment sexually, it would work. But no one could promise him that. He would just have to wait and see, which was agonizing. What he was planning to do, once he recovered, was what he had always done, throw himself full tilt into his work. More than ever now, it was all he had left.

After the doctor left, Bill lay in bed and thought for a while. He was severely depressed. A lot had happened in a few hours, and it was a great deal to absorb. It was hard to wrap his mind around the idea that he would never walk again . . . never walk again . . . he kept saying the words in his head. But he knew it could have been worse. He could have been totally paralyzed, or dead, his head injury could have left him permanently impaired mentally. But in spite of the mercies he knew he should be grateful for, the possible loss of his manhood seemed to outweigh them all, and he lay in bed, worried and depressed. And as he thought about it, his mind wandered to Isabelle again. He lay there and closed his eyes, thinking of the time they had spent together earlier that week. It was hard to believe it was only four days before. Four days ago, he had been dancing with her at Annabel's, feeling her close to him, and now he would never dance again, and she was hovering near death. It was impossible to believe that he might never talk to her again, might never hear her voice, or see her lovely face. Thinking about it, and everything that had happened to him, brought tears to his eyes. He was thinking about her, with tears running down his cheeks, when the nurse walked in. She knew the specialist had been with him for a long time, and that the news hadn't been good, and she thought he was disheartened over that, and gently tried to cheer him up. He was a handsome, vital man, and she could only imagine what it must mean to him to know that he would never walk again. The nurses had guessed it would turn out that way almost from the first day. His injuries had just been too severe.

"Would you like some pain medication, Mr. Robinson?" she asked, as he looked at her.

"No, I'm fine. How is Mrs. Forrester? Is there any change?" He asked every time he saw one of them, and none of them could figure out if he felt responsible for the accident in some way, because she'd been out with him, or if he was in love with her. It was hard to tell. The only one who knew was the one nurse who'd been there when he visited her the night before, and she had sworn to the doctor she wouldn't say a word about whatever she heard.

"She's about the same. Her husband was here for a little while, and he just left. I think he's going back to Paris for a few days. There's nothing he can do here." Except be with her, and talk to her, and beg her to come back. Bill hated Gordon as he thought of him. He was so icy cold, and so rotten to her. And then it occurred to him, if Gordon had left the hospital, then he could visit her again, and he mentioned it to the nurse. She knew he'd been in to see her the night before, and their mutual physician had allowed him to, but she had no idea what he'd think about Bill doing it again. But when she saw the look in his eyes, she could see what a hard day he'd had, and how affected he was by it, and her heart went out to him.

"I'll see what I can do," she said, and disappeared. She was back five minutes later with two orderlies, who unlocked the brakes on his bed, and rolled him slowly toward the door. She had to unhook some of his monitors, but he was well enough now to be without them for a little while, and she knew how determined he was to go across the hall and see Isabelle.

Her nurse held the door open for them, and the orderlies rolled his bed gently across the hall into the room, and placed it next to hers. The shades in her room were drawn, and the respirator was making its familiar whooshing sound, as the nurses backed away into a corner of the room to leave them alone. Bill turned toward her as best he could, which was extremely limited, and took her fingers in his hand again, just as he had the night before.

"It's me, Isabelle . . . you have to wake up, my love. You have to come back. Teddy needs you, and so do I. I need to talk to you, I miss you so much." Tears rolled freely down his cheeks as he talked to her, and after a while, he just lay silently holding her hand. The nurses were about to suggest that he go back, as he lay quietly in his own bed next to her, and he looked strangely at peace. He almost seemed about to drift off to sleep, when the door opened, and Gordon Forrester stood looking around the room. Both nurses gave a start, and the orderlies were right outside, as Gordon spoke sharply to his wife's nurse.

"Please take Mr. Robinson back to his room immediately." It was all he said, and Bill said not a word as they wheeled him from the room. There was no mistaking what was happening there, or why he had been brought to her, and as he rolled past Gordon, Bill felt a ripple of fear. He was sure that Gordon would insist that Bill not visit her again. But if he was leaving for Paris soon, Bill would see to it that he was brought to her again. He was lying in his room, thinking about it, and how lifeless she looked, when Gordon Forrester strode into his room.

"If I find you in her room again, Robinson, or hear that you've been there, I'll have you removed from this hospital. Is that clear?" He was shaking with rage, and his face was pale. Bill was poaching on his territory, and he wasn't going to tolerate it. As far as he was concerned, he owned Isabelle, and he was going to make it impossible for Bill to get anywhere near her, whatever the nature of their relationship was. She belonged to him.

"I'm not impressed, Mr. Forrester," Bill said quietly, looking him firmly in the eye. "I think Ambassador Stevens would have something to say about my being removed. But I don't need him to fight my battles for me. Isabelle and I are friends, we have been for a long time. She's never done anything you'd disapprove of, I can assure you of that," other than one kiss that night in the car, but Gordon didn't need to know that, it was only between them. "I'm concerned about her. You're a lucky man. She's a wonderful woman, and I want her to survive just as much as you do, maybe more. Teddy needs her, even more than you do. If talking to her, or being there, or simply willing her to live because I give a damn about her, can possibly help her now, then it's at least something I can do for her."

"Stay away from her. You've done enough. You damn near got her killed with you. What did you think you were doing, out at that hour? Didn't you have any idea how it would look?

You got yourselves photographed by the paparazzi, made fools of yourselves, and of me. I
suppose you thought you'd get away with it.
Well, you didn't obviously. And now the best
thing you can do is stay the hell out of her
room, and our lives. We don't need a scandal,
involving you."

"You don't have a scandal involving me," Bill
said, sounding fierce.

"I'm not so sure of that. And whether I do or
not, I forbid you to enter her room. Have I
made myself clear?"

"Why do you hate her so much?" Bill asked
as Gordon reached the door, and then froze and
slowly turned at his words.

"Are you insane? I don't hate her. She's my
wife. Why do you think I'm here?"

"What other choice do you have? Could you
actually not be here and still pretend that you
care about her to anyone? Hardly. We both
know why you're here. You're here for appearances, and because you have no choice. You're
responsible for her. You don't give a damn
about her, Forrester, and I doubt if you
ever did."

"You're a son of a bitch," Gordon spat at him,
and then walked out the door. But he couldn't
help wondering as he did if that was what
Isabelle had said to him, that her husband hated

her, and he wondered how much Bill knew about their domestic life. It sounded to Gordon as though he knew far too much.

Bill was still thinking about their exchange when Cynthia and the girls came back to see him that afternoon. The girls had been to the flea market and bought a pile of silly things they loved, and Cynthia had gone for a long, thoughtful walk, thinking of everything he'd said. But neither of them mentioned any of it, or their legal plans, in front of the girls. It was too soon. They stayed until dinnertime, and Olivia fed him with a spoon. He tried to feed himself, but with the cumbersome neck brace on, he spilled his food everywhere, especially the soup.

"What did the doctor say?" Cynthia asked him quietly before they left.

"That you'll be better off," he whispered to her, and she looked weepy again. "I'm just kidding. He said I could regain some of the use of my legs, with a lot of hard work. It's an interesting challenge. Who knows? Maybe they'll manage a miracle, and get me walking." He still wanted to believe that, although according to the doctor, it was by no means sure. "I start therapy and rehab in earnest in three weeks. They want to give everything a little more time to heal before they start."

"You can come home for that," she said softly. She was still feeling overwhelmed by his decision, and hoped he would relent in time.

"Maybe. We'll see," he said noncommittally. He didn't want to say too much in front of the girls. "What about you? When are you going home? Have you thought about it?" Bill asked her, looking subdued. It had been a tough afternoon for him.

"The girls want to stay for the week. I thought I might take them to Paris in a few days, if you're okay, and then I can come back to see you." She was still hoping he'd change his mind after everything he'd said, but his voice was firm. He had no regrets. He knew he was doing the right thing, for both of them.

"Don't," he said gently. "I'll be fine. You should go back with the girls. I know you have plans to go to see your parents in Maine." She had already decided not to come back to Europe again, and after Maine, she was going straight to the Hamptons. "I'll be back in the States soon." There was a lot he had to do. If he went back, he had to find a rehab facility where he could stay for a while, and then he needed to find an apartment and move out of their house. But it was early days for all that yet. And first, they'd have to tell the girls what they'd decided. He wasn't looking forward to that, and he wanted to tell them with her, so the girls would understand that he and Cynthia would still be friends. That mattered a lot to him, and would to them eventually too. He was sure of it.

Cynthia and the girls went back to the hotel to have dinner, and he lay in his room quietly all night. He would have liked to see Isabelle again, but he didn't want to push his luck, in case Gordon was still in town, and he was tired anyway. It had been a big day. He had been told he would most probably never walk again, "might" have sex again eventually although not certainly, had seen Isabelle, locked horns with her husband, and told Cynthia he wanted a divorce. Except for the accident that had changed all their lives irreversibly, that was about as big as it got.

Chapter Seven

Gordon Forrester left London for Paris early Monday morning. He called the hospital before he left, was told nothing had changed, and left for the airport. He was carrying with him all of Isabelle's belongings that she'd left in her hotel room. There was no point leaving her anything at the hospital, he decided. In the state she was in, she didn't need it. And as he flew over the English Channel, he knew nothing more than he had when he'd come. The doctors still had no idea if she'd live, or recover. Her internal organs seemed to be mending slowly, but there was considerable concern over her heart and lungs, and her liver would take a long time to heal. And the blow to her head, although less severe than the rest of the damage, was keeping her in a deep coma. They were sedating her to allow all her injuries to heal. But whether or not she would wake up, or die, or remain in a coma interminably, was a story yet to be told. There were still too many questions, to which no one had any answers. It was a hopeful sign that she was still alive five days after the accident, and certainly each day counted. But she was still in extremely critical condition. And Gordon knew, as he landed at Charles de Gaulle Airport in Roissy, that he could not put off telling the children any longer. He had waited from one day to the next, hoping for some improvement, but there had been none. And it seemed dangerous to him to wait any longer. Sophie was old enough to know the truth, that she might lose her mother, and whether he was ill or not, Teddy simply had to face it. Gordon was sure that Sophie would be of some comfort to him. He was going to wait until she returned from Portugal to tell Teddy, so that she could deal with her brother. It was not a scene Gordon was looking forward to, or the kind of situation he was good at. And particularly in this case, he had almost no relationship with his son.

As he put his bag and Isabelle's into a cab at Roissy, he thought of Bill Robinson again and their unpleasant encounter. He was still infuriated by the audacity and arrogance of Bill's question, about why he hated Isabelle. It was an outrageous suggestion, and he couldn't help wondering if that was what Isabelle had said. He didn't hate his wife. He had simply lost her in the chaos and abysmal years after Teddy's birth. He could no longer separate her in his mind from the horrors of the sickroom, and all that represented to him. In his eyes, she was no longer his wife, she was Teddy's nurse, and nothing more.

He wondered if perhaps in her mind, thinking that Gordon hated her justified the affair he suspected she'd had with Bill, or at the very least, the flirtation. If they had been to Annabel's together as the papers said, and the photograph indicated, clearly their alliance was not as innocent as Bill Robinson suggested. Gordon still had a thousand questions in his mind about it, but unless Isabelle recovered, he knew he would never have the answers. Bill Robinson was certainly not going to tell him anything. It bothered Gordon in principle, but in truth he had not thought of her romantically or sexually in years.

Gordon had left instructions at the hospital desk when he left, that Bill was not to be allowed in her room again. The nurse had written it all down very formally, but Gordon had had the uneasy feeling that none of his wishes were going to be followed. They seemed to have an inordinate amount of sympathy for Bill, and none for Gordon. Not to mention a huge amount of respect and admiration for who he was. Bill Robinson was a very important man.

When Gordon left the airport, he went straight to the office and made several phone calls. He explained the situation to his secretary, which he had not done previously, and she did not mention to him that she had seen the photograph of Isabelle and Bill in the *International Herald Tribune.* She knew better. And at his request, that afternoon, she handed him Sophie's number in Portugal. Isabelle had left it with her when she left for London, just in case.

Sophie was staying at a rented house with friends in Sintra, she was out, so all Gordon could do was leave a message for her. She called him back at six o'clock, just as he was about to leave the office. He took a sharp breath as he picked up the phone, and braced himself for what he had to tell her.

"How was London?" she asked cheerfully. "Did you and Mom have fun?"

"How did you know I went to London?" He had told virtually no one, except Teddy and his nurse.

"I called home over the weekend, and talked to Teddy. Didn't he tell you?"

"I haven't seen him yet. I came straight to the

office from the airport this morning," Gordon said coolly. He was stalling, groping for words.

"I'll call home then. I have to ask Mom something."

"She can't talk to you," he said cryptically, dreading this moment. It was a nightmare from which he could not wake. Instead he had to pull his children into it with him.

"Why not? Is she out?"

"No, your mother is in London."

"That's funny. She stayed?" It was unlike her mother to leave Teddy at all, let alone for six days. Sophie knew her mother had gone to London on Tuesday. "When is she coming back?" She sounded confused.

"We don't know yet." He took a final breath then and dove in. "Sophie, your mother had an accident." There was dead silence at the other end of the phone, as she waited, and her heart was pounding. Something about the way he said it was terrifying. "A very serious accident. I think you should come home."

"What happened? Is she all right?" She was so breathless, she could hardly squeeze out the words.

"She was in a car that was in an accident with a bus." There was no avoiding the truth now. "She's in a coma. They don't know what's going to happen. She has very serious internal injuries. She may not survive. I'm sorry to tell you on the phone. But I want you to make arrangements to come back to Paris as soon as possible." In spite of his feelings for Sophie, and allegedly for Isabelle, he sounded as though he were planning a business meeting. Gordon was doing everything he could not to feel his daughter's pain. It was an indulgence he could not allow himself.

"Oh my God . . . oh my God . . ." Sophie sounded on the verge of hysterics, which was unlike her. She was normally cool and calm and sensible and relatively unemotional, like her father. But what he had just said to her exceeded her worst nightmares. All her life she had been preparing to lose her brother, but never her mother, whom she loved more than she'd ever wanted to admit to herself. This had been the farthest thing from her mind when her father called her. "Oh my God, Daddy, do you think she'll die?" He could hear that Sophie was crying, and for a moment, he didn't know what to say.

"It's possible," he said, looking uncomfortable as he sat in his office staring into space. He was thinking back to when his own mother had died, and doing all he could to push the memories away. "It's a hopeful sign that she's still alive, but she's in very critical condition, and there's been no improvement," he said honestly as Sophie cried harder, and could not stop sobbing while he waited, and he could think of nothing to say to reassure her. He didn't want to lie to her and hold out false hopes, and the truth was that Isabelle could die at any moment. Sophie had to face that, as would Teddy.

And then she thought of something with a ripple of fear. "Does Teddy know?" He had sounded fine on the weekend, and he had never lied to her before. Sophie couldn't imagine Teddy keeping that kind of secret from her, or sounding as cheerful as he had when she called.

"No, he doesn't know. I want to wait and tell him when you get home. I think you should get off the phone now and make the arrangements. Can someone there help you?"

"I don't know," she said, sounding disoriented. "I want to go to London to see Mommy." She sounded like a five-year-old, and suddenly felt like an orphan.

"I want you to come home first," he said firmly. He wanted her with him when he told Teddy. He did not intend to shoulder that burden alone.

"All right," she said, still crying uncontrollably.

"Call me when you know when you're

arriving. I'll have someone pick you up." It never dawned on him to do it himself, even under these circumstances. Being distant and aloof was so natural to him that he found it impossible to break through his walls, even for his daughter, but she had always known that about him. They all did, although she was the closest to him.

"I'll try to come home tonight," she said, sounding distracted. She was two hours from Lisbon, but she might be able to catch a late flight out, if she hurried. Otherwise, she'd have to wait till the next morning.

They hung up a moment later, and Gordon had his driver take him back to the house. It was the first he had seen of Teddy in four days, and the boy seemed in good spirits, but he asked for his mother the moment he saw Gordon in the doorway of his room.

"Where's Mom? Is she downstairs?" His eyes filled with light as he said her name.

"No, she's not," Gordon said vaguely, trying to stall him by looking austere. "I think Sophie's coming back from Portugal tonight."

"She is?" The boy looked surprised, but the diversion had worked, for an instant. "Mommy said Sophie would be gone for two weeks. Why is she coming back early?" She hadn't mentioned it on the phone on Saturday, and instinctively he sensed something. And then, like a dog returning to a bone, he asked the same question again. "Where's Mom?" Gordon didn't dare tell him she was still in London, he'd know something was wrong. Teddy was too bright and sensitive to fool for long. All Gordon could hope was that Sophie would be home soon to help him tell the boy.

"I'll see you in a little while," Gordon said, without answering him. "I have to make some calls." And with that, he left Teddy's room and disappeared. But it was obvious that his son was worried. Gordon looked grim as he strode down the hall to his own room.

"Where's my mother?" Gordon heard him ask the nurse, as he closed the door. It was going to be a long night until Sophie got home. He decided to solve the problem by staying downstairs, in the library, and was stunned an hour later, when he looked up and saw Teddy walk slowly into the room. He had insisted on coming downstairs himself, and the nurse had been unable to stop him. He looked agitated and very pale.

"Something's wrong," Teddy said quietly, leaning breathlessly against a chair as he looked his father in the eye. Gordon had been dismissive of him all his life, but this time he was not going to be put off. He had a determined look that reminded Gordon of Isabelle. He had never seen Teddy look that way before. And for the first time, he noticed that Teddy no longer looked like a child. "I want to know where my mother is," he said as he sat down. He was prepared to wait all night, if he had to, for an answer. They would have had to drag or carry him from the room.

Gordon looked irritated to cover his own fright. The boy had always made him uncomfortable, he was so ephemeral and so frail, but he was looking better than he had in a long time. Six months before he would have been unable to come downstairs. But there was no avoiding him now, as Gordon sighed.

"Your mother is in London," he said honestly, and prayed he wouldn't have to say more. But that was almost too much to hope for as he met his son's eyes.

"Why?"

"She went there to see an art exhibit," Gordon said, looking away, and trying to will him into silence.

"I know. That was six days ago. Why didn't she come back with you?" With that, Gordon raised his eyes and felt as though he were seeing his son for the first time. He had spent a lifetime shutting him out and trying to resist him. And now he couldn't avoid Teddy's intense gaze.

He was a beautiful boy, but everything had always been wrong with him. And his infirmities had terrified his father. And now, in spite of himself, seeing the look of anguish in Teddy's eyes touched Gordon. He couldn't put off telling him the truth anymore, but he didn't want to be responsible for impacting his health. Teddy's existence always seemed to hang by a thread, and Gordon didn't want to be the one to sever his lifeline with disastrous news about the mother he adored.

"She had an accident," Gordon said in a low voice, and he could hear Teddy catch his breath, without looking at him. He couldn't bear the sight of what he knew he would see in the boy's eyes.

"Is she all right?" Teddy's voice was the merest whisper. He already knew something was wrong, but was terrified of what his father would say to him.

"She will be all right, I hope. We don't know yet. She's very ill. I'm sorry," Gordon said stiffly, but at least Teddy didn't cry. He just sat there breathing carefully and watching his father, as he waited for more.

"You can't let her die," he said in a whisper, as though Gordon had some power to change it.

"It's not in my control. You know I don't want anything to happen to her." But the look in Teddy's eyes spoke volumes. He knew too much about his mother's unhappiness, although she had never explained it to him. It was the second time in two days that someone had accused Gordon of being unkind to Isabelle, and he didn't like it.

"Is that why Sophie is coming home?" Teddy asked, and Gordon nodded. He sat across the room from the boy. It never dawned on him to walk across the room and put his arms around him. It would have been totally foreign to him to do anything like that, unlike Isabelle, who would have been holding Teddy close to her then, if Gordon had had the accident instead. Even Gordon knew that. "I want to go to London with Sophie, or with you," Teddy said with a determined look. "When are you going back?" He was sure he would. He couldn't bear the thought of his mother being there alone.

"I don't know," Gordon said honestly. "I thought I should come home to you." Teddy didn't acknowledge what he said. He was still trying to absorb and assimilate what his father had just told him. Gordon was stunned and impressed that the boy wasn't crying. Teddy was braver than he'd thought.

"I want to talk to her. Can we call her now?" Teddy asked, and his father shook his head.

"No, we can't. She's been unconscious since

the accident. She's in a coma, from a blow to her head."

"Oh, no!" Teddy said, suddenly envisioning her as desperately injured as she was, and he started to cry finally. The full impact had suddenly hit him. "I want to go now," he said, looking agitated.

"She won't know you're there," Gordon said practically, "and it wouldn't be good for you. You're not strong enough to make the trip." It was a reality of Teddy's life, no matter how sick his mother was, or how dire her condition. A trip to London was not an option for Teddy.

"Yes, I am strong enough," Teddy said ferociously, wiping his eyes bravely. "She needs us at the hospital with her. She's always there for me. We can't leave her alone, Papa. We can't do that to her." He suddenly looked like a child again as he cried, feeling helpless.

"Let's wait until Sophie gets home," Gordon said, looking tired. "Why don't you go upstairs and rest? This isn't good for you," he told him, as though he were an adult, but Teddy didn't care. All he wanted now was to go to his mother's side. Nothing was going to stop him. He was still talking about it as he walked to the little elevator they'd mounted for him at the side of the stairs. It had been there for years. And as Teddy lay on his bed, talking to the nurse, once he got back to his room, his eyes were wild. He couldn't stop talking, and after dinner, the nurse took his temperature and he had a fever. He had gotten too excited, which was dangerous for him. It was precisely the kind of reaction Gordon had expected Teddy to have when he heard the news.

Teddy was still wide awake when Sophie came home late that night. She had managed to catch an eight o'clock flight, and by midnight, she was back in Paris.

Gordon was waiting up for her, and he met her in the front hall when he heard the car outside. She catapulted into his arms the moment she saw him and started crying.

"Oh, Papa . . . please don't let her die. . . ." He had never seen her so upset, understandably, and as soon as she'd calmed down a little bit, she went upstairs to see Teddy. He was waiting for her in his bed. And the two embraced as though they hadn't seen each other in years. The most terrible, unthinkable thing had happened to them. Neither of them could imagine it. It was beyond bearing, beyond thinking. They cried for a long time in each other's arms, until their father finally walked into the room, looking exhausted. The emotions of the day had taken a toll on him, as well as his children.

"I'm coming to London with you to see

Mom," Teddy said to Sophie quietly, as their father stood watching them, looking grim. Their reaction had been even worse than he'd feared.

"I don't think he should," Gordon said somberly. "It'll just make him sicker than he is." He spoke of Teddy as though he couldn't hear him.

"Mom wouldn't like that," Sophie said, smoothing her brother's tousled hair, and just touching him, she could feel he was too warm. "She'd be very upset if you got sick, and that won't be good for her when she wakes up," Sophie said sensibly, stressing the word "when" and not "if." Teddy looked at her with huge eyes.

"I want to see her anyway, even if she's in a coma. She'll know I'm there." It was the same theory Bill had, but their father didn't agree. He thought that Teddy's seeing her was pointless.

"She doesn't know anyone's there," Gordon said calmly. He was sure of that, he didn't believe that people in comas heard things, or sensed what was happening. Especially after seeing her, he was convinced that was nonsense, and he was not going to allow the boy to go. It would be insane, and too great a risk for anyone to take him there, he was much too frail to travel, or even leave the house.

"Then why are you going if she won't know you're there?" Teddy asked Sophie pointedly.

"She's not sick," Gordon said sensibly. "And I think she should. I'll stay here with you."

"You're not going back, Papa?" Sophie looked shocked, but didn't say anything when he shook his head.

"Not yet. I'll wait till you come home. You can go tomorrow for the day if you want, or spend the night, whatever you prefer."

"I thought I'd stay a little while, maybe a few days."

"We'll see how she is, but don't stay too long," Gordon said, and then left the room. He had no intention of being alone in the house with his son for an extended period of time. He wanted Sophie to take over his care, and she couldn't do that if she was in London with her mother.

Sophie slept in Teddy's bed that night, with her arms around him, and she got up early the next day while he was still asleep. She showered and dressed, and she was ready to leave for the airport by the time he woke up.

"Are you going now?" he asked sleepily. "I want to come." But he was too tired and weak to move. The night before had taken a toll on him, and he looked less well than he had in a long time.

"I'll be back soon," Sophie whispered, and then left his room. She went to say good-bye to her father, but he had already left for the bank. A ticket had been arranged for her the night before, and she had a reservation at Claridge's. She knew the name of the hospital where her mother was. St. Thomas' Hospital. And she still had money left over from her trip. Her father's driver was waiting for her outside, and half an hour later she was at Roissy. There had been no traffic at all. And Sophie looked far calmer and more mature than she felt.

Her flight landed at noon local time, and a car from Claridge's drove her straight to the hospital. She felt very grown up going there, in a simple navy dress and a pair of shoes her mother had bought for her. Her hair was pulled back, and she was well dressed, but to anyone who saw her, even at eighteen she looked like a child, with huge frightened eyes filled with sorrow.

The nurses smiled at her when she spoke to them at the desk. She explained who she was, and one of them took her straight to her mother's room. The door across the hall was open, and she saw a man watching her. He had no other choice, they had turned him on his side, and he was looking toward the door, unable to move.

Cautiously, she stepped into her mother's room and was instantly shocked by what she saw there.

Her mother looked deathly pale, with a huge bandage on her head. A respirator was breathing for her, and there were monitors and tubes coming from every part of her. Sophie's eyes filled with tears as she approached the bed, and she stood there for a long time just looking at her and touching her hand, and then finally a nurse pulled a chair up to the bed for her, and Sophie sat down. Instinctively, Sophie started talking to Isabelle, hoping that somewhere, somehow, she could hear her. She told her how much she loved her, and begged her to live. There was no sign of life from Isabelle. The only thing that moved was the respirator, and the little lines of light on the monitors. There was no other sound or movement in the room. Her mother looked even more terrifying than she'd expected. It was hard to believe she'd survive it.

Sophie sat there for a long time, and then finally, around four o'clock, she walked out of the room. The same man who had watched her go in was looking at her again. The nurses had told him who she was, but he would have known anyway. She looked like a very young Isabelle.

"Sophie?" he called out, and she started at the sound of her name, surprised that he knew who she was. And she slowly approached and stood in his doorway.

"Yes," she said hesitantly, she was deeply upset by what she had just seen. He wished he could put his arms around her, for Isabelle's sake, and his own. There was so little he could do for her.

"My name is Bill Robinson. Your mother and I are friends. I was in the car with her," he said, as though to apologize for her being there at all. "I'm so sorry about what happened." She nodded, looking at him. She didn't remember her mother ever mentioning his name, but he looked like a nice man, and he was also obviously very badly hurt, but, unlike her mother, he was awake and alive.

"What happened to you in the accident?" Sophie asked carefully, she was afraid to enter the room. And she still didn't fully understand who he was, or why he had been with her mother.

"I fractured my neck, and hit my head. But your mom is in a lot worse shape than I am," he said, looking sad. "I'd give anything to change places with her, Sophie. I hope you know that. I'd give my life for her if I could." Sophie was touched by what he said, he seemed like a nice man. And she wondered how he and her mother had come to be friends. Her mother never went anywhere, because of Teddy.

"How is Teddy taking it?" he asked. "Does he know?"

"My father told him last night," she said, feeling strange. It was odd the way he seemed to know them all, without their knowing him. "He's very upset. He had a fever last night, but he wanted to come. I have to go home to take care of him tomorrow. I'd rather stay, but I think he needs me there." She was stepping into Isabelle's shoes, and Bill wished he could reach out and touch her, she looked so like her mother.

"Is there anything I can do for you?" Bill asked, feeling as helpless as she did. There was nothing anyone could do at this point. They couldn't change what had happened to them, and whether Isabelle came out of the coma or not was in the hands of God.

"No, I'm fine," she said. But she looked unspeakably sad.

"Where are you staying?"

"At Claridge's."

"My wife and daughters are there. If you have any problem tonight, give them a call." And just as he said it, Cynthia and the girls walked down the hall, and saw Sophie talking to him from the doorway of his room. He introduced everyone, and then Sophie said she should go. She didn't want to intrude. She thought his daughters looked nice, and guessed correctly that Jane was about the same age she was. Sophie said good-bye politely to all of them, and then walked away down the hall. She was going to come back later that night, to see her mother again. It was all she wanted to do.

"Is that her daughter?" Cynthia asked quietly.

"Yes, it is. She has a son too, but he's very ill." Cynthia made no comment, and started to straighten up his room, for lack of something better to do. And the girls chatted with him.

They had decided to leave the next day. They were going to Paris for a week, and they were going to come through London to see him on the way home. He thought it was a great idea, and wanted them to have some fun. He and Cynthia had agreed to tell them about the divorce on the way back, and then they could adjust to the idea of it once they went home. He didn't want to spoil Paris for them. And Cynthia was taking them out to dinner that night. They were going to use his membership at Harry's Bar. And just hearing that made him think of Isabelle, and going there with her.

Bill was lying quietly on his back, thinking about her that night, when Sophie came back to see her mother. And this time, she stopped and walked into the room to see how he was.

"How do you feel, Mr. Robinson?" she asked politely as he smiled at her.

"About the same. How are you?" She shrugged, and her eyes filled with tears. It broke her heart to see her mother like that, and there was no sign of her making any progress toward consciousness at all. She was suspended in a far-away, distant place, from which no one knew if she would ever return. The nurses had told him that she could live for years like that, and never come out of the coma before she eventually died. It was a hideous thought and a terrible waste of an extraordinary woman, and it seemed so desperately unfair. Ever since the accident, Bill had wished that he had died and she had been spared.

"How did you meet my mom?" Sophie asked, standing next to his bed. She had been wondering about it ever since she'd met him that afternoon. Her father hadn't said she was in the car with anyone, and Sophie had been surprised when Bill spoke to her.

"We met a long time ago, at the American Embassy in Paris." He suddenly needed to talk about her, and he was glad Sophie had asked. "We have lunch a couple of times a year, and we talk on the phone sometimes. And she tells me all about Teddy and you." Sophie wanted to ask him if he was in love with her, or her mother with him, but as they were both married, she thought it would be rude. But it seemed odd to her that she had never heard about him. Her mother had never mentioned his name.

"Do you know my father too?" she asked, and he smiled, and then invited her to sit down, which she did.

"Yes, I do. I think he's very angry at me since the accident. I think he believes that it would have never happened to her if we hadn't gone out to dinner. I would feel that way too in his shoes."

"It's not your fault. The nurse said your driver was killed. It's all so terrible. I don't understand how something like that can happen," and then tears filled her eyes again, "My mother is such a good person, this seems so wrong."

"Yes, she is a very good person." There were tears in his eyes too, and he stretched out a hand and held hers. In an odd way, it was like touching Isabelle, and for Sophie, this man who was a friend of hers was like a way of reaching out to her. They shared an unusual bond through Isabelle.

"I wasn't always nice to her," Sophie confessed after a while. "I used to get angry at her. She spent so much time with Teddy, when I was younger, I thought she didn't have enough time for me." It was a way of confessing her sins and the things she regretted now, and he understood.

"She loves you so much, Sophie. She never said anything about you except that you're a wonderful girl." All he wanted was to reassure her now. It was all he could do for her.

"Was she happy that night?" Sophie asked sadly. "Was she having fun?" It was an odd question to ask him, and all he could think of as she questioned him was their first and last kiss.

"Yes, she was. We went to see a wonderful art exhibit that afternoon, and she was excited about it. And then we went out to dinner. I was here to see the American ambassador," he stretched the truth a bit for both their sakes, "and we ran into each other at Claridge's and decided to have dinner." He had no reason to tell this child that they had met in London intentionally and he was in love with her. Isabelle wouldn't have wanted her to know, nor would he. "We hadn't seen each other in a long time."

"My mother never has much fun. She's always taking care of Teddy, and stays at home."

"I know. That's what she wants to do. She loves you both very much." Sophie nodded, and they sat there in silence next to each other for a while, and then finally Sophie stood up. She still didn't really know who he was, but felt she had found a new friend. She stood smiling at him for a moment before she left, and all he could see as he looked at her was Isabelle, and the woman Sophie would be one day.

"I'll come to see you tomorrow," Sophie

promised him. "I'll be here in the morning before I leave."

"I'd like that very much. Thank you for talking to me, Sophie." It had been a moment of comfort in a terribly lonely time for him, more than she knew, or he even understood. Life, as he had known it, was about to change forever. He would never again walk, or jump, or dance, or stroll down the street. His movements, like his life, would be complicated from now on. He had given up his marriage, and lost the woman he loved. He had nothing to hang on to at the moment, and was lost in an open sea with no sign of land around him. It was comforting to spend a few minutes with Isabelle's daughter as they tried to guess where their lives would take them now. Even if he never saw her again, which he knew was a distinct possibility, he was grateful that they had met.

Cynthia and the girls came to say good-bye to him the next morning, on the way to the airport. And Sophie arrived just after they left. She sat with her mother for over an hour, and then came to say good-bye to him. And she noticed that he looked depressed, she assumed because his family had left and he was alone again. She had no idea that it was far more because of her mother. She had no way of knowing that he was in love with her, although she suspected it.

"Good-bye, Mr. Robinson," Sophie said politely as she prepared to leave. "I hope you'll be better soon." He didn't ask her if she would be back again, it seemed inappropriate since neither of them knew yet if Isabelle would live.

"Take good care of yourself . . . for your mom's sake, Sophie. I know she'd be very worried about you now. Be good to yourself, and take care of Teddy," he said, with tears in his eyes. He sounded like her mother, as though she'd been leaving on a trip. "I'll be thinking about you."

"I'll say a prayer for you when I go to church," she said softly. She felt sad leaving him, as though she were leaving a piece of her mother. He was so nice, she was glad they'd been friends, and that she'd had a nice time with him.

"I'll say one for you too." He reached out and took her hand and kissed it gently, because he couldn't kiss her cheek in the contraption he was in. And then with a shy smile, she left him, and he lay there in his bed, with his eyes closed, thinking of her.

And a little while later, he had himself wheeled into Isabelle's room. She was as silent and removed as ever, but he lay in the bed they rolled next to hers, and he talked to her about his visit with Sophie.

"She's a wonderful girl. I can see why you're proud of her," he said, as though she could hear him, but he still hoped she did. And then he lay there for a long time, thinking strong thoughts for Isabelle, willing her to reach out and live again. He was tired when they wheeled him back to his room. His frequent visits to her had ceased to cause comment among the nursing staff. They had come to accept it as a loving gesture he made. No one asked the reason for it, or wondered what had happened between them, and there were a number of nurses who believed that if anything could bring Isabelle back, Bill could.

Chapter Eight

Sophie thought a lot about Bill on the way back to Paris, and she could understand why her mother had liked him. He seemed like such a decent man, and she felt so sorry for him. One of the nurses had told her he would never walk again. He seemed to be very philosophical about it, and he was devastated that Isabelle had gotten injured while she was out with him.

As they landed in Paris, Sophie's thoughts shifted to her mother and brother again. She felt torn now as to where she should be. She had decided to go home for a few days, and then she wanted to go back to London again to see her mother.

She took a cab from the airport, and the house was strangely quiet when she arrived. There was no sound in the house, and as she walked upstairs, she saw that it was dark in her father's rooms. And when she walked into

Teddy's room, she was shocked by the condition he was in. He was running a high fever, seemed nearly delirious, and the doctor had just been there, Teddy's nurse explained. She said that if the fever didn't come down that night, the doctor would put Teddy in the hospital the next day. Just thinking about it, after seeing her mother, was almost more than Sophie could bear.

"What happened?" Sophie sat down in a chair, looking drained, she felt as though she had grown up overnight. Teddy didn't even know she was there. He had been sedated, and was in a deep sleep.

"I think he's upset about your mother," the nurse said in a whisper. "He hasn't slept properly in days. He won't eat, he won't drink." She and the doctor had discussed starting him on an IV, but he had objected and cried so much when he heard them, that they had agreed to let it go another day, if he would promise to at least try to eat and drink. He looked as though he had lost weight to Sophie.

"Where's my father?" Sophie asked, running a hand through her hair, looking more than ever like Isabelle. She seemed to be resembling her more and more in the last few days.

"He's out for the evening," the nurse said, without comment. She hadn't seen him since the previous day, but she didn't say that to Sophie. "How was your mother?" the nurse asked, looking worried.

"Still the same," Sophie said, and thought about Bill. "No one knows what will happen. They said she could be in a coma for a long time, and still recover." Sophie looked hopeful as she said it, but they had also told her that Isabelle could die at any time. All they could do was pray and wait. "I'm going to go back in a few days." The nurse nodded, and then took Teddy's pulse again. It was fast and thready, and she frowned as she made a note for the doctor of what it had been. It seemed almost certain to her that they were going to be obliged to hospitalize him. And Sophie agreed. It seemed safest for him.

Sophie waited up for her father that night, to discuss Teddy's condition with him, and she was surprised at midnight when he wasn't home. She asked the nurse if he knew Teddy was ill.

"I spoke to him this afternoon in his office," she said without expression. "I'm sure he'll be home soon." But at three o'clock, Sophie was still awake and he wasn't in. She had called the hospital in London earlier, to check on her mother, and there was nothing new there either. For a moment, she'd almost asked to speak to Bill, just to say hello, but she was embar-

rassed to call him, and hung up without asking
for him.

Sophie woke up, still dressed and sitting in a
chair in Teddy's room the next morning, just as
she had seen her mother do so often when he
was ill. She hadn't even intended to, she'd been
waiting for her father, and finally fallen asleep.
She thought he had probably been careful not
to wake her, and didn't know she was waiting
in Teddy's room.

The boy was awake as she left the room to find
her father, and he looked a little better. The nurse
said the fever had broken, but he still didn't seem
at all well to Sophie. And as she walked down the
hall to talk to her father, she was surprised to see
that his doors were open, and when she looked
in, there was no one there.

She turned to the maid with surprise. "Did
my father sleep here last night, Josephine?" The
woman shook her head and disappeared down
the stairs. It was not an answer she thought appropriate to give his daughter at her age. But
Sophie could see for herself that he hadn't. The
shades and curtains were drawn, the lights were
off, and the room was undisturbed. No one had
been in his bed. And for an instant, she panicked. What if something had happened to her
father? They would be orphans, she suddenly
realized. She couldn't imagine where he'd been.

An hour later she called his office, and he sounded perfectly calm when he answered. He hadn't seen her since she left for London, and she was astonished he hadn't been home with Teddy. It seemed irresponsible to her.

"Teddy has been sick," she said with a tone of accusation, as though it was his fault, but he seemed unconcerned.

"I know. I spoke to Marthe yesterday afternoon. The doctor came to see him, and I spoke to him today." He was not about to accept a hint of reproach from an eighteen-year-old girl.

"You didn't come home last night," Sophie said tersely, and he almost laughed at the tone of her voice, but she was not amused.

"I'm well aware of that. I was with friends out of the city, it got late, and I thought it more prudent to stay there than drive home."

Sophie assumed he'd been drinking, and given what had just happened to her mother, she had to agree with him about driving home when he was tired.

"I just spoke to London," he said quietly, "there's no change."

"Oh." Sophie's spirits were further dampened by that news. But she was still upset that her father hadn't come home the night before. If something terrible had happened to Teddy, they would have needed him there. And no one knew where he had been. But he wasn't the least apologetic, and Sophie suddenly found herself wondering if he stayed out all night regularly. She'd never been aware of it before. And she couldn't help asking herself if there were things about her parents she didn't know, particularly since she'd met Bill. It still seemed odd that she had never heard of her mother's friendship with him, and it occurred to her that she never ventured into her father's rooms at night or in the early morning. Maybe there were other times when he hadn't been there. He went out a great deal in the evenings for business, and her mother rarely went with him anymore. Sophie suddenly had a sense of her whole life unraveling, not just because of what had happened to Isabelle, but because of what it had exposed. Sophie had always thought her father was godlike, and now she was wondering if he had secrets of which she was unaware. Perhaps there were more reasons than just Teddy that had kept her mother at home, and her parents sleeping in separate rooms.

"Will you be home tonight?" she asked her father, sounding nervous, feeling more like his wife than his daughter, but she was feeling very insecure. There were too many frightening things going on.

"Yes, I will. I'll be out for dinner. But I'll be home before you go to bed," he reassured her.

"If Teddy has to go to the hospital, I'll need you to be there," Sophie explained.

"The doctor seems less worried. I think Teddy's just had a shock and he needs time to recover from it."

"We all have," Sophie said sadly. "When are you going back to London?"

"In a few days. There's nothing I can do there. They'll call us if there's any change." But if she died, Sophie thought, no one would be with her, and if something happened to warn them of it, it would take them hours to get from Paris to London. Sophie wished she could just stay there, but she knew Teddy needed her too. And now that she realized that her father stayed out all night at times, she didn't feel she could leave. It was hard to know what was the right thing to do. Her father seemed far less troubled by it than she was.

Her father left for a meeting then, and Sophie spent the day with her brother, reading to him, telling him stories, and talking to him about their mother. She was doing the best she could, but they both knew she was no substitute for Isabelle. She felt like a zombie by the time her father came home after dinner. He seemed in good spirits, and sat down in the library to smoke a cigar. Sophie had heard him come in and found him there. She was surprised he hadn't come to find her upstairs. He had always been so pleasant to her and so interested that she was surprised by how distant he was being these days, particularly with her mother so ill. But suddenly, as she watched him, she wondered if his previous interest in her had been more show than real, and perhaps even to annoy Isabelle, and make her feel less important to him. Sophie had always been treated as his little darling, and he had been as cool and distant with his wife as he was now with Sophie.

"How was your day, Papa?" she asked cautiously. Hers had been pretty grim, between worrying about her mother and caring for a sick boy.

"Long. How was yours?"

"I was with Teddy all day." She expected him to ask more about it, but at the mention of her brother, her father looked instantly bored as he poured himself a glass of port.

"What else did you do?" he asked, focusing on his cigar, and it felt strange sitting there talking to him as though nothing had happened. Her mother was in a coma in a hospital in London, and her brother had been failing since he heard. And her father seemed astonishingly unconcerned. And as she looked at him, all she could think of was the look of devastation on Bill Robinson's face when he talked about her mother. She saw none of that in her father's eyes. He seemed distant and cool whenever he referred to her.

"That's all I did today, Papa. I stayed with Teddy. He's very upset." Gordon nodded, and didn't answer her. He seemed to almost forget she was there, and then the phone rang. And he told whoever it was that he'd call back. Sophie's heart had nearly stopped when she heard it. Every time the phone rang now, she was terrified that it was a call from London to tell them the worst.

"You should go to bed," Gordon said as he sipped his port, dismissing her. "You've had a long day." It was obvious he didn't want to talk, and Sophie was hurt. She had never felt as alone in her life as she did now.

"When are you going back to London?" she asked quietly before she left.

"When I think I should," he said tersely, frowning at her. She was annoying him. She had turned into her mother overnight.

"I want to go back with you," she said, aware of the fact that he wasn't pleased with her, but for the moment, she didn't care.

"Your brother needs you here."

"I want to see Mom again." She sounded young and stubborn, and he wasn't amused.

"She won't even know you're there. I need

you here. I can't worry about that boy and his nurses all day. They call me at the office all day long, I don't have time for that, Sophie. You need to take care of him." He didn't ask her, he just told her what she had to do, and expected her to do as he said.

" 'That boy' is your son, Papa. And he needs you too, not just me or Mom. You never talk to him." She was too tired to hold back anymore.

"He has nothing to say," Gordon said harshly, pouring himself another glass of port. "And it's not up to you to tell me what to do." It was a conversation Isabelle had had with him many times over the years, and she had given up long ago. For reasons of his own, based on past history among other things, Gordon was determined not to have a relationship with his son. And in her naïveté, Sophie could not change that. If Teddy had been healthy and strong and able to participate in things that interested his father, it would have been a different story. But as he was, as far as Gordon was concerned, the boy didn't exist and was of no interest to him. If anything, he was an irritant to him, although he felt sorry for him now. All Teddy was was an annoyance and a burden to his father. And as far as Gordon was concerned, he was Isabelle's job, not his. And in her absence, he was Sophie's.

Just hearing the way her father spoke of him

made Sophie sad as she went to her room. She and Teddy had talked about it over the years, and he always said things like that about their father, and she had argued about it with him. But now she saw it was true. Teddy said their father was mean and selfish and cold and hated him. And now she could see that Teddy knew a side of him she had never wanted to see. As far as Gordon was concerned, having a son like Teddy was no credit to him. He preferred to shut him away and forget him, just as he had his wife.

Sophie put her nightgown on in her own room, and then went back to Teddy's room. The nurse said he had a fever again, and Sophie climbed into his bed and cuddled up next to him. She felt as though they were two children who had lost their mother for the time being, and she had never felt as sad or as lonely in her life. And all she could hope, as her tears ran into her pillow, was that their mother would wake from her coma soon. She couldn't begin to imagine what their life would be like if she died.

Chapter Nine

Things moved along at the hospital in London.
Physical therapists came to assess Bill and plan a
rehabilitation program for him. They were
turning him frequently in his bed to keep his
circulation moving, and prevent pneumonia,
but the days were boring for him. And once or
twice a day he had his bed wheeled into Isabelle's room. The nurses had paid no attention
to Gordon's instructions, and several of them
hoped it would do her good to be visited by
Bill. It did no harm in any case, and it raised
Bill's spirits noticeably. He always felt better
when he visited her. He missed their late-night
talks terribly. And he lay in his hospital bed for
hours, thinking about her just across the hall.
He looked forward all day to the few minutes
he could spend at her side.

His own injuries were starting to heal a little
bit. His neck and spine still caused him a lot of

pain, but he was able to move more than he could before, and he had some vague phantom sensations in his legs. But in spite of that, the prognosis for him had not changed. He was trying to keep his spirits up, and think about what he was going to do when he got back to the States, but the changes he was facing now were unspeakably hard.

He had become a favorite with the nursing staff, and there were whispered exchanges as people tried to guess what his relationship with Isabelle was, but there was no easy explanation for what they saw. Most of them guessed that he'd been having an affair with her, and one of the nurses had overheard him telling his wife that he wanted a divorce, but whatever his situation was, or had been, with Isabelle, they knew that they liked him, and thought him a very nice man.

"I'll take him!" one of the nurses said while talking to a group of her co-workers in the cafeteria. "He's a good-looking guy." But he hadn't made advances toward any of them, he was never fresh, rude, ungentlemanly, and everyone who talked to him genuinely admired him. They also noted that the American ambassador had come to see him several times.

"What does he do?" another nurse asked, looking confused, she couldn't remember what she'd heard, although they knew that he was an important man.

"Something in politics," one of Isabelle's nurses said. "He must have been crazy about her. It's such a shame." They were all in full agreement on that.

Gordon hadn't been back to see his wife yet, and neither had Sophie when Cynthia and their daughters came back after their Paris trip. They were in high spirits when they arrived, and they looked sobered when they left, after Cynthia and Bill told the girls that they were getting divorced. Olivia and Jane were shocked.

"Why?" Olivia sat in her father's hospital room and cried. "You guys love each other . . . don't you? Mom? . . . Dad?? . . ." The girls had always thought that they did, but Bill tried to explain that they had drifted apart over the years, and he thought it was better for both of them if they parted ways. He didn't want to tell them about their mother's affairs, or how unhappy they'd both been. They'd kept it to themselves for years. And he had to admit, he thought things were better in some ways since he'd told her it was over for him. He felt more honest and open with her now. But Cynthia made it clear to him before they left that if he changed his mind, she would prefer to stay married to him. But Bill was gentle but firm.

He no longer wanted to be married to her. All his dreams now were of Isabelle.

"It's better this way," he insisted, but Cynthia was very upset by the reaction of the girls. He didn't want to explain that he couldn't see her married to an invalid, or someone handicapped at best. But more than anything, he just wasn't in love with her anymore. What he had felt for Isabelle had told him many things about himself and what he didn't have. He didn't want to live a lie anymore. He knew he would never have a life with Isabelle, whether she recovered or not, but the fact that he was and had been in love with her was enough to tell him that it was time for him to get out of a loveless marriage he'd been willing to settle for, for too long.

He was quiet and pensive after they left. And he had promised to call the girls often when they got home. They asked their mother on the way back to the hotel if they thought their father was a little crazy from the accident, or the bump on his head, and if she thought he might change his mind. She smiled sadly and shook her head.

"He's not crazy. I guess I was for a long time. I wasn't a very good wife to him," she confessed. "I took him for granted, and I resented his success and independence, which was lousy of me." They had seen none of it, which was something at least, and they were crushed at the thought that their parents would live in separate homes.

"How's Daddy going to take care of himself now?" Jane asked, looking worried. His injuries were serious, and they had been told that he might not be able to walk again.

"I don't know," Cynthia said with a sigh. "He's very proud, and very capable. He'll figure something out. But in answer to your question, Jane, no, I don't think he'll change his mind. He never does. Once he gets an idea in his head, he usually sticks with it, no matter what. He won't even admit it if he's made a mistake, he'll just live with it. But as much as I hate what he's doing, I don't think it's wrong for him." In a way, he had done what he wanted to, he had preserved their friendship by ending their marriage, and in spite of her regrets, Cynthia admired him for it. She just felt sorry for the girls, it was a real blow for them, and she was frightened for herself. She knew she'd never find another man like Bill.

"Do you think he was having an affair with Isabelle Forrester?" Olivia asked her honestly, and Cynthia thought about it. She had pondered it a lot herself.

"I just don't know. He says not, and he's never lied to me, that I know of anyway. I think he's in love with her, but I don't think they did anything they shouldn't have. She's very much married to Gordon Forrester, from what your father says. I think maybe they were infatuated with each other, or just friends."

"Do you think Dad would ever marry her, if she survives?" Jane asked, looking concerned.

"I don't think that's an issue now," Cynthia answered, the poor woman was almost dead, "but no, I don't, even if she lives. Your father says she'll never leave Forrester, and her whole life revolves around an invalid child."

"What do you think Dad's going to do now, after he gets home . . . I mean, back to the States . . ." Olivia looked sad as she asked.

"I don't know. Get an apartment, I guess. Go back to work. He's going to be in rehab for a long time. I don't think he'll even come back for a couple of months. They want to work with him here." The girls nodded and were quiet the rest of the way back to the hotel. They still couldn't believe what they'd just heard. And Cynthia still couldn't quite believe the decision he'd made.

It was so like Bill to do what he thought was the right thing, no matter how difficult it was. She had come out of their marriage with a deep respect for him, and she knew there would never be another man like him in her life. She just wished now that she'd figured that out before. She knew that most of the responsibility for the divorce was hers, no matter how much of the blame he was willing to take himself.

They left for the States the next day, so early that they didn't have time to stop and see him at the hospital before they left. Cynthia and the girls called him from the airport to say good-bye, and both girls were crying when they hung up. And he didn't say it to anyone, but after they were gone, he was sad. It was lonely for him, and he was beginning to understand the long hard road he had ahead of him. He was facing at least a year of excruciating rehabilitation work, maybe more. But he had no choice. He made some business calls from time to time, and a few people had heard about the accident and called him. But for the most part, he felt as though he were living in a cocoon, surrounded by nurses and doctors, and Isabelle still in a coma across the hall. It was not an easy time for him.

By two weeks after the accident, Bill was making a reasonable recovery, and Gordon Forrester still hadn't been back to see his wife. Bill had developed his own little routine of being rolled in to see her morning and night. He would lie there in his bed and talk to her for a while, in the hope that she could hear him in her deep sleep, and then he would go back to his own room.

The nurses had told him that Forrester couldn't come because their son was ill, and Bill worried about Teddy all the time on her behalf. He hoped the situation wasn't too bad. And he thought about Sophie frequently too, and hoped she was all right.

He had almost given up any hope of Isabelle coming out of her coma by the third week after the accident, and he wondered if Gordon was just going to leave her there, forgotten and unloved. There was no way to move her back to Paris, on the respirator, it was too dangerous for her, and Bill had started worrying about what would happen to her when he went back to the States. The doctors thought he might be able to go back in another month or so. He couldn't bear the thought of leaving her, with no one to visit her, talk to her, comfort her, care what happened to her. He couldn't imagine how Gordon could abandon her now, but he had. Bill was thinking about it one night as he lay in his bed next to her, talking to her and holding her hand. The nurses no longer found it unusual anymore. They just smiled and chatted with him, when he visited her, as though they expected to find him in her room several times a day.

He was telling Isabelle how beautiful she was, and how much he missed talking to her on a warm, balmy night in July. The windows were open, and they could hear sounds from outside. And he found himself thinking of the night they'd gone to Harry's Bar, and then Annabel's afterward. All he wished now was that he could turn back the clock, and step backward in time to that night.

"Do you remember what a good time we had?" he murmured to her, stroking her fingers and then kissing them as he held her hand. "I love dancing with you, Isabelle," he said. "If you wake up, we can go dancing again someday." But for him, that was only a memory, and a distant dream. He was still talking to her and reminding her of that night, when he felt a gentle pressure in the palm of his hand. He thought it was a reflex at first, and went on talking to her, and then he felt the same gentle pressure again. Distracted by it, he stopped talking for a minute, and glanced at the nurse when she walked in. He didn't want to say anything, but his conversation with Isabelle continued in a slightly more determined way, and then he stopped, and tried to position himself so he could look at Isabelle.

"I felt you squeeze my hand just then," he said clearly to her. "I want you to do it again." He waited for what seemed like a long time, as the nurse watched them both, but nothing happened, and the nurse looked away. "Do it again, Isabelle. Squeeze my hand, just a little bit. . . . I want you to really try." And then, as though she were reaching back toward him from another world, she did, almost imperceptibly. His face broke into a broad smile, and there were tears in his eyes. "That was wonderful," he encouraged her, overwhelmed by what he had just felt. "Now I want you to open your eyes. Just a tiny bit . . . I'm looking at you, Isabelle. And I want you to look at me." There was no sign of life in her face, but then her fingers moved again, and he wondered now if it was just a random reflex after all. And just as he was getting discouraged again, she wrinkled her nose, but her eyes were still closed. He could feel his heart race. She was coming back. "What was that? That was a funny face, but it was very good. How about a little smile?" There were tears rolling down his cheeks as he spoke to her, and all his efforts and strength and love were concentrated on her. The nurse in the room stood frozen in place as she watched. But she had clearly seen the quick grimace Isabelle had made. That was definitely not a reflex. "Can you smile for me, my love? Or just open one eye. . . . I've missed you so much. . . ." He was begging her, willing her to come back to him, he wanted to just reach down into the abyss where she'd been and pull her back safely to him. He lay there talking to her for another half hour, with no results, and he looked exhausted and spent, but he refused to give up. "Isabelle . . . all right, make that funny face again . . . come on . . . wrinkle your nose." But this time instead she lifted one hand several inches off the bed and then let it fall, as though the effort it had taken was simply too great. "That was very, very good. And very hard work. Rest a minute, sweetheart. Then we'll do it again." He wanted to gather all the signs from her he could, to keep her engaged until she came back to him, and to life. He talked to her endlessly, trying to get her to blink, to move some part of her face, to open her eyes, or squeeze his hand again. And for a long time nothing moved, and then he saw the faintest fluttering of her eyes.

"Oh my God . . ." he whispered to the nurse, and she hurried out of the room to find one of the doctors to see what was happening. After three weeks of hovering near death, Isabelle was coming back. It was Bill who was lovingly, painstakingly bringing her home.

"Isabelle," Bill said more firmly then. "You have to open your eyes, my love. I know it's hard. You've been asleep for a long time. It's time to wake up. I want to see you look at me. I want to see you, and I know you want to see me. Just open your eyes a little bit," and a moment after he said it, she did. He hadn't even been expecting it. After all this time, he was willing to be satisfied with any sign she would make. But she had gone all the way this time, and the long-sleeping eyes opened just a crack. "That's it . . . that's right . . . can you open them more now . . . work at it, my darling . . . open those beautiful eyes. . . ." The doctor had joined them in the room by then, but he stood back and did not interfere. Bill was doing fine on his own, and the doctor didn't think he could do as well. "Isabelle," Bill tried again, "I'm waiting for you to look at me. I've been waiting a very long time," and as he said it, there was a long, graceful sigh from the bed, and with only a slight flutter, she opened her eyes, and without looking at him, she closed them again, as though the effort was too much. "Come on, sweetheart, keep them open long enough to look at me. Please, my love . . ." Watching her come to life slowly as he talked to her was like watching her float slowly to earth from a distant place. And then finally, finally, she opened her eyes again, turned her head, and looked straight at him as she gave a small moan. He suspected the movement had made her head hurt. But then she smiled, with her eyes closed again, and seemed to struggle with a single word. She worked at it for a long time, and then finally, as she opened her eyes again, she said his name in a voice that was barely more than a croak.

"Bill . . ." He kissed her hand as she said it, and had to choke back a sob so he could talk to her. He wanted to reward her for what she'd done.

"Isabelle, I love you so much. . . . What a good girl you are. You worked so hard to come back."

"Yes," she whispered to him as her eyes closed again, and this time she opened them on her own. "I love you . . ." she whispered, and then said his name again, as though she were savoring the word.

"I think this is where we left off," he said, smiling through his tears. It had been a lifetime and more since the night they'd kissed and been hit by the bus. "You've been gone too long, my love. I missed you so much."

"Talk to me . . ." she said softly, with a smile, as Bill, the nurse, and the doctor laughed. He had been talking to her for three weeks, and for hours that night. It was as though he had known all along that he could bring her back. He had never given up, although recently he had gotten discouraged, but he had never stopped. "Like . . . to hear you . . . talk," she said, as though she was immensely tired, which Bill realized she probably was. She had worked hard.

"I like to hear you talk. I've waited a long time to hear you talk to me. Where have you been, my love?" he said softly, still holding her hand.

"Gone," she said, and smiled again, and then looked at him with a thousand questions in her eyes. She knew he had the answers she did not. "How long?"

"Three weeks," he answered her honestly, and she looked surprised.

"So much?" She seemed to be struggling to find the words, but she was doing fine, and the doctor watching her thought so too.

"So much." There was so much to tell her eventually, so much to share, but it was still too soon. She had just landed from a very distant place.

And then she thought of something and looked at him with worried eyes. "Teddy . . . and Sophie?"

"They're fine." He hoped he wasn't lying to her, since he didn't have recent news, and he knew Teddy hadn't been well. But he was sure that once he knew his mother had come back, the boy's condition would improve. "Sophie was here. She came to visit you. She's a won-derful girl, and she looks exactly like you." Is-

abelle smiled and closed her eyes, and when she
opened them, there was another question in
them. Bill knew what the question was, he
could almost read her mind. "He was here."
She nodded, and then quickly winced.

"My head . . . hurts."

"I'll bet it does." That was easy to believe.

"Other . . . things . . . too." The doctor was
interested in hearing about that, and he asked
her a few questions then, but he was enormously pleased, and suggested that they should
both get some rest, they had had a big night. Isabelle looked worried by what the doctor said,
as the orderlies came to take Bill away. "No . . .
don't go. . . ." She held his hand more tightly
than she had been till then. And Bill looked at
the doctor questioningly.

"Could I stay here?" There was a long pause
while the doctor considered it. There was no
real reason why they couldn't do that. They
were adults, and friends, and the nurses could
keep an eye on both of them. It seemed a suitable reward for what Bill had done for her that
night, and there was something about it that felt
right to him.

"I think that's a fine idea." Bill wasn't on the
monitors anymore, all he needed was his IV
pole next to his bed, and pain medications if he
asked for them, which he seldom did.

"I want you to sleep here," Isabelle said, clinging to his hand, as Bill beamed at her. She was back, she was alive, she had come back to him. It was the happiest night of his life. They were both smiling as the nurses settled them. The doctor examined Isabelle carefully, and he was satisfied. He asked her a few more questions, and she talked to him about how her head felt. She said her body felt too small now, everything inside felt too tight, and he explained that she was feeling her internal injuries and would for a while. There was plenty of time to examine her further the next day. What they both needed now was rest.

The nurse turned off all but one small light, and another nurse came to help turn Bill onto his side. He was pleased because he could see her better that way. He didn't want to sleep, he just wanted to look at her all night, and see her face, touch her hand. She was still holding his hand, as they lay facing each other, and she looked like a child as she smiled at him. It struck him that she was the image of Sophie.

"You're so beautiful," he whispered to her, "and I love you so much." She'd been worth waiting for, for the past three weeks, and a lifetime before that.

"I missed you while I was gone," she whispered to him.

"How do you know?" he whispered back, while the nurse smiled from the corner of the room.

"I just do." They were like two children at a slumber party, whispering in the dark, as the doctor and the other nurse left the room. They were both smiling and exchanged a long look outside. They were a beautiful sight to see. None of them had expected Isabelle to survive.

The doctor called Paris that night to tell Gordon that his wife was no longer comatose, he felt he owed him that. But Gordon was out, and the doctor told the woman who answered the phone, Teddy's nurse, to tell Mr. Forrester that he'd called. He didn't want to leave any further message, and Bill and Isabelle would have been grateful to him if they'd known.

It felt as though they had always slept together, as they lay there facing each other. Isabelle tried to turn on her back once, but it hurt too much to move her head, so she turned back again toward Bill, and he was wide awake, watching her.

"What happened to you?" she asked, she had just noticed the enormous brace around his neck, she hadn't seen it before. There had been too much going on, but now she looked worried about him.

"I hurt my neck, and my back. I'll be fine," he

said, smiling at her. He would now. This was all he had wanted for three weeks.

"Are you sure?"

"I'm sure. I've never felt better in my life than I do right now."

"Me too." And then she looked at him pensively. "I don't remember anything . . . how did we get here?"

"That, my love, is a very long story we can talk about tomorrow. We got hit by a bus." He wasn't going to tell her for a while that eleven people had died, and she had very nearly made it twelve. "The last thing I knew I was kissing you, and then I was here."

"I remember that too," she smiled sleepily, as she yawned. He would have liked to kiss her again, but he couldn't move. He could only lie as he was, and all he could do was touch her face or her hand. "One of these days, I'd like to kiss you again," she said dreamily, and Bill didn't respond. There was a long pause as he contemplated the possibility that, in his own eyes, he might no longer be a man. And he quietly held her hand. It was all he could offer her now. "I hope the children are all right," she said, thinking about them, and unaware of Bill's terrors about his ability to perform.

"They will be when they hear about you," he reassured her.

But for an instant, she looked sad, and tightened her hold on Bill's hand. "And then he'll come back again, won't he?" He didn't want to tell her that her husband hadn't been back to see her in two weeks. He didn't think it was his place, and he had come to hate the man, for everything he didn't do for her, and the ugly things he did.

"Let's not think about that now," Bill whispered to her. "Why don't you close your eyes and try to sleep." He wished he could stroke her hair.

"I thought you wanted me to wake up," she teased. She was definitely going to be all right, after three weeks in a coma, and an accident she almost hadn't survived, she hadn't changed. Her spirit was still strong. In the end, that and his love were what had brought her back.

"Go back to sleep, you talk too much, you're going to wear yourself out." He couldn't stop smiling as he looked at her. She seemed even more beautiful to him than she had before.

"I want to talk to you all night," she grinned, and then remembered something else. "I want to go dancing with you again." He smiled at her, he felt as though he were.

"We will one day."

"And I want to go back to Harry's Bar." She was making a wish list for him, and he smiled.

"Now?" he teased, happier than he'd ever been. He loved lying next to her and talking to her.

"All right. Tomorrow. And then Annabel's. We have to make up for lost time. I haven't been dancing in weeks," she said with a contented sigh.

"You'd better behave yourself, or the doctors are going to put you to sleep again."

"I just want to lie here with you." And then she laughed softly in the darkened room. "Now we can say we've slept with each other, can't we?"

"You're very badly behaved for a woman who's been very sick for three weeks. I don't think you should be thinking about things like that," he scolded her, and wished he could put his arms around her, but in his heart, he was. In his heart, she would always be his. She had become his that night, and whatever came now, he knew that would never change. She had walked through the darkness to come back to him, and whatever happened, wherever they went, he knew he would never lose her again.

"I walked into a very bright light with you . . . we were going somewhere, on a narrow path . . . and the children started calling us, and you made me turn back." He felt as though he'd been struck by lightning when she said those words. He had had the same memory, precisely as she had just described, when he woke from unconsciousness himself.

"What was it like?"

"Very bright . . . and I was very tired . . . I sat down on a rock. I didn't want to come back, but you kept pulling me. You said we could go there another time. . . . I didn't want to, but I let you pull me back." And he had again, that night. The first time he had brought her back from death, and the second time from the deep darkness where she slept endlessly. But what she was describing about the rock and the bright light was exactly what he had seen himself.

"Isabelle, I was there too." He looked thunderstruck, and she didn't know why. "I had the same dream you did. Exactly the way you described."

"I know, you were there," it seemed normal to her, "I saw you, and I held your hand, and I came back with you."

"Why?" He was searching his own memory, and he wanted to understand what had happened to them. He didn't think this was any ordinary thing. People talked of these experiences, but most people didn't share the same bright light in the same dream, the same rock, the same path, the same memory. He realized then that somewhere, in some deep, meaningful way, their souls had met and joined. In another life, they had met and become one.

"I came back because you told me to," she said quietly. "But then I got lost again after that. I think I fell asleep next to the path."

"You certainly did, and if you ever do that again, Isabelle, I'm going to be seriously angry at you. Don't you ever get lost on me again."

"I won't," she said, and kissed his fingers and hand. "Thank you for waiting for me, and for bringing me back." She was getting sleepy then, and yawned several times, and before he could say anything more to her, she had fallen into a peaceful sleep holding his hand. And as he looked at her, he had a perfect memory of what she had described, their walking toward the bright light, with Isabelle just ahead of him on the path. It had taken all the strength he had to bring her back from that light, and tonight she had come back to him again. He wasn't sure what any of it meant, but he knew that something extraordinary had happened to them, and as he lay watching her sleep, he knew that in spite of everything that had occurred, he was a very lucky man.

Chapter Ten

The doctor called Gordon Forrester at eight o'clock the next day to tell him the news, but the same voice told him he was out again. And he finally reached Gordon in his office at ten. He sounded startled to hear the news, and said he was very pleased. He asked if he could talk to her, but as yet she had no phone. The doctor said he would have one put in for her, and Gordon could call her in her room that afternoon.

"I'm sure the children will want to talk to her," he said, looking distracted as he sat at his desk, thinking about her. He had already made his peace that she would never come out of the coma, and he was amazed to hear that she had. Although he was certainly relieved for her, it took a little readjustment on his part.

"How did it happen?" Gordon asked innocently, and there was a moment's pause at the doctor's end. He didn't want to tell him about

Bill Robinson, he didn't think they'd want him to, and he was right.

"She did it on her own," he said. It was all Gordon needed to know.

"Well done," Gordon said as though talking about a golf tournament or a tennis match. In sharp contrast to Bill's tears of joy the night before, Gordon sounded dispassionate, as though he were talking about a distant friend. It was hard to believe she was his wife. But perhaps that explained her relationship with Bill. There were questions the doctor didn't want to ask, and after seeing them together the night before, he didn't need to now. He could see it all. He wondered how long it would be before Gordon came back to London to see her again. For Bill and Isabelle's sake, he hoped it wouldn't be too soon. He had fallen in love with them, it was impossible to resist a love like that, that had gone to the edge of death and beyond and back again. It was something the doctor knew few people ever shared, and it was infinitely precious when they did. "Tell her I'll call her this afternoon when I get home" was all Gordon said, and the doctor assured him he would.

The nurse passed the message on to Isabelle when they plugged in her phone. She was looking forward to talking to the children, but not to him.

"What are we going to do now?" she said to Bill that afternoon, as he sat in his bed in her room, and he kept her company while she ate her first lunch. They had brought her Jell-O and a bowl of very thin soup. It had been a long time since she'd seen food, and it had no appeal at all.

"What do you mean?" Bill asked. "You mean croquet or golf, or a stroll in the park?" He was teasing again, but this time she didn't smile.

"Gordon is going to want to take me back to Paris when I get well." She wanted to see her children, of course, but she didn't want to leave Bill.

"I don't think that'll be for a while," Bill said, trying to stay calm himself. "I don't think you can just hop out of bed and run out the door." She still had a lot of healing to do internally, and they wanted to be careful about her head. The doctor had told her that morning that he ex-pected her to be there for roughly another four weeks. It was about as long as they planned to keep Bill.

"And after that?" she asked him as the nurse fed her the soup. Her hands weren't strong enough to do it yet. She was amazingly weak, which surprised no one but Isabelle.

"We'll figure it out." He hadn't told her yet that his legs were permanently compromised, and he wasn't sure he would ever walk again. He wanted to think about it. He wasn't sure she needed to know. Unless things had changed radically while she was comatose, he knew that she would go back to Gordon, to take care of her sick child. He could of course still call her, and see her from time to time, but he didn't want her pity, if he was in a wheelchair. All he wanted was her love. He was thinking now that if he could truly never walk again, perhaps he wouldn't see her after they left the hospital, and they would continue their relationship on the phone. He wasn't sure yet what he would do, or how often he could see her after she left. For the moment, she thought his situation was temporary, and he was inclined to keep it that way. She wouldn't worry about him, she couldn't pity him, and he also hadn't told her about his divorce. He didn't want her to think he was putting pressure on her. He fully understood that she had to go home to her family eventually. All he wanted was to enjoy the time they had.

She was in her room that afternoon, and so was Bill, when Gordon called. He told her that he was very relieved to know that she was getting well. He made it sound as though she were recovering from a sprained ankle, or a bad fall. In fact, he felt as though she had returned from the dead. By the time she woke up, he hadn't expected her to live, or to come out of the coma. He had begun to think of himself as a widower, and he had to mentally turn the clock back again, to resume his marriage to her. He sounded very strange, and she correctly guessed that he was angry about Bill, and punishing her for it. He sounded awkward to her, but there was no awkwardness when she talked to Teddy and Sophie. Sophie cried when she heard her mother's voice, and all Teddy could do was gasp for air and sob. Isabelle thought he sounded terrible, and she asked Gordon about it when her children got off the phone. She was still crying from the overwhelming emotion of hearing them. She had been so worried about both of them.

"Teddy will be much better now," Gordon said casually. Sophie had said she wanted to come to see her, but Gordon said her mother would be home soon enough. "How soon will they let you leave?" he asked matter-of-factly. There was no point in his going to see her, he said, if she was coming home.

"They said in about four weeks, depending on my liver, my head, and my heart." They were hardly small things to contemplate, but

Gordon didn't seem impressed. Now that she was out of the coma, he was dismissive of the rest.

"Four weeks sounds a bit long, doesn't it? I'm sure they'll let you go sooner if you ask." He sounded faintly suspicious of her, and wondered if she was dragging her feet, because Bill was still there. Gordon was not going to tolerate that. "I'll talk to the doctor myself. You can get all the medical attention you need here." She felt panicked when she got off the phone, and she told her doctor that Gordon was going to call to press him into sending her home.

"Is that what you want, Isabelle? We could probably transfer you to a hospital in Paris in a week or so. You're not ready to be at home yet."

"I want to stay here," she said, looking worried. They both knew why.

"I'll take care of it," he said reassuringly. He was willing to do that for her and Bill, he liked them both. They'd been to hell and back, and her children could wait. But later, she admitted to Bill how worried she was about Teddy. He hadn't sounded well on the phone, and it was the one thing that made her feel she should try to go home sooner than planned. It drove her crazy knowing how badly he needed her and how long she'd been gone, although she

knew he was in good hands. Bill was sympathetic, as always, when they spoke of it later on.

"I'm sure this has been terribly traumatic for
him. God knows what Gordon said to him
about the condition you were in. But now that
he's heard your voice, and knows you'll be
home in a few weeks, I'm sure he'll improve
every day." She felt reassured by what Bill said.

"I hope so," she said fervently. "Thank God
Sophie is there. She wanted to come to see me,
but I don't think she should. Teddy needs her
there, more than I do here." And she had Bill.
She wanted this time with him before they left
each other and she went back, but not at her
children's expense. "What about Cindy? Do
you think she'll come back to see you here?"

"No," he said simply, without explaining why.
And the girls would be busy all summer. "I told
them I'd see them when I get back." He had
also told the doctor not to tell Isabelle how extensive the damage was to his spine, and that he
wouldn't be able to walk. It was the one thing,
other than the divorce, that he didn't want her
to know. He wanted time to see how much
better he could get. She thought it would take
him a long time to heal, like six months or a
year, so she wasn't surprised that he couldn't
walk.

If she had been willing to leave Gordon, it

could have been different for him. He might have told her the truth then about his legs. But since she was determined to go back to Gordon, Bill didn't want her worrying about him. She had enough on her plate with her sick child. And now that he'd seen Gordon at close range, he knew what she was up against, and it made him sick to think of her with him. Gordon seemed to have no regard for her, no love, no kindness, no respect, no warmth. As far as Gordon Forrester was concerned, his entire world revolved around himself, and all Isabelle was was a convenience and a pawn, and a caretaker for their sick son. He had no appreciation whatsoever, as far as Bill was concerned, of the gem he had. And he was worried that she was going to have a hard life with him, perhaps even harder than before. Gordon was suspicious of her now, and angry about Bill, and Bill was worried that Gordon would punish her for the sins he thought she had committed behind his back. She was going to have to be careful of him now, and stand up for herself, or he would turn her life into a nightmare of torment and disrespect. He couldn't even be bothered to stay with her in London, when she appeared to be comatose and dying, for more than a few days, and he hadn't returned since. And now that she was awake, and she and Bill were together again, that was just as well.

When the doctor spoke to Gordon on the phone later that afternoon, he insisted again that Isabelle could not be moved for at least another four weeks. Her husband was not pleased. He thought they were being unreasonable and overly cautious about it, but in the end the doctor frightened him with hideous complications he claimed she could develop, and even suggested she might slip into a coma again. "I should lose my license over this," he laughed as he told Isabelle and Bill later on. But he thought they deserved some small chance for happiness at least, and a reward for the agony they'd survived. And Bill's torments weren't over by any means. The doctor knew only too well how long and hard his rehabilitation was going to be. He had already set it up for him to go to a hospital in New York, where they would help him regain as much use of his legs as he could. Neither Isabelle nor Bill had any real idea of what was in store for Bill there.

For now, they had four weeks, to sit together, and laugh and talk and revel in the love and comfort they derived from each other. The hospital was a safe haven for both of them, after the trauma they'd been through, and before they both went back to their own lives. Reality was going to hit them both soon enough.

They slept together cautiously in her room again that night, and they tried his after that. They were both free of monitors, and they spent long hours throughout the afternoon talking about their lives and hopes and dreams. The time they were sharing was a rare gift, and for both of them, it had been hard won.

They played cards, they read books, he taught her to play liar's dice. They sat and talked for hours, they took their meals in the same room. Her liver was getting better, and healing slowly on its own. Her heartbeat was still irregular, though less so than it had been. And she had ferocious headaches sometimes. She tired easily, and slept a great deal, most of the time lying in bed next to him. His neck was still locked in the terrible brace he had to wear, and as his spine healed, he had pains in his back sometimes, and she would gently rub his shoulders and his arms. She had noticed how little use of his legs he had, but Bill kept assuring her that he would be walking by the next time they met, and she believed him, because she wanted to. It seemed reasonable to her that he still couldn't walk. It had only been a month since the accident, which wasn't very long. They talked very little of their assorted aches and pains. Most of the time, they shared confidences, talked endlessly, and made each other laugh.

She had been out of the coma for a full two weeks when they were lying on his bed on a sunny afternoon in July. The windows were open, and the day was warm, and they were telling stories about their childhoods, as she lay on his bed with him. She was careful not to bump into him, or touch anything that still hurt. She was particularly careful about his spine. And as she told him about her time with her grandparents in Hampshire, she was running her fingers lazily down his arm. She had scratched the back of his neck for him, and after his arm, she ran her fingers lazily across his shoulders and down his back where she knew they wouldn't do any harm, and as she did, he looked at her with an air of longing, and then smiled, looking like a mischievous little boy.

"Why are you looking like that?" she asked, wondering if he was laughing at her. "I was being serious about my grandfather. He was a very nice man."

"I'm sure he was. I stopped listening to you about five minutes ago," he said honestly. "Wanting you is driving me insane."

"What did you have in mind? Liar's dice again?" He beat her constantly, and refused to tell her how he could tell when she lied. She was a terrible liar, which he liked. Unlike his former wife.

"Better than that," he said, kissing her gently on the lips. He had figured out how to lean forward just enough so that they could kiss, and they had done a lot of it, particularly at night, lying side by side. "Isabelle," he said quietly, "I'm not sure how this is going to work, but I want to make love to you." He had been having overpowering sensations for the past half hour. And he was so comfortable with her now, he was willing to try. They were both still pretty fragile, but he had wanted to make love to her for a long time. Since long before the accident, and he would never have asked her then, but there was a hopeful look in his eyes that went straight to her heart.

"It's all right, my love." It was something she wanted to do for him, even if all they did was lie in each other's arms. She understood perfectly now what he had in mind. "What do you say we lock the door?" There were locks on their doors that no one ever used, but this seemed an excellent time to start.

"Do you suppose they'll throw us out of the hospital?" he asked with a grin, as she got up and locked the door. He could hardly move, but he had had an irresistible desire for her for the last half hour, and it was all he could think of now. He had been so worried about it for so long, and he was nervous about trying it out with her, but neither of them could resist. Their relationship was tender and passionate and solidified by mutual trust.

"I'm not sure this is what they had in mind when they let us sleep in the same room," Isabelle said cautiously with a mischievous smile.

"That was silly of them," he said, looking more than a little nervous. "This is the best part." Or at least he hoped it would be. But what if it was not? He quivered at the thought.

She stopped him for a moment then, looking serious, and she gently kissed him on the lips. "I just want to tell you that the best part is what we already have . . . loving each other, being together . . . holding each other . . . I love everything about you, Bill. Whatever comes now is just an added gift, but it's not the best part. You are."

He had no idea if he could make love to her, but he wanted so badly to try. The doctor had told him it was possible, and Bill hoped he was right. And if it was, he wanted to share that with her. If not, he felt sure it would be a huge disappointment to both of them, and a failure on his part. But he did not voice his fears to Isabelle. He was afraid she'd worry or feel sorry for him. It was the latter he feared most.

She was infinitely gentle with him as she removed his hospital gown, he had a beautiful body, and he was aching for her. There was no shame between them, no modesty, they had been through so much, it was as though they had always been together, as she stroked and caressed him and he looked concerned. He felt everything she did emotionally, but he was not yet sure of the rest. She took her own nightgown off as he held her breasts in his hands. The bodies that had been so badly broken and abused suddenly forgot all their pain, and ever so gently, she began kissing him, first on the mouth, and then she worked her way artfully down. They knew how much they loved each other, and this was the last secret garden where they hadn't been, they discovered it slowly together, and he was overwhelmed by his feelings for her. She was infinitely careful as she tried to arouse him, careful not to put any weight on him, just enough in the right places, and he felt the exquisite pleasure she intended for him, but the desired effect did not take place, much to his dismay.

Even as he felt it, Bill was aware that what he felt was muffled somehow. And although he felt overwhelming passion for her, at the same time he had a sense that he was not in control of himself. Something was disconnected in him, and he wasn't sure if it was his brain or his spinal cord. And in spite of the intensity with which he wanted to make love to her, he felt raw fear slowing him down. He began to realize as she lay poised over him that it wasn't going to work, and he felt not only foolish, but insane for having tried.

Isabelle was remotely aware of what was happening to him, but she was so in love with him that all she wanted was to make him happy and feel loved. She had been well aware herself that it might not work, ever, or certainly the first time. He had been severely traumatized, and it was reasonable to expect that it might take patience to bring his sexual abilities back to life again. She hadn't wanted to present a challenge to him, but to give him hope, and life. But instead of hope, she could see despair in his eyes, as his efforts to consummate their passion failed.

"It's all right, my love . . . it's all right . . . give it time," she whispered as he clung to her, and then she felt him pull away from her and turn away. He was devastated by not being able to make love to her. All Bill could think as he lay next to her was that he had failed, and nothing she could say altered that fact. He vowed to himself, as he held her close to him, that he would never try again. Despite her tenderness and her love for him, he felt humiliated and more despondent than he had since the accident. It was the worst day of his life. He was no longer a man. And nothing on earth, he told himself, would induce him to try again. And surely not with her.

"Put your clothes on," he whispered to her, and she hesitated, wanting to do anything she could for him. But she could see how depressed he was, and any effort to please him, or comfort him, or caress or fondle him would only have upset him more. She slipped under the covers with him, and covered herself with the sheet as she lay close to him.

"It's all right, Bill," she whispered tenderly. "It will happen eventually," they both knew how deeply he felt for her, but he had wanted more than that, for both of them. "This is only the beginning," she said, kissing him gently on the cheek and trying to take his hand in hers, but he pulled it away. He was fighting back tears, and all he wanted was to run away, and there was no chance of that.

"No, it's not the beginning," he said angrily. He was furious with himself, not with her. "It's the end." The end of his life as a man, as far as he was concerned.

"It's not the end of anything," she said as she would have to a child. "The doctor told you it could take time to get things going again." But Bill was terrified his failure to perform was permanent. It would have been hard for any woman to imagine what his failure to make love to her represented to him. It was not something she could simply kiss away. All he could see ahead of him was a terrifying future without sex, and knowing that he could no longer function as a man. Like any other man, it had happened to him from time to time in his life, when he had been too tired, or too upset, too worried about politics, or when he had had too much to drink. But this had been his watershed, his epiphany, the first time he had ever made love to Isabelle. And after the accident, it had been, in his eyes, his one chance to prove that he was still a man, whether or not he could walk. What he had discovered changed everything for him, if not for her. Isabelle was understanding and decidedly calm about it. She was certain that it would work eventually. And even if not, she was prepared to accept whatever limitations he had, and love him anyway. It changed nothing for her, but it changed Bill's entire world. He was certain if he didn't recover his manhood, if not his legs, there was no way he could remain in her life. He had lost a lot that night, his self-respect, his self-esteem, his sense of his own masculinity, and all hope of any kind of a future with Isabelle, if his abilities were gone for good, which he feared they were. It would have seemed insane to her to come to those conclusions because of one failed attempt to make love to her. But Bill's fears were overpowering. He was terrified it would mean the end of the road for them, although his inability to make love to her meant nothing to Isabelle. If anything, as a result, she loved him more, and felt infinite tenderness for him.

Chapter Eleven

Bill's spirits took a hard hit after their failed attempt at making love. And although they continued to sleep in the same room, he was adamant about not trying again. He had risked all the humiliation he could bear, and Isabelle tried to encourage him to be optimistic, but she didn't force herself on him. She was careful not to, in fact. She was quiet and calm and supportive, and insisted, when he allowed her to talk about it, that with time and patience, his sexual abilities would very probably return. He had felt far too much, even during their brief attempt, to suggest that he would be forever numb. But Bill refused to accept even the remote possibility that there was hope for him. As far as he was concerned, the door to his life as a man was closed. He and Isabelle remained close to each other, and derived enormous comfort from each other, but he had no intention of trying to make love to her again.

As Bill and Isabelle grew even closer to each other emotionally, time seemed to move at an ever faster speed. The physical therapists were beginning to work with Bill, and Isabelle underwent a battery of tests, which covered everything from EEGs for brain function to sonograms for her heart. Little by little, they were advancing in their recoveries, and they were increasingly aware that their days together would soon end. The accident had been a high price to pay to spend nearly two months together, but as time went on, they were almost beginning to feel married.

They sat in each other's rooms all day, he accompanied her for her tests, they read the newspaper and had breakfast together in the morning, and at night they slept in two hospital beds that had been placed side by side. The only thing missing from their conjugal life was sex, still a sore subject for him. Although even without a physical side to their relationship, Isabelle had never been happier in her life.

"I feel like I'm running a beach resort here," one of the nurses teased amiably as they came back from sitting in the sun. Isabelle had had a headache that day, and they had done a brain scan on her before lunch, but the doctor said it looked fine. They were following her progress carefully, and she had done remarkably well.

Gordon was pressing her about when she was coming home. She knew, as Bill did, that her return to Paris was only weeks away. She wasn't hoping for complications for either of them, but she dreaded leaving Bill, not knowing when she would see him again.

She talked to her children every day, and she thought Sophie sounded incredibly stressed, which worried her. The full responsibility for Teddy was on her shoulders, and although Isabelle talked to him constantly, the boy was not doing as well as he had been before his mother left. Isabelle felt guilty for staying away from them for so long, but at the moment, she had no other choice, other than to be in a hospital in Paris. But she knew that as happy as she would be to see her children again, it was going to be excruciatingly painful to leave Bill.

They talked about it sometimes, and she said that perhaps in the future they could continue to meet somewhere, as they had in June. She didn't know how she'd get away, but she thought she could. What she shared now with Bill was not something she was willing to give up easily, even if they only met a few times a year. Bill was vague when she talked about meeting him every few months. He couldn't even think about it now, although he was making steady progress, his recovery had been far slower than hers, and his spirits had been flagging. He didn't want to commit to seeing her until he saw how his rehabilitation went. He continued not to want to be a burden to her. Nor did he want to give up seeing her. And after what they'd shared in the hospital, and the time they'd spent, it was hard to imagine that phone calls would still be enough, for either of them.

"I'm not sure you're being realistic about our meeting in Paris," Bill said once quietly. "Gordon doesn't know what happened here, but he does know we were together that night. He told me to get out of your room, in no uncertain terms, when he was here. I don't think he's going to just sit by while you go wandering off. I think he's going to be highly suspicious of us, and of you." Bill realized he might even monitor her calls. Gordon had been shocked to realize that she had developed a friendship with a man right under his nose.

And Bill didn't say it to Isabelle, but he had made a decision weeks before that if he was to be confined to a wheelchair for the rest of his life, he refused to be a burden to her, or anyone else. It had been a factor, although not the most important one in their case, in his divorcing Cynthia. And if in addition, he could not be a man with Isabelle, in every sense of the word, he was going to end it between them.

If he could learn to walk again, he would meet her quietly somewhere in France when she could get away. But the sexual issue remained a question mark for him. If the rehabilitation center in the States was no more successful at getting him on his feet again than the doctors in England thought it would be, he was not going to see her again. Sex would not even be an issue then. He was not willing to burden her with his limitations if he was wheelchair-bound for the rest of his days. He was tormented by both issues in their final days in the hospital, whether he would ever walk again, and whether time would restore his manhood. He was not willing to inflict either problem on Isabelle, and she had no idea how intensely and how hopeless he felt about it. Bill was careful not to express to her how pessimistic he was, although at times she sensed it without words.

He admitted to his doctor once that he had attempted to make love to her, and how devastating his failure had been, and the doctor had reassured him as best he could.

"I'm not surprised, you know," the surgeon said to him, with uncharacteristic understanding. "It actually sounds fairly hopeful, for the first time, after such an extensive trauma. Give it time, I think you may be encouraged by what happens. It is still very reasonable to expect that you would achieve both erection and orgasm within the first year. I think you may have been a little too enthusiastic and optimistic a little too soon. It's still very early days." But in spite of the potential comfort of the doctor's words, Bill didn't believe him. He continued to cling to his terror that the situation was hopeless, and it would never work. And he was absolutely determined not to try it again anytime in the near future, although Isabelle was more than willing to be creative with him, but Bill was not. He had abandoned all thought of a physical relationship with Isabelle for the time being, and maybe forever. And he had no idea when, or if, they'd have the opportunity to try again.

But in spite of the torture Bill was putting himself through, he and Isabelle were still sharing a room, and she was contemplating what to do with her life. She knew she would never leave her marriage, because of Teddy and Sophie, but nor was she willing now to give up Bill. Being his lover was a life she had never envisaged for herself, but it was what she wanted now and all she could have. She and Bill shared something that she had never known before. She often felt as though they were two bodies with one soul. And nothing on earth was going to make her give that up.

She spoke to Gordon every few days. He had
his secretary call the nurses' station every day
to check on her condition, but more often than
not she called him, usually at the office, out
of respect for him, and to check how Teddy
was. Usually, Sophie called her about him. And
Isabelle called Teddy herself every day. And
when Isabelle spoke to Gordon, as always,
he sounded distant and cool. Most of the time,
she had the feeling that she had interrupted
him and had called at an inopportune time.
He had very little to say to her, since the accident. And she could sense that he no longer
trusted her, although he never said as much.
She felt as though he were punishing her, and
she knew that once she was back in Paris with
him, she would have some serious explaining
to do. The fact that she and Bill had been to
Annabel's and Harry's Bar, and had been together at that hour when the bus hit their car,
spoke for itself. He said only once to her, during one of their calls, "You're not the woman I
married, Isabelle. In fact, I'm not sure I know
who you are." She felt guilty about it at times,
and she knew it wasn't right to pursue her relationship with Bill, and yet it was like a drug to
her now, her life depended on it, and she didn't
want to give it up.

She was talking to Bill about it one night, as

she massaged his legs for him. He said they still felt mostly numb, but he had some sensation, as he did elsewhere, and they ached sometimes, almost as though he'd been walking for a long time. She was telling him about the conversation she'd had with Gordon that day. He had been particularly short with her, and she sighed when she hung up the phone.

"I don't think he'll ever trust me again," she said to Bill. "And he's right, of course. I can't even imagine what it's going to be like going home. What about you? How angry is Cynthia?" Isabelle had noticed that he never talked about her, only the girls. But their relationship had been very different than hers and Gordon's was, they led far more separate lives, and there was little if any pretense of a relationship between them anymore. He still had not told Isabelle about the divorce. It was the only secret he had kept from her. He didn't want her to know he was soon to be free. He didn't want her to feel pressured. He knew she was staying in her marriage, and it seemed best to him if she believed he was married too.

"I don't think she was happy when she left," Bill said honestly. "I was honest with her about my feelings about you. And I didn't have to be. But she knows me, and she knew how worried I was about you."

"That didn't bother her?" Isabelle asked, looking surprised.

"I'm sure it did, but she knows better than to make a big fuss. She has enough secrets in her past." He smiled at Isabelle. "You can't put a man in jail for being in love. And Cynthia has led her own life for a long time. She hasn't let the grass grow under her feet for the last ten years."

Isabelle was pensive as she listened to him. "I don't think Gordon has ever cheated on me," she said quietly. "He's far too conservative and proper and sensible to do anything like that." From what Bill knew of their marriage, he wasn't as sure, but he didn't want to say that to her. It seemed odd to him for a man to be as cold and even cruel to her as her husband was, and not be finding comfort and consolation somewhere else. On the contrary, when he'd met him, he didn't think Gordon looked like the kind of man to be faithful or loyal to anyone. He was entirely out for himself. And Bill thought a mistress hidden somewhere would have explained Gordon's appalling behavior to his wife.

"What makes you think that?" Bill asked cautiously, he didn't want to stir things up, particularly since she was going back to him. He wanted her to have a peaceful life, not assist her in waging war on a man who could far too easily be cruel and damaging to her.

"Affection isn't important to him, neither is sex," she said very openly. "We haven't slept in the same room for years." He knew what she meant by that, and he smiled at her. She was very proper and shy in some ways, verbally at least. But she was very open and comfortable with him. And she was also naïve about her husband, he felt sure.

Bill and Isabelle were happy together in every way, but by the following week, they were both beginning to look strained. She had a battery of tests scheduled, and if her doctors were pleased with the results, she was going home. It was late August by then, and they had been in the hospital for two months. Gordon was getting angrier every day, and accusing her doctors of dragging their feet in releasing her. And the rehab center where Bill was scheduled for the next several months was waiting for him. She had to go back to Paris, and he was due to return to the States. Their strange idyll was about to end. It wasn't easy for either of them to face.

"Do you swear you'll call me every day?" she asked, looking sad one night as they lay in bed. She was due to have her last brain scan the next day. Her liver was healing, her heart had looked normal on the last sonogram, and her lungs had finally cleared.

"I'll call you ten times a day if I can," he said, pulling her closer to him. "You can call me too, you know."

"I will. I'll get up very early so I can call you before you go to sleep at night." But she also knew that if she called too often, Gordon or his secretary would see the number on their bills. She wasn't as free to call him as he was to call her. She was also aware of how duplicitous it was to continue their relationship by phone, but she couldn't bear the thought of being out of touch with him. They had been living together for two months.

They had gotten spoiled during their time in the hospital, and the thought of their being apart now frightened her. She had no idea when she'd see him again. The doctors had told him to expect to be in the rehabilitation center in New York for six months to a year. It sounded like a life sentence to both of them.

"You have to hurry up and get well," she told him as she kissed his chest, leaning over onto his bed. "I want you to come to Paris as soon as you can." There was no way she could come to New York. Sophie had had the burden of Teddy's responsibility for long enough, and she was about to go back to school. Isabelle knew it would be a long time before she could leave Paris again. She was desperate to see Teddy for herself. He had been sounding weaker and weaker on the phone.

But Bill said nothing when she mentioned his coming to France, and she didn't notice it. He had promised himself that he would phase himself slowly out of her life if he couldn't walk, or worse, be a man with her. It was a deal he had made with himself, and he had said nothing about it to her. He had never told her how grim his own prognosis was, and how much he feared that he would never walk again. He wanted to see what they said when he got back to the States. He still didn't quite believe that he would be confined to a wheelchair. But if he was, she had one invalid in her life, and he wasn't going to allow her to have two.

Bill couldn't tolerate the idea of her pitying him, or taking care of him as she had her son. She had spent fourteen years with a mortally ill child. And he didn't want her to have to take care of him, or even think about him that way. But even if he never saw her again, he couldn't imagine not talking to her on the phone. He could no longer imagine waking up in the morning, or the night, without having Isabelle next to him. It pained him just thinking about her being so far away, not being able to watch over her, or take care of her, or see her smile at him when she walked into the room. The time they had spent together had been the happiest in his life. He only wished it could have turned out differently, that Teddy were healthier, and Gordon had less of a grip on her. He had a myriad of wishes about her, and feared that none of them would come true.

The last few days in the hospital seemed to fly by them with the speed of sound. All of her tests were clear, and she had regained some of her strength again. She was ready to leave the hospital, and all the arrangements had been made. Gordon was supposed to come from Paris to take her back, but at the last minute, he told them to hire a nurse to make the trip with her instead. He said he had too much to do. But Isabelle preferred it that way, she didn't want anyone or anything keeping her from Bill on her last night with him.

The nurses left them alone on their last night. They just wanted some quiet time alone, to be peaceful and close. She was leaving in the morning, and Bill the following week. He still had a few last tests to do.

"I can't imagine leaving you tomorrow," Isabelle said unhappily. She had climbed into his bed, and they held each other close. She would have loved to find a way to make love to him, but she didn't want to upset him if it didn't work, particularly on their last night. She couldn't imagine going back to Gordon now, and she was relieved that she and Gordon kept so much distance between them. She could hardly remember what it was like living with Gordon, she felt far more married to Bill.

"I want you to take care of yourself, my love," he said, holding her close. They had switched his enormous neck brace to a smaller one, and he could move his head just a little bit. It allowed him to turn his head and look at her more easily, and all he could see now was the look in her eyes. Neither of them needed words for what they were feeling. They had come much farther than that. And now they had to go farther still. They had to learn to live without seeing each other every day, without touching each other, without her gentle hands on his shoulders when he was exhausted, or his arm around her when she fell asleep. She couldn't imagine it, but she knew it would be all too real the next day as she stepped into the house on the rue de Grenelle. It broke her heart to think of leaving him.

"I can't do this," she whispered softly as tears ran down her cheeks and she lay next to him. "I can't do it without you."

"Yes, you can. I won't be any farther away

than the phone." But they both knew it would be different now. And she had an odd feeling about returning to Gordon. He had been so icy with her on the phone that she knew he was going to punish her for her transgressions, and being in the accident with Bill. As though what had happened that night hadn't been punishment enough. But she sensed correctly that he was furious about her being in the car with Bill, and all he assumed it had meant, and now did.

They lay there in silence for a long time, watching a full moon in the night sky. And morning came far too soon. They lay together for their last few minutes, and a nurse came in to remind Isabelle that she had to get up. She showered and dressed, and had breakfast with Bill. But neither of them could eat. They just sat looking at each other, as Isabelle choked on a sob, and then she held him in her arms, as he comforted her.

"It'll be all right, Isabelle. I'll call you tonight," he said, steeling himself. "Don't cry, my love. . . ." She sounded like a heartbroken child, and in many ways was. Leaving him was worse than leaving home. He was the only source of comfort and love she had.

Gordon had sent her some clothes from Paris: a plain black Chanel suit that hung on her now, and a pair of flat black leather shoes that felt too big. She had lost a lot of weight, and her body seemed to have changed. She was rail thin, but she looked more beautiful than ever to Bill. She was wearing her long dark hair pulled back in a neat ponytail, and no makeup, just lipstick. And seeing her that way reminded him of when they'd arrived in June, their first day when they'd gone out for lunch, and Harry's Bar that night. So much had happened, so many bridges had been crossed. It was incredible to think that they'd nearly died, and then found each other again. And now their dreams were about to end. They both had to go back into the real world, a world in which they could not be to-gether, and in fact would be lifetimes apart.

"Take good care of yourself," she said as she hugged him close. "Come back to me soon," she whispered as he smiled through damp eyes. "And don't forget how much I love you."

"Be strong, Isabelle. . . . I love you too," he said, and feeling as though she were tearing herself away from him, she walked resolutely to the door, stopped, took a last look at him, and smiling through her tears, she left.

She thanked the nurses, said good-bye to both doctors who had come to say good-bye to her, and the nurse they had hired for the trip stood close to her in case she fell, and accompanied her to the elevator. And all the while, all she wanted was to run back into his room, to turn back the clock, all the way to the coma if necessary, anything to stay with him. She got into the elevator with her head bowed, and they could all see she was crying as they waved and the doors closed.

No one walked into Bill's room after she left, out of respect for him. No one saw him cry, or turn his eyes toward the ceiling with a look of anguish as he thought of her. If anyone had listened outside his door, they would have heard him sob for a time. It was a sound of dying hope, and lost dreams. It was the sound of a man who knew he would never see the woman he loved again. And when the nurses finally went in to check on him hours later, he had cried himself to sleep.

Chapter Twelve

The flight that Gordon's secretary had booked Isabelle on touched down at Charles de Gaulle shortly after two o'clock. She had no luggage with her, and only one small carrying bag, with her toiletries and a few books, and some pictures of her children and Bill. She had never gathered any real belongings at the hospital, and with a glance at her passport, the immigration officer waved her through. There was no one to meet her. Gordon hadn't come, and he hadn't told Sophie what flight her mother would be on.

By the time she got in the car Gordon had sent, she was amazed by how exhausted she was. She could hardly put one foot in front of the other. She knew that some of it was emotional, but it was also an enormous change for her to be out in the world again. The nurse escorted her through the airport in a wheelchair,

as Isabelle sat quietly thinking of Bill. She'd
tried to call him before they got in the car, but
the nurses in London said he was asleep. She
didn't want to wake him up, and she had nothing to tell him anyway, except that she loved
him and she hated being away from him. She
was already lonely for him, and she wasn't even
home yet. But she knew that once she arrived,
she would be happy to see her children again.

The nurse said very little to her on the ride
into Paris. They had hired her at the hospital,
and she worked privately. She was booked on a
flight to go back to London at six o'clock that
night. She was just a baby-sitter for the ride, as
Bill had said, and he thought it was a good idea
since Gordon wasn't accompanying her. If Isabelle got dizzy, if she fell, if she got frightened
or confused, it was better for her not to be
alone. She had been very ill for a very long time
and had sustained an enormous shock. The
woman had asked her a few pertinent questions
about the accident, she had read the chart anyway, and after a while she lapsed into silence,
and on the plane she'd read a book.

Isabelle felt oddly depressed as they drove into
town. It did not give her a thrill to see Paris
again, and when she saw the Tour Eiffel, it
meant nothing to her. She wanted to be on the
other side of the English Channel, in the hospi-

tal with Bill. She forced herself to think of Teddy and Sophie as they reached Paris, and crossed onto the Left Bank. And it gave her a strange feeling of excitement suddenly when they turned onto the rue de Grenelle. All she could think of now were her children, she could hardly wait to see them again, and at the same time, she was aware of an overwhelming feeling of longing and sadness as she thought of Bill.

The huge bronze doors to the courtyard were standing open, waiting for her. The guardian was watching for the car, and as it drove into the courtyard, Isabelle looked up at the house. She couldn't see anyone. But the children's rooms faced the garden, just as hers did, and she didn't expect Gordon to be home at that hour. He had told her he'd be home at six o'clock, as he always was, he had a busy day scheduled at the office, and she had said she understood. There was more power for him in not being there than in picking her up or meeting her. It was his way of showing her that she did not control him and never would. And there was no one to welcome her as she stepped out of the car.

The guardian bowed and touched his cap without saying a word, she nodded at him, and the driver turned the car around, as the nurse followed her up the short flight of stairs into the house.

Isabelle rang the bell, and for a moment no one came, and then Josephine, the housekeeper, appeared. She took one look at Isabelle, burst into tears, and threw her arms around her.

"Oh, madame . . ." She had thought Isabelle would die, and she was genuinely happy to see her. She'd been with her all the years of Isabelle's married life. And she dabbed at her eyes as Isabelle hugged her and smiled.

"It's so good to see you," Isabelle said, and walked into the familiar hall, and looked around. It looked different than she remembered it. Bigger, darker, sadder somehow. It was strange how the mind played tricks, but the house no longer felt comfortable, it felt strange, like being in the wrong house. She wondered if her accident and head injury made her feel that way, or if it was real. She had been gone for a long time. It had been more than two months since she left to spend two days in London in June. So much had happened, and it felt so odd now that she was back. She felt as though she no longer belonged, nor wanted to be, in the house on the rue de Grenelle. And the only thing that kept her there was her kids.

She thanked the nurse for bringing her home, left her with Josephine, and walked slowly up the stairs to see her children. She stood at the top of the stairs for a moment to catch her breath, and she could hear voices in the distance. For an instant, everything around her faded, except the voice of her son. She could hear him talking to someone. And on silent feet, she walked to his room, and opened the door.

Teddy didn't see her at first, he was lying on his bed, and talking to his favorite nurse, Marthe. Isabelle could hear without seeing him that he sounded tired and plaintive. She said not a word to warn him, and walked into the room with a smile.

He glanced at her at first, seeming not to register what had happened, and then with a great whoop of glee, he leaped off the bed and ran to her. And he hugged her so hard, he almost knocked her down.

"Mom!! You're back!!" He was hugging and holding her and pulling at her and kissing her so hard, she thought they would both fall, and she tried to steady him and herself, as the nurse warned him to be gentle. Just holding him like that, and feeling him and touching him and smelling the fresh scent of his hair brought tears to her eyes.

"Oh my God, I've missed you so much. . . . I can't believe it. . . . Teddy, I love you. . . ." She was like a mother with a young pup, as he pulled and tugged, and kissed and loved. It suddenly brought home to her as nothing else could how much she had missed him, and when she pulled away from him a little bit, and sat down on his bed, still holding his hands, she could see how pale he was. He was thinner and looked more frail than when she had left, and he started to cough as he sat down next to her, and she saw that it was difficult for him to stop or breathe.

Isabelle glanced at the nurse, and there were tears on her cheeks as she watched them. But the boy's mother could see from the vast array of pills and syrups next to his bed that he hadn't been well. He'd been in such fine form for once when she left him. But the last two months had taken a heavy toll.

"What are you doing in bed at this hour?" she asked him, her eyes worried, and he smiled at her happily as he crawled back up the bed and lay against his pillows, just looking at her.

"The doctor won't let me get up," he said, as though the entire matter were unimportant. Now that she was home, he didn't care how sick he was. "I told him it was stupid. I wanted to go out to the garden yesterday, and Sophie said I couldn't. She's even sillier than you, she worries all the time. And she doesn't let me do anything at all."

"That sounds sensible," his mother said, beaming at him. "It sounds like she took very good care of you for me while I was gone."

"Are you all right?" he asked her, looking worried. The coughing had stopped, but when she looked more closely, she saw that there was a tremor in his hands. She suspected it was caused by one of his medications, but she didn't like it anyway. Some of the breathing medicines he took had made him shake before. What Isabelle didn't like about them was that they were too hard on his heart. But Sophie couldn't have known that, and Isabelle was sure she had done a good job. "Papa said you were in a coma, and then you woke up, and now you're fine."

"That's about right. It wasn't quite as quick as all that, I'm afraid. But I'm fine now."

"What was it like in the coma? Was it beautiful?" he asked, with a strange wistful look in his eyes. "Do you remember it?"

"No, I don't. I only remember one dream I had, and you were in it. There was a very bright light and I was going away, and you made me come back, so I did." It was the same dream Bill had had that they had talked about many times. But she couldn't tell him about Bill. And she felt a pang of missing him now as she thought about it. She wished that he could see Teddy, they had talked about him so much, it seemed so unfair that they couldn't meet, although she hoped they might someday.

"Did you hurt very much?" He was very worried about her. He looked like the Little Prince in Saint-Exupéry's book, as he sat cross-legged on his bed, with his silky hair in soft curls around his face. He looked and seemed a great deal younger than he was. At fourteen, he had never been to school, rarely left the house, and had no friends. All he had were Sophie and his parents. And it was Isabelle he had always relied on most of all.

"It only hurt in the beginning. After that, I just had to rest a lot, and have tests, and take medicine, and get well so I could come home to you."

"I missed you," he said simply. His words didn't even begin to describe to her how he had longed for her, and how frightened he had been that she'd never come home again.

"I missed you too." Isabelle looked around then, as she lay across his bed. She felt comfortable in this room, far more so than she had felt in the front hall, or would in her own room. This was where she always spent her time when she was home. "Where's Sophie?"

"She had to do some errands. She's going back to school next week. It's a good thing you came home. Papa has been out all the time, and Sophie was mad about it."

"Then you and I will do lots of reading, and some wonderful puzzles. If everyone else is so busy, we'll have more time just for us, won't we?" she said, looking unconcerned, but she couldn't help wondering where Gordon had been. She also knew that that was Teddy's perception, and he probably hadn't been out as much as Teddy said.

They were talking and laughing and hugging when Sophie walked into the room with a stack of magazines for Teddy, and she gave a little scream when she saw her mother lying on the bed beside him.

"Mommy!" She ran to her and almost threw herself on her, and then suddenly worried that she might hurt her. Not unlike her brother, her mother looked very frail to her. "You look so thin!"

"The food at the hospital was awful." Isabelle smiled at her. She didn't tell her that on several occasions Bill had had some excellent meals sent in. But she hadn't been hungry, and she had a pitifully small appetite these days. The clothes she had worn home were hanging off her.

"Do you feel all right?" Sophie asked, looking worried. She had become the family caretaker while her mother was in the hospital in London.

"I feel wonderful now that I can see you two

again." Isabelle was beaming, as they were. It was another hour before she went back to her own room to lie down for a little while. She was absolutely exhausted, and Teddy's nurse Marthe said she would look in on her.

Isabelle lay down on her bed, and kicked off her shoes, and as she lay there, she glanced around. The room was all done in flowered silks that were very delicate and pale. There were pinks and whites and pale lavenders on an ivory background. And the furniture around the room was all Louis XV. In some ways, it felt good to be there, and she realized that she felt complete again, now that she had seen her children, but at the same time there was a piece of her missing. She felt overwhelmed by how much she missed Bill. It almost gave her a feeling of panic. They had been so brave when she left, but she had no idea when she would see him again. At best, it was going to be a very long time. She longed to hear his voice, to see him smiling at her, or just touch his hand. And she felt strangely lonely in this house she lived in with her children and the husband who had long since become a stranger to her.

She only meant to rest for a few minutes, but in spite of herself, she fell asleep, and she awoke only when Sophie came in and gently touched her shoulder.

"Are you all right, Mom?" She had grown up too much over the summer, she seemed to have jumped from childhood into all the burdens of adulthood. And listening to her, she seemed more the parent now than the child. Isabelle rolled over on her back and smiled up at her. Without even saying it, she felt a new closeness between them.

"I'm fine, darling. I must have dozed off. I'm just a little tired."

"Don't let Teddy wear you out. He's so happy to see you, he's like a big puppy. He's had a fever again for the past few days," Sophie said, looking worried.

"He looks very thin," Isabelle commented, patting the bed next to her so Sophie would sit down beside her.

"So do you," Sophie said, looking at her mother more closely. She looked different than she had before, as though something enormously important had happened to her, and it had. She had nearly died, and been reborn. And she had fallen deeply in love with a wonderful man. The changes in her were visible even to her eighteen-year-old daughter.

"You've done a wonderful job with Teddy," Isabelle praised her, and it was much deserved. She knew better than anyone that caring for a child as sick as Teddy was no easy job. He was loving and always appreciative of the things people did for him, but he had enormous needs, and had to be constantly tended to and monitored and watched. It was a life of eternal vigilance and literally no rest for those who cared for him. "I'm sorry it took me so long to come home," Isabelle said softly.

"I'm just glad you're alive," Sophie said with a tired smile.

"I want you to relax now," Isabelle said, looking concerned about her. "I'll keep Teddy company again tomorrow. I want you to have some fun before you go back to school." And this time, when Sophie smiled, she looked like a girl again. She didn't want to complain or tell her mother how hard it had been, or how lonely. She'd had no one to talk to or share her worries with, except her friends when they called. They came to visit her now and then, but after a few weeks they got tired of how tied down she was. And for most of the summer, her friends had been away. It had been a long, lonely, hard two months for her. And her father had been no help at all. It was as though he didn't want to know anything about Teddy. He had a sick wife, a sick child, and a life of his own. He had scarcely talked to Sophie while her mother was gone, and she had felt more like an overworked employee than his daughter.

Isabelle got up, washed her face, and combed her hair, and she thought about calling Bill, but she didn't think she had time before Gordon came home. As it turned out, he only came home at seven. Isabelle was in Teddy's room, reading a book to him, when she saw a tall, dark figure walk by. He must have recognized her voice, but he simply walked on without stopping to look into the room or greet her.

Isabelle finished the page, and put the book down. Teddy had eaten dinner on a tray an hour before, and after the emotion of seeing his mother again, he was tired. Sophie had gone out with friends for the evening, for the first time in two months. And after kissing Teddy gently on the cheek, and promising to come back, Isabelle walked quietly down the hall to see her husband. When she found him, Gordon was in his dressing room, making a phone call. He looked surprised to see her standing there, as though he had forgotten she was coming home. She knew that wasn't possible, but it was his style not to make a fuss about arrivals and departures. He rarely said good-bye when he went on a trip, never did when he left for the office in the morning, and when he returned, he usually went to his own rooms to relax for a while before seeing Isabelle or his children. And tonight was no different. He had assumed correctly that she was with Teddy, and knew that he would see her, in good time. He was clearly in no hurry.

"How was your trip?" he asked, smiling at her, from a distance. He made no move to come toward her as she stood cautiously in the doorway.

"Fine." It was as though the past two months hadn't happened. She felt suddenly as though she had only been gone for two days, and he took no notice of the fact that she'd been gone for two months and had nearly died during her absence. Since she had still been comatose when he left her in the hospital in London, she had not seen him since she left Paris. "The nurse was very helpful. It would have been hard to travel without her. The children seem fine," Isabelle said quietly, if you discounted the fact that Teddy had lost weight and was running a fever, and Sophie had aged five years in two months. Other than that, everything was "fine." But she knew he wouldn't want to hear about it. As far as Gordon was concerned, matters that concerned the children and the house were not his province or concern.

"How do you feel?" He looked worried as he asked her, which surprised her. She had expected him to want her to pretend that she hadn't been ill at all. He hated illness and sick people so much,

he thought it was a sign of weakness when people were ill. And as they both knew, illness of any
kind reminded him of his mother, and was
painful for him. In his mind, his entire childhood
had been hampered and tainted by her illness.

"I feel all right. Just tired. I think it will take
me a while to feel like myself again." She had to
see a specialist the following week for her heart
and her liver, and the doctor had warned her
that if she had headaches, even mild ones, she
would have to be seen immediately by a doctor.
The doctor in London expected her full recovery to take close to a year, if not longer.

"You look very well," Gordon said pleasantly,
wanting it to be so. For a variety of reasons, he
wanted the past two months to have never happened. He still hadn't gotten up to hug her or
kiss her. And he made no move toward her as
they spoke. He was an entirely different animal
from Bill. And once again, she wondered if
Gordon was angry at her. He knew of her
friendship with him, and Bill had told her that
Gordon had banished him from her room. But
he asked her no questions, and made no mention of him. She knew that Bill Robinson was
now a subject that was entirely taboo between
them. Gordon did not have to warn her, she
understood it. "Have you had dinner?" he
asked coolly.

She shook her head, and as it always did now, it gave her a slightly dizzy feeling. She had to remind herself not to make any sudden moves with her head, at least for a while. "Not yet. I was waiting for you. Teddy's eaten, and Sophie is out with friends." Gordon frowned as she said it.

"I assumed you'd want to go to bed when you arrived, Isabelle. This has been a long day for you, for your first day out. I have a business dinner tonight, with an important client from Bangkok."

"That's all right." She smiled at him. She was still standing near the doorway. He had never actually invited her to come in, and it was a formality she respected. He had always made it clear to everyone that one needed an invitation from him to enter these rooms, and that applied even to her. "I'll have Josephine bring me up a tray. I'm not hungry anyway." All she wanted was some soup, or maybe toast and eggs.

"I think that's an excellent idea. We'll have dinner tomorrow." In the past, it wouldn't have surprised her that he had made no particular fuss about her return after her long absence. But now that she knew Bill so intimately and how he treated her, it startled her that Gordon was so distant and so cool. The two men couldn't possibly have been more different. There was no acknowledgment of her illness, no celebration, no flowers. He didn't even come to hug her before she quietly left his room. And she knew she would not see him again that night. She was actually surprised when he stopped in to see her for a minute on his way out. He was wearing a dark blue suit, a white shirt, a navy Hermès tie, and smelled of cologne. He looked like he was going to a dinner party, but she didn't ask him.

"Have you eaten?" For Gordon, the question was a sign of unusual solicitousness, and she was touched by the attention. These were the crumbs of affection she had been satisfied with in the past.

"I had eggs and some soup," she said politely, and he nodded.

"Get some rest. Don't stay up with Teddy tonight. He has a nurse for that." She would have liked to be with Teddy, but knew she didn't feel up to it yet.

"He's already asleep," she told Gordon. She had just checked on him, and gone back to her own bed, before Gordon walked in to talk to her.

"You'd be wise to do the same," he said, once again not approaching her bed. He rarely touched her, never hugged her, hadn't kissed her in years, and kept a noticeable distance from

her when they were in the same room. The
only time he was ever affectionate with her was
when they were out in public. Years before, she
had been fooled by it, thinking he was warming
up to her, and then when they got home, he
would be cold to her as soon as they closed
their bedroom door. Being close to anyone was
the hardest thing in the world for Gordon,
which was in sharp contrast to Isabelle, who
was warm, affectionate, and loving. It was also
light-years from what she had just experienced
with Bill, who constantly wanted to hold and
touch her. "See you tomorrow," Gordon said,
hesitating slightly. For an instant, she thought he
might walk fully into the room, and approach
her, but without saying anything more, he
turned on his heel and left. It was not the marriage she had ever dreamed of having, but there
was no point thinking about it now, it was the
only one she had. All she had to do now was
readjust to it, after her months with Bill. It was
no small feat.

A few minutes after Gordon left, she picked
up the phone and dialed London. And when
the switchboard answered, she asked to speak to
Bill. He sounded depressed when he answered,
and as soon as he heard her voice at the other
end, he beamed.

"I was lying here thinking about you," he said

easily, and his tone was in sharp contrast to the greeting she'd had from Gordon. "How are the children?"

"Wonderful," she smiled just hearing him. He sounded like a husband on a trip checking how her day was. "They were so happy to see me. Poor Sophie looks exhausted."

"How's Teddy?"

"Very thin. He's getting fevers again. But he seemed a bit better tonight. I'm going to spend the day with him tomorrow."

"Don't overdo it. You're not up to full speed yourself yet."

"I know, sweetheart. How was your day?" It had been awful, as far as he was concerned, but he didn't say that to her. He'd been lonely all day after she left, but he knew he had to get used to it. All they had now were phone calls. Just like the old days. But after nearly two months of living together, the phone calls seemed like so little to both of them. They both longed for the warmth and closeness they had shared.

"It was all right," he lied. "I missed you. They're trying to get me ready to leave next week. I feel like I'm going to boot camp." He was going to the rehab center with the most rigorous program, because he thought they might get the best results. His future depended

on it, and theirs. And in spite of what they had
told him in London about his legs, he was
hopeful. He still felt sure that in the States they
might tell him something different. He had
more faith in them.

They talked for a while about her homecom-
ing, and the kids, and he had had a call from
Jane that afternoon, which had cheered him up
a little. And it was only at the end of the call
that he asked her about Gordon.

"How was he?"

"He was Gordon. He came home late from
the office, and he's out tonight. It doesn't matter." She had left her heart with Bill in London,
except for the part of her that belonged to her
children. But there was nothing left for her
husband. It was too late, and too much had
happened over the years. Even if she never saw
Bill again, she knew that it was too late for her
and Gordon. All they had now was the shell of
an empty marriage, the appearance of it, and
not the substance.

"Does he seem angry at you?" Bill had been
worried about it. He had seemed so angry to
Bill during those first days in London.

"No, he doesn't. But he'd never show it. If he
is, it'll come out sometime when I don't expect
it. That's how he works. He saves things. The
payback always comes later." But she didn't have

any sense of it. He seemed detached from her, but he had been for years. There was nothing different about it. It was all very much the same.

"I just don't want him taking it out on you because you were with me during the accident. I know he was very upset about it. With good reason." And even better reason now, but he didn't know that.

"Did you talk to Cynthia?" she asked, trying to sound casual. She had noticed in London that his wife never called him. He had had several conversations with his lawyer in the hospital in London and had filed the divorce papers without telling Isabelle. "Jane said she's in South Hampton. I'll see her when I'm in the hospital in New York."

"I should hope so." Isabelle was shocked at her lack of attention.

He promised to call Isabelle the next day then. She said she'd be home all day. It was easy for them now with only an hour's time difference between Paris and London. It would be harder when he was in New York, but Isabelle knew they'd manage just as they had for years. Bill told her he loved her when he hung up, and as she lay in her bed that night, in the house that was supposed to be her home, she felt as though she were in a strange place. She felt as though her home was with Bill in London.

She didn't hear Gordon come in that night, but she was sleeping soundly in her own room. And she ran into him in the hall the next day, when she was on her way to see Teddy. She had slept later than usual, and it was nearly nine o'clock when she got up. She was wearing a dressing gown, her face was washed and her hair combed when she saw Gordon, rushing toward the stairs with his briefcase. He didn't talk to her, but he waved as he ran down the stairs. He was talking on his cell phone, and a moment later she heard him drive out of the courtyard.

She and Teddy had a good day. She read to him a lot, lay on the bed next to him, and it reminded her a little of her time with Bill in the hospital in London. They read and talked and played games, and after lunch, he had a long nap, and after that the doctor came to see him. He found the boy vastly improved now that his mother was home, but as Isabelle walked the doctor out, he turned to her with an odd expression.

"You know he's deteriorating, don't you, Isabelle?" She had been afraid of that, but she thought it was only temporary. Now that she was home, she was going to put her full efforts into getting him back to the place where he'd been two months before, when she left for

London. And she was sure she could do it. Sophie had taken good care of him while she was
gone, but she didn't know all the tricks Isabelle did.

"He looks pale, and he's lost weight, but he
seemed better this morning," she said, looking
hopeful.

"He's happier. But he's getting weaker. You
have to face that. His heart function is getting
worse, and his lungs were bad all summer."

"What are you saying to me, Doctor?" She
looked worried.

"That his body is struggling to keep up with
him. As he gets bigger, his heart and lungs face
an ever-greater challenge."

"And a transplant?" she asked again.

"He would never survive it." And without it,
she knew his days were numbered. It was a lot
to face so soon after she got home, and she was
still frail herself. The doctor reminded her not
to overdo it. "I'd like to see him gain some
weight," the doctor said, "and you too, Isabelle." He was concerned about her. Her body
had sustained a terrible shock, and she
looked it.

"I'll work on it. We'll go on a fattening
regime together." She smiled, pensive about
what he had just told her. It had been a hard
summer for Teddy, for both of them, but now

that she was home, she was determined to turn things around again, she felt sure she could.

"I'll come back to see him in a day or two, and if you have any problems, call me."

But the problems she had were not related to Teddy. They were with Gordon. He came home looking sullen that night, and offered no explanation for it. He had dinner on a tray in his room, and did not come downstairs to dine with her. He never spoke to her, and never came into her room. And later that night, as she lay in her bed thinking about it, she heard him go out. She had no idea where he went when he went out at night, and she didn't see him again until the next morning. She ran into him when she went downstairs for breakfast. He was sitting in the dining room, reading the paper and drinking a cup of coffee. And for a long time, he didn't acknowledge her, until he put down the paper and finished his coffee. She had the impression he was angry at her, and she had no idea what she'd done to annoy him.

"Have you heard from your friend in London?" he asked her bluntly, and she was startled by the question. She didn't want to lie to him, but she didn't want to tell him Bill had called her twice the day before either.

"Yes, I spoke to him" was all she said. She was surprised to hear him mention Bill. He hadn't said a word about him on the day she came home, but now Gordon looked furious about him.

"Don't you think it's inappropriate for him to call you here, Isabelle? I would think he'd be embarrassed to. He damn near killed you."

"The bus nearly killed both of us. It wasn't his fault."

"If you hadn't been out with him, it wouldn't have happened. I don't imagine you'd like your children to know that you were out with another man when the accident occurred." There was an implied threat that he would tell them, and she understood him. It was a warning.

"No, I wouldn't. But it wasn't the way you make it sound. We were friends," she said calmly, although her heart was pounding.

"Are you telling me the friendship is over?"

"I didn't say that. We went through a lot together." She looked at her husband carefully. She knew how vindictive he could be, and she didn't want to start a war with him. She knew that if she did, he would win it. He always did. Gordon was all about power and control, and she knew he wasn't going to tolerate her crossing him. She didn't want to have a showdown with him, if she could possibly avoid it. "You have nothing to fear from him, Gordon. I'm home now."

"That's not the issue. I'm telling you to leave that alone, Isabelle. You're taking a great risk if you make me angry. I wouldn't suggest it."

"I have no desire to make you angry. I'm sorry that it created a very awkward situation." She lowered her eyes as she said it.

"That's an interesting choice of words." His eyes bored into her, and they were giving her a warning. "I'd say having you in a near-fatal accident while you were cheating on me is definitely 'awkward.' "

"I wasn't cheating on you. I was having dinner," she said softly.

"And dancing. You were out at two o'clock in the morning." She didn't ask him where he'd been the night before, or where he went when he left the house late at night. She had never asked him. She wouldn't have dared. He had established early on in their marriage that he made the rules, and he was free to do what he wanted. He expected her to toe the line, and it was silently agreed between them that she was not to ask questions, or challenge his authority or his independence. The punishment for it would have been extreme if she'd dared. That much had always been understood between them. There had never been any pretense of equality in their marriage. He had never offered it or promised it, and he didn't intend to start now. She understood that too. The only thing that surprised her now was that she had always been willing to accept his authoritarian rule. She saw now that it was a dictatorship, not a marriage. "You're a married woman," he reminded her, "and I expect you to behave that way. I hope you learned a lesson." And what was that, she wondered. That she'd be hit by a bus if she dined with another man? She wondered what he'd do to her if he knew she was sharing a room with Bill in the hospital in London, or if someone had told him. He was making himself very clear to her. He was not going to tolerate anything other than exemplary behavior from her. Anything less than that would be punished, by silence, by threats, by rejection, by insults if necessary, or perhaps by banishment, maybe even without her children. And if he divorced her, she had no way of taking care of Teddy, which was the only thing that mattered to her.

"You're lucky I'm willing to forgive you. But if I discover that you're misbehaving, or that he's visiting you here, things are going to go very badly between us. And I suggest you tell him to stop calling." But she knew she would never do that. Their calls were all she had now. There was certainly going to be no warmth or support from Gordon. He got up from the table then, picked up his briefcase, and walked out of the room. He had delivered his message, and she heard him leave for the office a moment later.

She sat in the dining room for a while, collecting her thoughts, and feeling shaken. She had wondered if he was going to punish her, and now she knew. She was a prisoner, a convict on parole, and if she broke the rules again, and he found out, God only knew what he would do to her. He might even divorce her and keep custody of Teddy. That would be her worst nightmare. And she knew he was capable of making it happen. She wanted to call Bill, but she didn't dare. She waited for him to call her. He did, at noon, after his morning of physical therapy. He sounded tired, but in decent spirits, and he was happy to talk to her.

"Hi, baby, what are you up to?" he asked cheerfully, and as soon as she spoke to him, he could tell that something had happened. "What's wrong? You sound worried."

"No, I'm fine," she lied, and then broke down and told him when he pressed her. She told him about the exchange with Gordon that morning.

"He's just trying to scare you. Reign by terror." Bill hated everything about him, and he realized now that Gordon had never come back to see her at the hospital to punish her and frighten her, and make her feel insecure and uncertain. What Gordon didn't know was that it had been a gift to her, and to them, and had turned out to be a blessing. "He can't do anything. He can't take Teddy." He tried in vain to reassure her, but as they talked, he realized that Isabelle was genuinely afraid.

"The courts here favor the father. Maybe he could convince them I'm an unsuitable mother." It broke Bill's heart to hear her sounding so worried. She had been upset about it all morning.

"How can he convince anyone you're 'unsuitable'? By telling them you've spent fourteen years taking care of him night and day? Sweetheart, don't be silly. He's just trying to terrorize you, and he's succeeding." It was an unfounded fear, but Gordon always frightened her. He seemed so all-powerful and all-knowing.

"He's very impressive." And in her eyes, always had been.

"He doesn't impress me," Bill said, sounding angry. He would have loved to confront him about how badly he treated his wife. Gordon Forrester was a bully. "Just try to ignore him, and go about your business."

"That's what I'm doing."

"Are you having dinner with him tonight?"

"I don't know. He never tells me."

It drove Bill crazy to hear what she was going through, but he was helpless to do anything about it. He wished she would divorce him, but he knew she never would. She had too much at stake there, and she was too afraid of what he would do to her, and that was exactly what Gordon wanted. Bill tried to explain it to her, but she pointed out to him that she was entirely at his mercy. She had no money of her own, and she had a child who was an invalid, and needed extremely costly medical attention. Hearing her say it upset Bill terribly. He would have liked to marry her, and take care of the boy. But it was too late now, for the moment at least: He couldn't ask her to marry him if he was going to be an invalid. His hands were tied. And men like Gordon always found the right weapon to wield at their victims. In this case, it was fear. He wondered how long it had been like that, and how much abuse she had taken over the years. It seemed to be unlimited, the man had been allowed to run roughshod over her for years, and with her meeting Bill in London and getting exposed by the accident, she had loaded the gun for him. It was unfortunate that he had found out about it.

"Try to stay out of his way. And I'll call you." He knew it was best if his phone number didn't appear on her bills. That would have been all

Gordon needed. "Only call me if you absolutely have to," Bill told her. "I'll call you." She felt lonely and isolated as she realized the situation she was in. She was in disgrace, even more than he knew, and Gordon was prepared to exact the ultimate price for it. To the uttermost farthing.

They talked for a while, and he had to go back to therapy again. He promised to call her later in the afternoon, before Gordon came home from the office.

But this time he surprised her. Instead of late, he came home early. He came home at four o'clock, looking as though he expected to surprise her in some wrongdoing. But Bill had already called her. And she was stretched across Teddy's bed playing cards with him. Teddy had a passion for gin rummy. He liked to play solitaire too, but he much preferred to play games with his mother.

Gordon waved as he walked by the room, but he didn't stop to speak to the boy, or Isabelle. It was exactly the same behavior Sophie had seen all summer. It had given Sophie a new view of her father, and she didn't like it. She hated the way he would talk to her, and completely ignore Teddy, as though he were invisible or had never existed. The boy was inadequate in Gordon's eyes, and severely flawed, and he dismissed him. He wasn't worthy of his attention, and Teddy knew it. For years now, he had had absolutely no respect for his father, and little affection. Gordon showed him none at all, nor did he show Isabelle any, and hadn't for years. Sophie had only just begun to understand that. And Sophie commented on it later that afternoon, when she was visiting her mother before she went out for the evening again with friends.

"Why do you let him treat you that way?" Sophie accused her. She wanted her mother to stand up for herself, and was upset that she didn't. Although she had battled with her for years, Sophie was now potentially her strongest ally.

"He doesn't mean any harm by it, sweetheart. That's just the way he is." Isabelle was always quick to defend him to the children, no matter how right they were when they complained about him. "He's not a demonstrative person," she explained, and Sophie looked angry. She had learned a lot about him that summer, more than she wanted. It had destroyed all her illusions about her father. Her sympathies were now entirely with her mother. Isabelle had become a hero to her.

"He demonstrates indifference and rejection and meanness constantly. He's awful to you, and he doesn't care about Teddy," Sophie said angrily.

"Of course he does, Sophie." Isabelle looked

nervous as she listened to what Sophie was saying, although she knew there was a great deal of
truth to it.

"He only cares about himself. He doesn't care
about me either."

"He's very proud of you." Sophie didn't challenge her about that, but she also didn't believe
her.

"Even if he is, he has no right to treat you
that way, or Teddy." He was slightly better to
Sophie than the others, but he had been less
nice to her lately, and it hadn't gone unnoticed.
He had never thanked her for the efforts she
made, the opportunities she gave up, or the love
she showered on her brother in their mother's
absence. Sophie had come to see her father as a
cold, hard, unfeeling, ruthless man, which was
precisely what he was. It had gotten him a long
way in business, but it definitely wasn't winning
him any medals at home with his wife and
children.

"Please don't worry about it," Isabelle urged
her. "Your father is a good man." But even as
she said it, she knew it was a lie, and so did Sophie. He was anything but good, or even kind.
"Your father and I are used to each other. We
know what to expect, and how we feel about
each other. It's not as bad as it looks from the
outside." But Sophie knew it was worse. She

now understood why they had separate bedrooms, and she realized that her father was out
all the time. He had hardly spent an evening at
home while Isabelle was in the hospital in London, and more than once she had discovered
that he was out for the night, but she didn't tell
her mother that. She knew she would have
been terribly hurt by it. Sophie didn't think he
had a girlfriend. He didn't seem the type. But
she had no idea where he went. He never left
any numbers with her. "Everything's fine," Isabelle reiterated, but she didn't convince her
daughter. There seemed no point in Isabelle's
mind to tell her just how unpleasant the situation was.

"Was he always like that?" Now that she
thought about it, and had for the past two
months, she couldn't remember her father ever
treating her mother any other way. She couldn't
remember a time when there had been warmth
and affection between them. She couldn't recall
her father ever giving her mother a kiss or a
hug. And they had had separate rooms ever
since Teddy was born. Her mother had said it
was so she could take care of Teddy and not
disturb their father, but now Sophie realized it
was due to far more than that. And she couldn't
understand why she herself hadn't been shocked
by it sooner. She had always favored her father

since her earliest childhood, and now she felt guilty about it. She had learned a lot, and grown up, while her mother was gone. And nearly losing her in the accident made Sophie cherish her more than she ever had. "Was he different when you got married?" Sophie asked, looking sad for her. She felt so tender toward her mother now.

"He was very protective when we got married. Very strong, very determined, I thought it meant he loved me. I was very young. And he was wonderful when you were born. He was so happy." She didn't tell Sophie that Gordon had wanted a boy. She'd had a miscarriage after that, and then finally four years after Sophie, Teddy was born. And everything had gone sour after that. He reproached her for Teddy's early birth, insisting that she must have done something to provoke it, and it was all her fault.

Gordon had disengaged himself from the ailing baby right from the first. And within months, he had detached himself from Isabelle as well. She had wanted his support and his love, it had been a hard time for her. They had almost lost Teddy several times during the first two years of his life, and it terrified her. He was so tiny and so frail and so much at risk, but Gordon had let her know again and again that he thought it was all her fault. He told her constantly how inadequate she was, how incapable, how wrong. He had completely undermined her self-confidence, and any belief she'd had in herself, as a mother, as a woman, as his wife. And within two years of Teddy's birth, he had completely shut her out. She had never really understood why, but she had somehow come to believe that it was her fault. And she still felt that way now at times. She always had the feeling that if she'd done things better, he would still love her, and all would have been well with them. Just as he had this morning about her behavior and the accident in London, he invariably blamed her, and she was willing to accept both the blame and the guilt. Except finally, thanks to Bill, less so this time. She knew she had been wrong to meet him in London, in a clandestine way, but at that point at least, she had done nothing wrong. She intended it to be an innocent encounter, and she had told him that she honored her marriage. It was only in the hospital, after the accident, that everything had changed. And she loved Bill so much now, she was willing to bear the guilt, just to have him in her life. There was no way she could give him up now.

"I don't know why you married him, Mom," Sophie said as she got ready to leave and meet her friends. What she had discovered that summer about her father, among other things, was that he was mean to the point of being cruel at times. And she hated that about him.

"I married him because I loved him." Isabelle smiled sadly. "I was twenty-one years old, and I thought we were going to have a wonderful life. He was handsome and smart and successful. My father thought the sun rose and fell on him. He told me he would be the perfect husband for me, and I believed him. He was very impressed by your father. He was a very accomplished man." At thirty-eight, he was already the head of the bank then, and Gordon had been very impressed by her royal and social connections. She had been able to enhance his life at first. Through her parents, she had friends who were useful to him. But once he knew them himself, he pushed her away. It became impossible for him to show affection or love for her. He had been so charming at first, and so cruel so quickly after, and totally self-involved, as though she didn't exist, except to serve him.

Five years later, he was no longer interested in wasting his charm on her. And he certainly wasn't now. By the time her father died, the marriage had become a nightmare, but she would never have admitted it to anyone. She was too ashamed, and Gordon had convinced her by then that it was her fault. Ever since then, she had poured all her love into Sophie and Teddy. At least, she thought, she had done that right. And in sharp contrast to her experience with Gordon, Bill seemed to think she did everything right. It was still hard to believe that two men could view her so entirely differently. But it was Bill she trusted now, and whose opinions she respected. But she had made a decision to stay with Gordon in spite of it, for her children's sake, and she had to make the best of it.

Sophie left the house a little while later, and Gordon and Isabelle had dinner in the dining room. But after the tone of their exchange that morning, very little was said by either of them. Isabelle didn't want to anger him further, and his entire aura warned her not to talk to him. It was never said, but understood, as though even conversation with him were an imposition, and wouldn't be of any interest to him. All she ever talked about were the children anyway, which bored him. Isabelle said not a word all through dinner, and after coffee, she went back upstairs to Teddy's room. Gordon barricaded himself behind his doors as usual. As he left her, he said only that he had work to do. And as she lay in her bed later, she was thinking about everything Sophie had said. She was a bright, healthy, perceptive girl, and her father's behavior and attitudes appalled her, but her mother's bothered her more. She wanted her to stand up to him, and instead Isabelle defended him, no matter what he did to her. It made Sophie sad for her.

Isabelle never heard Gordon leave that night. But she discovered that his bed hadn't been slept in when she went to find him for an important phone call from New York in the morning. She couldn't imagine where he'd been, and there was no one to ask. She was startled by what she saw, and then suddenly wondered if he did that often. She had never been aware of it before. But she was far more willing now to open her eyes. She said nothing to anyone, and told the people on the phone to call him at the office. She would have liked to call him and ask him herself where he'd been, but she wouldn't stoop to that. Instead, she went about her business through the day, as Bill had suggested, took care of Teddy, and waited for Gordon to come home again in the evening. And when he did, she asked him nothing, said nothing. Confrontation wasn't her style, and Gordon's rejections no longer mattered to her. She had Bill, and the love they shared. She went to bed after dinner, and long after she was asleep, Gordon went out and closed the door quietly behind him, careful so no one would hear.

Chapter Thirteen

Bill left the hospital in London five days after Is-abelle had gone back to Paris. The days there without her had depressed him immeasur-ably. He was so lonely without her, but he knew he had to get used to it. And in his own life, he had Mount Everest to climb now. The therapists had mapped out what he would have to do in the coming year, but even as they de-scribed it to him, they warned him not to set his sights too high. The likelihood of his regain-ing the use of his legs would have to be a mira-cle, they felt, and although they admired his determination, they didn't want him to be crushed if all he did was manage to stand on braces and on crutches, or have to resign him-self to permanently being in a wheelchair. They were almost certain he would remain confined to the wheelchair. They thought it extraordi-nary that he had any sensation at all, given the extent of the damage to his spine. But there was a big difference, they explained, between having some feeling in his legs and being able to walk on them.

The nurses all hugged him and cried when he left. They had all fallen in love with him, and had been touched by his deep attachment to Isabelle. They thought that the fact that they had lived through their accident was one of life's great gifts. And it had given them all new faith and hope. Everyone in the intensive care ward had been amazed that they had both survived.

He promised to send them all postcards from New York, and ordered gifts from Harrods for each of them. He bought them all beautiful gold bracelets, and his doctor a Patek Philippe watch. He was generous and kind and thoughtful and appreciative, and he would be sorely missed. A nurse and an orderly took him to the airport and settled him on his plane, representatives of the rehab center were picking him up at Kennedy in New York.

Bill had called his daughters to tell them he was coming in, and both of them had promised to visit him the next day at the rehab center. He didn't call Cynthia, intentionally, he was trying to keep some distance between them. He thought it was better that way, given the divorce. He had settled a considerable amount of money on her, given her their estate and several cars, and an impressive investment portfolio. He had filed the divorce the month before. She had been stunned by the speed with which he'd moved, and his generosity, and she still believed it was because he was hoping to marry Isabelle, but Bill had told her clearly and honestly that he was not. And if Cynthia hadn't seen how in love Bill was with Isabelle, she would have believed him.

He was able to sit in his seat on the plane comfortably for the first few hours, but after a while his neck and back began to hurt. He was wearing braces on both, and he stretched out, grateful to be traveling on his own plane. It made an enormous difference for him. His doctor had suggested that he refrain from eating or drinking on the flight, which he did. They had also suggested he take a nurse on the flight, but he had resisted the idea, and regretted it once they took off. But he had wanted to prove to himself how independent he was. He was absolutely exhausted and in considerable pain by the time they landed in New York.

There were two male nurses and a driver waiting for him at the airport. He was whisked through customs without having anything checked, and there was a van outside fitted with a gurney. The nurses had taken him to the bathroom first, and he thought about stopping to call Isabelle, but he decided to wait until they reached the rehab center. He was in too much pain, and he was anxious to lie down in the van.

"How's that? Better?" one of the nurses asked as they settled him in the van, and Bill smiled.

"That was a hell of a long flight." Even lying down for part of the trip, it had been hard for him. He had reclined his seat into a bed, but even doing that, it had been at a slight angle, which had caused him excruciating pain. It reminded him again, very unpleasantly, that he still had a long way to go in his recovery, but he was still certain he would get there eventually. But it was upsetting to him to realize how far he had to go.

They had brought him a Thermos of coffee, some cold drinks, and a sandwich. And he felt a lot better by the time they pulled out. It was a beautiful fall day, and the air was still warm.

It took them half an hour to get to the rehab hospital, it was a large sprawling place with manicured grounds on the outskirts of New York. It looked more like a country club than a hospital, but Bill was too tired to look around when they arrived. All he wanted was to get to bed. He signed in and noticed men and women in wheelchairs and on crutches all around.

There were two teams playing basketball from wheelchairs, and people on gurneys watching as they cheered the teams on. The atmosphere seemed friendly and active, and people seemed to be full of energy for the most part. But it depressed Bill anyway. This was going to be his home for the next year, or at best nine months. He felt like a kid who had been sent away to school, and he was homesick for Isabelle and St. Thomas', and all the friendly familiar faces he had come to know there. He didn't even let himself think about his home in Connecticut. That was part of the distant past now. And when he was wheeled into his room, there were tears in his eyes. He had never in his entire life ever felt as vulnerable or as lonely.

"Is everything all right, Mr. Robinson?" All he could do was nod.

It looked like a standard room in a clean, respectable hotel. Despite the price, which was exorbitant, it wasn't luxurious, there were no frills, and few comforts. There was decent modern furniture, clean carpeting, a single hospital bed, like the one he'd slept in next to Isabelle, and a single poster of the South of France on the wall. It was a reproduction of a watercolor that looked familiar to him, and he thought he recognized Saint-Tropez. He had his own bathroom, and the light in the room

was good. There was a fax in the room, a
hook-up for a computer, and his own phone.
They told him he couldn't have a microwave in
the room, not that he cared. They didn't say it,
but they didn't want clients isolating and eating
by themselves. They wanted him to eat in the
cafeteria with everyone else, join the sports
teams, use the social rooms, and make friends.
It was all part of the process of rehabilitation
that they had established for him. And socializ-
ing in his new circumstances was part of it. No
matter who he was, or had been, or perhaps
would be again, they wanted him to be an active part of their community while he was
there.

Seeing the hook-ups in his room reminded
him that he needed to call his secretary. His political pursuits had dwindled to almost nothing
in the past two and a half months. He couldn't
do what he needed to from his bed, and she'd
had to cancel everything for him. There was no
way he could introduce people to each other,
plan campaigns, or shepherd his protégés
through the process of running a successful
campaign. For that, he needed to be hands on
and very much on deck. And he realized again,
as he looked around his room, that if he were
even able to go back to it, that part of his life
would have to lie dormant for another year.

There was a small refrigerator in his room filled with the same things as a minibar in a good hotel, sodas and snacks and chocolate bars, and he was pleased and surprised to find two half-bottles of wine. And as he popped open a Coke, after the nurses left, he took a sip and looked at his watch. He wanted to call Isabelle, but he was also afraid that Gordon might be home. But he was too lonely this time not to call. He was planning to hang up if Gordon answered the phone.

The phone answered on the second ring, and he heard her voice. It was eleven o'clock at night for her, but she sounded wide awake. Her familiar soft voice went instantly like a knife to his heart, as he longed for her.

"Is this a good time?" he asked immediately, and she laughed.

"For what, my love? Actually, it's a very good time, I just wish you were here. Gordon is in Munich for the night. How was the trip?"

"Painful," he said honestly, without whining about it. "I'm in jail." He looked around the room again, and although he knew it wasn't bad, as those things went it was top of the line, but it depressed him profoundly anyway. "I hate it here," he said, sounding like a homesick kid calling from boarding school.

"Now come on, be a good sport. It'll do

wonderful things for you," she encouraged him, just as she would have Sophie when she went away to school. "You'll get used to it, and before you know it, you'll be all through. Maybe you'll only have to stay a few months." She was trying to encourage him, but he sounded very down, and her heart went out to him. She wished there were something she could do for him, but at this distance, it was very hard. They both had to fight their battles on their own. And in many ways, his was much tougher than hers.

"What if I'm here for two years?" he asked, sounding like a kid again.

"That won't happen. I'll bet you're finished in no time. What kinds of people are at the center?" They had both been afraid it would be full of elderly people recovering from strokes, and he'd have little in common with them. But from the little he'd seen, most of the patients he'd observed on the way in looked young, even younger than he. Many of them were there as a result of skiing accidents, or disastrous dives into pools, car accidents, gymnastic tragedies. The people who were motivated to be there were, for the most part, young, with long, potentially productive lives ahead of them.

"They look okay, I guess." He sighed, and

looked out the window at the Olympic-size outdoor pool, and he could see a number of people swimming and wheelchairs parked all around. "I just don't want to be here. I want to go back to Washington and work, or be in Paris with you. I feel as though life is passing me by." But neither of the places he wanted to be were possibilities for him. And what he feared most was that they never would be again. He would have to be able to sit for extended periods, to hold up for long hours, travel freely on his own, take care of himself, and have endurance, mobility, and clarity of mind, if he was to return to his career. And he was also afraid that there would be some psychological resistance to him now. People's perceptions could be very strange, and maybe they would feel that if he was in a wheelchair and impaired in any way, he might not be able to run a successful campaign. It was hard to predict what strange turns people's prejudices would take. It was of quintessential importance to him, for an abundance of reasons, to get back on his feet and walk again.

In Isabelle's mind, as far as she was concerned, she didn't care if he never did, but she wanted that very much for him. But her love for him was going to be in no way affected by whether or not he walked again. She had told him as

much, but it was an obsession with him. He refused to be dependent on anyone. Not Cynthia,
not his children, not his co-workers or friends,
and certainly not Isabelle. If he couldn't protect
her, take care of her, stand up like a man next to
her, and make love to her, then he had no intention of being in her life. There was a lot riding on his recovery, in his own mind, and
although he hadn't spelled it out fully to her, Isabelle sensed that the stakes were high. All she
could do now was be there on the phone and
pray for him.

"How is Teddy?" he asked solicitously. "And
how are you?"

"I'm fine. Sophie went back to school yesterday. Teddy is still very tired, and I'm worried
about his heart. Sometimes I think he's getting
worse, and then he has a good day and feels
better. It's hard to say. But his spirits are good."
They had been ever since she'd gotten back, but
her instincts told her that the doctor was right
and Teddy was weaker than he'd been in a long
time. He had lost considerable ground.

"Olivia and Jane went back to college last
week, but they said they'd come to see me this
weekend."

"Will Cynthia come too?" She was somewhat
jealous of her, though she hated admitting it to
him. He knew it anyway, and it flattered him.

And actually, Cynthia had offered to come with the girls, but he thought it better not. He didn't explain it to Isabelle, because he hadn't told her about the divorce. He still believed that it put less pressure on her if she thought they were both married. She wouldn't think he was waiting for her that way, or looking for someone else. If she ever got free of Gordon, he'd be waiting for her. But he thought it would only complicate things if he told her that. So he continued the fantasy with her that he and Cynthia were staying married and all was well.

"I think Cynthia's out of town for a few days," he said casually. Isabelle always thought it singularly callous of Cynthia to make such a point of leading her own life, but she made no comment about it to him.

"Gordon's in Munich for the night, he's at some conference for the bank. He's coming home for the weekend. I think he has plans," she filled him in, but she was never included in Gordon's plans anymore, and she had no real desire to be. Ever since London, and Bill, she felt entirely separate from him, and it no longer irked her that Gordon didn't invite her to anything. He just assumed that she'd want to stay home with her son, and he was right. And she was still very tired. She went to bed early at night, and sat with Teddy all day. She'd gone out to lunch with Sophie before she left, and just that effort had left Isabelle feeling drained. It was going to be several more months, the doctor said, before Isabelle felt like her old self. And even longer for Bill. He knew that now. The plane trip had been torturous for him, he hadn't been in that much pain in months, and he still felt it as he talked to her.

"What are you going to do tonight?" Isabelle asked in a gentle voice. She could hear how tired and sad he was, and she was worried about him.

"Go to bed, I think. There's no room service, but I'm not hungry." He was in too much pain to eat, and he didn't want to take painkillers. He had weaned himself off them weeks before, and had worried all along about getting addicted to them. He hadn't, fortunately, but he didn't want to start taking them again.

"Maybe you should take a look around." She didn't like the idea of him staying alone in his room, it sounded too lonely, and she was afraid he would get too depressed.

"I'll do it tomorrow. They don't give you much choice. I start therapy tomorrow at seven A.M., and I won't get back to my room until five o'clock." It was a strict regimen, but he had chosen the hospital for just that reason. He thought if he worked harder, he'd get quicker results. And all he wanted now, even before he started, was to leave. "I'll call you in the morning when I get up." It would be noon for her, and he knew that was a good time. If he called her when he got back to his room at the end of the day, it would be eleven o'clock at night, and if Gordon answered, it could cause problems for her.

"I can call you sometimes," she offered, but he said it was probably better for her if he called, which was true.

"I'll call you tomorrow, sweetheart," he said finally, too exhausted to talk anymore, even to her. His back was killing him, his neck was stiff, his spirits were down, and he felt like he was on another planet from her and the life he had once known. He was back in the States finally, but it didn't do him any good. He was out in the middle of nowhere on a desert island, as he saw it, and he was condemned to be there for a year. It was not a cheering thought.

"I love you, my darling," she whispered into the phone. And after they hung up, she lay on her bed and thought about him for a long time. She wished that she could put her arms around him and hold him and comfort him, but at this distance all she could do was love him and send him good thoughts.

Bill got up the next morning at six o'clock. He

had never gotten up out of bed after he talked to her. He had just rolled over and gone to sleep in his clothes, and he woke up when the alarm went off. He was jet-lagged and tired and he could hardly move. He rang for an orderly to help him get into his chair again, and make his way into the shower. Half an hour later he felt better, and he called Isabelle before he left the room.

"How do you feel, sweetheart?" she asked, sounding concerned. He sounded brighter and in better spirits than he had the night before.

"A lot better than last night. I was wiped out."

"I know you were." She was smiling. Teddy had woken up in good spirits, and it was a beautiful September day. It was noon for her.

"I'm sorry if I whined at you last night. I felt like a kid in boarding school." She smiled as he said it, he had sounded that way to her too.

"I know. I wanted to fly over and bring you home," she said sympathetically.

"That's what mothers do. Fathers just tell the kid to shape up. It's a basic difference between the two sexes. The girls always got homesick when they went to camp. Cindy always wanted to pick them up early, and I thought they should stick it out."

"Who won?" Isabelle sounded amused. It was a softer side of Cynthia she had never heard him talk about, and she liked her better for it.

She would have said the same thing. She had never sent either of her children away until Sophie went to university, and Isabelle thought that was too soon. She had wanted her to stay in Paris and go to the Sorbonne, instead of going to Grenoble.

"She did, of course. I was always away and couldn't enforce my rules. By the time I'd get back, they'd be home."

"Good for her."

"Well, I'd better get going, and see what tortures they have in store for me. I'm sure they've honed it to an art form here." But he was in no way prepared for the intense regimen they had planned for him.

After the moderate therapy they had started in London, this was like joining the Marines. He did calisthenics as best he could, from his chair. They had him lifting weights to strengthen his upper body, and working with exercise machines. There was special therapy for his neck, a long workout in the pool, and special exercises for his legs. He had half an hour for lunch, and barely had time to get to the cafeteria, or speak to anyone, and by five o'clock when he got back to his room, he was so tired, he could hardly move. He couldn't even get out of his chair to get on the bed, and he had to ring for an orderly, who smiled when he heard Bill groan.

"Had a good workout today, Mr. Robinson?" He was a young African American who had trained with the Jets, and been injured himself five years before. He was studying to become a physical therapist. Bill was encouraged to see that there was no sign of his previous injuries and he was in fantastic shape, he was only twenty-six years old.

"Are you kidding?" Bill looked at him miserably. "I think they tried to kill me today."

"You won't even feel it a couple of weeks from now. It'll be a piece of cake for you." It was hard to imagine, and he offered to give Bill a massage. And after he left, Bill decided to skip dinner and stay in bed. He was dozing off, when there was a knock on his door that roused him again, and he asked sleepily who it was. When he opened his eyes, a young man in a wheelchair was already in his room.

"Hi. I'm Joe Andrews. I'm in the room next to you. Can I talk you into a basketball game at eight o'clock?" Bill groaned as he looked at him, and then laughed. Andrews was sitting at ease in his wheelchair, and appeared to have the use of only one arm. He was a handsome boy and looked to be in his early twenties. He'd been in a car accident that had killed four other people six months before.

"A basketball game? Are you kidding? You

could use me as the ball. I don't think I'll ever be able to sit up again, let alone move."

"It's tough at first," Joe Andrews said as he smiled at him. "It gets easier after a while. It's a great place. Six months ago I was strapped to a body board, and all I could move were my eyes. I thought I'd be happy if I could just scratch my nose." It was sobering to think of him that way, and with another moan, Bill sat up.

"You've got age on your side," Bill pointed out to him, but he had always been in great shape until he got hit by the bus. "I'm an old man."

"There's no such thing here. The captain of the basketball team is eighty-two, he had a stroke. He played for the Yankees sixty years ago."

"I'm out of my league. I should have just enlisted in the Marines."

"It would have been easier, but it's not as much fun. There are some really nice-looking women here." It was like going to college in a funny way, and Bill decided instantly that he liked the boy. He had laughing eyes, and a nice smile and bright red hair.

"Sounds like you've been busy here." Joe hadn't been, but he was looking again at least. The girl he'd been engaged to had been killed in the car accident, but he didn't mention it to Bill.

"I go to New York on weekends. Maybe you'd like to come with me sometime. It takes twenty minutes on the train."

"That's a thought. Right now, I don't think I can move."

"Why don't you come watch? I'll introduce you to some of the guys." He was determined to bring Bill into the center of things. Joe was the senior floor rep, and he had volunteered to do just what he was doing with Bill. It was important for morale to get clients involved in more than just their own therapy. It was what had saved Joe's life. When he'd gotten to the rehab center, he'd been contemplating suicide after the accident. And now he'd come through the worst of it, and was on his way, and back into life.

"What about the girls?" Bill teased.

"Are you married?" Joe asked, drawing him out. He was great with people, and Bill could see he was a really nice kid. It saddened him to see him sitting in a wheelchair.

"Nope. I'm getting divorced."

"That's too bad. There are a couple of girls on the team. One of them is eighteen."

"I think I'd like to stay out of jail, if I can manage it. How old is the other one?"

"Sixty-three." Joe grinned.

"I'll take her. She's more my age."

"How old are you?"

"Fifty-two. Going on ninety today."

"Have you had dinner yet?"

"I thought I'd skip it tonight." He had skipped it the night before too. It was just too much trouble to go out again once he was in his room.

"That's a bad idea. I'll pick you up at six-thirty, you can decide about the game after that." He didn't ask, and before Bill could object, Joe had left his room.

He had done his job well, and in spite of himself, Bill was back in his wheelchair at six-fifteen, and he felt better than he had an hour before. He'd showered and shaved and combed his hair. He was wearing a T-shirt and jeans, and he and Joe looked like two kids as they headed to the dining hall together. Joe seemed to know everyone on the way, and introduced Bill to everyone he could. Bill knew by then that Joe was twenty-two, from Minneapolis. He had graduated from college, and wanted to go to law school the following year. He had two sisters and an identical twin who had been in the accident with him. His twin and his fiancée had been killed, and both people in the other car. Joe's twin had been driving, when the other car hit them head-on, on a snowy night. A lot of the people at the hospital had tough stories, kids who had just been fooling around and doing nothing more serious than most kids did, a woman who'd been shot in the spine during a convenience store robbery when she stopped in the middle of the day to buy Cokes for her kids, people who'd had accidents and traumas of all kinds. Many of them were not only in physical therapy, but getting psychiatric help as well, like Joe and the woman who'd been shot in the spine. When they left the hospital, the idea was that they would be able to lead full, productive, astonishingly normal lives.

There were two hundred residents, and another three hundred or more came to the facility on an outpatient basis every day. But the ones who lived there formed a core of people for the most part who cared about each other and became like family during their extended stays. The noise in the cafeteria reminded Bill not so much of college, but of a cocktail party in full swing. Everyone was laughing, talking, making plans, and either bragging about their victories of the day, or complaining that they were being worked too hard. But Bill realized he hadn't seen that many smiling faces in a long time. It wasn't at all what he'd expected when he arrived.

"There's a tennis tournament next week, if

you play." Joe filled him in as he talked to about six people at once, at least four of them girls. But he wasn't unusual there, there were a lot of good-looking young guys in wheelchairs, Bill guessed that about half of the people he saw were in their twenties and male. The other half covered a wide range of ages, and less than half of them were women or girls. Three-quarters of the population were male. They seemed to get into more trouble, or had worse luck, drove their cars too fast, took greater risks, or played dangerous sports. But there were also a number of men and women Bill's age. And at their table there was a beautiful girl whose face was ex- quisite and whose speech was slurred. She was a model and had fallen down a flight of marble stairs at a shoot and gotten a tremendous head injury. She'd been in a coma for eight months, and as Bill talked to her, he realized how fortu- nate he and Isabelle had been. The girl's name was Helena, and her best friend in the rehab center was a young ballerina who'd been in a car accident, and was determined to dance again. They were people who had faced re- markable challenges, and were making an as- tonishing effort to overcome the hands they'd been dealt. Bill was overcome with admiration for them.

By the time dinner was over, he was feeling

better again, and Joe and Helena had talked him into coming to the game, but he didn't want to play. He just wanted to watch.

"They're pretty good," Helena smiled at him and commented in her slurred speech. She was in a wheelchair too, but only because she had vertigo from her head injury and sometimes fell with no warning. She felt safer in the chair. Bill was struck by how beautiful she was, and thought she looked like Isabelle. He knew from Joe that she'd worked in New York, Paris, and Milan, and been on the cover of *Vogue* and *Harper's Bazaar* before her accident. According to Joe, she was doing really well. "Next time you should play," she encouraged Bill.

"Why don't you?" he teased, she was taller than several of the men, he could tell by her endless legs. She was wearing shorts and sandals as she sat in the chair next to his, and her toes were impeccably pedicured, and she had bright red polish on her nails. A lot of the young men were keeping their eyes on her, but her boyfriend was the photographer she'd been working for the day of the shoot, and he was incredibly devoted to her. They were getting married when she got out of the hospital, and she was wearing an engagement ring Cynthia would have described as the size of an egg.

They sat watching the game side by side, and

there was lots of screaming and shouting and encouragement for both teams. Everyone seemed happy and excited no matter who scored. The fact that they were playing at all was a victory for all of them. And Bill was impressed by the spectacular gym.

"Are you married?" Helena asked casually. Everyone knew she was engaged, and crazy about her fiancé. She was just curious about Bill. He was a handsome man, and in another life she would have been attracted to him, but she was happy now with her fiancé.

"Divorced. Almost. In a few months."

"That's too bad," she sympathized. "You'll be very popular here," she grinned. But Bill thought he'd never seen so many good-looking men in one place, and most of them half his age. He wasn't worried about it, he didn't consider himself available. He was in love with Isabelle. "Do you have a girlfriend?" He was about to say no, and then decided to be honest with her.

"Yes."

"Are you going to marry her?" She cut right to the chase.

"No." And then he threw caution to the winds. He had no need for secrets here. "She's married to someone else, and she's going to stay that way. It's just as well now."

"What does that mean?" She looked intently

at him, and missed seeing one of the major scores in the game. The din around them in the gym was deafening, but she was more interested in what Bill had just said.

"It means that she doesn't need my problems added to her own. She has a sick kid. She doesn't need a husband in a wheelchair." It seemed obvious to him.

"Why not? What difference does that make? You'd better get over that. Is that how she feels?"

"Probably not. But it's how I feel. I'm not going to be a burden to her."

"That's nice of you. What about them?" She pointed to the guys in the game, crashing into each other, rolling around the court at full speed, with wide smiles and sweat running down their faces. They were having a great time. "Do they look like a burden to you?"

"I'm not married to them. But maybe I'd think so if I were. Look, Helena, I can't dance, I can't stand, I can't walk down the street, I don't even know if I can still work anymore. I can't inflict that on someone else." And he didn't even mention to her that the last time he had made love, he had failed.

"What were you? An ice skater?" she asked, raising an eyebrow at him. She was a bright girl, and he already liked her style.

"I'm in politics."

"Is that something you can't do sitting down? That's news to me."

"You know what I'm talking about."

"Yeah, I do. I used to feel that way too, and then I figured out how stupid it was. I talk funny now. I forget things sometimes, I fall down in the middle of talking to someone. Pretty embarrassing. And I don't know if I can work anymore either. But I'll be goddamned if I'm going to give up my life over it. I'm better than that. I can do other things. I still look halfway decent," she said modestly, and he rolled his eyes, they were friends now. Friendships here formed quickly, it was like shipboard, and the bond they had in common held them fast. "I'm still smart, even if I sound stupid. And if that's not good enough for someone, then to hell with them. My fiancé doesn't give a damn about all this, and if he did, I wouldn't want him anyway. Maybe you should give the lady a chance to make up her own mind."

"It's a little more complicated than that."

"What isn't?" Helena said, unimpressed, watching the game again for a minute, and then she turned her eyes back to Bill. "Just make sure you don't decide that for the wrong reasons. I'd bet my ass that if she's worth your loving her, and she probably is, she wouldn't give a damn if you can walk or not." He knew that what she was saying was true. But for Isabelle there was still the problem of Teddy. And for Bill, whether he continued seeing her or not depended on whether or not he could walk again. It was a condition he had imposed on himself, unbeknownst to Isabelle.

"You know, Helena, that's a bet I'd like to take," he was teasing her right back. But he had heard everything she'd said, and was profoundly touched, not only by her own courage, but for her candor with him.

"What bet?"

"Your ass," he said, and she laughed out loud.

"Calm down, big boy. You're in love, and I'm engaged."

"It's a damn shame," he said with good humor. They sat together like old friends for the rest of the game.

Joe's team had won when he finally joined them again. He was happy and sweaty, and a gorgeous kid, Bill noticed again as the three of them went back to the cafeteria for something to drink afterward, and most of the members of both teams and their supporters were there. It had been a fun evening, and when Helena left them finally to go back to her room, Joe grinned at Bill.

"So, is she breaking her engagement?" Joe asked with a grin. "We've all tried."

"I'm working on it, but not yet." They both knew he was only kidding. She was madly in love with her fiancé, and Joe said he was a great guy. They were planning to be married in the spring, and Helena was determined to walk down the aisle under her own steam. And from what he'd seen that night, the indomitable spirit that shone from her like a beacon, Bill figured she could do it. She was a terrific girl.

"She has a sister who comes to visit her," Joe commented to Bill as they rolled back to their dorm. "She looks like a frog." Bill laughed out loud. "They must have had a different mother or something. Helena fixed me up with her, and I was really surprised. But she's very nice." The two men exchanged a very male glance, and Bill laughed again.

"It works that way sometimes."

"So will you play with us next time?" Joe asked as they rolled down the hall to their rooms.

"I think I'd rather watch." He had enjoyed the conversation with Helena, and was thinking about what she'd said, but he still didn't agree with her. He was not going to be a burden or an invalid in anyone's life, and surely not Isabelle's, even if they only met a couple of times a year. That was a headache she just didn't need. She had enough in her life without that.

"Do you want to come into New York to-morrow? Some of the other guys are coming with me. We're going to dinner and a show."

"I'd love to," Bill said kindly, "but my daughters are coming to see me. They're coming up from school." Olivia was coming up from Georgetown, and Jane from NYU.

"How old are they?" Joe asked with interest. He was definitely interested in girls, although he hadn't actually dated anyone since the death of his fiancée.

"Nineteen and twenty-one. I'd like you to meet them if you're around when they get here."

"We're not going to the city till six o'clock," Joe said as they got to Bill's room. "I've got a swim meet tomorrow, but I'll be here." He had been the captain of his college swimming team.

"I'll look for you," Bill promised, and then they both went to their rooms. Bill felt bad because he hadn't had time to call Isabelle that night, but it was too late to call her now. It was five in the morning for her. And then he decided to wait an hour and call her when she got up.

He lay in bed and read for an hour, trying not to fall asleep, and then at midnight, he called. She was very quick to answer the phone, and she sounded relieved to hear his voice.

"Are you okay? I was worried about you."

"I'm fine. I went to watch a basketball game. They're running my ass ragged here. But it's a very impressive place." He told her about the people he'd met and the stories he'd heard, and the therapy he'd done all day.

"My God, I don't think I could do any of that," she said, impressed.

"I'm not sure I can either. You only get one day off. The girls are coming tomorrow, it'll be good to see them." He hadn't seen them in two months, and he missed them both. He was surprised to find he missed Cynthia too. But he didn't tell Isabelle that. After thirty years, Cynthia's presence had become a habit in his life that was hard to break, even if it was a habit he felt no longer belonged in his life. "How are you, sweetheart?"

"I'm fine. I just got up. Teddy's still asleep." They chatted for a little while, and then finally hung up when she heard the boy stir, and she was still thinking of Bill when she went to check on Teddy. She gave him his morning medications, and he went right back to sleep. She went to her own room and dressed, and stood looking at the garden for a long time, thinking of Bill. It saddened her to realize that it would be a long time before they saw each other again, but it was for a good cause. But she knew it might be as long as a year.

And in his own bed that night, Bill smiled to himself as he thought of her and drifted off to sleep. Helena's words came back to him just as he was dozing off, and they made sense to him, but he still thought she was wrong for him. He didn't belong in Isabelle's life, or anyone's, if he couldn't learn to walk again. He believed it to his very core, although his belief was counter to everything he was seeing here. But Helena was beautiful and young, and a woman . . . she just didn't understand how he felt . . . it was different for him . . . he was a man. He knew that if he couldn't walk back into Isabelle's life, he couldn't be there at all.

Chapter Fourteen

When Olivia and Jane came to visit Bill the next day, they were thrilled to see him, and they both thought he was looking well. He showed them around the hospital and the grounds, introduced them to the people he'd met, and then found a quiet corner to sit with them outside in the warm September air. It was a sunny afternoon, and both girls were looking happy and well. They had a lot to say, they talked about their mother a lot, and said they'd missed him, and wished he'd come home. They were still both very upset about the divorce, but they were both distracted by school.

They went to the cafeteria for a hamburger in the late afternoon, before they left, and when they got there, they ran into Joe. Bill introduced the three young people to each other, and they seemed to hit it off immediately. Olivia knew someone he'd gone to school with in Minneapolis. The world of college kids was small. And he asked Jane how she liked NYU, he was thinking of going to law school there. She told him she loved it, and the conversation continued at a lively pace without further input from Bill. Joe joined them for a hamburger, and they talked about all the subjects that interested them. And the fact that Joe was in a wheelchair seemed entirely irrelevant to all of them. No one noticed, no one cared, and Bill observed as they left the cafeteria and walked back to his dorm, Olivia walked alongside her father, and Jane was walking along next to Joe. He seemed to be very taken with her, and asked if she'd like to go to a movie with him and some of his friends that night in New York. But she said she had other plans, and seemed sorry she couldn't go. She told him to call her another time, or she'd call him. They seemed to have a lot in common, and he hung around almost till they left, and then discreetly left them to their family gathering. He was sensitive and polite and intelligent, and Bill commented on how much he liked him once Joe left.

"He's nice" was all Jane contributed, and Olivia laughed at her.

"Never mind 'nice,' he's hot!" He was a great-looking kid, and Bill was amused by how they all related to each other at that age. They reminded him of puppies at play.

The girls were on their way to stay with their mother that night. And Bill went back to his room when they left. And when he got there, Joe was waiting for him, looking concerned.

"I'd like to ask you something," he asked nervously.

"Sure, Joe, what's up?" He assumed it was another basketball game.

"I wanted to know if . . . actually . . . what I was thinking was . . ." This was serious, the bright personable boy was suddenly severely tongue-tied, and blushing to the roots of his red hair.

"This must be good," Bill teased. "It sounds like you want to borrow my car. I don't have one, and neither of us can drive."

Joe Andrews laughed. "I was wondering if you'd mind if . . ." He took a breath and plunged in, ". . . you'd mind if I call Jane sometime? I won't do it if you'd rather not, and she may not want to see me anyway . . . I mean . . . you know . . . it . . . well . . ."

"I think that's a great idea." She'd had a boyfriend they'd all hated for two years, and much to Bill's delight, they'd broken up the year before, and she hadn't been interested in anyone else since. "As far as I know, she's free and not spoken for, though I'm not always privy to those details. You'll have to check it out with her."

"She said I could call, and she gave me her mom's number and her number at school. But I wanted to ask you first." It was a nice thing to do, and Bill was touched.

"I'd say that's a hopeful sign," he smiled at the boy. "Better than Helena's sister then?"

"Are you kidding? You can't even compare the two of them. Jane is great! I mean . . . Helena's sister was a nice girl, but . . ."

"I know. She looked like a frog."

"Don't tell Helena I said that, she was a really sweet girl, and very smart." He looked panicked at the thought that Bill would tell Helena what he'd said.

"I promise I won't. I'm flattered you liked Jane. I'm very proud of both of them." Joe could see why. He had liked Olivia too, but she seemed older and more mature, and more reserved. He was more comfortable with Jane, and bowled over by her looks.

"Maybe I'll call her tonight."

"That's up to you," Bill said, looking fatherly. "From here on, I'm out of the loop. She's a big girl." But it touched him that this boy whom he liked so much had felt some kinship with Jane. It would be good for both of them, he thought. She needed someone bright and decent and kind in her life, and he deserved some happiness after what had happened to him. It never occurred to him for a moment that the match was unsuitable because he was in a wheelchair. He felt that way about himself, in terms of Isabelle, but for Joe and Jane, he thought it was fine. The dichotomy between those two ideas never even dawned on him.

The girls were pleased with their visit with Bill. And they both called him before they went back to school the next day. Jane didn't mention Joe again, so Bill had no idea if he'd called, and he didn't want to pry. And Cynthia got on the phone before they hung up, and asked if she could visit him that week. He hesitated and then agreed. There was no harm in it. After all, he'd told her himself that he was divorcing her so they could stay friends. Like the girls, he hadn't seen her in two months.

Two days later, on Tuesday, Cynthia came to have dinner with him. And when he rolled into the cafeteria next to her, she was amazed. People were smiling and laughing and looking happy, and it didn't seem to matter if they were walking, or in wheelchairs, or on gurneys strapped to body boards, everyone seemed to know each other and have something to talk about. It was one of the liveliest places she'd ever seen.

Helena stopped by to say hello to him, and he introduced her to Cynthia, who he explained was his wife.

"Who was that?" Cynthia asked afterward. "She's incredible looking."

"She's a model."

"Are you going out with her?" she asked, with a flash of jealousy in her eyes as he laughed.

"She's engaged."

"Lucky guy." Cynthia sounded relieved.

"That's what I said." Bill laughed. They went back to his room then, and talked for a while. She looked all right, but she sounded unhappy when they talked about the divorce.

"Are you sure that's what you want?" she asked him again. "It seems such a stupid thing to do now, at our age, after all these years."

"There was nothing left, Cyn. You know that." He was gentle but firm.

"Yes, there was. There still is. Look at us now. We've been talking for hours. I still love you, Bill. Can't we give it another chance?"

"I don't have anything left to give," he said honestly. "I love you too, but I ran out of gas. I'll always love you, but if we tried again, I think it would turn out the same way. If I go back to work, I'll be gone, you'll be pissed, you'll be doing your own thing again," he didn't spell it out, but they both knew what he meant. She'd be having affairs. "And if I can't go back to work, I'd be sitting around the house moping while you lead your life, and this time I'd be pissed. I'm better off on my own. And so are you, until you find the right guy."

"You were the right guy," she said, looking sad. She couldn't tell him he was wrong. But she felt bad leaving him on his own.

"Maybe I was, and maybe I wasn't. If I had been, it would have worked better than it did."

"I was stupid then. I've grown up."

"We both have. So let's be grown-up about this." She didn't say anything for a minute, and then sighed. She could tell he'd made up his mind. And once he did, Bill never changed course. That was just the way he was.

"What about Isabelle?" Cynthia asked then.

"What about her?" Bill didn't want to talk about her with Cynthia. "There's nothing to say."

"Why not?" Cynthia was surprised. He had been so obviously in love with her, it was hard to believe he was willing to let that go too. She wondered if he was depressed.

"She's married. I'm here. That's where it ends."

"It's not like you to give up that easily. Why are you doing that? She can't be happy with that iceberg I saw in London. He looks like a real son of a bitch."

"He is. But she has a very sick kid. I told you that. She can't leave Forrester, she thinks it would be too traumatic for the boy, and she can't provide for him. Believe me, Cyn, it's complicated. And besides, it's a moot point. I'm not going to inflict my problems on her on top of it. She deserves better than that. And so do you."

Cynthia looked at him carefully. "Is that why you wanted a divorce?" She was horrified at the thought.

"In part," he answered honestly, "but we have other reasons too. I did it for myself. And I'm going to stay away from her, for her sake. Unless they can work a miracle here."

"You know what they told you in London," she chided him, "that's not going to happen. You're not going to walk out of here on Rollerblades, Bill. Don't do that to yourself. Don't expect too much."

"I'm not. I figure whatever I get will be an improvement. I'm just saying that as long as I am like this, I'm out of her life."

"Does she know that?" Cynthia looked upset for him. It was a terrible reason to leave someone you loved, worse by far than the reasons why he wanted a divorce. And in some ways, she thought he was right to want a divorce, although she wouldn't have admitted it to him. If he'd have been willing to come back to her, she'd have taken him in a flash. But she knew only too well how indifferent she'd been to him for years. She only realized now fully what a great deal she'd had. And it was too late for them. "Does she know why you're ending it?" She felt sorry for them.

Bill shook his head. "She doesn't even know I am ending it. But you can only keep something alive at this distance, without seeing each other, for so long. We'll drift apart eventually. I'm going to be here for a long time. She has her own life. She'll get over it."

"I'm not so sure. It sounds like she doesn't have much else in her life. And more importantly, will you get over it? And why should you? If she's half the human being I suspect she is if you're so crazy about her, she's not going to give a damn what state you're in. You're better than most guys standing on two feet." It was exactly what Helena had said to him. "That's not what love is all about."

"Maybe not. But it's who I am. I will never do that to her. She's not leaving Forrester anyway. She can't." It didn't sound like a happy situation to Cynthia, and Bill was quiet for a long time after she left. Why was it that everyone was so insistent that it didn't matter if he was in a wheelchair permanently? It mattered to him. And he knew that, in the long run, it would matter to Isabelle. He refused to go down that path, with her or anyone else, no matter what Cynthia said. She had no idea what it was like. And he knew damn well that she could never have put up with it. She would have wound up hating him in the end for all that he wasn't and could no longer be or do. And he would never do that to Isabelle, not even if it meant lying to her and telling her he no longer cared. He was determined not to go back to see her in Paris if he couldn't walk off the plane. And as Cynthia had reminded him, there was almost no hope of that. If he had wanted that, he should have gone to Lourdes.

As time went on, the weeks at the rehab center went incredibly quickly for Bill. He was so busy, so tired, working so hard at all his therapies, that he hardly had time to come up for air.

Bill liked most of the therapists he worked with, they were bright and energetic and young, for the most part, and cared deeply about their patients. He was impressed with them right from the first. There was only one that he was unsure about, and he was unhappy when he was assigned to her. She was a sex therapist named Linda Harcourt, and he told her the first time they met that he had no interest in discussing therapy with her.

"Why not?" she asked, looking at him calmly from across her desk. She was a striking-looking woman, with good looks and an intelligent face, about his age. "Are you planning to give up sex?" she asked with a smile. "Or is everything okay?" He thought about lying to her, but something about the honesty in her eyes stopped him. He didn't want to talk to her about his nonexistent sex life, but something about the way she watched him told him she would think less of him if he ran away. And he couldn't think of a single reason why he should care what she thought of him, but for some unknown reason, he did. She was a person who commanded attention and respect. She seemed like a no-nonsense kind of woman, and at the same time, like the other therapists at the hospital, she seemed caring and warm. "I see on your chart that you're married," she said easily, "do you think your wife would like to speak to me?" She was almost certain that his sexual function had been affected by his injuries, and if he didn't want to discuss it with her, maybe his wife would. It was not unusual for men to feel cautious about speaking to her about their sexual issues at first. Sometimes talking to their wives, when they had them, was a gentler way in. But Bill was quick to shake his head.

"I'm getting a divorce," he said simply, closing that door firmly in her face.

"That's interesting. Was the accident part of that decision?" Bill looked away, didn't answer for a minute, and then shook his head again.

"Not really. We should have done it years ago. The accident just kind of brought things to a head."

And then the doctor became a little more direct. "Have you had intercourse since the accident, or tried to?" she asked so noncommittally that he was surprised himself when he answered her.

"Yes." There was no hint of how it had gone in the single word.

Her voice was gentle but not overly sympathetic. She was practical and down to earth, and there was nothing to suggest pity in her face. "How was it?"

"How was it for me?" He laughed at the old saw, and she smiled. It was what men usually said, particularly when it hadn't worked. She knew then what he would say next. "It wasn't, actually."

"No erection, or no ejaculation, or both?" she asked matter-of-factly, as though asking if he wanted cream or sugar in his coffee or both. It made it easier to answer her than he would have thought.

"Both. We never got that far."

"Was there sensation?" He nodded again. "Muted or distinct?"

"Distinct, actually. But I never got an erection, I could feel everything . . . well, almost everything. But it still didn't work."

"Often that takes time. Even with what you're telling me, it's still possible for things to improve to the point that you could have a relatively normal sex life later on. A lot of it is in how you feel about it. Success in this area can be a very creative thing." Just listening to her made him feel depressed. He didn't want to be "creative" or redefine his definition of "success." In fact, he didn't even want to try again. And who would he have tried with? Isabelle? She was in Paris, he wouldn't have been willing to inflict another fiasco on her, and he had no desire to ever sleep with Cindy again. It would have been even more humiliating to try it with her. He was no longer in love with her. "Do you have a partner?" Dr. Harcourt asked simply.

"No, I don't."

"That's all right. We can talk about it, and you can do some experimenting on your own.

A lot of this is how you feel about it, and how you deal with it, not just what you feel physically, or how you perform."

"I don't want to deal with it at all," he said bluntly, making a mental note to tell his doctor he didn't want to see the sex therapist again. "I don't think it's relevant for me at this point."

"Or ever?" Her eyes met his squarely, and he nodded.

"That's right, Doctor. I'm not going to make a fool of myself, knowing it won't work."

"What if it did? That's an important part of life to give up at your age."

"Sometimes things work out that way. I'm very involved in my work."

"So am I," she smiled at him, and handed him a book across her desk. It looked sensible and very medically oriented, he hesitated and then took it from her. "Required reading. There will be a quiz next week." He looked panicked at what she said, and she laughed. "Not really. But you might find it interesting."

She brought the meeting to a close then, they had gone far enough for the first day. She knew what his outlook was, what his experience had been the one time he tried it after the accident, and he had something worthwhile to read. She had time in the coming months to work with him, and she was far more optimistic than he was when he went back to his room. He tossed the book onto his bed with an angry expression, and sat staring out the window for a long time. He didn't want sex therapy, or to learn how to be "creative." He wanted to be a man, and if he wasn't going to be one, he had every intention of turning his back on everything he held dear, or Isabelle at least. And he certainly wasn't going to start dating, and experimenting to see if he could achieve and maintain an erection. He was determined to preserve his dignity, if nothing else.

He didn't tell Isabelle about meeting with Linda Harcourt the next time he spoke to her, it was the only facet of the rehab hospital that he did not share or describe to her. But he was still upset about his meeting with the sex therapist, and it was days later when he finally picked up the book, and was surprised at how informative it was. According to what he read, his first experience had not been atypical, and might still lead to considerable improvement as his injuries continued to heal. But he was still skeptical when he finished the book. He still believed he could turn out to be one of the vast category of men who had sensation but inadequate control, and erections that easily disappeared. And he had no desire to check for improvement, either with a partner or alone. It was easier for him, he insisted when he saw Linda Harcourt again a week later, to simply close the door on that part of his life. He also told her he didn't want to meet with her again, and after giving him two more books, she suggested they meet just once more. She said she wanted his feedback on the books, they were new to her. She was a very clever woman, and had an easy, open way. He actually liked her, he just didn't want to discuss his potential sex life with her. As far as Bill was concerned, he had become a eunuch, and he intended to stay that way. Humiliation, failure, and disappointment were of no interest to him. He preferred to stay celibate, and alone.

Some of his political pals had discovered he was there by then. A couple of them flew up from Washington to see him, and several others drove up from New York. They seemed to disregard his physical situation entirely once they were there, and spent all their time asking for his advice. And by Christmas, he was getting constant calls. It was hard enough to concentrate on his varied forms of therapy, and he tried to keep the political issues down to a dull roar. But his old cohorts were determined to pull him back into politics again. If nothing else, it was flattering, and he loved hearing about what everyone was doing, their hopes, and strategies, and plans. What they wanted from him, as they always had, was his help to assure the results.

He had agreed to have Christmas at the mansion in Greenwich with Cynthia and the girls. He had arranged for a limousine to take him there on Christmas Eve, and he had promised the girls he'd spend the night. He felt a little odd about it, but Cynthia had said he could stay in one of the two guest rooms on the main floor. He had heard from the girls that she had a new man in her life. Bill was happy for her, everything seemed to be going fine.

The car came for him at four o'clock, and an hour later, he was in Greenwich, pulling up the familiar drive to his old house. It was large and imposing, and he had always loved it, but it gave him a strange feeling being there, a nostalgia for times past. But as soon as Bill saw the girls, he felt better again.

They were decorating the tree when he rolled into the living room. There were Christmas carols on the stereo, and Cynthia looked better than he'd seen her in years. And when he turned to say hello to Olivia and Jane, his eyes grew wide as he saw Joe Andrews in the living room, in his chair.

"How did you get here?" Bill asked, looking amazed. He had seen him that afternoon in the dining hall, and Joe laughed and looked sheepish as Bill grinned. Joe was relieved that he didn't seem upset, and Jane came to stand next to Joe and held his hand.

"Jane picked me up on the way home from school," Joe explained. "We wanted to surprise you." The two of them were beaming, and Bill was intrigued. Joe hadn't said a word to him about Jane since the first time they'd met. He had no idea they'd been seeing each other, and things seemed to have advanced nicely in the last three months.

"Well, I am surprised." Bill smiled at both of them, he was pleased too. He thought Joe was a great kid.

They all had dinner together that night, and went to church afterward, and the next morning he and Joe wheeled into the living room as the girls came downstairs. Cynthia had already made breakfast for them, and her new friend joined them for lunch. He seemed like a very pleasant, intelligent man. He was a widower with four grown kids, and he seemed very fond of Cynthia, which pleased Bill. He was surprised himself to find that he felt neither jealous nor possessive about her, which confirmed to him once again that the divorce had been the right thing.

He and Joe rode back to the hospital together

on Christmas night, and talked about what a wonderful holiday it had been. The only thing missing for Bill had been Isabelle. He had called her several times, and she said that everything was fine there, but he could hear in her voice that she was unhappy and stressed. Gordon had been very difficult with her for the past two months. He was still punishing her for the affair he was sure she'd had, as though the accident hadn't been punishment enough. And Teddy seemed to be slowly losing strength. Sophie had come home for the holidays, and the day after Christmas she was going skiing with friends in Courchevelle.

"You're not upset at me for seeing Jane?" Joe asked Bill cautiously on the ride home, and Bill smiled at him and shook his head.

"She deserves a nice guy like you, and you deserve a lot better than a girl who looks like a frog." They both laughed at the memory of his blind date with Helena's sister. Helena had gone to New York for Christmas with her fiancé. They had all exchanged small gifts before they left.

Bill was sure that neither Jane nor Joe was serious about their relationship, so he wasn't concerned. They were too young to even think about it, but they were nice young people, and it was good to see them together. And Olivia had confessed that she had a new beau too. He was an assistant to a senator Bill knew. And it struck him on the way home that everyone had someone in their life, except him. He was still in love with Isabelle, but sitting in Paris with Gordon and her kids, she seemed light-years away. And for the first time in a long time, he felt lonely and sad when he got back to his room. Joe had gone off with friends as soon as he got back, and Jane was coming to see him the next day. Bill got into bed, and tried reading a book, but he couldn't keep his mind on it. And it was a relief when Jane called late that night.

"Are you mad at me, Daddy?" she asked cautiously. She had the same voice she'd used when she'd crashed his car in her junior year of high school, and he laughed easily.

"Of course not. Why would I be mad at you?" He smiled, thinking about her, and the good time they'd just had.

"I didn't know how you'd feel about me and Joe."

"How do you feel about him?" He was beginning to wish they'd had this conversation earlier at the house, so he could see her face while they talked. Her voice had a serious tone.

"I love him a lot. I've never known anyone like him before."

"I like him too. And he's been through some very tough things." Losing the use of his legs, the trauma of the accident, losing his fiancée and his twin. A whole life forever changed.

"I know. He told me all about it. Daddy, the girl he was engaged to died in his arms. He says he'll never forgive himself."

"From what I know of it, the accident wasn't his fault. What he has is survivor guilt because he's alive and other people died. He'll get over it in time."

"I want to be there for him, Dad." There was a long pause as Bill absorbed the full weight of what she'd just said.

"What are you saying to me, Janie?" All of a sudden he wondered if she was telling him they were getting married, and he didn't think it was a good idea. They were both too young, and Joe had a hard road ahead of him. There was no hope of his ever walking again. And Bill felt that was too much responsibility for her. As a romance, it was fine, a couple of years even, if it worked out for them, but he thought that any-thing more serious than that would be wrong for both of them.

"I think I'm telling you this is serious, Dad."

"I'm beginning to get that message. Does he feel that way too?"

"I think he does. We haven't really talked

about it, but he's that kind of guy." Bill liked that quality about him, Joe was a man of substance unquestionably. But he still didn't think it was right for them.

"I don't think you can consider anything too serious right now. You're still in school, and well . . . we'll talk about it sometime." He changed the subject then, and they talked about what a nice holiday they'd had, just like old times, only better actually. There had been no tension between him and Cynthia, and Bill liked her new friend. And then Jane said she'd stop in to say hi, when she came to see Joe the next day.

The conversation gave him a lot to think about when they hung up, and he told Isabelle about them late that night when they talked.

"I don't even want her to think about marrying that boy," he said honestly. "It's a shame too, because he's a great guy."

"Then why couldn't they get married one day? Lots of people get married at their age. They're young, but she sounds very mature for her age, and he's been through so much, poor boy."

"It would be a disaster for her, Isabelle. She needs someone who can keep up with her. She loves to ski and run and ride a bike. She'll want to have kids one day. He'll be stuck in that chair for the rest of his life. She deserves more than that." So did he, but he had no choice. Jane did.

"That's a terrible thing to say," Isabelle said, sounding upset. "What difference does it make, if she skis with friends, or dances with someone else? Are you telling me that if they love each other, you wouldn't want them to marry because he can't ride a bike? That's incredibly limited of you. I can't believe you mean something as stupid as that."

"I know what I'm talking about," he said stubbornly, frowning at his end.

"No, you don't!" she said firmly. It was the first argument they'd ever had. "I hope Jane's mother is smarter than you are. I've never heard anything so stupid. I hope you don't say that to Jane. She'd never forgive you for it, and she would be right."

They passed on to other subjects then, and they both calmed down. He told her about sharing Christmas with Cynthia and the girls, and of course didn't mention Cynthia's new man, since Isabelle didn't know Bill was out of her life. She told Bill that Gordon was leaving for Saint-Moritz the next day, to go skiing with friends. She was staying in Paris with Teddy, and they were going to see the New Year in alone. Sophie was already away.

Bill never ceased to be amazed by how inattentive Gordon was to Isabelle. But he was also relieved that Gordon wouldn't be there to torture her. His absence was a blessing in disguise. They talked for a long time that night, Bill was feeling open and vulnerable and a little sad. He hadn't seen her in four months, and missed her terribly, as she did him. They couldn't even talk about meeting again, he still had months of rehab ahead of him.

After the call, he lay there for a long time thinking about what Isabelle had said about Jane and Joe. He still disagreed with her, she didn't know what she was talking about, or how great the challenges could be for them. He wanted something far simpler for Jane, no matter how much he liked Joe. And for once he disagreed with Isabelle vehemently. She was too kind and idealistic to understand the implications of what she had said. And Bill was determined to say something to Jane about it, if need be. At least they didn't seem to be in a rush to make any decisions so far. And Bill hoped they'd come to their senses before they did.

He fell asleep dreaming of their Christmas tree, and for the first time in a long time, he dreamed of the white light again. He was walking toward it, holding Isabelle's hand, and when she turned toward him, he kissed her, and even in his dream he was disturbed to see Jane and

Joe coming toward them on the same path. He was in his wheelchair, and she was walking along slowly beside him, looking pained, and when she stopped in the dream, she turned to her father and asked why he hadn't warned her how hard it would be.

Chapter Fifteen

When Gordon left for Saint-Moritz, and Sophie for Courchevelle, the house was deadly quiet, as Isabelle sat in Teddy's room all afternoon, reading to him. It was a dark day outside, and the weather was unusually cold. It was drafty in the house and she had bundled Teddy up in a sweater over his pajamas, and tucked him in under a quilt.

He'd had a good Christmas, and got a ton of books and new games. She'd bought him a big teddy bear to keep him company. And all Isabelle wished she could have given him was good health. He was a constant source of worry to her.

Bill called Isabelle more frequently since he knew that Gordon was gone, and she called him once or twice. Bill was calling her twice a day. She longed for the days when they were in the hospital together, and could talk to each other anytime. She had no desire to go out, or see friends. And when she opened the mail right after Gordon left, she was surprised to see an invitation addressed to both of them. It was from a couple Isabelle knew were very fashionable. The wife was the head of a couture house, her husband was very old, had a title, and had been the head of an important bank. Isabelle couldn't recall ever meeting them but she assumed that Gordon had met them through some of his social activities that didn't include her, or perhaps he knew the husband from the bank. The invitation was very beautiful, and it was for their daughter's wedding in January. Isabelle made a mental note to send the bride a gift, and then forgot about it. She never went to events like that anymore, and Gordon no longer invited her to join him when he did.

She spent the next few days with Teddy, and talking to Bill. He was staying at the rehab center for New Year's Eve, and they were planning all kinds of festivities. He promised to call her at midnight in Paris on the thirty-first, so they could see the New Year in together, and she was going to call him at midnight in New York. She was waiting for his call when the telephone rang, and a woman at the other end sounded startled to hear her voice.

"Oh, how stupid of me!" she said, "I'm terribly sorry, I dialed the wrong number. I was calling to say I missed my flight." And with that, sounding even more confused, and a little drunk, she hung up. Who she was, and where she was flying to was a mystery to Isabelle. And she assumed the woman had dialed a wrong number entirely, and Isabelle hung up.

Bill called promptly, as he had said he would, they toasted the New Year in Paris, and Teddy was asleep by then. And Isabelle called him back at six in the morning, her time, when it was midnight for him. It had been a funny thing to do, but it amused them both. And after she spoke to him, she went downstairs to make a cup of tea, read the newspaper, and then came back upstairs. She had given Teddy's nurse the day off for New Year's Day, and she was happy to take care of him herself.

He slept late that day, and she started reading the paper again, and was surprised to see Gordon's name in a gossip column, mentioning his stay in Saint-Moritz. It said that he was there with friends, it mentioned the Aga Khan, Prince Charles, and a number of notables. And then she noticed another name. The column said that the Comtesse de Ligne was expected to join them for New Year's Eve as well. She was the woman who had invited them the day before to her daughter's wedding, and Isabelle could only assume that she and Gordon were friends. And then, as she thought of it, she remembered the call the night before, from the woman who said she had missed her flight. And for the oddest moment, the hair stood up on the back of Isabelle's neck. Why would the woman have called Gordon's house? And why on earth would Isabelle assume it had been the Comtesse de Ligne? Her first name was Louise. Isabelle couldn't imagine that she was involved with Gordon in any way, she was probably a friend of the other people going to Saint-Moritz. But the coincidence of it haunted her all day. And at six o'clock, Isabelle decided to do something totally insane. She had nothing else to do, and she wanted to hear Louise de Ligne's voice. She called information and got the number easily, sat thinking about it for a long moment, and then dialed. The phone answered at once at the other end.

"Allo? Yes?"

"Is this Madame de Ligne?" Isabelle asked, eliminating her title.

"Yes."

"I'm calling to confirm your flight to Saint-Moritz," Isabelle said, with no idea what she'd say after that.

"I told you an hour ago, I can't go now until tomorrow. My husband is very ill," she said, sounding irritated, but Isabelle had heard what she wanted to know. It was the same voice as the night before when the slightly confused, seemingly inebriated voice had called to say she'd missed her flight.

"Oh, I'm terribly sorry. That must have been my co-worker. Of course. I apologize, Madame de Ligne."

"Do I need to confirm it again?" the countess asked, sounding somewhat imperious. It was odd, she had the same dismissive quality of arrogance in her voice that Gordon had, Isabelle noticed. They sounded like twins.

"No, you don't. Have a good trip," Isabelle said pleasantly, and then hung up. And she didn't know why, but she was shaking at the other end, trying to figure out what she had learned. She had no idea why she'd been suspicious of her, but she knew she was. And suddenly she couldn't help wondering why the countess had called Gordon the night before. She didn't want to jump to conclusions, but it seemed obvious to her. She had a sixth sense that Gordon was having an affair with her. She had meant to call him in Saint-Moritz to tell him she'd missed her flight, and she'd obviously been drinking and called the Paris house instead.

"Who was that?" Teddy asked as he wandered into his mother's room, which he seldom did.

But he was startled when he saw the look on her face. "Is something wrong?"

"No, I . . . I was just calling Papa in Saint-Moritz. He was out."

"He's probably skiing, or gone to a dinner party," Teddy said sensibly, and she nodded her head.

And when Bill called later on, she mentioned it to him.

"It sounds pretty far-fetched to me," he said cautiously. "But women have amazing intuition about those things. I trust your gut more than my head. I've always known when Cynthia was sleeping with someone. She always looked different to me, she was friendlier and more jovial. I guess she was having more fun than she did with me." It had happened to him a lot, and he was almost always right when he guessed about her affairs.

"I don't even know why I called. It could have been a wrong number, but she was too polite about it. If it had been, she would have just hung up. And why would she invite us to her daughter's wedding?"

"If your theory is right, he probably told her you wouldn't come, and she wants him there. She screwed herself with good manners," Bill commented dryly, "she should have just invited him."

"I should frighten them both and accept," Isabelle said.

"Do you care?" Bill asked, curious at her reaction. He knew she hadn't slept with Gordon in years, but she was still married to him. And Gordon had been so nasty with her since the accident, that in some ways it would have been a relief to have something on him. It wasn't a nice way to look at it, but that was how she felt. He'd been acting like outraged virtue ever since she'd come back from the hospital, and Isabelle was sick of being treated like a criminal in her own home.

"I don't know what I feel," she told Bill honestly. "Angry, hurt, relieved, avenged, humiliated, I'm not sure. Maybe they're just friends and I'm wrong."

"It would be interesting to know," Bill said quietly.

"How would I ever find out? If I'm right, he's not going to admit it to me. He'd be crazy to. I have no idea what he does, where he goes, or who he sees." He hadn't shared any of that information with her in years.

"Hire an investigator," Bill suggested practically.

"That would be too rude. And he'd be furious if he found out. He'd torment me even more to cover his guilt." Bill agreed that that was probably true.

"Well, keep your ear to the ground. Maybe something will come out in the press after she's been to Saint-Moritz."

"Gordon's too smart to expose himself that much," Isabelle said, thinking about it. And after they hung up, she had another idea. There was a woman she had known years ago, in the haute couture world. They'd gone to school together and been good friends, but Isabelle hadn't seen her in years, ever since Teddy was born prematurely and was so sick. Her name was Nathalie Vivier, and as young girls they had been very close.

Isabelle called information again, and got Nathalie's number. She had never married, and was a considerable force in the haute couture. She was basically of equal importance to Louise in a rival house. Isabelle felt as though she were unraveling a great mystery, and she was compelled to find out whatever she could about Louise de Ligne. In the past twelve hours, it had become an obsession with her.

Isabelle waited till a respectable hour and called Nathalie. It was a Saturday, and she answered the phone herself. She was stunned when she realized who it was.

"My God, I haven't talked to you in years . . . how is your little boy?" Isabelle explained that he had been ill for fourteen years and had become her whole life.

"I had a feeling something like that had happened. Everyone says you've become a recluse. Are you still painting?"

"I don't have time." They checked up on each other's news for a while. Nathalie's mother had died, her father had remarried, she had lived with a senator for ten years, and he had gone back to his dying wife. She'd never married or had children, and she said she still loved her work. It was as though no time had elapsed since they last saw each other. They had been best friends in school, and then drifted apart when she and Gordon married. Nathalie had detested him, she thought him pompous and arrogant, and was convinced he had married Isabelle for her social connections. She had never trusted him, but she didn't remind Isabelle of it now. It was Isabelle who first mentioned his name.

"I have a terrible thing to ask of you. You don't owe me anything, Nat, I just want to know something, and I don't know how else to find out." There was a long silence on the other end, as Nathalie wondered how honest she could be. She had wondered if she would ever get this call, and was not entirely surprised to hear from Isabelle. Although it seemed odd that she would ask now, after all this time.

"What do you want me to do?" Nathalie asked quietly.

"I want to ask you about someone, I won't ever say I asked you. And I'd like you to tell me the truth. What do you know about Louise de Ligne?"

There was a brief sigh at the other end, and Nathalie decided to play it straight initially. "She's very talented, very difficult, very bright, nice looking, though a little older than we are, sometimes very rude. Rather cold. And very ambitious, I think. They say she's the money behind the house where she works. I think her husband bought her a big piece of it, he's about a hundred years old, completely gaga, I assume, and very sick. She'll inherit the money when he dies. He was married before, and his kids hate her guts, from everything I hear. But she's clever enough to cut them out, to the extent she can. She's already bragged that she has. She married him for the money when he was about eighty years old and had a kid to assure her future with him. He's well into his nineties now. He can't last much longer. He's one of the biggest fortunes in France." It was all interesting information, but not entirely what Isabelle wanted to hear.

"What else do you know?"

"Isabelle, don't look for things that will hurt you. Life is painful enough. Why are you asking me this?"

"Because I want to know. You know something, don't you?"

There was a long silence and another sigh. "It's not exactly a secret. Half of Paris knows." Isabelle could feel her heart race at the words.

"Is she involved with Gordon?" Isabelle finally asked what she wanted to know, and Nathalie laughed. Isabelle was still so naïve after all these years. It was what Nathalie had loved about her in school. There was an innocence to Isabelle that touched one's heart. But she was about to grow up. Maybe it was time.

"She's been his mistress for roughly the last ten or twelve years. They go everywhere together. I'm surprised no one's ever told you before. They go out socially quite openly, and have for years. Everyone knows."

"I don't know anyone anymore," Isabelle said, sounding stunned. "Are you serious?"

"Yes, I am. He buys her jewelry, he bought her a car. I think they have an apartment together somewhere, on the Left Bank. Rue du Bac, I think. They go to the Hotel du Cap in the summer. I ran into them in Saint-Tropez last year." He had a whole life, a whole world with her, that Isabelle knew nothing about. It was far worse than she had feared. "Is he leaving you?" Nathalie asked practically. "If he is, you should get a hell of a settlement out of him.

From what I've heard, he's spent a fortune on her."

"I can't believe this, Nathalie. How is this possible? Are you sure?"

"Positive. If you don't believe me, call ten people you used to know, they'll all tell you the same thing. They've been a couple for years."

"He's not leaving me," Isabelle said thoughtfully. "I just figured it out yesterday, or I guessed at it, but I didn't think it was anything like this." At worst, she had imagined a recent indiscretion, or a casual affair, not a whole other life that had gone on for a dozen years while she was home nursing her son.

"He has no reason to leave you yet. She can't go anywhere till her husband dies. When he does, though, my guess is that Gordon will want to nail her down. She's powerful and rich. Who knows though, maybe she's tired of Gordon by now. You never know. Watch out for her, though, she's a real bitch. If she thinks you're a threat to her, she'll go after you. I've seen her do it in the haute couture. She's a real piece of work. She was a little seamstress in some backwater somewhere when she met the old man, and he made her a countess and bought her that fancy job. She's good at it though, I'll give her that. But she's nothing to mess with if she decides you're a threat. She'll wipe you out in the blink of an eye, whatever she has to do. If she wants him, she'll take him right from under your nose." And in fact, they both knew now, she already had.

"I'm no threat to her," Isabelle said, sounding pained. She felt like a total fool. And on top of it, he had been cruel to her for years. It had been a rotten thing to do.

"She may not see it that way. I'm sorry, Isabelle." Nathalie hated being the one to give her the bad news. She had always been fond of her.

It was amazing to think of Gordon allied to another woman to that extent. Isabelle couldn't help wondering if it was her fault because she was so involved with her son. Nathalie had said it had been going on for ten or twelve years. And Gordon had shut her out of his room, and his heart, and his life at precisely the same time. It all made perfect sense.

"You'll be better off without him one day, Isabelle," Nathalie said honestly. "And for that matter so would she. He's entirely self-serving, and I've always thought he hated women." Isabelle told her about the accident, but not about Bill, and they promised to call each other again soon. Isabelle was grateful to have heard the truth, however painful it was. After she hung up, Isabelle sat staring into space for a long

time, and then she called Bill. She woke him
out of a sound sleep, but she couldn't wait to
tell him all she'd heard.

She rattled it all off to him while he tried to
wake up, and by the time she was finished, he
was sitting up in bed, wide-eyed and stunned. It
sounded very French. Long-term mistresses for
a decade or more were unusual in the States.
Most people got divorced. But the countess was
waiting for her husband to die to collect the
inheritance.

"That's a hell of a story. Are you sure she's
right?" It confirmed what he'd suspected, what
a bastard Gordon was.

"Nathalie always knows everything. Why
didn't anyone ever tell me before?" It was humiliating to realize that everyone in Paris had
known. It made her feel like such a fool.

"They probably thought you knew and had
decided not to rock the boat. A lot of people do
that, especially in Europe, but they do it here
too." No one had ever told him about Cynthia's
affairs either, he just knew.

"They don't do it as much anymore, now that
people can get divorced. What do you think I
should do?" She had no idea how to use the information she had gleaned.

"What do you want to do?" Bill asked
sensibly.

"I don't know. I'd love to just hit him with it the minute he gets home, or call him in Saint-Moritz, but I know that's not smart." She knew he would come after her like a tiger, if she did.

"I think you should wait and let him have it the next time he goes after you. Do you want to leave him?" She did, but she didn't think she should. The change would still be too hard on Teddy, and there was no guarantee Gordon would give her enough to support the boy. And his girlfriend couldn't get married anyway, so he wouldn't be anxious to divorce Isabelle, or be generous with her if he did. He wouldn't want a scandal, particularly given his prominence and impeccable reputation at the bank. It seemed smarter to just keep quiet and wait, as Bill said. She had a lot to think about, and a lot to decide. "Well, you've got some ammunition now, in any case. Maybe the smartest thing you can do is keep it under your hat until the right time, and then let him have it right between the eyes."

"If everyone knows anyway, it wouldn't be much of a scandal if we got divorced, would it?"

"Yes, it would. It's one thing to have a mistress on the side, even if it's public knowledge behind closed doors. It's another thing entirely to have an irate wife blow the roof sky high, talk to the press, make public accusations, hit him up for a lot of money, turning public opinion against him. You look like the Virgin Mary with a sick kid, for chrissake. I've been there in politics before. If one of my candidates had a mess like this, I'd be telling him to run for cover and hide, stay married to you, look respectable as hell, start feeding orphans or adopting blind nuns. But I sure wouldn't tell him to blow his cover, tell all, and get divorced. He'll want this whole mess to disappear as quietly as it can, and that depends on you, my love. The ball, or his balls, if you'll pardon me for saying so, are in your hands. The one thing he won't want is a public scandal, or a divorce. Especially if she's not free yet. He'll want to get out as quietly as possible when she is, and not a moment before. And knowing the personality, I don't think he's going to be apologetic and get nice to you in any case. In the end, he'll always try to blame you. The more he has to hide, the more vicious he'll be. If you confront him, he's going to threaten the hell out of you, and convince you how mean he's going to be, and try to scare you off from blowing the lid off this. Be very careful, sweetheart. If you corner him, he'll rip out your throat. I know his type, and he's not going to back down, or go quietly into the night, he'll kill you first. For whatever reason, this marriage has served a purpose for him, and whatever it is, he doesn't want you messing with that. Maybe she wants you married, for the sake of her respectability. She's not going to want to piss off the old man before he dies. I think there's a lot going on here you don't even know, be very careful, and don't push him too hard." It was sound advice, and Isabelle knew he was right, she just didn't know what to do with the information now. But she realized, as she thought about it, there were probably many nights when he didn't sleep at home and was living with the countess in the apartment Nathalie had alluded to. She had only begun to suspect recently how often he slept out, and so had Sophie. She thought back now over trips he took with friends, and vacations he went on "alone," parties he went to, places he went, and Nathalie was right, it all went back about a dozen years.

"It's certainly interesting, isn't it?" Isabelle said, still sounding shocked. Gordon suddenly seemed like a stranger to her. And Louise de Ligne was so much racier and more sophisticated than she had ever been. Isabelle felt utterly stupid for what had gone on under her nose for all those years.

"I want to give it some more thought. Don't do anything yet," Bill said pensively. Most of all, he didn't want her to get hurt in any way, and she easily could.

"I won't."

"Remember, if you corner him, he'll strike. That much I know for sure." She agreed with him a hundred percent. Gordon could be incredibly vicious if you attacked him about anything. She had discovered that about him years ago.

For the next few days, she and Bill talked about it, but they came to no new conclusions, and when Gordon came home, he looked happy and tan, and was surprisingly friendly to her. He even asked how Teddy was, and she assured him he was fine. She didn't say a word about the Comtesse de Ligne.

The only bit of mischief she caused with him was when she handed over his mail to him. She had removed one piece, since it was addressed to both of them, and ever so casually she mentioned that they had been invited to a wedding by the Comte and Comtesse de Ligne. She said she'd accepted it for them both, and it sounded like fun. She looked entirely innocent, and nothing showed in his eyes as he listened to her. He seemed to have no reaction at all.

"Teddy's doctor says I should get out a bit more, and he's right. I assumed you know them, and since it came to both of us, I thought you wouldn't mind if I go," she said sweetly with wide eyes.

"Not at all," he said, looking totally uncon-

cerned, and for a moment she wondered if
Nathalie was wrong, and then he turned to her
with an odd expression. "They're a bit tedious
though, they're both very old. I think you
might be bored. If you're going to start going
out again, I think you ought to choose something a bit more fun." He seemed solicitous
rather than scared.

"How old can they be with a daughter getting
married?" Isabelle asked innocently, and Gordon shrugged.

"I don't think she's a very young girl, she's
probably an old maid, and very unattractive. It
doesn't sound very amusing to me."

He was very determined that Isabelle not go,
and for the first time in years, when dealing
with him, she was amused.

"You're right, that doesn't sound like much
fun. Should I write and tell them we can't go
after all, or would that be too rude?"

"I'll take care of it. Where is the invitation, by
the way?"

"It's on my desk."

"I'll pick it up on my way out. I'll have my
secretary take care of it."

"Thank you, Gordon. I'll send them a nice
gift to apologize."

"I'll have Elisabeth take care of that too. You
have enough to do."

She thanked him sweetly, and he left for the office with the invitation still in his hand, and Bill laughed when she told him about it when he called.

"You're a monster, you are. But remember what I said. Be careful with him, he's no fool. He may be watching now, to see what you do. He may think someone told you something, if your friend is right, and everyone in Paris knows."

"I won't do anything." For the next few days, all she did was check to see if he was in his room late at night, and in the early hours when she got up. It was exactly what she'd thought, he didn't come home all night, and didn't expect her to know, since she was tacitly forbidden to come to his rooms. He was presumably at the apartment on the rue du Bac with Louise.

Isabelle and Gordon played cat and mouse with each other for the next month and nothing changed, but then again, it hadn't in years. He had a life with the woman, an apartment, a relationship, in some ways he was more married to her than he was to Isabelle. Just as in some ways, she felt more married to Bill.

He had been at the rehab center for five months by then, and he was stronger, and felt healthier than he had in years. His neck hardly caused him any problem anymore, his shoulders had grown, his hips were slim, and in a bathing suit, when he swam, he looked like a very young man. More of the sensation in his legs had returned, and he could move more easily in his wheelchair, but not only could he not walk, he couldn't stand. His legs just didn't have the strength, and they collapsed under him when he put any weight on them at all. Even the braces they'd fit him for didn't work. He fell even faster when he wore those. And the deal he'd made with himself about Isabelle wasn't looking good.

He was still meeting with Dr. Harcourt, the sex therapist, despite his initial resistance. He still insisted that sex was over for him. It had been too traumatic for him when it hadn't worked with Isabelle, and he was convinced nothing would change. But he enjoyed talking to Linda Harcourt anyway. She gave him a constant flow of interesting books. But he remained unconvinced.

To complicate matters further, Jane and Joe came to him in March, and told him they wanted to get engaged. Although he liked Joe very much, Bill was upset about it, and had several long talks with Cynthia on the phone. She was much more understanding about it than he, and they argued about it for several weeks. And in the end, Bill had a long talk with Jane when she came up to see him from NYU.

"Daddy, we know what we're doing. We're not kids. I've been around here for seven months. I know what I'm getting into." Because of the nature of his injuries, Joe wore diapers, took medications, and only had the use of one arm. His limitations were more extensive than Bill's. He had been accepted for law school in the fall, and he had a fine mind. And the doctors thought, but were not certain, that he could have children eventually. Linda had explained to Bill that some men, although unable to perform sexually on their own, were still able to impregnate their wives, with medical help. It was not clear if Joe was one of those. He was one of her patients too. But as far as Bill was concerned, Joe had youth on his side. At Bill's age, he was no longer willing to be "experimental" or make a fool of himself. He was prepared to abstain entirely from sex for the rest of his life. He accepted that as an inevitability, unlike Joe.

"You don't know what you're getting into," Bill argued with her. "He's going to be completely dependent on you, physically and emotionally."

"That's not true. Joe takes care of me, he's the only man who ever has, except you. He's going to be a lawyer, he invested the settlement money from the accident, he has a million dollars in blue chip stocks, and some very good investments. Mom's stockbroker looked at it, and he said Joe's done all the right things. And if he can't go rock climbing, or do the waltz, I don't care."

"Maybe you will one day."

"You and Mom didn't make it, and you could walk then. What's so different about this? Why are we so much worse off than you were, when you got married?"

"Because he's handicapped," Bill insisted, "that's going to be a tremendous burden on you. Your mom and I didn't make it when I could walk, as you put it, I wouldn't even consider marrying her the way I am today."

"That's pathetic. I can't believe you think that way." He was suddenly sorry that she'd ever come to the hospital, and he'd introduced her to Joe. He had thought it was harmless, but he'd been wrong. He argued with Isabelle and Cynthia, and both his daughters for the next two weeks, and finally he sat down and talked to Joe. He expected a lot of sincere, earnest pressure from him, and it was obvious that Bill was upset before the conversation even began. But he wasn't prepared for what Joe had to say.

"I know how you feel, Bill," Joe said quietly. He had heard it all from Jane. She was furious with her father over it, and wanted to elope with Joe. But Joe respected her and Bill too much for that. "I can't tell you you're wrong. I can't tell you it will be an easy road, we both know it's not. I know. I understand that better than Jane. And we're both young. Marriage isn't easy at the best of times. My parents are divorced, you and Cynthia are too. There are no guarantees in life. Nothing is a sure thing. But I also think that Jane and I share a special bond, I honestly think we can make it work. I'm going to do everything I can to protect her and love her and take care of her," there were tears in his eyes and Bill turned away, he didn't want to be swayed. "But I also respect you too much to do something you don't want. I trust your judgment, even though I think you're wrong about this. I think you and I have as much right to a good life, and a good marriage, as anyone else. Just because I can't walk or use my left arm doesn't mean I have no right to love. I hope you believe that too, for your sake. But if you don't want me to marry her, if you say no, I'll tell her I thought about it and changed my mind. If that's what you want, I'd rather she hate me than you, you're her father, she needs you, maybe even more than she needs me. And I don't want to be part of your family if you don't want me to be. It's up to you." Bill felt sick as he listened to him. He wanted it all to be true, but he just thought it was too hard for both of them, and he wanted to protect his little girl. He wanted her to have a man who could walk into the sunset with her, under his own steam.

"What if you find out you can't have kids after you try?" That was a big issue to him, and he knew it would be to Jane one day.

"Then we'll adopt. Jane and I have talked about it. There are no guarantees for anyone. A lot of couples who don't have our challenges find out they can't have kids. We'll do whatever seems right to both of us."

Bill knew he couldn't ask for more from any man. Joe was decent, loving, crazy about Jane, intelligent, polite, considerate, educated, financially sound, but he was confined to a wheelchair for the rest of his life. It was the hardest decision Bill had ever made. He listened to Joe for a long time, and then with tears in his eyes he held out his arms and the two men embraced.

"All right, you little shit," there were tears in their eyes, and Bill's lip was quivering as he struggled to talk. "Go for it. But if you ever make her unhappy, I'm going to kill you."

"I swear, I'll do everything I can for her for the rest of my life." It was all anyone could ask of the man marrying his daughter. Both men wiped their eyes and smiled, as Bill took out one of the half bottles of wine from the fridge in his room.

"When do you two want to get married?" Bill asked, pouring them each a glass of wine. He felt as though he'd climbed the Alps in the last half hour, and Joe felt that way too.

"We thought June or July. I'll be going to law school at NYU, and we can get married housing, that way it won't interfere with her going to school." She'd be twenty and a junior in the fall. He was twenty-three. They were young, certainly, but others had done it before, and succeeded. Bill hoped they'd be among the lucky ones, that was all he wanted for them.

"When are you getting out of here?" Bill asked.

"In a month or two. I've been here for a year, and they think I'm about cooked. I thought I'd go home to Minneapolis for a while." Bill nodded. It all sounded sensible, if you could call it that. If Joe weren't in a wheelchair, Bill would have been jumping for joy. But at least he'd agreed.

They both got a little drunk, and Joe called Jane when he went back to his room. He was feeling absolutely drained. He'd been terrified of what Bill would say, but it had gone astonishingly well. And as soon as she heard, Jane burst into tears of relief. Her father's blessing meant the world to her. She didn't want to get married unless he approved, nor did Joe.

Five minutes after Joe left the room, Jane called Bill, she was crying and laughing and thanking him, and then she got off the phone and Cynthia got on.

"You did good. I was a little worried about you for a while, but you did the right thing." She sounded remarkably calm and mature. They had all grown up in the last year, not just the kids.

"What makes you so sure?" Bill asked, still sounding concerned.

"I just know. So do you, you're just scared. He'll be good to her." That was all they could ask. The rest was up to the Fates.

"He'd better be. He has me to answer to."

"I'm proud of you," Cynthia said.

"Don't be, he's just such a nice kid, I couldn't say no."

"I'm glad," and Isabelle said the same thing when she called to find out how it had gone.

"I would never have forgiven you if you'd said no," she said fervently. She'd been worried about it all night, and got up at four A.M. so she could call. Everyone had been rooting for them. There was nothing more irresistible than love, and one thing was for sure, Joe and Jane loved each other. Bill just hoped that life treated them well. Joe at least had paid his dues.

Spring had come to Paris by then, and nothing had changed for Isabelle in the past two months. She had never confronted Gordon about her discovery. She was biding her time. But everything had changed for her since she'd found out about Louise. She no longer felt guilty about what she felt for Bill, and she stayed away from Gordon most of the time. She made no apologies, expected nothing from him. He was simply a man she no longer knew who lived at the same address. Bill was only worried that Gordon would sense something too different in her. But so far, he seemed to have no clue.

Bill was still calling her every day, but he knew he had to make some decisions soon. He had been at the rehab facility for seven months, and although he was stronger and healthier, nothing significant had changed. His body had healed, and he had originally planned to stay for a year, but his therapists were telling him that he'd be ready to leave soon. He was tentatively thinking of leaving in May. They had told him finally that there was nothing more they could do. He was bound to his wheelchair for life. There was no miracle, no surgery they could offer him. He had to make his peace with his life as it now was, and would remain. It was the cruelest blow imaginable for him. The only one worse would have been if Isabelle had died when they were hit by the bus. His not being able to walk, to him, meant never seeing her again. He would rather have died than burden her with his infirmities. And he felt as though he had died when they told him there was nothing more they could do. He hadn't told her it was over yet, but knew he had to soon, so he wouldn't change his mind. He had vowed to bow out quietly sometime soon.

His friends were still calling from Washington, and an important senatorial candidate was asking him to take his campaign on in June. He had his eye on the presidency in four years, and he knew Bill was the man to make it happen for him. Bill had all but promised him he would.

He had talked about it with Isabelle, and she had come to believe it would do him good to go back to work. She could tell that he was discouraged at times that he hadn't made more progress in the rehab center, but they had taken him as far as they could. And she sensed correctly that he was stalling about moving on. Leaving the rehab center was a little bit like leaving the womb.

Her own wounds had healed by then. Her tests were normal, she seldom had headaches anymore. She had made a remarkable recovery, and there was no remaining sign of the accident, except for a long thin scar along her left arm where the severed artery had been sutured. There was no other remnant of it, except for the relationship that had been born in the hospital between them. She still missed him terribly, and she had asked him to come to see her when he got out of the rehab facility. But whenever she asked him about it, he was vague. She knew it was too soon for him to make travel plans, but she hoped he would soon. She hadn't seen him in seven months, which seemed an eternity to her. And it did to Bill too.

He tormented himself over it constantly as time went on, and had been for a while. He wanted to see her, but it didn't seem right to him. Once he truly understood and accepted the fact that he would never walk again, it changed everything for him. And their calls didn't seem as innocent to him anymore. He felt as though he were misleading her, given the decision he'd made. In his eyes, he had nothing to offer her now, except his emotional support, and whatever stolen moments they could eventually share, a few times a year. He had too little to give her, he could offer no future as long as she was married, no safety from Gordon, or for her sick child. He had nothing to give her except words. The one thing he didn't want was her pity. He couldn't have borne it. And he knew that, if he chose to leave her, for her sake, she had to believe he was whole. If she didn't, and thought he needed her, she would never let him go. He knew that much about her. But every time he thought of leaving her, or not calling her anymore, he felt as though his heart would break. He didn't want her to feel abandoned, but, he told himself, in the long run it was best for her. If he could have given her a future, the kind he wanted to, he would have waited forever for her, but now that he knew he couldn't and would be in a wheelchair forever, he told himself he had to let her go, for her sake. Even more so, if he could not make love to her. Even if Joe and Jane were crazy enough to try and build a life together, as far as he was concerned, he would never do that to Isabelle. It was becoming a wrestling match between Bill and his conscience every day.

The one blessing, other than Bill, in her life, was the fact that Teddy had improved radically in the past two months. She didn't know if it was the weather, or just blind luck, but he seemed stronger and better than he had all year. He had even come downstairs to have dinner with her in the dining room several times. And in April, she drove him through the Bois de Boulogne for the first time in years. They stopped for an ice cream in the Jardin d'Acclimatation, and she was ecstatic when she called Bill. She hadn't done anything like it since he was a very little boy. And she thanked God for the blessing he was in her life, when he turned fifteen on the first of May.

It was the following afternoon that Bill called, and began laying the groundwork for what he had convinced himself he had to do. He told her the first lie he ever had. He had thought about it long and hard. And however terrible it seemed, he knew he was doing it for her. He loved her enough to sacrifice himself for her. Teddy was better, Gordon had left her in peace for several months. He was almost never there. And Bill knew that there would never be a good time to do what he believed he had to do, but this seemed better than most. With a pounding heart, he called to tell her that he had fantastic news, and tried to make himself sound convincing. She knew him so well, he was afraid she'd know it wasn't true. But by some miracle she believed him when he told her he had walked that day, and that he had finally made the connection between his brain and his legs. She sounded astounded to hear what he said, and burst into tears, she was so happy for him, which made him feel even worse. But in his mind, there was nothing else he could do. He knew now that he had to let her go, for her sake, and to convince her that he was whole. She had Teddy to take care of, she didn't need the burden of Bill too. As he was, he felt he had nothing to offer her, no matter what eventually happened with Gordon. Bill would not do this to her. He refused to destroy her life and turn her into his nursemaid one day. Unlike Joe and Jane, Bill knew better. He could not let her pity him, rescue him, take care of him. If he wasn't able to walk, he refused to stay in Isabelle's life. And what he had just told her, about having walked that day, was the first step toward setting her free. In his mind, it was all he had left to give. It was like freeing a beautiful bird.

They talked for a long time, and she asked him how he had felt when he took his first steps, if it had been terrifying or wonderful, and he elaborated endlessly on the theme. And every day after that, he solidified his story. He felt sick when he called her now, hated lying to her. He felt he had no choice, but it tainted all their phone calls, because he was lying to her. She was warm and wonderful and vulnerable and trusting, and he loved her so much. Enough not to stay in her life as he was. He saw himself now as a half person, or less, who had nothing to offer a woman anymore. Even if parts of him worked, there were others that did not, and never would. In effect, in his eyes, the prognosis the therapists had given him had destroyed what was left of his life, and what he shared with Isabelle.

And when Bill wasn't talking to her, he was setting up his future life in Washington. He was finally starting to make plans for when he left the rehab center. He had promised to take on the senatorial candidate at the end of June.

He had to get an apartment before that, and he wanted to spend time with the candidate and learn everything he could about him. And before he went back to work, there was Joe and Jane's wedding in June. She was having half a dozen bridesmaids, Olivia was the maid of honor, and they were planning to hold the reception at the house in Greenwich. They were having three hundred guests in a tent on the front lawn. There was a lot going on, and Cynthia was going crazy making arrangements with caterers and florists, and going to fittings for the dresses with the girls.

Joe and Jane were beside themselves. They had signed up for married housing at NYU. She had gone to Minneapolis to meet his parents. And they were going to Italy for their honeymoon. As he listened to Joe when he went to therapy with him every day, Bill felt sicker and sicker about what he was about to do to Isabelle. But he had made his decision. He felt certain it was his only choice, and the right thing to do. For him, the decision had been made. All that was left to do was to tell her.

"Are you okay?" Joe asked him one afternoon as they headed back to their rooms. "You've been so quiet lately." Joe was worried about him. He seemed strange. He knew Bill had hit a wall in his recovery, and was concerned about the effect it had had on him. They had all been there at some point, when they had to face reality and the truth.

"I'm getting ready to go back to the real world. I have a lot of work to do right after the wedding," Bill explained, but Joe had noticed that his future father-in-law had lost his interest in therapy almost completely in the last month. And he had finally stopped seeing Linda Harcourt in therapy sessions. He had nothing left to say, and no interest in her books. He had given up all hope of a life with Isabelle. Bill had agreed to stay at the rehab center for another month, but his heart no longer appeared to be in it in any way. He had already moved on, in his head. He seemed distracted and quiet, and when he wasn't paying attention to the people around him, which was frequently now, he looked depressed, and was.

At the end of May, Bill ran into Helena on her way back from the dining hall, and she was crying. She was heading his way, and she almost ran him down as she sped past him in her chair.

"Hey, hit-and-run is a felony!" Bill shouted at her, and she slowed to a stop without turning to look at him and then put her face in her hands and started sobbing. He moved his wheelchair next to hers, and touched her shoulder. "Can I help?" She shook her head for a minute, and didn't answer. And then she looked at him with ravaged eyes. And as she took her hand away from her face, he could see that her ring was gone, the enormous diamond she'd been wearing since he met her nine months before. It was easy to guess what had happened. "Do you want to come talk for a while?" he offered, and she nodded. They went back to his room then, and he handed her a wad of tissues. And after she'd blown her nose, she thanked him with a teary smile.

"I'm sorry. I'm a mess," she apologized. She was as beautiful as ever, even when she was crying. She was a spectacular-looking girl, regardless of the fact that she was in a wheelchair.

"Should I guess, or do you want to tell me?"

"It's Sergio. He called . . . things have been weird lately. He's been working in Milan, and he's been away a lot. We put the wedding off a few months ago, because he thought we needed more time. . . . Shit, Bill, we've been going out for six years . . . but we never got engaged until after the accident. I think he just did it because he felt guilty that I fell when I was working for him. That day, he kept making me step back further and further, and then I fell backward down the stairs . . . and . . . he just told me he can't do it, that it's too hard, and I need too much attention. He says he needs someone in his life who's more independent. It's because of this," she slapped the sides of her wheelchair, and started crying again, as Bill put an arm around her shoulders. The slurring of her speech had improved immeasurably in the past nine months, but the rest of her situation had not and never would. It was exactly what he was afraid of for Joe and Jane, and why he wanted to free Isabelle now before she came to hate him for all that he no longer was, or couldn't do.

"It probably scared him," Bill said sensibly. Sergio was one of the most successful young photographers in the business, and he was only twenty-nine. But he could also have any model he wanted, even one not in a wheelchair. It would have been nice if he could have lived up to his promise to Helena, but if it was too much for him, Bill told her, it was better that he speak up now. "You know, if he can't do it, Helena, then he's done the right thing. You don't want him to walk out after you're married. If he's not the right guy, better you know now." It was his theory with Isabelle too, although he knew she would never have walked out on him, but Bill thought she should. And if she didn't have the sense to do it, he did, for her sake. He had worked himself into a frenzy over it in the last weeks, and convinced himself he was right. What Sergio had just done to her confirmed everything he thought, that "whole" people did not belong with people who were anything less than that. "Helena, believe me, one day you'll be glad this happened," he said, and she started to cry harder. It didn't make any sense to her. She loved him, and thought he loved her too. She already had her wedding dress, the caterer, the photographer, the band. But marriage was a lot more than that, particularly in circumstances like theirs.

"Why would I be glad this happened?" What Bill was saying just didn't make sense to her.

"Because you don't want to be a burden to him. He'd only come to hate you that way."

"I'm not a burden," she said, looking incensed. "I'm no different than I was before the accident. I'm still the same person." Joe and Jane would have applauded what she was say-

ing, but Bill did not. He had exactly the oppo-
site point of view.

"None of us are the same. We can't be. We
have limitations. There are things we'll never
do again," Bill said quietly, thinking of Isabelle.

"Like what? Dance? Ski? Roller-skate? Who
cares?" She blew her nose again.

"He does apparently, that's my point. At least
he was honest, you have to admire him for
that."

"I don't admire him. He's a shit. I didn't do
anything wrong for him to walk out on me."

"No. You just had rotten luck. We all did.
That's why we're here."

"Are you telling me no one will ever love us
because we're like this? Because if you are, I
think you're wrong, and that's a rotten thing to
say. What about Joe and Jane? Look at them."

"You're old enough to be smarter than they
are." She was twenty-eight, and she wanted a
life and a husband and kids. "I still think they're
making a mistake, and one day they'll pay for it.
Maybe one day Jane will do what Sergio just
did. And then what? By then they'll have a
couple of kids, and they'll screw up everyone's
lives."

"Is that what you think? That no one will
ever stay with us or want us? That's bullshit, and
you know it. Or at least I hope you do. We

have a right to the same things everyone else does."

"Maybe not," he said, looking grim. "Or at least I don't. I can only speak for myself. But I don't feel like I have a right to inflict this," he waved at their wheelchairs, "on someone else. It wouldn't be fair." They both knew he was speaking of Isabelle, and Helena looked even more upset.

"Have you talked to the shrink here lately, Bill?" she asked, suddenly more concerned about him than about herself. "I think you need to, because I think your attitude stinks. I think Sergio is an asshole, and maybe you're right, maybe I'm better off than if he walks out on me later, but I don't think it should have anything to do with this," she waved at his wheelchair the way he had, "I think it should have to do with whether or not he loves me, and what kind of wife he thinks I'm going to be. Maybe he thinks I'm not good enough for him."

"That's my point," Bill said smugly, and Helena looked angry at Bill.

"No, it isn't, Bill. You're confused. You think we lost our right to be loved the day we wound up in a wheelchair. I don't believe that, and I never will. There are too many good people out there who won't give a damn if we're standing up or sitting down. I don't like being like this either. I'd much rather be running around under my own steam, and wearing high heels. But I'm not. So fucking what? Are you telling me you wouldn't love a woman in a wheelchair? Are you that small? I don't think you are." She looked pointedly at him.

"Maybe not," he said, dodging her question, but knowing in spite of himself that there was some truth to what she was saying. Because if it were Isabelle who'd wound up in the wheelchair, he would have loved her just the same, maybe more. But that wasn't his point. "I guess I'm just saying that some people aren't big enough to do this. And even if they are, you have to take a good look and figure out if that's what you want to do to them. Do you really want to subject them to that, or do you love them enough to give them up?" He was talking about himself, and Helena was looking confused.

"Why don't they just put us all out on an iceberg somewhere? That might solve the problem. Then we wouldn't be a problem for anyone, they wouldn't have to be decent human beings, or have any compassion, or even grow up. You know what? I admire the hell out of Jane and Joe for what they're doing. They believe in each other, and they're right. They love each other, and that's worth everything.

The rest of it, the chair, or the crutches, or no chair or no crutches, it doesn't mean a damn thing. At least not to me. I don't care if the guy I marry is deaf, dumb, and blind, if he's a good person, and we love each other, and he's a decent human being, then that's good enough for me. This wheelchair wouldn't mean shit to me if someone else were in it instead of me."

"Good. Then marry me," Bill teased her, and she sat back in her chair and smiled through her tears.

"You'd be a huge pain in the ass," she laughed at him. "And your outlook stinks. I still think you should talk to the shrink before you leave, or you're going to do some really stupid stuff." She was one of Linda Harcourt's patients too, and had done well with her, because she wanted to.

"Like what?" He looked defensive. He liked her, she was a very bright girl, and they had become good friends.

"Like walk out on people who love you, because you think you're a burden to them. Why don't you let them figure that out, instead of deciding for them? You have no right to control what they think, or make decisions for them."

"Maybe I know better. If you love someone, you want to protect them from themselves."

"You can't protect people," Helena said clearly. She had done a lot of work on herself and faced a lot of things, more so than Bill. He had spent all his time lifting weights, and had eventually avoided the shrink. Helena could see that. "People have a right to make their own choices. You can't take that away from them, just like they can't take that away from us. It's a question of respect."

"Maybe you're right," Bill said, looking pensive. "I don't have the answers. I just have the questions. And I'm a lot older than you are. Maybe at your age, I'd be braver too. Maybe you're right, maybe Sergio is a shit. But if he is, you're better off without him, and you're better off knowing it now."

"That, I agree with," she said sadly, "but it hurts anyway."

"Yeah," he said, "it does. But so does life. There's a lot of stuff that happens that hurts like hell. Some people never fail to disappoint you. It's nice to weed them out early on," he said, and she nodded. He was thinking of Cynthia, and that had had nothing to do with his chair.

"I guess Sergio is one of those," she said philosophically.

"Maybe next time you'll get a smaller ring, and a bigger guy." She nodded, and they chatted for a while, and then she went back to her own room, but she reminded Bill again that she thought he should see the shrink before he left. And when Isabelle called him later that night, he sounded troubled. Some of the things Helena had said had confused him again. She was so emphatic about their limitations not making a difference to the people who loved them, that he almost wondered if she was right, but not quite. She was a young woman, and if a man wanted to take care of her, it was one thing. He was a man, and he felt he had to be able to offer more than that.

"You sound tired," Isabelle said, sensing instantly that he was feeling down. "Did you walk around too much and wear yourself out today?" She had believed him totally, about his being able to walk again. And he looked at his wheelchair feeling guilty as he listened. It was the lie that made it impossible for him to see her again. Like poisoning his food, he couldn't go near it again. But that had been his plan. And he had no intention of backing out now, no matter what Helena said. It had already gone too far, and he still believed that leaving her was the right thing to do. The only question in his mind was when.

"Yeah, I guess so. I have a lot to do before I leave," he said, sounding vague.

"They did a great job," Isabelle said, sounding

gentler than ever, and as trusting, and just hearing her ripped out his heart. However mis-
guided, what he wanted was to give her the gift
of freedom, from a burden he felt certain would
ruin her life. And he knew Helena would have
told him Isabelle had the right to make her own
choice, and he was taking away that right. But he
was convinced he knew best, and Isabelle was
too kind to ever walk out on him. But for days,
she had heard something odd in his voice, and
she couldn't tell what. He sounded different and
distant and unhappy. All she could guess was that
he was nervous about leaving the protected en-
vironment of the rehab facility and starting a new
life. But now that he could walk again, as far as
she knew, it was all going to be so much easier for
him, and she was so relieved.

"How's the wedding coming?" she asked a
few minutes later, hoping to distract him from
whatever was bothering him.

"Cynthia's going crazy. I'm trying to stay out
of it. All I have to do is pay the bills. That's the
easy part." The hard part was what he was planning to do to Isabelle. But she didn't know that
yet. "How's Teddy?" He rapidly changed the
subject. She noticed that he was doing that a lot
these days, hopping from one topic to another,
as though he was uncomfortable suddenly talking about anything in depth. It was so unlike

him, and the conversations they'd shared for nearly five years. She knew him better than he thought, better than he wanted her to.

"He's terrific," Isabelle said, which reassured him. He could never have ended it with her if Teddy had been failing. She was sealing her own fate by telling Bill he was doing well. "He's never been better."

"Good." And then he told her he was going to Washington to look for an apartment the following week. It made her ask him about Paris again.

"Maybe you can come over after the wedding, if you're not too tired. Just for a few days before you start work." It was a lot to ask of him, but she was afraid he wouldn't have time to do it after that. She knew just how busy things got for him, and would now.

"I'll have to see. I may be starting on the campaign that week." It was another lie. He wasn't starting on the campaign until the end of June, and he would have had time to come over, but he wasn't walking, and he couldn't tell her that. He had made it impossible for himself to visit her. "We'll figure it out" was all he offered, and when they hung up this time, she was worried. She had the distinct feeling he was avoiding her, and she didn't know why. It had started happening from one day to the next, literally overnight. What she didn't know was that his vagueness had started the day his therapists had confirmed that he would never walk again. That had been the turning point for him. He had always promised himself that when that happened, he would stop calling her, and never see her again. But he couldn't bring himself to stop calling her yet. At her end, Isabelle was worried that she had said something that offended him. But he didn't seem angry at her, just distant. It had been nine months since she'd seen him, and she had no idea when he was going to come to Paris to visit her. And there was no way she could go to Washington or New York to see him. She couldn't leave Teddy for that long or venture that far away.

By the time the wedding came, Isabelle was panicked. He had missed calling her a few times, and when she asked him about it, he said he'd been too busy. He had found an apartment in Washington, and met with the young senator about his campaign. He sounded excited when he talked about that. And for two days after the wedding, Bill didn't call her at all. And for some odd, instinctive reason, she suddenly didn't dare call him. He had suddenly put up walls to keep her out.

It had been a beautiful wedding, and everyone had cried when Joe and Jane exchanged their vows. With Joe in his wheelchair, and Jane standing next to him, holding his hand, it had been incredibly touching. And no one cried more than Bill, sitting in his wheelchair, next to Cynthia, at the end of the first pew.

"Are you okay?" she asked him at the reception. He was sitting next to her, and she found him unusually quiet. "You look stressed."

"Just thinking about work. I'm leaving the rehab and going to Washington in a few days. You know how I am." Physically, he looked terrific, but she could see that something was bothering him.

"You seem upset." In the end, she assumed that it had gotten to him watching his baby get married.

Olivia came and sat with him some of the time, and when Jane was supposed to dance with him, she danced with her grandfather instead while he and Joe watched, smiling at her. It didn't seem to bother Joe, but it bothered Bill. A lot. It was a beautiful wedding, a great party, and everyone had a great time. And as he rode back to the rehab facility that night, all Bill could think about was Isabelle.

He stayed in his room and didn't even go to physical therapy for two days, and then he finally got up the guts to make the call. She was worried about him by then, and he hadn't answered his phone when she finally called him. It had rung several times in the past two days. He knew it was Isabelle. And he just lay on his bed, thinking about her, and wishing he were dead.

"Where have you been?" she asked, with a note of panic in her voice when he finally called. "I thought you went on the honeymoon with them," she teased. But he could hear that she was worried and hurt and hated himself for it. He knew that the concern she had felt was nothing compared to the pain she was going to feel. After five years of talking to her, it was inconceivable to no longer have her in his life. But he was certain now that it was the final gift that he owed her. "How was the wedding?" she asked innocently, and he sighed.

"It was beautiful. Everyone cried at the ceremony, and after that they had a great time."

"Tell me about it." Teddy was still asleep, he was sleeping later these days, and she had lots of time.

He did, and then he took a breath. It was like jumping off the high dive. "Isabelle, there's something I have to tell you." She could feel her heart stop. She knew before he said another word that something was terribly wrong.

"Why do I not like the sound of that?" She held her breath, waiting for the other shoe to fall.

"Cynthia and I renewed our vows." There was an endless silence at her end while she absorbed what he had just said to her.

"What exactly does that mean?" She was trying to be polite, but she wanted to scream. As always, she was gracious and waited for him to explain.

"We made a recommitment to our marriage." It was the second- worst lie he had ever told her. The first one was when he told her that he could walk again. "Things have changed since I've been at the rehab facility. We thought it was important for the girls." One was married and the other was twenty-two years old. How important could it be to two grown women for their parents to renew their vows? But Isabelle didn't ask the obvious, the fact that they'd done it was all that mattered and that she heard.

"When did you decide this?" Her whole body was shaking, but she sounded deceptively calm.

"In the last few weeks." He sounded almost cavalier and forced himself not to think of what it was doing to her.

"I knew something was wrong." She was right about that. She knew him well, which was hardly surprising after five years. "Is that why you wouldn't make plans to come to Paris?" It explained it to her now. She knew he was worried about something, she just hadn't known what. "What does that mean for us?"

"I don't think we should talk to each other anymore." His words hit her harder than the impact of the bus. She couldn't even speak for a moment, and she thought she was going to pass out. She couldn't get air in her lungs, and she could feel her heart for the first time since the accident. It was as though he had dropped a wrecking ball on her, and she was too crushed to answer. But she knew she had to say something. She hadn't expected this. But she could hardly blame him. She had refused to leave Gordon, for Teddy's sake. She had so little to offer Bill, except their calls. It made sense to her for him to recommit himself to Cynthia, no matter how much it hurt her. It seemed right for him, and she loved him enough to want the best for him.

"I don't know what to say. I'm happy for you, Bill." He had recovered not only his legs, but his marriage, and she wished him well. He could hear that she was crying and he wanted to die. But he knew it was the right thing for her, whether she knew it or not. Only his love for her had led him to do such an awful thing. He knew that with what he'd said, he had destroyed part of his own heart. It was the ultimate sacrifice he could make for her, and she for him.

"I want you to take care of yourself. Don't let Gordon get the upper hand. Save your ammunition, and if he tortures you, use it on him. He won't bother you after that. As long as Louise's husband is alive, he'll want to stay married to you." He had thought a lot about it, and it was the only thing he was worried about now. He didn't want Gordon tormenting her, and he would no longer know about it. He couldn't protect her from him anyway, except with his love, which seemed too little to him now anyway.

"It's nice of you to worry about that," she said, sounding shocked and confused. "I don't understand . . . you didn't tell me things were better between you and Cynthia. How did that happen? And when?"

"I don't know. Maybe when the kids decided to get married, we figured we needed to clean up our act." In fact, their divorce had come through in March right after Jane and Joe told them they were getting married. Cynthia appeared to be very serious now with the man she'd been seeing for nine months, and Bill was happy for her.

"I want you to be happy, Bill," she said generously, "whatever that means to you. And for what it's worth, I love you with all my heart."

"I know you do," there were tears rolling

down his cheeks, but he couldn't let her hear it in his voice. Her freedom depended on his convincing her, and he was determined to do it right. "I love you too, Isabelle." He wanted to tell her he always would, but there was no way he could say that. "Take good care of yourself. If you ever need anything, call me. I'll always be there for you."

"I don't think Cynthia would like that."

"Thirty years is a long time. It's hard to walk away from that." But he had walked away from that too. For similar reasons. But it was Isabelle who owned his heart, and he knew she always would. But only he knew that.

"I'm going to miss you terribly," she said, beginning to sob. "But I want you to be happy . . . be happy . . . be good to yourself, Bill. You deserve so much." He knew he deserved to burn in hell for what he was doing to her, but he was still convinced that the gift he was giving her was greater than the pain she had now. She'd see that one day, he was sure.

"Good-bye," he said simply, and then gently hung up, and as Isabelle put down the phone, she began to cry long wracking sobs. It sounded as though someone had died, and she had.

"What's wrong, Mommy?" Teddy came running into her room with terrified eyes. He had heard her from the hall, and he'd never seen her like that. He was breathless when he got to where she sat, after she'd hung up the phone.

For a moment she couldn't speak, but she knew she had to pull herself together for him. "An old friend of mine just died." She didn't know what else to say to him, and in a way, he had. Bill was dead to her now. Gone. Lost to her. She couldn't imagine living without him, couldn't imagine what her life would be like without his calls. It was like a death sentence in a life where she already had so little. All she had were her children now. And as Teddy watched, she got up and got her coat and then came to give him a hug. "I'm fine. I'm just sad. I'm going to go for a little walk." She took him back to his room, and settled him in his bed. And then she went out, and walked for hours. It was nearly lunchtime when she got back, and she looked deathly pale, almost gray. And even Teddy's nurse was frightened for her.

"Are you all right, Mrs. Forrester?" she asked respectfully. In all the years she had known her, she had never seen her look so ill. Isabelle quietly nodded, with a wintry smile. Her eyes were two deep pools of pain.

"I'm fine," she said mechanically. There was nothing else she could say. But that afternoon, as she read to her son, there were little rivers of tears that kept sliding down her cheeks, and

Teddy quietly patted her hand. He didn't know what to say to her. And when she hugged him when he went to bed that night, she choked on a sob.

"I'm sorry, Mommy," he said gently, hugging her tight, and she nodded with a sad smile.

"So am I, sweetheart."

All she could think of that night was Bill. She was devastated, more than she'd ever been in her entire life. He had taken away hope and laughter and love and comfort on dark days. She had no one to turn to now, and knew she never would again. She would die Gordon's prisoner, and she no longer cared. About anything. She would live to serve Teddy and Sophie, and somehow get through the rest of her days.

And in his room at the rehab facility, Bill lay in the dark. He hadn't moved since he'd called her. He hadn't slept all night. He just lay there and cried. But it was the right thing to do. Knowing and believing that was the only consolation he had.

Chapter Sixteen

For Isabelle, the days were endless after Bill left her life. There was no beginning, no end, no part of the day that offered any relief. She took care of Teddy as she always had, and now it was she who looked ill. She didn't eat, she didn't sleep, she said very little, although she tried to make an effort for Teddy. But she felt as though she'd been dropped down an abyss where there was no sunshine, no light. She longed to hear Bill's voice, but she didn't even know where he was anymore. She knew he had gone to Washington, and she wondered if Cynthia had gone with him. But wherever he was, he no longer belonged to her, and she knew now he never had. He had been a temporary gift in her life, and she was grateful for him. But the pain of losing him was so acute that she wondered daily if she'd survive. Losing Bill was much harder than surviving the bus. The impact this time was to her soul.

Even Gordon noticed it during the little time he spent in the house. He wondered if her obviously failing health was related to her accident, and when Sophie saw her when she returned from school, she was terrified. Isabelle looked as though she were dying.

"Are you ill?" Gordon finally asked her one day over breakfast. He had actually spent the night in the house. He still didn't know that Isabelle was aware that he often slept out. But Isabelle had lost so much weight that her clothes hung on her more than they had after the accident.

"I haven't been feeling well. I'm having migraines," she said to explain the gray color of her face. She could see it too, but she couldn't seem to eat or sleep anymore.

"It must be a recurrence of your injury," he said, looking vaguely concerned. "I want you to call the doctor." It was the first sign of interest he had shown for her in months. "I'm going away next week, and I think you should see about it before I leave." She wondered if he was going away with Louise. She had long since realized that the previous summer when she was in the hospital with Bill, he had probably spent the entire time with Louise. Her absence had been a blessing for him, she was sure. And his failure to come back and visit her had had nothing to do with her, or Bill, or any anger about that, it had to do with his own involvement with Louise, and the time he wanted to spend with her, and could with Isabelle away. But she no longer cared about that. It was simply a fact of their life, and apparently had been for years.

"Where are you going?" she asked, trying to look interested, but she wasn't. In anything anymore. It was all she could do to take care of Teddy now, and she was relieved that Sophie had come home for a few days.

"To see clients in the South of France." She was sure the "client" was Louise, but of course she didn't ask. "I want you to call the doctor today," he reminded her when he left, but she didn't. She knew what was wrong with her. Her heart was broken, it had nothing to do with the accident the year before. It had been exactly one year. It was hard to believe Bill was out of her life. And lately, she found herself wishing she had died during the accident. It would have been so much easier than what she was going through now. She wondered if the pain would ever stop, and doubted it. Each day was worse than the one before. She had nothing to look forward to, nothing to wish for, nothing to hope, nothing she believed in anymore, no faith that life would be kind to her.

Bill had taken it all with him and left her nothing but memories and grief. And the worst of it was that she wasn't even angry at him. She just loved him, and knew she always would. She was like an animal who had lost its mate and was looking for a quiet place to die.

"Mommy, what's wrong?" Sophie asked in a worried voice when they met outside Teddy's room that afternoon.

"Nothing, darling. I'm just tired." She looked terrible, and everyone could see it. Sophie and Teddy's nurse Marthe had been talking about it that afternoon. Teddy said that she'd been looking ill ever since she got a call that a friend had died. But the others sensed that the cause of Isabelle's despair ran far deeper than that, and they were all seriously afraid not only for her health, but her life.

When Gordon inquired that night, she said the doctor had said she was fine. She hadn't even bothered to call, and she knew Gordon wouldn't check to see if she had.

It crossed his mind that some very intense emotional pain must have been the cause of it, a failed love affair, a broken heart. A warning bell in his head made him think of Bill, and he rejected the idea just as fast. She wouldn't dare start that again, Gordon knew, after the warnings he'd given her. But he understood nothing about the force of her love for Bill, or who she really was.

The next day, Gordon left for the South of France, looking unconcerned. The number he left was the Hotel du Cap. He was planning to be away for three weeks, and Isabelle didn't question it. It was a relief to have him gone. She no longer had to make excuses to him for how ill she felt, or how bad she looked. It was far easier to be alone.

And when he returned three weeks later, he was shocked to find her looking worse. He looked healthy and tanned, and she looked as though she were suffering from a terminal disease. She and Teddy looked equally sick. Sophie cried when she talked to him about it. But he said that her mother had seen the doctor several weeks before, and he had declared her fit. He didn't want to know more than that, or face the possibility that he might have another invalid in the house.

Gordon left again in August, on a lengthy business trip in Italy and Spain. Sophie had gone to Brittany for a few weeks, to visit friends. And Isabelle was content to be alone with Teddy. She was reading to him again and making an effort for him, in order not to worry him, but she couldn't imagine ever being herself again. It had been easier to get over the accident than to lose Bill. She woke every morning now thinking of him, and wishing she were dead.

And it was while Gordon and Sophie were gone that Teddy caught a nasty summer flu. It seemed like a head cold at first, and then went straight to his chest. He ran a high fever, and the doctor put him on antibiotics to make sure it wouldn't get worse. But the fever kept rising, and nothing Isabelle or the nurse did brought it down. By the third day, he could hardly breathe. Even the doctor was concerned by how unresponsive he was. And at the end of two more days, he had pneumonia. He was rapidly going from bad to worse. Five days after it started, the doctor put him in the hospital, and Isabelle stayed there with him. She thought about calling Gordon, but it seemed wrong to bother him. He was never involved in Teddy's miseries anyway. They always fell to her.

"Am I going to die?" Teddy asked her with huge glassy eyes in the hospital, as she stroked his head, and put cool cloths on his forehead and wrists. The nurses were grateful for her help.

"Of course not. But you have to get well now. This is a silly bug, and you've been sick long enough." But he had a 107-degree fever that night. And Isabelle called Gordon the next day.

"I don't know what it is. It's some kind of virus. But he's very sick." She sounded even more exhausted than before, and looked worse.

"He's always sick," Gordon said, sounding annoyed. He was in Tuscany, and it was hard for Isabelle to imagine what kind of business he had there. It was another vacation with Louise undoubtedly, but Isabelle no longer cared. "There's nothing I can do from here."

"I just thought you'd want to know," she said, wondering why she'd even bothered to call. It had been a courtesy, rather than a plea for help.

"Call me if he gets worse." And then what would he do, Isabelle thought to herself. What if he dies, should I call then? Or would that be an imposition too? But she didn't say anything to him.

She waited two more days, and then called Sophie. Teddy was delirious by then, and Isabelle was panicked as she tried to talk to him. They were giving him intravenous antibiotics, but by then his lungs were failing, and the doctor was worried about his heart. She was suddenly terrified that this was the moment she had always feared. And unlike her father, Sophie came home that night from Brittany. The two women sat with him for hours, neither of them slept, and they each held one hand, standing on either side of his bed, as he dozed. He talked in his sleep at times, but very little of what he said made sense.

He looked peaceful finally the next morning when he woke. It was a hot, muggy day, and he was blazing to the touch, but he kept saying he was cold. It was nightfall before he spoke to them that day. The doctor came and went, and the nurses checked on him, and late that night, the doctor told Isabelle that things didn't look good. He was getting worse.

"What do you mean?"

"I'm worried about his heart. It can't stand so much strain. He's a very sick boy." She knew that already, but she was frustrated that they couldn't seem to do anything for him.

And much to her horror, they spent another week that way, with Teddy seeming to hover between life and death. Both Sophie and Isabelle were beyond exhausted by then. They looked almost as bad as he did. And Isabelle was horrified that Gordon had never called to ask how Teddy was, after Isabelle's call to Tuscany nearly two weeks before. She imagined that he just assumed that Teddy had recovered. And as the third week began, Teddy slipped into unconsciousness. He had several seizures, and his pneumonia was worse. Isabelle couldn't imagine how he'd survived this long, and she just sat in the hall and cried, and then went back in the room to sit next to him. And that night she called Gordon again.

Just as she'd guessed, he had assumed that the child was fine, and was startled to hear how ill he still was.

"I didn't know if you'd want to come home."

"Do you think I should?" He didn't sound enthused by the idea, but he did sound concerned. The situation was far worse than he'd expected it to be by then.

"That's up to you. He's very sick." He hadn't regained consciousness since the night before, and the doctor was no longer sure he would again. Gordon said to call him the next day.

Isabelle and Sophie sat with Teddy all that night, and at five in the morning, he opened his eyes and smiled at both of them. They both cried with relief and thought it was a good sign. But the nurse said his fever had gone higher during the night. It was close to 108. But he was talking to them. This time, when the doctor came, he shook his head. The boy's heart was giving out. It was the moment Isabelle had dreaded all his life, and now it had come. She looked devastated, and felt strangely calm, as she waited with her son for whatever hand Fate would deal them.

He was talking to her clearly now, and holding her hand. He looked at Sophie with an angelic smile. Isabelle kissed his cheek, and felt how hot and dry it was until it was bathed by her tears. She couldn't stop crying.

"I love you, my little one." He had always been so loving to her, so patient and so sweet. He had had a lifetime of pain and never complained. And he didn't complain now. He just held her hand in his and drifted between sleep and waking. She had an uncontrollable urge to hang on to him, to keep him from the edge of the abyss where his soul was dancing. She couldn't bear the thought of losing him. But there was nothing she could do to stop what was happening to him.

He looked at her then and smiled. "I'm happy, Mommy," he said quietly, and then turned to his sister, "I love you, Sophie," and then with the smallest of sighs, he was gone, as they each held his hands. It was peaceful and simple, the release of his soul from the body that had tormented him all his life, and Isabelle took him in her arms and held him as she cried. Sophie watched them and sobbed, and then Isabelle hugged Sophie. Teddy looked beautiful as he lay on the bed, and the two women hugged him and kissed him for a last time, and then walked quietly out of the room. It was a hot sunny day and Isabelle felt lost when she reached the street. She couldn't believe he had left them. It was unimaginable, unthinkable, unbearable. He had looked so sweet. She knew she would remember his last expression all her life. She stood in the street sobbing and hugging her daughter, as Sophie clung to her.

The two women hailed a cab and went home, and Isabelle broke into sobs when she saw his room. He had truly been like the Little Prince in Saint-Exupéry's book, and now he was gone to his own world, a world he never should have left. But he had given her so much joy during his brief lifetime.

She made Sophie a cup of tea, and then called Gordon, and she sounded amazingly calm. He was stunned when he heard the news. He said he'd be home that night. He didn't cry or tell her he was sorry. He said almost nothing and hung up. And Isabelle thought of calling Bill, but she knew there was no point, he was no longer there for her, and he had never met the boy. She knew she had to let Bill go. She felt she no longer had a right to call him and intrude on his life.

She and Sophie went to the funeral home that afternoon and made arrangements for him. They picked a simple white casket, and Isabelle ordered flowers, lilies of the valley and white roses, and she knew no one would come to his funeral but them, and his nurses. He had never gone to school, had no friends, and Isabelle had led a secluded life for years. They were the only ones who had known and loved him. Isabelle couldn't imagine what she would do without him. He had been not only her life and her heart, but her job for years. Isabelle was crying softly, and Sophie was inconsolable when they went home. And Gordon arrived from Rome late that night, looking somber and subdued.

He went to the funeral home with Isabelle and Sophie the next day. Isabelle had asked that the casket be closed. She couldn't bear to see him that way, although he had been as beautiful in death as he had been in life. Gordon had said he didn't want to see him, which Isabelle understood. He had never been able to tolerate Teddy's frailty or illness, and although he was his father, he barely knew him. He had resisted knowing him all his life, and it was too late now.

The three of them had dinner in the dining room that night. Isabelle said nothing as Sophie and Gordon talked. No one spoke of Teddy, it was just too painful. Isabelle went to her room afterward and lay down on the bed, and all she could think of was the child she had borne whose life had always been so fragile. He was like a butterfly who had finally escaped them, and flown away. She was grateful to have loved him and known him at all.

The funeral the next day was in the chapel of their church, and the eulogy was written by a priest who never knew him, and mispronounced his name. But it was the ride to the cemetery that nearly destroyed Isabelle, she couldn't bear to leave him there and she wanted to throw herself on his casket. She touched it a hundred times before she left, and took one of the delicate white roses with her to press in a book. She felt as though she were moving underwater or recovering from another coma. She had no idea how ill she looked by the time they got home. She could hardly breathe or move. Every instant was intolerably painful.

It was late that afternoon when Gordon came into her bedroom, and frowned as he looked down at her. She was lying on her bed and her face was the color of white marble. "I don't know what's wrong with you," he said, looking more annoyed than concerned. He was beginning to hate being around her. She always looked so ill and had for a while. "You look like we should have buried you today instead of Teddy. What's wrong with you, Isabelle?"

"I just lost my son." Her eyes were broken as she looked at him, unable to believe what she was hearing.

"So did I. But you've looked like this for two months."

"Have I? I'm sorry." She turned her face away from him. She didn't want to see him, and wished he would leave.

"It's very hard on Sophie to see you looking like that."

"It's very hard on me to lose my son," she said without expression in her voice.

"We've expected this for years," he reminded her, "although I know it's a shock, particularly after the blow to your system you had last year." He was beginning to think now that she had never regained her health. But she was struck, as she watched him, by how totally cold and unemotional he was. No one would have believed that he had also just lost his son. He seemed more a visitor to the house than a member of the family, and certainly not the child's father. He looked at Isabelle almost with curiosity and asked her a strange question. "What are you going to do now?"

"About what?" His room? Her life? His clothes? She couldn't bear to think of it.

"Taking care of Teddy is all you've done for the past fifteen years. You can't just bury yourself with him now."

Why not? But she didn't say the words. With any luck at all, she thought, she was truly going to die. After losing Teddy, and Bill, she had very little to live for, except Sophie. But Gordon stunned her with what he said next. "I think you should go to stay with Sophie in Grenoble when she goes back to school in two weeks. I really think it's an excellent idea. You need to get out of this house finally, and it will do you good to be with her." What Isabelle understood instantly was that he was banishing her to the provinces so he could stay with Louise. It was a very clever plan, and so easily explained because of Teddy's death. He was brilliant.

"Are you serious?" She almost laughed at the look on his face. He seemed so solicitous, but so desperate for her to leave. He must have been terrified that, without Teddy to keep her busy, she would try to reclaim her place as his wife. "What on earth do you expect me to do there? I'm sure Sophie would be horrified, justifiably, to have me underfoot." It was the last thing Isabelle wanted to do now.

"Well, you can't just lie around here," he said, looking annoyed again.

"Is that what you think I do?" There was an edge to their conversation. Isabelle had had enough of the pretense and the sham they had already played out for too many years, and she wasn't going to be fobbed off now on the pretext that he thought she should be with Sophie. She was devastated by losing Teddy, but she was not going to become a nuisance to her daughter while she grieved him. She had more sense and more dignity than that. And she was too smart not to see through what he had in mind for her.

"I have no idea what you do," he said unpleasantly, "other than take care of that child."

" 'That child' was your son, and he's dead now. Have a little respect. For him. And for me." It was the first time she had dared to speak to him like that. And he was not pleased.

"Isabelle, don't tell me how to behave. If you'll recall, I tolerated a great deal of bad behavior from you last year, around the time of your accident. And I'm not going to put up with any more nonsense from you."

"Really?" Isabelle asked, with dangerously glittering eyes. He was coming across the line of what she could tolerate, and at an astonishing speed. "And what kind of bad behavior was that?"

"You know exactly what I mean. I put up with your affair with Bill Robinson. You were very lucky I didn't divorce you." The weapons had just been unveiled. But for once, having lost so much, Isabelle was no longer frightened of him. With Teddy's death, Gordon had lost his hold on her. Perhaps forever, and surely for now.

"And you're very lucky that I've put up with the way you've treated me for the past twenty years, and the appalling way you treated your son for the last fifteen." They were locked in deadly combat, Isabelle hadn't anticipated having this conversation with him so soon after Teddy's death, but she was ready for him. And she remembered what Bill had said when he left, about saving the ammunition until Gordon attacked her again, and he finally had. On the day of Teddy's funeral. It was an appalling cruelty and disrespect, but not surprising from him.

Gordon stood looking at her as though he wanted to slap her, but didn't dare. "I won't tolerate this from you. You'll find yourself in the street with your hat in your hand, Isabelle, if you're not careful."

"You don't frighten me anymore, Gordon." She had nothing left to lose. She didn't need to protect Teddy anymore, and she no longer cared if Gordon threw her out. It would be a blessing for her in the end if he did. "You don't frighten me at all." He could see that she meant it.

"And where will you go if I throw you out?" He spat the words at her, and Isabelle looked remarkably calm, as her eyes met his and held firm.

"Perhaps you and the Comtesse de Ligne would be kind enough to let me stay in your apartment on the rue du Bac? I assume, if you 'threw me out,' she would be staying with you here?" She said it in a quiet, ladylike voice, and Gordon let out an irate roar. He sounded like a wounded lion, and he came so close to her, she could see his every pore. He was so angry, he was shaking.

"You don't know what you're talking about!" he shouted at her, stunned by what she had just said. It was a blow he hadn't expected, and for a moment, it knocked him off balance.

"Maybe not, but apparently half of Paris knows, and has for the last ten years. She called here by mistake, on New Year's Eve. I think she was drunk, but it opened my eyes to what I should have seen years ago. So don't speak to me about Bill Robinson, Gordon. He's beside the point."

"Is he still in your life?" He had no right to know, but she told him anyway. He was staggered that she knew about Louise, and had never said a word to him.

"No, he's not. But I gather the countess is very much in yours. I assume she was in Italy with you." He didn't admit it to Isabelle, but her assumption was accurate, and a number of people knew it. "I've been told she can't or won't marry you until her husband dies. That must be difficult for you. And what were you planning to do with me then, Gordon? How were you planning to get rid of me, other than shipping me off to Grenoble to stay with Sophie?"

"You're insane! You're deranged by the loss of your son. I won't listen to this nonsense." Gordon looked like he was about to walk out. He did not want to hear another word from her.

"No," she said calmly. "I'm heartbroken, but not insane. I must have been though not to see what you were doing for all these years. You weren't even sleeping here, and I was too stupid to know it, because you were so busy terrorizing me. Well, those days are over."

"Get out of my house!" he barked at her. He was shaking with fury.

"I will, but not until I'm ready to. And in the meantime, I suggest you stay with her." He stormed out of her bedroom then, and a moment later she heard him slam the front door. It had been an incredible scene, and she suddenly realized he had walked out on her, and she didn't even care. It was as though losing Teddy had finally freed her. She had lost so much when she lost Teddy and Bill, she had absolutely nothing to lose anymore, except Sophie. And in leaving, Gordon had released her from the misery and lies they had shared for far too many years.

"What did he say to you, Mom?" Sophie

asked quietly. Isabelle hadn't seen her slip into her room. She had come in after her father left, and she looked frightened. She had never heard them fight like that in her entire life.

"It's not important," Isabelle said, sitting down on her bed again. She felt shaken, but relieved.

"It is important," Sophie said. "Mom, he's horrible to you. He's my father, and I love him, but I don't want him to be mean to you anymore." Particularly today, after Teddy's funeral, it was outrageous.

As she looked at her daughter, Isabelle suddenly realized all that had just happened. "He just told me to move out." She was oddly quiet and composed as she said it. And Sophie needed to know what had happened.

"Do you have to do that?" Sophie's eyes were enormous in her face, and Isabelle thought about it. Sophie looked terrified, but Isabelle did not. She was strangely calm.

"I suppose I do. It's his house." Their marriage had ended on the day of Teddy's funeral, which was right somehow. It was over at last.

"Where will you go?" There were tears in Sophie's eyes.

"I suppose I'll get an apartment. I should have done it a long time ago, but I couldn't have taken care of Teddy without his help." Sophie nodded, as Isabelle understood that everything was ending around her. She had lost so much. Teddy, Bill, her home, her marriage. Everything she had known or loved or cherished or counted on or believed in had come to an end. There was nothing left for her to do but begin again. And as she looked at her daughter, Sophie came and put her arms around her, and the two women hugged without saying a word.

It was Teddy who had freed her from Gordon finally. Teddy who had taken her by the hand and led her away. Bill hadn't been able to do it, and he had left first. And she would never have had the courage to do it herself. But Teddy, in freeing himself of the earthly body that had been such torture to him, had finally freed his mother from the life that had tormented her. It was almost as though she could feel him next to her, happy about what he had done. After all she had done for him for fifteen years, it was his final gift to her. She was free at last.

Chapter Seventeen

Gordon didn't return to the house on the rue de Grenelle for several days. Isabelle knew she could have found him if she wanted, but she didn't try. She had no reason to. They had nothing left to say, and she was sure he was with the Comtesse de Ligne.

Isabelle wandered around the house aimlessly for a while, absorbing all that had happened. She sat in Teddy's room for hours, and cried, and then suddenly smiled through her tears as she remembered things he had done or said. She seemed lost in another world. And by herself, late one night, she began to pack up his things. He had so little, as though he had only been passing through this world. He had books, puzzles, toys from his childhood, endless nightclothes, some religious articles the nurses had given him over the years. Isabelle sniffed his clothes and his pillow before she put them

away. But in effect, he had very little. The only
things that had really mattered to him were
photographs he had of his mother and Sophie.
And there was a very handsome one of Isabelle
and Gordon on their wedding day. It was the
only photograph of his father he'd ever had, or
wanted.

She packed it all up, and stayed up until
morning to do it, and by the time Sophie got
up in the morning, it was done. There were
neatly packed boxes stacked in his room. And
when she was finished, Isabelle went back to
her own bedroom and went to sleep.

She heard from Gordon finally late that afternoon. He wanted to know what her plans were.

"I haven't figured that out yet. I've been
packing Teddy's things."

"That's a morbid pursuit, why don't you have
the nurses do it?" She had done it herself out of
respect for the child she had loved so much. But
Gordon couldn't understand that. He loved no
one except himself, and never had. Isabelle
couldn't imagine what his relationship was with
Louise. She was sure it was based on her social
importance, and her title. They were the same
things that had once drawn him to Isabelle. But
he couldn't tolerate the person, or the reality.
He had no use for them. "You behaved abom-
inably the other night," he accused her, trying

to intimidate her with his tone. She had heard it so often, it no longer impressed her. And what he had been so horrified by was that she dared to bring up his affair with Louise. It seemed amazing to him that she had finally discovered it after all these years. And when he'd asked Louise if she'd actually called his house on New Year's Eve when she missed her flight to Saint-Moritz, all of which he considered most unlikely, she had admitted that she probably had. It was an innocent mistake. But it had unraveled and exposed ten years of his carefully constructed lies. He hadn't dared complain to her about it.

"This has been an abominable situation for a long time," Isabelle said simply, which was the truth. "I always thought that I had somehow failed you and that's why you were so cold to me. I thought it was my fault, because I was always so wrapped up in Teddy. But I finally understand it had nothing to do with me, or with him. You simply didn't want to be here."

"It had everything to do with you," he said. "If you'd taken the time to be a decent wife, it would never have happened." He was admitting nothing to her, and blaming her for everything, which was typical of him.

"I have been a decent wife to you, Gordon. I was always here for you. I actually loved you in the beginning. You were the one who shut me out, who put walls up between us, who moved out of our bedroom and rejected me. But none of that had anything to do with me, and I think you know that."

"You can't absolve yourself so easily. I would never have done any of those things if you had learned what you needed to in the beginning."

He was the teacher, and she the pupil, and he wanted her to know she had failed the course abysmally. All her love and decency and heart counted for nothing with him. He didn't know or care who she was. That much was clear. She had done backward somersaults for him for years, while he shouted "higher," "faster," and it was never good enough for him. Once he had taken advantage of her background and connections, and had established himself, he had no further use for her. And she knew he would do the same thing to Louise. Once the world knew he had married a countess, and that she was a very rich and successful woman, and he had used her to his satisfaction, he could throw her away too. Isabelle could no longer imagine Gordon caring about anyone, not her, not his children, not even his mistress probably. He was narcissistic in the extreme.

"I think you've been brain-damaged ever since your accident," he said coolly, and she suddenly saw the picture he was going to paint, that she had never been quite right after her coma, that she had always been a little odd, and had finally become severely disturbed after her son's death. It was the perfect excuse for disposing of her. It was like suddenly catching a glimpse of a deep dark cave, and seeing the monster who lived there. In the old days, it would have terrified her, but it no longer did. She wanted nothing to do with the monster anymore. "I expect you to move out quickly," he said coldly. He had dispensed with her, and all he wanted was for her to disappear. It was so perfectly convenient. She served no purpose and had become a problem. And he wanted her removed. She had exposed him, and he couldn't tolerate that. She had shined a far too bright light on him, and refused to be fooled. She had been duped by him for far too long, but no more.

"I'll move out when I find an apartment, Gordon," she said, sounding tired. She'd been up all the night before, packing Teddy's things. "You do realize, don't you, that if you throw me out in the street right after Teddy's death, that people are going to say ugly things about you."

"I will tell them that you were crazed over his death, and ran away for reasons that are unclear to me, aggravated of course by your brain injury." It was brilliant actually, and he'd worked it all out. She couldn't help wondering if he'd had help from Louise.

"You're assuming that people believe you, and I'm not sure they do. Some may, but anyone who knows me knows that I'm not *la folle de Chaillot* hiding away in the attic, I'm a woman you've lied to and cheated on and treated very badly. One day, people will see who you are, just as your children finally did. You can't fool people forever, not even me." But his betrayal still felt like a terrible blow to her. And what he was doing now seemed almost worse, given the shock of Teddy's death. She had been abandoned by Bill, after five years, and now by Gordon, who had actually abandoned her emotionally years before, and Teddy had left her because he had no choice. But however Isabelle looked at it, they were hard hits for her. Very hard. And she knew, as she listened to him tell her how he would destroy her reputation, that she would never recover entirely from the betrayal of people she had once loved so passionately. It dissolved any faith she'd once had in life being fair, and things ending happily. There were no happy endings in her world. She didn't even expect them anymore. She just wanted peace.

"Move out when you want. Just let me know when you do. I called my lawyer today. He's going to draft settlement papers for you." He had moved very quickly. She wondered if the Comte de Ligne was failing. Gordon seemed to be in a rush suddenly. And it would have been so perfect for him if she'd been willing to disappear to Grenoble. He could have said she was in a sanatorium, or had gone mad, or was suffering from depression. He could have said almost anything, as long as no one saw her anymore. But she had no intention of making things that easy for him. And she realized, as she listened to him, that she had to find an attorney. And then Gordon issued her yet another warning. "Be clear when you pack, Isabelle, that you can only take what's yours, whatever you brought to the marriage. The rest belongs to me."

"That was my intention," she said coldly. How quickly it was all reduced to what belonged to whom. All she wanted were her clothes, Teddy's things, some of her parents' paintings and antiques, and the few pieces of jewelry Gordon had given her. She never wanted to see the rest of it again, and she was only taking the jewelry so she could give it to Sophie. "I'll let you know when I find a place to live."

She looked frantically for an apartment for the

next few weeks, and it was easier once Sophie went back to school. Sophie was so distraught over everything that had happened, that Isabelle didn't want to upset her further. But in late September, Isabelle found a very suitable apartment for them on the rue de Varenne, not far from the house she and Gordon had shared on the rue de Grenelle. The apartment had two bedrooms, a large sunny living room, a small dining room, a somewhat antiquated kitchen and pantry, and a terrace overlooking the Musée Rodin. It was actually the third floor in an old *hôtel particulier,* there was garage space for one car in what had been the stables, and it was in fairly decent shape. The house itself had been elegant once, although like so many of the beautiful eighteenth-century houses on the Left Bank, the people who had owned it for generations had run out of money to maintain it long since. There was a tiny elevator that looked like a bird cage, high ceilings, beautiful but battered floors, and the landlords were an aristocratic family she had once met. It was a good neighborhood and a good address, and she knew she would feel safe there. And she knew she had just enough furniture from her parents to decorate it decently. She called Gordon's attorney once she signed the lease for the apartment, and told him she was going to move in two weeks. And then she called Sophie.

For Sophie, it seemed like a mixed blessing. She was happy her mother had found it, but it was going to be strange living somewhere else. She would stay at the rue de Grenelle when she visited her father, but with her mother and Teddy gone, it depressed her just thinking about it.

Isabelle had had the settlement papers from Gordon by then. He was offering her a small settlement, which in no way reflected the life they had shared for twenty-one years. And his attorney suggested she get a job, which she intended to do anyway, rather than ask Gordon for support. Everything in the offer they made was slanted toward him, and it was, in effect, an enormous slap in the face. In truth, she wanted nothing from him, and it confirmed everything she'd thought when she'd been afraid to leave him because of Teddy. He would have starved them to death if she left. She wanted very little from him now, just enough to cover her, in case something untoward happened to her or she got sick.

Her own lawyer was outraged by what he'd offered, and wanted her to fight for her fair share, and even try to win the house on the rue de Grenelle. But Isabelle knew it would be a hollow victory. As best she could, she wanted to walk away with a bare minimum to meet her needs, and nothing more. She wanted almost nothing from him.

She moved to the apartment on the rue de Varenne in mid-October, and was surprised by how pretty it looked once she got it fixed up a bit. And the only painful part of leaving her old house was leaving the rooms where she and Teddy had spent his entire life. But she knew that she was taking her memories with her, and with a last sad look over her shoulder, she walked out, as Josephine the housekeeper cried. Isabelle promised to have her come to visit at her new address.

And even Sophie was surprised the first time she came home for a weekend. It was the long All Saints' Day weekend, and she had four days off from school.

"It looks wonderful, Mom!" Sophie beamed when she saw her room. Isabelle had used some fabric she'd put away, it was all done in lavender silk with lilacs and violets on it. And she'd had the walls painted a warm ivory, with a thin line of lavender trim. It was a perfect room for a girl. She had done her own room in yellow, and the living room was filled with antiques that had been Isabelle's mother's, they were very fine pieces, mostly Louis XV and XVI. She had only been there for two weeks, and it already felt like home. In some ways, far more than the rue de Grenelle. It was hers.

Most of all, Isabelle was surprised by how easily she had adjusted to her new life. She didn't miss Gordon, the only one she missed incredibly was Teddy, her heart ached for him constantly. The new apartment had given her some distraction, but there was no hiding from the fact that he was gone. In some ways, it was easier being in a new place, she couldn't wander the halls that he had once walked, or sit in the room where she had sat with him for hours. And in spite of her new location, she had not only taken her grief for Teddy with her, her endless longing for Bill had followed her there as well. It was inconceivable to her that she would never see him again, and that, after five years of talking to her, advising her, comforting her, being her mentor and best friend, and finally lover, he had simply shut her out and left. It was the last thing she had ever expected of him, the only cruel thing he had ever done. In its own way, it was the cruelest of all. She knew it would take her a lifetime to forget him, if she ever did. And she couldn't imagine ever loving or trusting anyone again. In the end, it was not so much Gordon who had broken her heart and destroyed her faith, because she expected nothing of him anymore, and hadn't in years, but Bill had hurt her more, because she had truly loved and trusted him. But she knew it was something she had to live with, at whatever cost.

Two weeks after she had moved into the apartment, even before Sophie came home for the Toussaint, she saw a photograph of him in the *Herald Tribune.* The article talked about the upcoming elections in the States, and his part in an important senatorial race. It was very flattering to him, and she sat and stared at the photograph for a long time, and thought he looked well. She couldn't tell precisely, but it looked as though he were standing in a group of men, and the candidate whose cause he was championing was standing next to him. It even mentioned briefly that he had had a near-fatal car accident in London the year before and had made a remarkable recovery, and returned to politics stronger than ever. Although it didn't say he was walking or running marathons, the article seemed to support what Bill had said when he lied to her about being able to walk again. It sounded like he was perfectly fine and fully restored. In the end, after staring at it for two days and torturing herself over it, she threw the newspaper away.

Sophie had just gone back to school after the Toussaint weekend, when Isabelle saw Bill on CNN. He was at a Senate hearing in Washington, seated at a long table, addressing a committee on Senate appropriations. What they were saying sounded extremely technical and boring to her, but she was mesmerized the moment she saw his face. She'd been having a very bad day over Teddy, and finally gave up trying to cheer herself up. She'd gone to bed and turned on the TV to distract herself. She couldn't take her eyes off him as he talked and moved, made an impassioned speech, and then turned right toward the camera, as though he were speaking to her.

"You bastard," she whispered softly. She wanted to wish him well with his renewed vows to Cynthia, but she couldn't. She was still too hurt by what he had done to her. She could still remember every word he had said to her when he had told her it was over between them. She hadn't deserved that, she had loved him so much, and they'd been so happy. She was agonizing, remembering all of it, when the camera pulled back at the end of the speech, and she saw someone wheel him away. Her mouth fell open as she watched it. He had told her the use of his legs had fully returned, and it was obvious from what she was seeing that he was still confined to a wheelchair. But why? Why would he tell her he could walk if he couldn't? What purpose could it possibly serve? And then as she watched him disappear off the screen with a wave to several people in the crowd, she remembered what he had said from the first. Already in London, he had hinted darkly that if he couldn't walk again, he wouldn't stay with her, so as not to be a burden on her. He had never spelled it out to her, but she had understood what he meant, and thought he was just depressed. She hadn't really believed him then, and thought he was dramatizing, but she suddenly wondered if he'd meant what he said. It was as though she could hear his words now, as clear as could be. She had never even thought about it, because he had been so clear that he was walking again. And suddenly she wondered if he had lied about everything else.

She sat in her bed for a long time, wondering what to do next, how to find out what had happened. She wanted to pick up the phone and ask him. But if he had wanted her to know the truth, he would have told her five months before, instead of lying to her. She was completely confused. She tossed back the covers and got out of bed, and began pacing her bedroom as the television droned on. She turned it off so she could think more clearly, and then looked at her watch. It was noon in Washington, and six o'clock at night in Paris. And then she had an idea, ran to the kitchen, and grabbed the phone.

She dialed Washington information and asked

for the number of his office, and was instantly rewarded. She wasn't totally sure what to do next, but when a voice answered, sounding busy, she asked for Mr. Robinson's assistant, and a male voice came on the phone. She explained that Mr. Robinson had encouraged her to call for her committee on literacy in children in the Deep South, and she could hear the assistant pay attention to her. Isabelle knew that literacy all over America was of great importance to him, and he urged all his candidates to espouse it as a valuable cause.

"Of course," the assistant said, validating Isabelle's idea.

"We were hoping that he and his wife would attend our event in December. We'd like his wife to be our honorary chair." There was a brief pause while the assistant caught his breath and Isabelle regrouped, praying that she was right.

"I'm sure Mr. Robinson would like to. I'll check his calendar when you give me the date. But I'm afraid that . . . er . . . Mrs. Robinson won't be able to chair the event. Or actually, she might, but . . . well, they're divorced. In fact," he sounded slightly embarrassed, "she's getting remarried next month. I'm sure she'd be very interested if you'd actually prefer to ask them. I can give you her number if you'd like to call her. Otherwise, I think Mr. Robinson would be interested in chairing your event, if you'll send me some material on it, and give me the date."

"Absolutely. I'll get it out to you today." Isabelle's hand was shaking as she held the phone and closed her eyes. He had lied to her about both things. He and Cynthia were not together, and he could not walk, and she felt certain now of what he had done. He had freed her, for her sake, out of some crazy lunatic idea he had that he owed that to her, because he loved her. Or maybe he didn't love her anymore . . . but two things were sure, he was no longer married to Cynthia, and he was still in a wheelchair.

"Thank you so much," she breathed into the phone to his assistant.

"And what was that date again?"

"December twelfth."

"I'll calendar that for you and let him know."

"Thank you."

"And your name? I'm sorry . . . I didn't catch it. . . ."

"No problem. Sally Jones."

"Thank you, Miss Jones. Thank you for your call."

She sat in her bed for a long time afterward, pondering what to do next. She just sat there, thinking about him, and ever more certain of what he had done and why. She felt as though everything had changed in the blink of an eye. But this time, instead of wanting to die as she had for the last five months, she felt alive again.

And at midnight, after thinking about it for hours, she knew what she had to do. She picked up the phone and called the airline, and made a reservation for the following afternoon. His elections were only four days away, and the timing was probably awful, but she couldn't wait. She booked a seat on the two o'clock flight the next day. And then she called Sophie and told her she was going to Washington for a few days.

"Why?" Sophie sounded surprised, but she was pleased. Her mother had been so lifeless, so sad, and so distraught for months, and especially after Teddy died, that it was a relief to know she was willing to go anywhere.

"I'm going to see an old friend," Isabelle explained.

"Anyone I know?" Sophie asked, trying to figure it out. Her mother was acting a little crazy, and sounding strange. She sounded excited and happy and scared.

"Bill Robinson. We were in the accident to-gether," Isabelle said gently, and Sophie smiled at her end.

"I know, Mom. He was nice to me in London

when I visited you in the hospital. He has two daughters and a nice wife."

"That's about right." Minus the wife.

"He liked you a lot," Sophie said innocently, and Isabelle smiled.

"I like him too. I'll call and let you know where I am, and when I'm coming home. Okay? Take good care of yourself, sweetheart. I'll be back soon."

"Don't rush back. I'm not coming home till Christmas. Have a good time."

"Thank you," Isabelle said, and hung up.

She couldn't sleep that night, and left for the airport the next morning at eleven o'clock. She had to be there at noon. And she could hardly contain herself on the flight. She had no idea how to see him, or what to say to him when she did. Maybe he'd be furious with her for finding him out and hunting him down. If he had wanted to be with her, she told herself, he would have been. He had made himself perfectly clear, she argued with herself all the way across the Atlantic. But he was wrong. That was the whole point. He was entirely, totally wrong. He didn't have to do that for her, didn't have to sacrifice himself. She didn't give a damn if he never walked again, except for his sake, but not for her own. All she could do now was find him, and tell him that. But she knew it would be no easy thing. He was a very stubborn man. She remembered all too vividly his many objections to Joe marrying Jane.

As the plane landed at Dulles Airport, Isabelle closed her eyes and said a silent prayer that he would listen to her. She had no idea if he would. But she was going to give it one hell of a try.

She had his office address in her pocket, and trembling in the chill air, she stepped into a cab, and gave the driver the address of the Four Seasons Hotel in Georgetown, where she'd made a reservation the night before. All she had to do now was find out where he was.

Chapter Eighteen

It was nearly four o'clock when Isabelle settled into her room at the hotel. And she knew she had to call his office soon if she was going to find out where he was going that night. Or maybe she should just walk in on him in the office. Maybe she was totally crazy to have come. There were a thousand scenarios in her head, and she had no idea how any of them would work out. And as she stared at the phone, she was beginning to think she'd made a terrible mistake. Maybe he had just fallen out of love with her. Finally, after another half hour of total terror, she picked up the phone.

A receptionist answered, and Isabelle made herself sound busy, crazed, and stressed.

"Hi, I'm with security for tonight. What time will Mr. Robinson arrive?" She forced herself to sound American, so the woman wouldn't know she was French.

"God, I don't know," the girl said, sounding even more stressed than Isabelle could pretend. "They're going to six different events. Who is this again?"

"Security. You know, for the dinner."

"Oh, of course . . . damn . . . I thought he canceled that . . . no, that's right . . . okay . . . he's coming to you at nine o'clock . . . he's sorry to be late, but he just can't get there any sooner. You'll be his fourth event. And he can't stay long . . . now, you know he's in a wheelchair, right?"

"Right. I've got that in my notes," Isabelle said, sounding official and informed.

"You need to take away the chair at the table so he can wheel himself in. He doesn't like to make a fuss. And he doesn't want to be photographed in the chair. Very low profile. He and Senator Johnson want to come in a side door, and they'll leave the same way."

"Right," Isabelle said, but she still didn't know where the dinner was and she couldn't ask.

"Senator Johnson has his own security, and they'll meet you at the side entrance of the Kennedy Center just like last time. . . ." Thank you, God, Isabelle whispered to herself. The Kennedy Center.

"Will he be in black tie? . . . just so we see

him right away . . ." She needed to know what to wear.

"No, he's very sorry . . . he won't . . . I'm sure that's all right."

"It's fine."

They went over the details for another ten minutes, and Isabelle no longer cared what the receptionist said. All she needed to know was that he'd be at the Kennedy Center at nine o'clock that night. And he would be leaving at ten o'clock for his next event. She could either confront him on the way in, or the way out, or she could make a scene at dinner, hide under his table, or pull a gun on him . . . the possibilities were endless, and most of them sounded absolutely hopeless to her now that she was here. She had no idea how to do this, but she knew she had to try.

In the end, she decided to meet him outside, after the dinner, on his way out. That would mean ten o'clock. It was six hours away. The longest six hours of her life. She called the concierge and hired a limousine for that night. And after that she sat in her room worrying about what she was going to say to him, or if he'd even give her a chance to speak. It was a distinct possibility that he would just brush her off and tell her there was nothing to say. It was

Bill who had said that he never wanted to see her again, but he had lied to her. He had told her he could walk and that he and Cindy had renewed their vows. She hadn't been able to understand for five months how he could just sever all ties with her like that. But now she understood perfectly. It was all about not being a burden on her. That was why he hadn't wanted to see her in Paris, she realized, because he didn't want her to know that he still couldn't walk, and never would. She had figured it all out. What she hadn't figured out was how to convince him to change his mind. And she knew she'd only have minutes with him, with the senator standing by, before he got in a car and drove away. She had no idea what she was going to say. I love you was a start, but he knew that anyway, and had when he ended their affair, and it hadn't stopped him then. Why would it now?

There was so much he didn't know, about Teddy, that she had left Gordon and moved out. He didn't know that he'd broken her heart when he left. And most of all, he didn't know that she didn't care that he was in a wheelchair for the rest of his life. All she wanted was to be with him, and love him for as long as he lived.

As she sat there, thinking about him, she began to wonder if it was a mistake trying to see him that night. Maybe she should try and see him in the office, or call him on the phone. She knew he must be crazed, with the election only three days away. She could wait until afterward, she told herself, but he might leave town, or disappear. She didn't want to wait. They had waited long enough.

She couldn't eat that night, she tried to take a nap and was wide awake. In the end, she took a bath and dressed, and at nine-thirty she was in the limousine, speeding toward the Kennedy Center, and then panicked when they reached the side entrance. What if he had already left? She was numb with worry by the time she got out of the car, and went to stand off to the side, where she could watch the entrance, and see him when he came out. It was freezing cold, but she didn't care, and then like some kind of terrifying omen, it started to snow.

Big lacy flakes began drifting down from the sky. They were the kind that stick to your clothes and your lashes and your hair. They came with no warning, and there was a brisk wind that seemed to blow them everywhere. By ten-fifteen there was no sign of him, and she was sure he had left by some other door. Maybe there had been a change of plan. Isabelle was wearing a big heavy black coat and a sable hat, warm black suede boots, and gloves. She was still freezing cold anyway, and covered with snow.

By ten-thirty, she had lost hope. She knew she would have to find some other way and try again. She'd have to attempt some other ploy the next day. She told herself she'd stay until eleven o'clock, just so she could tell herself she had, but she was sure that Bill and the senator would be long gone by then, to their next event.

But at ten to eleven, there was a flurry of activity near the door. Two off-duty policemen came out, looking fairly obvious, a uniformed security man with a wire in his ear, and then a good-looking man with his head down against the wind who strode out of the building and headed toward a waiting car that had appeared from nowhere. Isabelle hadn't seen it before. He looked vaguely like the senator to her, but she wasn't sure from the angle of his face. She watched him for a moment, and no one else came out. She was wondering if Bill hadn't come at all, or had decided to stay. And as she watched, she saw a wheelchair roll slowly out. There were people talking intently to him, and he was nodding, listening to what they said. He was wheeling the chair himself. He was wearing a thick scarf and a dark coat, and she saw instantly that it was Bill. She could feel her heart pound as she watched him wheel himself toward the steps, and then take a ramp down toward where she stood. He hadn't noticed her, and the others left him and ran back inside to escape the snow. The senator and his men were already in the limousine, and they were waiting for him.

And feeling as though she were taking her life in her hands, she walked to the ramp, and began walking up to where he was. She met him halfway, standing squarely in his path. His head was down against the wind, and all he saw were her coat and her legs, and he muttered "excuse me" absentmindedly, but she didn't move away.

Isabelle looked at him, and he heard her voice before he saw her face. "You lied to me," she said in the voice he had dreamed of for five months, and told himself he would never hear again. His eyes rose to hers, and he couldn't say a word. He just looked at her, stunned, and tried to regain his composure as quickly as he could.

"Hello, Isabelle. What a coincidence to see you here." He assumed instantly that Gordon had come to town on business and she had accompanied him. He made no explanation as to why he was in the wheelchair, in spite of what he'd told her months before.

"Actually, it's not a coincidence," she said

honestly. It was far too late for more lies. "I flew here from Paris to see you." He didn't know how to answer her, as the wind whipped their faces, and the snow collected on her hat. She looked like a Christmas card, or a Russian princess to him. She looked so beautiful, it broke his heart, but nothing showed in his face. He forced himself to look dispassionate and unconcerned, and to hide everything he felt. He had become a master of that.

"I have to go. Cynthia is waiting in the car for me." It was the only excuse he could think of for a rapid escape. He knew he needed to get away from her as quickly as he could, before he lost his resolve.

"No, she's not," Isabelle said, pulling her coat tightly around herself. "You're divorced. You lied about that too."

"I guess I lied about a number of things. Except that it was over for me. That part was true." Everything about him resisted her, but his eyes gave him away.

"Why was it over for you?" She was relentless in her pursuit of the truth, and if he could tell her he didn't love her, she would walk away forever. But she had had to see him this one last time. She had taken this chance when she came. But if he was going to send her away again, she at least wanted him to look her in the eye.

"It happens that way sometimes. How's Teddy?" he asked, to break the tension between them, and put her off the scent, but he wasn't prepared for what came next.

"He died three months ago. He caught a very bad flu. I'm sorry you never met him," she said sadly, fighting to keep her composure. She had no intention of burdening him with her grief, but she thought he should know.

"I'm sorry too," he said softly, looking stricken for her. For a moment, he was overwhelmed by the blow he knew it must have been for her, and his own guilt for not being there for her at the time. "Are you all right?" He wanted to reach out to her, and put his arms around her, but he didn't dare. It was embarrassing too to have been caught in his lies, and to have her see him in his chair. He had been so convinced their paths would never cross again, and she would never know.

"Not yet, but I will be eventually. I miss him a lot. I miss you too." Her voice was soft and sad. "How are you?" She wanted to ask if he missed her, if he regretted what he'd done, but he seemed anxious to move on. She knew that the senator was waiting for him. But this was her only chance.

"I'm fine. Better than ever. I'm back at work. The election is three days away." He glanced at his watch then. They were an hour late for their next stop, and he looked at Isabelle apologetically, but there was no sign that he wanted anything from her. "I've really got to go."

"I still love you, Bill," she said, feeling desperately vulnerable, but this was why she had come. She wanted him to know. "I don't give a damn that you can't rollerblade or dance. I'm not a great dancer anyway, I never was."

He smiled at her nostalgically for what seemed like an eternity, and then reached out and touched her hand. "Are you serious that you came here to see me?" His voice was gentle, it was the voice she remembered too well, and had for a long time. All she could do was nod as tears filled her eyes, and then she recovered, as a few stray tears slid down her cheeks and she wiped them away with a gloved hand.

"I saw you on CNN yesterday, and I thought I knew why you lied to me. I wanted you to know I don't care."

"I know you don't," he said softly, "you never did. But I do. That's what matters. I would never let you do that to yourself. I love you too much to let you destroy your life by being saddled with this," he glanced down at his chair. "Even if you left Gordon one day, especially then. Is he treating you decently?" He had looked around for him at first, and realized he wasn't there. She had obviously eluded him somehow, or left him at the hotel.

She smiled at his question. "I used the ammunition on him, as you told me to, when Teddy died. He threw me out. Sophie and I have an apartment on the rue de Varenne." A great many changes had happened in both their lives. But it didn't change the way he felt, or the decision he'd made. In fact, seeing her strengthened it. She was free now, and she deserved a lot more than he had to give, or so he thought.

"I'm glad you're okay." But he refused to say more.

"I know you have to go," she said, brushing the snowflakes away from her eyes, "I'm at the Four Seasons Hotel. If you'd like to talk, give me a call."

All he did was shake his head. There were snowflakes all over his hair, and she realized he must be cold. "I won't call you, Isabelle. We did the right thing five months ago. I did the right thing. For both of us. We have to live by it now."

"I don't agree with you, it was entirely the wrong thing. For both of us. We have a right to love each other, Bill. And even if you stay out of my life, I won't stop loving you. I never will."

"You'll forget eventually," he said, and she

shook her head and stepped aside. He looked at her long and hard. "Take good care of yourself." He wanted to tell her again he was sorry about Teddy, but he didn't. There was nothing more he could say. He just wheeled himself the rest of the way down the ramp, without looking back at her, and got into the car. He apologized to the senator for the delay, and said he had run into an old friend. He didn't say another word all the way to their next stop, and the senator sensed the somberness of his mood. He seemed a million miles away.

It was after midnight when Bill got home, and he didn't call her. It was too late, and he had told himself again that he never would. He believed in what he'd done for her and knew it was the loving thing to do. If he had loved her any less, he would have inflicted himself on her, but he loved her far too much to do that, and knew he always would. He was heartbroken for her about her boy, he knew how much Teddy had meant to her, and he could only imagine how devastating his death had been to her. He was relieved at least to know that Gordon was out of her life. He felt certain she'd find someone else soon. He had never seen her look as beautiful, or as sad, as she had standing there in the snow. It was all he could think of as he lay in his bed that night.

The snow was still falling as Isabelle sat in her hotel room and thought of him. And she knew now that he would never call her again. Everything she had seen in his face had spoken of his resolve not to get involved with her again. Only his eyes told her he still cared. She had to accept it now. Even if he had lied to her, this was what he wanted in the end. She had been right months before, there were no happy endings. There were only lessons and losses, and she had had a lot of those.

She was awake most of the night, and when she fell asleep at last, she was dreaming of him. She was in a deep sleep when the phone rang at her bedside at four A.M. It was Bill. Even wrapped in the mists of sleep, she would have known his voice anywhere.

"I'm sorry to call you so late. Were you asleep?" He sounded as tormented as she had felt before she finally went to sleep.

"Just." She was wide awake the moment she heard his voice. He sounded so agonizingly familiar to her, and then she thought of something. "Where are you?" she asked softly, and heard him hesitate.

"Downstairs. In the lobby of your hotel. I'm as crazy as you are, but I didn't know when you were leaving, and I have to be in New York tomorrow. I thought if you really came all the way from Paris, maybe we should talk." The insanity of the hour didn't seem to bother either of them.

"I'm glad you're here. Why don't you come upstairs?"

She combed her hair and brushed her teeth, and splashed some water on her face while she waited for him to come up. Five minutes later, there was a knock on her door. Bill was looking at her from his chair, and wheeled slowly in as she held the door open for him, and then closed it softly behind him. She wanted to reach out and touch him, but she didn't dare.

"I'm sorry to come here at this hour, Isabelle. I couldn't sleep. It was a shock seeing you there tonight. And kind of a crazy thing for you to do." But he didn't look unhappy about it, he was touched, but upset about it too. It had awakened a myriad of barely sleeping feelings that he had spent months trying to flee. And then seeing her there outside the Kennedy Center in the snow brought it all back to him. "I'm so sorry about Teddy. What happened?"

She sat down on the couch facing him, and told him briefly about her son's final days. There was a catch in her voice as she talked about it, and her eyes were filled with unshed tears, and then she brushed away a lone tear

that trickled down her cheek. Without thinking, he held out a hand and touched hers.

"I'm sorry," he whispered.

She smiled through her tears. "Me too. Other
people say it's a mercy for him, and I suppose it
is, but he had some happy moments too. And I
miss him so much. I never realized how much
of my life revolved around him. I don't know
what to do with myself now that he's gone, and
Sophie is away at school."

"It'll take time to adjust. You'll get used to it.
It's an enormous change for you." Everything
had changed about her life, her home, the divorce, the death of her son, losing Bill. She had
done nothing but face agonizing changes in the
past year. And so had he. "I don't know what to
say to you," Bill said, looking unhappy. "I never
thought we'd see each other again. I didn't
think we should. I didn't think I had a right to
ruin your life, Isabelle. You deserve so much
more than I can offer. You need someone wonderful in your life, someone whole . . . not
someone like me."

"You are whole," she said softly, her eyes
riveted to him. She wasn't sure yet what he was
saying to her, and she wasn't sure she wanted to
know. It sounded like good-bye again, or more
excuses about why he couldn't be with her. But

at least they weren't lies this time, only what he perceived as the truth, however distorted it may be.

"We both know that's not the case." He didn't want to remind her of their disastrous attempt to make love in the hospital in London. And unlike his son-in-law, he felt his handicaps presented too big an obstacle to overcome to marry her. And he didn't want to offer her less than that. He was convinced he had nothing to give that would be fair or reasonable for her. He vaguely remembered everything Helena had once told him, but she was young and idealistic too. Maybe love was only for the young. In any case, he had come to the hotel that night to see her, and explain things, and say good-bye to her decently. He at least owed her that, he had told himself before coming to the Four Seasons. He knew that the way he had left her before had been inordinately cruel. And she didn't deserve that either, particularly now after losing Teddy too. "I just wanted to say good-bye to you, and tell you I'm sorry. I never should have encouraged you to go to London. I feel like it was all my fault right from the beginning."

"You gave me the only real love I've ever had from a man," she said gently. "That's not something you owe me an apology for, Bill."

"I'm sorry I can't be more than I am. . . ." There were tears in his eyes as he looked at her and held her hand. "I'm sorry about all this," he said sadly, and with that, she leaned forward and kissed him as he sat in his chair, and he gently pulled her toward him, and she sat on his lap as he kissed her. Their kisses were filled with tenderness and passion, and the memory of all they had hoped for, barely tasted, and lost too soon. And as he held her, for an instant he forgot his lost manhood, and felt desire race through him like a tide that could not be turned back, and neither of them had any inclination to. The force of what they felt for each other was irresistible and overwhelmed them both. And suddenly, for one single shining instant, he was no longer afraid. They kissed for a long time, and they were both breathless when he pulled away from her, and without explaining it, or saying anything to each other, she helped him onto the couch, and gently took off his clothes, as he slipped the satin nightgown off her shoulders and it fell to the floor.

For the merest moment he hesitated, but he couldn't stop himself this time. With every ounce of his body and soul, he was starving for her. And this time, there was no question about what happened. He couldn't remember ever making love to anyone like Isabelle, or wanting any woman more. It was everything they had both dreamed of and hoped for, and the kind of longing and openness and passion he had never experienced before in his life. Not even before the accident, or in his youth. There was no one in the world like her. She made him feel like a man again, and they were both overcome by desire.

And afterward, he lay with his arms around her and smiled. His worst fears had vanished, swept away by her tenderness and love. Everything that had just happened between them was better than either of them could have imagined. It was obvious that whatever had remained of his injuries before had been healed. Even if he could not walk, he felt whole, and was.

"Wow!" she said softly afterward as she clung to him, and he smiled. He felt like a boy again in her arms. "That was amazing."

"So are you." But after she wheeled him into the bathroom an hour later and left him there, and he emerged fully dressed forty minutes later, she saw a look in his eyes that worried her.

"It was crazy of me to come here," he said somberly, already in the clutches of guilt and the throes of his own fears. "I shouldn't have done that." He didn't want to mislead her or give her false hope. He still was adamant that she deserved a better life than he could give her, and making love to her would only complicate things for both of them. He had spent half an hour in the shower, agonizing, and berating himself, but also immensely relieved about what he had shared with her. His legs were gone forever, but his manhood had returned full force.

"I don't see why we shouldn't have done that," Isabelle said calmly. "We're both adults, we're free. You're divorced, and I nearly am. My divorce will be final in a few months. We don't have young children who might object. We don't have to create problems that don't exist. Life is complicated enough without making it worse. And," she said seriously, looking into his eyes, "life is precious and short. We could have died together in London, or worse, one of us. We didn't. Perhaps we should not waste the blessing that was bestowed on us."

"I'm not a blessing, Isabelle," he said with a look of determination. "Life with a man in a wheelchair is not a blessing, by any means."

"Life between two people who love each other is." They had been to hell and back, and Isabelle felt they had a right to a small piece of Heaven together, however unusual it may be. She loved him, just as he was, without hesitation or reservation, and was more than willing to stand beside him for the rest of her life, and wanted to.

"I can't let you do this to yourself, Isabelle," he said firmly. "I won't do it. No matter what just happened here. I shouldn't have let that happen. It was stupid and irresponsible of me."

"And human. Do you ever leave yourself room for that? Can't you just let yourself be happy once in a while and not beat yourself to death?" He smiled at what she said, knowing that some of it, if not all, was true. "Why do you have to make this difficult, when it isn't, and doesn't need to be? We love each other. Can't you just let that be enough?" She was making a lot more sense than he.

"Sometimes love isn't enough. You don't know what you'd be getting into, Isabelle."

"Yes, I do," she argued with him. It was nearly six o'clock in the morning, and she knew he had to leave soon. "I spent fifteen years taking care of Teddy. I know what caring for and loving someone truly sick means. You're not sick. You're strong and healthy and whole. You can't walk. That makes no difference to me. I wouldn't have cared if you couldn't make love again. That's a lovely bonus, but I would have been willing to live without that too. What we have together means more than that to me."

"I wouldn't have let you," he said firmly, beginning to look grim. "But I can't let you take this on either. I'm not willing to. I came here to say good-bye to you, and that's what we have to do."

"That's so stupid, and such a waste. I won't let you do that."

"You have no choice. I won't see you again." And they both knew he was capable of it.

"And then what? You condemn us both to be lonely for the rest of our lives, to think of what we had and lost, and could have had if you weren't so stubborn? To what end? Where is the victory here? Do they give us rewards in Heaven for punishing ourselves and each other, for depriving ourselves? All right, maybe it won't always be easy. It will not be 'perfect.' But nothing in life is. And as far as I can see, this is as perfect as it gets, what we have between us. Why can't you just let us have what we deserve and want? You've been punished enough, how much more misery do you have to inflict on yourself, and on me? I've lost enough in my life, so have you. For God's sake, be sensible. . . ." Tears filled her eyes and ran down her cheeks as she looked at him, but he was unmoved.

"I'm sorry," he whispered, kissed the top of her head, and then wheeled himself to the door and turned around to look at her.

"Why did you do this?" She was crying as she asked him. "What was the point? Just to torture both of us? To remind us both of how much we love each other and take it all away again, so we can live in darkness and sorrow forever? Why, when we are so happy together and love each other so much? Why can't you let us have that? Is that so hard for you?"

"Maybe I don't love you enough," he said sadly, "or myself, and maybe you wouldn't be able to love me as much as you think."

"Don't make it so complicated. It isn't. I love you. That's all that matters. And however much you love me, that's enough for me."

"I am not enough for you, that's the whole point," he said, looking agonized from the doorway, wanting to come back and hold her in his arms again, but he wouldn't allow himself to.

"Let me decide that. Let me be the judge of who I love, and who I don't. You don't have the right to make that decision for me."

"Yes, I do," he said, looking at her one last time, and wheeled out of her room. The door slammed behind him a second later, and Isabelle sat crying on the couch, and didn't move.

Chapter Nineteen

Isabelle stayed in Washington for four days. The senator won the election, and she was pleased for Bill. She saw him on the news sitting in his wheelchair off to the side, the power behind the scenes. He never called her, and she didn't call him again. She believed him now. And she knew that, no matter how wrong she thought he was, she had to respect how he felt. It was hard to believe he was willing to be so stubborn and sacrifice everything they had. But he seemed willing to give up all that he could have had with her. It broke her heart to accept it, but she couldn't force him to come back to her. She had to accept the choice he'd made, no matter how much she disagreed with him. It was his right, just as it was hers to believe that they could have had a wonderful life. She would have been proud to be with him, wheelchair or not. It made no difference to her, but it did to him. It was his right to live as he chose.

She called Sophie on Tuesday night after the election, and told her she was coming home. Isabelle sounded sad, and Sophie didn't ask why. They had more than enough reason to these days. Sophie had struggled with her brother's loss, nearly as much as her mother had.

"Did you see your friend?" she asked, trying to cheer her up.

"Yes, I did," Isabelle said quietly. "He looks great."

"Is he walking again?"

"No."

"I didn't think he would. He was in pretty bad shape when I saw him at the hospital, but so were you."

"He seems fine in every other way. I'll be home tomorrow night, sweetheart. If you need me." She liked Sophie knowing where she was at all times. It was a hangover of her years of being constantly responsible for Teddy, and the truth was, Sophie didn't really need to know where her mother was every minute, but it made them both feel secure. "I'll see you in a few weeks."

"I'll call you this weekend, Mom. Did you have fun?" Sophie hoped she had, but her mother sounded very subdued.

"Not really," Isabelle said honestly, "but I'm glad I came." It had forced her to accept what she hadn't been able to in all this time. And she had gone to some museums and galleries. She was planning to go back to work restoring paintings at the Louvre after the first of the year, and she was steeping herself in art again. It had reminded her of her days in London with him more than a year before. Everything reminded her of Bill. Paintings, museums, Harry's Bar, dancing, music, laughter, air. Maybe it would finally stop one day. She hoped it would. If he wasn't going to be in her life again, she had to forget him as soon as she could. Maybe she'd even stop loving him one day. It would be a mercy for her when she did.

On Wednesday morning she packed the few things she'd brought, and called the bellman to collect her bag. Her flight was at one o'clock, and she left the hotel at ten. And as she closed the door to her room, the telephone rang. It took her a minute to unlock the door again, and when she got there, it had stopped. And when she checked out, the desk clerk told her he had just called to ask what time she was leaving the room. They already had someone waiting for it.

The ride to the airport was quiet and long. It had snowed again the night before, and Washington looked beautiful under a blanket of snow. She checked in for her flight, and after a while, went to buy some magazines and a book, so she'd have something to read on the plane. She felt quiet and sad, and free in a way. She had let him go at last, and she was glad she had come. She hadn't expected to feel as peaceful about it as she did. And she forced herself not to think about him as she paid for her magazines and books. She was thanking the woman for her change, when she heard a voice directly behind her.

"You know you're crazy, don't you? I always knew you were." She closed her eyes, this couldn't be happening. It wasn't possible. But it was, and when she turned, she was looking at Bill. "You're not only crazy, but you're wrong," he said quietly. He looked so familiar and powerful just sitting there, she smiled in spite of herself.

"Are you following me, or leaving on a trip?" Her heart pounded just seeing him again. She didn't know if it was coincidence or a miracle, and she didn't dare ask him which.

"I called you at the hotel, but you'd left."

"That's funny, I must have missed your call," she said, trying to look nonchalant. Her hands were shaking as she clutched the magazines and books she'd just bought. "The desk clerk said he'd called about the room."

"I must have called right after he did." She assumed he had called to say good-bye, but why was he here? "I know I did the right thing," he said, moving his chair out of the way, as she stood facing him. People were eddying around them, but neither of them seemed to care. Their eyes were riveted to each other, and Isabelle looked pale. He looked as though he hadn't slept in days. "You deserve better than this."

"I know that's what you think," she said, feeling her heart ache again. How many times was he going to tell her the same thing? "But there isn't better than this. This is as good as it gets . . . or at least it is for me. I lost Teddy. I lost you. I've got nothing to lose anymore, except Sophie. I don't think you walk away from love. Or one shouldn't anyway. It's too precious and too rare. But apparently you do." She knew there was nothing she could do to convince him or change his mind. He was going to think what he wanted to. And so was she.

"I want better than this for you. I want you to have a real life with a guy who can chase you around the room, and dance with you on New Year's Eve."

"I want a lot more than that. I want someone I love and who loves me, someone I can respect and take care of and laugh with for the rest of my life. I can love just as easily sitting down as

up. Maybe you can't," she said, accept-
ing the fate he had chosen for both of them.

"What makes you so sure?"

"Would you love me if I were sitting there
instead of you?" There were tears in her eyes,
and her voice was soft, as he nodded and didn't
say anything. And then he answered her, and finally understood.

"Yes, I would."

"You must not think much of me if you think
I can't too."

He didn't say a word to her, he just pulled her
down on his lap and looked at her, put his arms
around her, and kissed her on the mouth, and
she was breathless when he stopped.

"Why did you do that?" she had to ask. "Was
that hello or good-bye?"

"You choose. You know what I think. I love
you. You have a right to make up your own
mind." Helena had told him that so long ago,
and she had been right, he had finally figured
out. He had tried to protect Isabelle, but he
couldn't anymore. She had a right to choose her
own fate, and this time maybe even his.

Isabelle smiled at him, and whispered "hello"
as she kissed him and he held her tight.